THE WAYWARD HAUNT SERIES

I0593157

THE
DARK
DIVIDE

CAS E. CROWE

Author: Cas E. Crowe

Editor: Kristin Scearce, Hot Tree Editing

Book Cover Design: Miblart

Title: The Dark Divide

Paperback ISBN: 978-0-6488765-6-4

Hardback ISBN: 978-0-9756135-0-4

E-book ISBN: 978-9-6488765-7-1

THE DARK DIVIDE

Book Three

THE WAYWARD HAUNT SERIES

CAS E. CROWE

CAS E. CROWE

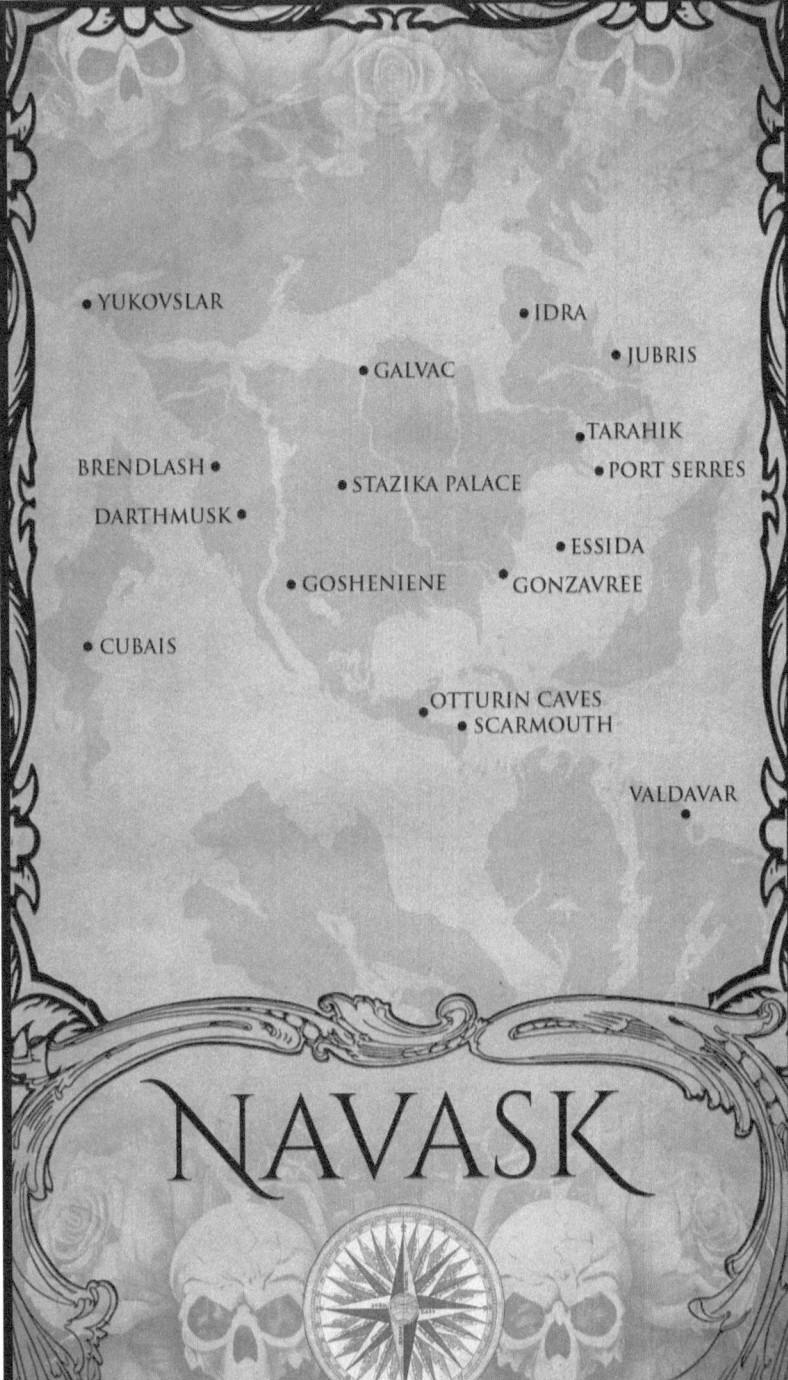

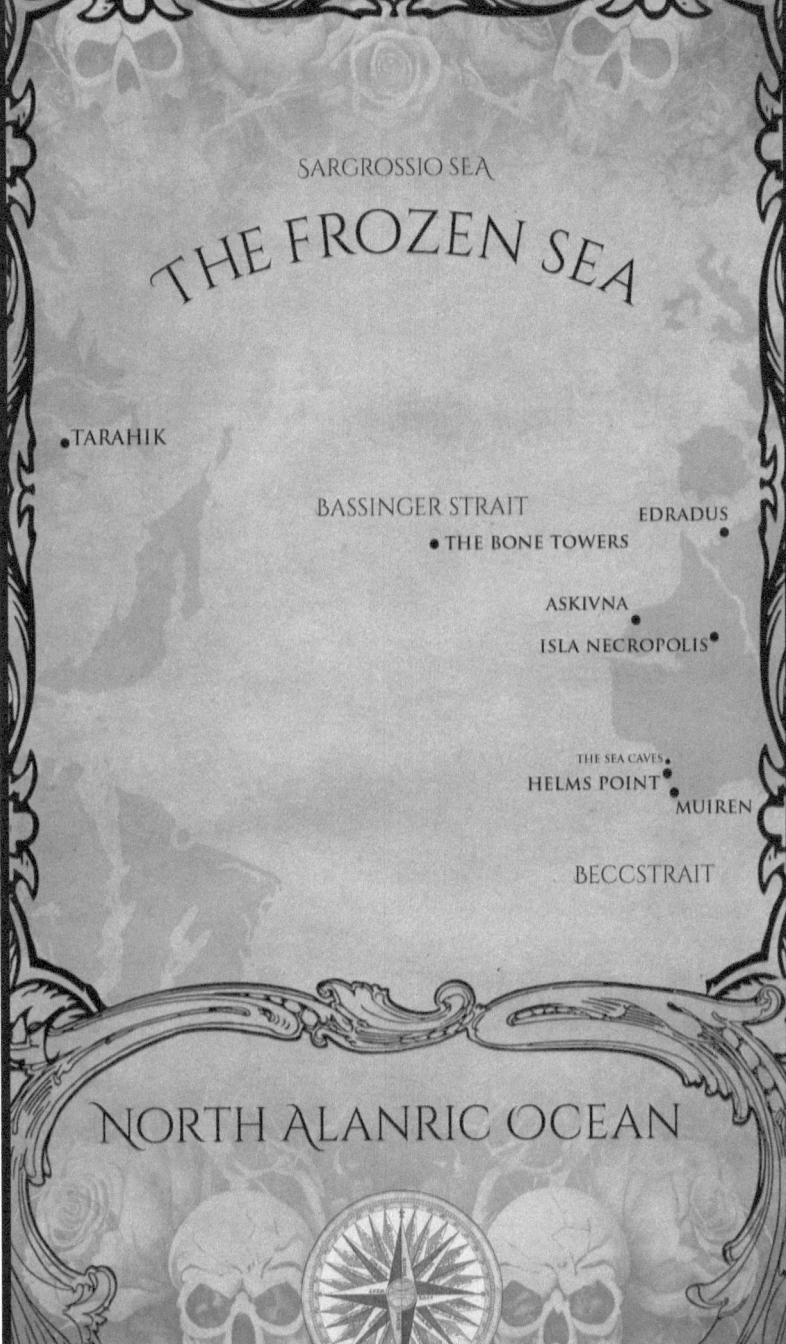

EDRADUS

ASKIVNA
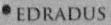ISLA NECROPOLIS

THE SEA CAVES
HELMS POINT
MUIREN

VUKOVAR

CHAPTER 1

Bronislav Olski fidgeted outside the doors of the imperial palace. He'd heard it called many names. The Palace of the Kings. The Home of the Royal Sovereigns. The Grand Citadel. But Bronislav only ever referred to it as the White Palace. Sentinels of the Royal Haxsan Guard stationed at the doors watched him with curious interest, their brows raised in arrogant amusement. He was only a soldier, a young man whose station meant he had no right to be standing among such greatness, and yet he'd been chosen to relay the news, to convince the sovereigns that the threat from the north was real.

Bronislav swallowed, his dry mouth tight. Fifteen sentinels in total. Flag-bearing guards who probably knew nothing about defence, but they were there to be imposing. Bronislav supposed they did a decent job, considering no one in the history of Navask had entered the palace without invitation.

That could change.

He ground his teeth at the unpleasant thought. The sun was insufferably hot. Sweat glazed his bronzed skin, and his short crew cut did little to insulate his head from the humidity. Bronislav stepped toward the shade. The guards clutched their cast-shooters, watching him with keen vigour.

On second thought, maybe I'll just stand here.

He didn't fancy being shot down by caster-fire.

Embroidered in white on the breast of the guards' black uniforms was the Infinite Eye—a triangle with a hexagon-shaped eye in the centre—that caught the sun like glittering diamonds. White was always reserved for the royals and their imperial guards. Bronislav's own uniform, which was shabby and in need of stitching, was embroidered in blue. He was beneath these guards in the hierarchy, but he knew he had more combat experience than all of them combined. Bronislav felt honoured, yet unsure why he was the bearer of this responsibility. General Kravis should have relayed the threat from the north to the Council of Founding Sovereigns. Even the general's personal emissary should have been chosen over Bronislav.

Why did he send me?

The two sentries who stood on either side of the hefty doors stomped their spears in pompous ceremony. The doors groaned open to reveal a footman attired in a cream suit, his insignia embroidered in gold. He offered a brief bow, but Bronislav didn't miss the way the man examined his threadbare uniform.

You can't fight wars and be fashionable.

The footman addressed Bronislav with a disinterested frown. "The Royal Advisers to the Sovereigns will see you now."

Finally.

He'd only waited half an hour in the blazing sun, and before that several hours in an army vehicle to cross the celestial shield. All the Free Zones were protected by an invisible forcefield that would blow off your toe at the slightest misstep. He'd grimaced when he realised that a large troupe of province dwellers—casters dressed in dark cloaks —had been granted access to the Free Zone before him. The visitors brought in carts, vehicles, and truckloads of plants for the annual Spring Carnival of Flowers. It had taken time and patience that Bronislav didn't have. When he'd finally been admitted through the celestial shield, he'd thought it peculiar that every caster hid their face with their heads bowed. It was a hot day. Even celestial shields couldn't prevent the rising heat or the sun. But still....

He tapped on his driver's shoulder. "Who are those casters? Why are they so... secretive?"

His escort turned with vague interest. "Priests from Celaniti, sir. Hundreds of them have arrived for the carnival these last five days. Apparently, it is customary for them to keep their heads down."

Bronislav opened his mouth but paused.

Why are priests being allowed entry?

Religion had been stripped from the world after the change, an event that had occurred so long ago that no one knew if the reshaping of the continents had been the result of human misguidance or if nature itself had decided to take charge and hit the reset button. Whatever it had been, over the centuries, both humans and casters had dared to fashion new social movements. Movements that had resulted in cults. They'd all been wiped out by the Council of Founding Sovereigns and the Haxsan Guard. The Seven Sovereigns and their Council were the only faith that humans and casters should allege themselves to. Period.

Bronislav sidled closer to the window to get a better view. The priests lumbered slowly up the hill as they dragged their carts. Their feet left strange watermarks on the ground, the path becoming a sloppy mud trail up the track.

His toes curled in his boots.

Probably wearing cilice chains for penance.

He'd heard the pain could make its wearer sweat or bleed. Even urinate.

Bronislav turned away to evade the shiver that snaked up his spine. He had more to ask the driver, but then the city walls appeared, the White Palace materialised in the distance, and he forgot about the priests entirely. He could see the Roski River that dipped in and around the city buildings like a silver serpent. Even at this distance, the air still held a taste of its salty waters. Beneath that smell were the wonderous aromas of spices from faraway provinces, the tantalising scent of pastries and bread, and the fatty waft of sausages and meat. When the vehicle drew closer to the palace, Bronislav inhaled and was greeted with the fragrant scent of blooms: jasmine, gardenia, and honeysuckle. The combination of sweet, velvety perfumes reminded him of home in the Flore Valley. He wondered if any of the flowers today had come from that province. Quite possibly. The Spring Carnival of Flowers was a city event, a celebration, a festival of everything that was Navask. No expense was spared.

If only they understood what was coming.

He saw the parks alive with street performers, the markets and shopping district packed with bargain hunters, and the little food outlets crammed with hungry consumers. Families explored the exhibits and watched the parade, taken in by the attraction's hyper-bright colours. These humans didn't live in fear like the rest of Navask. It was another confirmation of their surety that the celestial shield would protect them. The shield had done so for centuries; why should a rumour from the north concern them now?

They have to believe me. They have to.

Now, standing in front of the White Palace, Bronislav shook off the morning's events and rubbed the sweat from his hairline. It landed on the pavers and evaporated.

I just need to convince the most powerful men and women in the world that they need to evacuate this Free Zone. Simple.

His bitter sarcasm did nothing to allay his nerves. He inhaled a breath and stepped into the palace. Every wall, staircase, and doorway was embellished with gold leaf. Most of the furniture was elaborately carved wood, the chairs upholstered with velvet cushions. Chandeliers hung from the cavernous ceilings, crystal bouncing the sunlight in a multitude of directions, giving the impression of some kind of heavenly glory, if such a thing existed.

Bronislav now understood why the citadel was referred to as the crowning achievement of Navask. The building served as a political, symbolic, and cultural epicentre of the continent's history. In the last two centuries, it had become a place to welcome the masses and their enlightened thinking—if you were a human or a prestigious caster. The so-called lesser casters—those from the provinces, like him—were never welcome and were told to keep quiet.

Bronislav was led to an oak door varnished in dark red. His heart sprang and danced.

The Crimson Cabinet. I'm finally here.

He entered the stately room, eyes wide with unabashed wonder. The Crimson Cabinet was an octagonal hall with a ceiling fresco that depicted battle scenes of military might. Gilded floor lamps sent gold streams across the red walls, which were decorated with rich mouldings, trophies, and bronzed carvings.

The excitement in Bronislav's chest plummeted the moment he saw what he was up against. The Council of Founding Sovereigns were meant to be in attendance—senators, ambassadors, chancellors, captains of the sovereigns' guard, even emissaries from other Free Zones—but most of the chairs around the circle table were empty. It was a room that could seat over a hundred people. Bronislav was greeted by five elderly human men in grey robes, half asleep in their chairs.

His eyes darkened. "Where is everyone? Who are you?"

I am meant to be meeting with the Seven Sovereigns and their Council.

He struggled to remember what the footman had told him.

He did say the Seven Sovereigns, didn't he?

The men startled awake.

One of the advisers with thinning white hair offered a polished smile. His saggy cheeks and crumpled lips quivered as he did so. "Did the footman not tell you? We are the Royal Advisers to the Sovereigns. Spiritual advisers."

Bronislav blinked. He wasn't sure if he'd heard correctly. "I'm sorry. Did you say spiritual advisers?"

As in, spiritual advisers to magic?

Physical strain, stress, and mental fatigue could drain a caster of their powers. Bronislav was positive the sovereigns—who were human —would need their royal court—casters—well rested and performing magic at all times. He couldn't believe it. Five human men employed to offer advice on magic, something they definitely were not qualified to do.

Bronislav bristled, his spine taut.

The man with thin white hair widened his smile. It was one a snake would be proud of. "My name is Tiska. I am the chief spiritualist and was directed to remain at the White Palace. We now administer control over the Free Zones in all of Navask."

Is this a joke?

Bronislav's anger loosened his tongue. "Where are the sovereigns? The captain of the imperial guard? I came here with troubling news from General Kravis that requires immediate action."

Another of the advisers, with sickly yellow skin and an enormous jaw, waved Bronislav's words away with a lazy hand. "The Council left the palace two days ago to board a ship to Vukovar. This rumour from the north that Morgomoth has awoken, which of course can't be true because he was executed years ago, required the sovereigns' immediate relocation to the Black Palace. From there they can assess the situation and make the proper arrangements."

The Black Palace?

The sovereigns and the Council have relocated to the Black Palace?

In Vukovar?

Every continent had its own citadel for the sovereigns to reside in on their travels. They moved from location to location as was fit, but the capital was in Navask. The White Palace was where the sovereigns should have remained, but instead, they'd run away like scared dogs with their tails between their legs. If Navask fell, it wouldn't be long till the other continents fell with it.

Bronislav stared with his mouth open. He could have slapped the men who gazed at him with their foolish leers. "If it's true? I saw it with my own eyes. Morgomoth has returned. There are two dozen witnesses, survivors from Stazika Palace—which now rests in ruins, I might add—who have confirmed he's back. Morgomoth wants to eradicate humans from every continent on this earth. He has an army to achieve it. Spies have sent word that the United League of Dissent is moving toward the Free Zones in the north. The Four Revenants are said to be spreading darkness through the northern provinces with chak-lorks at their side. And you're sitting here, telling me the sovereigns have gone on holiday. How does leaving the continent help the people in Navask?"

Three of the advisers—the less smirky ones—flinched. Their frail bodies shook in rapid trembles.

The man with the enormous jaw raised his hand. "Could you not speak so loudly? Nothing has been confirmed, and until it is, we'd rather like to keep discussions within these walls." He lowered his voice. "You never know who may be listening outside."

Bronislav slammed his palms onto the table. "I am here to confirm it. What is your name?"

The adviser shook his head, shaking like a leaf about to break free from its branch. "It's Rudoll. You would be wise to hold that tongue, sir. While the sovereigns are absent, we are the highest authority in Navask. We demand respect. We are—"

"Wasting time." Bronislav's internal body temperature rose. His blood pounded in his ears. "You need to prepare the underground caverns and evacuate every human who is living in this Free Zone. If there are casters here, you need to get them prepared."

Tiska laughed, a high-pitched chuckle that would have annoyed Bronislav on a good day. "Prepared for what?"

"Battle." The word made Bronislav sick. Any decent caster would have been dispatched with the sovereigns and the Council. The casters who remained, if there were any, would never be able to defeat what was coming.

We're doomed.

The chief spiritualist stood and drew himself to full height, which wasn't considerable. He eyed Bronislav with a narrow glare. "The underground caverns are catacombs. They have never been used. We can't send our people down there. If the United League of Dissent are coming, our celestial shield will protect us. It has done so for centuries." The veins in his temple pulsed, his skin turning the colour of cooked lobster. He pointed a nasty finger at Bronislav. "Fearmonger. Alarmist. That is what you are. You're trying to frighten us."

Bronislav was ready to throttle him. "Did you not hear anything I said about Stazika Palace? The celestial shield was destroyed. I was there. Morgomoth has a way to bring the shields down. His necromancy has created chak-lorks. They are dead, unnatural creatures who were once human. They can turn into water at will and enter celestial shields. Do you understand what I'm saying? They can bring the shields down from the inside."

Bronislav froze, realisation slapping him in the face.

The Celaniti priests.

Pressure knotted his chest.

It can't be.

That's far too easy.

Far too clever.

Tiska swallowed. His stubby little fingers tapped nervously on the table. "What's wrong? You look ill."

Bronislav spun around. He threw the doors back and sped out of the Crimson Cabinet. In the hall, he surprised two young guards who must have had their ears pressed against the entry. They scrambled back into position, pretending to be none the wiser. Bronislav disregarded them and headed to the nearest window, the one that would give him the clearest view of the city. The advisers hurried after him, their long robes making their footsteps clumsy across the marble floor.

Rudoll could hardly catch his breath. "What is... the meaning... of this?"

Tiska's voice was a nasty cry. "This is very unorthodox. No one leaves the Crimson Cabinet when a session is in place."

Bronislav ignored the whining spiritualists and their outdated traditions. He scanned the city, its skyline, the carnival, and the exuberant parade. He imagined families picnicking in the parks, admiring the flowers and blossoms, unaware of what was about to come.

And all the while, those priests had stood and waited.

Please let me be wrong.

The moment the thought crossed his mind was the second the screams started.

He forgot to breathe. One scream was horrible. Thousands were earth-shattering. Bronislav discerned every terrified cry as they ricocheted across his bones. It reached into his ears, filling his head with such bloodcurdling resonance that his heart spasmed. He wanted to look away, but he couldn't. Explosions rippled across the skyline. The most terrifying roar he'd ever heard ruptured over the Free Zone.

The celestial shield... it's breaking apart!

Bronislav had always thought of the shields as a dome, a bubble that was invisible but, if scanned close, reflected swirls of colours caused by the sun. He watched the magic crumble now like a star imploding. It burned as it rained down onto the streets and buildings, igniting the urban landscape in an inferno. Smoke as thick and black as an electrical storm blocked out the sun, sinking the world into darkness. Flecks of ash fell like snow. Bronislav tasted it on his lips.

Darkness.

Sobbing.

Screams.

All caused because no one had bothered to check what these Celaniti priests really were. Too late, Bronislav realised he should have paid more attention to the water that had trailed out behind them.

They were Chak-lorks. All this time.

Corpses that could dissolve into water and emerge reformed. It was a truly frightening trait, and one Morgomoth had employed to great effect.

Bronislav remembered his driver's words, only now their meaning held more enormity. *"Hundreds of them have arrived for the carnival these last five days."*

Five days!

Meaning the sovereigns and the Council were aware. They had abandoned the White Palace because they knew the fox was already in the hen house. General Kravis had known.

That's why he insisted I attend in his place. A low soldier he didn't care to lose.

Bronislav's blood fizzed with rage.

Is Kravis on that ship to Vukovar too?

The advisers behind him covered their ears and cried. Their city, their home, was burning.

Bronislav stared at the atrocity before him. The devastation had become a churning cloud of darkness that swept across the ruins of the Free Zone.

Please let the radiation leak in fast. Don't let it be slow. Don't let it be painful.

Unlike casters, humans couldn't survive the radioactive contamination that had resulted with the change. That's why they had celestial shields to protect them in the first place.

Thump.

One of the advisers dropped to the ground. Another man soon followed him, and another. Tiska and Rudoll looked at their dead companions, their mouths rounded into perfect expressions of terror. It would have been a kinder mercy if they'd dropped dead too—spare them what was to come next. Enormous red blisters spread across their exposed skin and ruptured like pustules. The oily pus burned their flesh where it touched. Bronislav's training meant he knew what happened to human skin when it met radiation, but seeing it was another horror entirely. Rudoll and Tiska were being dissolved by their own bodily fluids.

He looked away. The sight was too horrible. Even hearing Tiska and Rudoll slowly die—the screams that flattened into wet gurgles—was something he would never be able to erase from his memory.

If I survive.

Bronislav stared at the approaching storm and closed his eyes as the darkness engulfed him.

CHAPTER 2

Zaya

I stirred at the soft crunch of footsteps that drew close. No matter how hard I tried, my body wouldn't wake. It had been this way for weeks now. Or months. Time worked differently in the Dark Divide. Sometimes, like now, the mysterious place allowed me to return to my body. My useless, immobile body. I was literally a sleeping beauty, which was ironic because as a child, that had been my least favourite human folktale.

The one mercy was that I still had my hearing. Whoever had entered the room—I assumed I was being kept in a room—had arrived to examine my sleeping state and apply more magical nutrients to my body. It sucked that I couldn't distinguish who they were. They pricked and prodded at my veins. At least, that's what I imagined they did. There was no sensation. Annoyance channelled through me, building into impossible energy I couldn't use. I wanted to move. I wanted to jog. Sprint. Dance. I wanted to see the world again.

But I couldn't open my eyes.

Whenever this frustration occurred, the Dark Divide would tug my soul back like a tide from the beach, drawing me into the deep. At least in the Dark Divide—this limbo—I could move and touch. I could speak. Not that there was anyone to have a conversation with. Whenever I returned to the Dark Divide, I'd wake on a stone slab. It was an altar that would have been more at home in an ancient tomb.

Maybe I am in an ancient tomb.

My eyes flew open. Musty air filled my nose.

I'm back.

Except for the chill and scent of decay, there wasn't anything about the Dark Divide that was vaguely familiar. It consisted of endless shifting tunnels that changed every time I appeared. The tunnels might have been made out of rock, hewn into the stone, or the natural formation of caverns. It wasn't light enough to ever get a clear view. This place was a world of shadows, every part just beyond reach.

This visit was no different.

They'll be here soon.

I shivered and rubbed my arms for warmth. The very thought of *them* sent an icy rivulet across my bones.

A ghostly, mournful howl ricocheted through the tunnels.

Wraiths.

Or at least what I thought were wraiths. They materialised around my altar, their skin puckered and grey, as though they'd soaked too long in a bath, their eyes sunken hollows.

I focused on the apparition closest to me. He stared, his lips shrunken and his cheeks pasty. These condemned souls had nowhere to go but wander aimlessly through the tunnels. I hoped they drew near because they were curious and I was a novelty to them, but I didn't think it was that simple. They wanted something. They wanted *me* to do something.

Their hands clutched uselessly at my hair and arms, brushing straight through me. The sensation doused my skin like cold raindrops.

I drew backward. "What? What do you want?"

I wished they'd go away. They made the tunnels smell of rot, as though the very air were dead. One of the wraiths, a woman with long hair that resembled wet reeds, released an indescribable wail and pointed in the direction of a tunnel.

Maybe it's best to appease them. It's not like I'm doing anything, anyway.

I ducked their outstretched hands and wandered to the earthen passage. It reeked of mould and dust, and… sulphur.

Great. Rotten eggs.

I cowered at the entrance. The wraiths were behind me now, hovering close, their faces sagging into what remained of their skulls.

They're forming a wall around me. They don't want me to escape.

Their long, tapered fingers, which reminded me of knotty branches that could break off in one snap, pointed into the cavern.

I threw my hands up in surrender. "Fine. I can take a hint. I'll go in there."

The tunnels had never actually hurt me. At least, I didn't think they had. Now that I thought on it, I couldn't remember ever leaving these underground passages. The memory was like a dream in reverse —instead of not being able to remember how it started, I couldn't recall how it finished.

I stood there, deliberating what to do.

Maybe this isn't a good idea after all.

My hesitance upset the wraiths. They assailed in a white blizzard, lips pulled back, forcing a snakish hiss through their stubbed teeth. Their ghostly forms had no substance and drifted right through me, leaving my skin damp and cold, as though I'd stepped through roiling mist at the foot of a waterfall.

I swallowed the protest on the tip of my tongue.

Better to just appease them.

And keep my wits.

I knew the stench of sulphur meant there was a lack of oxygen in the tunnel, but apparently in this place, my spiritual form didn't require it. The ground was wet and slippery. Moss covered the rock walls. Some kind of black liquid that could only be described as snot drips hung off the ceiling, dribbling onto the ground in fat puddles. The wraiths clung together in a twisted mass, fencing me in. Even though they were translucent and could diminish in a wisp of smoke, I knew they'd become solid the moment I changed my mind and tried to step out of the tunnel.

Great. There really is no turning back now.

I continued my trek deeper into the underground. The darkness was suffocating, and in places, I couldn't see anything beyond my own hands. Every so often, something pale would ripple through the shadows, sending flickering rays of light across the walls. Sometimes the tunnel was wide and expansive, other times narrow and winding, the ceiling so low I'd have to duck my head.

What am I doing here?

What am I even looking for?

The wraiths had a reason for sending me down here, right? This wasn't some elaborate hoax? I knew from experience that ghosts had a wicked sense of humour when it came to haunting, but there was always a reason behind it. This couldn't be any different, surely?

There's something in the tunnels they want me to see. Something they want me to find.

The white dress I wore—highly inappropriate for a place like this—trailed behind my feet and caught on rocks. I really hoped my body wasn't wearing this gown in the real world.

Please don't have me garbed like a tragic princess asleep in a glass coffin.

That was the exact kind of thing Talina would do.

Talina.

The thickness in my throat tightened. I missed her so much. I longed for her sweet, benign company. She was the exact opposite of me: kind, caring, and considerate, whereas I was mistrustful, impatient, and rash.

A deep, unsatisfied longing to see all my friends crept through me. Was Marek taking care of Talina? I knew he wanted to. His feelings for her went beyond friendship. Were Macaslan, Harper, Darius, and Macha working miracles to get me out of here?

They better be.

I reached out to steady myself against the cave wall, shutting my eyes for a moment. A gnawing pain churned inside me whenever I thought of Jad. His absence made me so heartsick I wished I could exchange my memories for a blank canvas. Thanks to me being cursed asleep to the Dark Divide, things had been left unsettled between us. I didn't know what we were. What we could be. This place had taken that from us.

No. Morgomoth did.

He was the one who'd cursed me to this place. I'd refused to stand by his side, so he'd made me weak. He'd made me worthless. Damaged. Killing me would have been too merciful. Morgomoth wanted me to suffer the same way he had.

And I did suffer. I was a mouse trapped in a maze with no place to go but endless dead ends. How had Morgomoth survived so many decades in this place without going stir-crazy?

Correction: Morgomoth is crazy. And that probably means at some point you're going to wind up crazy too.

I slid down the cave wall, curling into a pathetic heap on the ground.

I will not cry. I will not cry.

But misery crushed me. I wiped the watery haze from my eyes.

How had everything gone so horribly wrong? I had tried and fought so hard to get my friends to Port Serres and on a ship to Vukovar. In the end, it had all been for nothing. Edric was dead. Lainie had abandoned us and joined the United League of Dissent. Her betrayal still hurt, but I understood why she did it. Just like everyone else, she'd been afraid. She'd lost hope in the Council and the Haxsan Guard long ago, and she'd allowed anger and resentment to make her decision for her. Morgomoth's proposition at Stazika Palace had been a tempting offer. He could take the pain away. Provide a new life in a safer world where casters were the dominant species and humans had been eradicated. He'd known exactly what to say at the right moment. He'd caught everyone in a sea of gloom and reeled them in.

Fools.

No. Not fools.

Desperate.

Fragmented memories of Lainie drifted back to me. Our journey running from the Four Revenants had been a difficult and laboured one, and for its entirety, she had been scared and dejected. A strange part of me screamed that I had no right to be mad at her. Maybe if I'd taken more notice of what she was going through, if I'd supported her more, she'd be with my friends now trying to find me a way out of this place.

I squeezed my eyes shut, a poor attempt to dry the angry tears.

She made her decision. It was her choice. None of us could have prevented it.

So why did I feel responsible?

Great. I'm going to cry again.

Thick, heaving sobs curdled in the back of my throat. I'd survived two years in the Gosheniene labour camp on my own, but this....

The separation from everyone I loved and cared about was agony. The Dark Divide had no beginning or end. The tunnels drifted on and on. I had lost all motivation to move on or even hope to find a way out.

Hope.

A twisted laugh coursed through me. Wasn't that what my name was meant to mean? The Zaya star in the sky represented hope. Professor Gemmell had explained its origin in class back at Tarahik. It was ironic that my parents had named me Zaya. They'd been dissent rebels who'd sided with the United League of Dissent. At least, that's what Vulcan had told me. My parents had been willing to sacrifice me to awaken Morgomoth.

Well, they got what they'd hoped for. Here I am trapped in the Dark Divide while Morgomoth is awake doing providence knows what to the outside world.

I rubbed my arms. The temperature had plummeted again. In this flimsy dress, the chill drilled right into my marrow.

The muffled weeping of lost and damned souls drew closer.

Eerie, childlike voices brushed my ears. *"Zaya. Zaya. Zzzaaayyyaaa."*

They swept past, my name becoming a lost echo down the tunnel.

A powerful urge to follow the wraiths' calls consumed me. I stood, following without volition of my brain.

Have I been spelled?

The tunnels became increasingly claustrophobic, the walls tighter, my arms brushing against the rock. Long, droopy spiderwebs hung from the ceiling, creating white curtains ahead. Water trickled into my ballet flats—a ridiculous excuse for a shoe—freezing my toes. At least I prayed it was water.

"Zaya. Zaya. Zzzaaayyyaaa."

The voices grew from a whisper into something deeper and more powerful.

Wailing.

These ghosts… were crying.

Was that the reason they'd brought me here? To help? Surely that's all they wanted—the assistance of a necromancer.

I stumbled around a corner, blinded by a searing light. The tunnel had led me into an underground canal filled with black water. Silver-blue radiance danced on the surface. A path ran around the pool to a vast bronze door that stood like an imposing entrance to a temple. Behind the door, blue light, luminous and dazzling, pulsed. I cautiously took the path around the canal toward it.

A door?

Could this be the way out?

Hope, which I thought I'd seen the last of, flared inside me.

The door bore gilded panels, carved with scenes of a long-ago battle. In the centre was a demonic gargoyle holding a circular handle in its gaping jaws. Energy and magic thrummed behind the entry. I sensed the power vibrating in my chest, streaming through every fibre of my body. This was power that couldn't be ignored. Whatever it was behind the door, it wanted me to greet it on the other side.

My fingers inched toward the handle.

"No!"

The voice startled me.

A translucent hand slapped my fingers away.

I gasped.

Lunette hovered beside me. Her eyes bored into mine with such despair and panic that it sucked whatever warmth I had left out of my body. *"Don't open the door,"* she cried. *"Not now! Not ever!"*

CHAPTER 3

Lunette grabbed my wrist. Her pale hand felt more unyielding than I'd ever experienced before, her fingers biting into my own with icy determination. Was it this place? Did the Dark Divide make wraiths stronger?

Her eyes were still that beautiful sapphire blue, but the skin around them had sunken. Her framed pixie cut hung in wet strands around her white face.

I swallowed my shock. Lunette was… wearing her death wounds.

But she moved on.

I saw her find peace.

She shouldn't look like this.

The horrific injuries Melvina had inflicted on Lunette when she'd murdered the poor girl had returned. Lunette's skin was damp. Ice ran in tiny rivulets along her body. It was like looking at someone who had their veins on the outside, only instead of blood flowing through them, it was frost.

She must have read the horror on my face and guessed what I was thinking.

"It's this place, Zaya." Her voice was scratchy, her tone uneven. *"The Dark Divide is a wasteland for lost souls. It returns us back into the form we died in."* She closed her eyes. *"It hurts to be here."*

The air seemed to press in tight around me. "Then let's leave. Now."

I reached for the door handle.

"Zaya." She caught both my wrists. Her nails left crescent shapes on my skin. *"Never open that door. Understand? If you do, it will change everything."*

I flinched. It wasn't just Lunette's words that had unsettled me. The indescribable wailing that had led me into the cavern was now accompanied by a voice. A familiar voice. One that had haunted my dreams and tormented my waking mind.

And it called my name.

"Zaya. Zaya. Zzzaaayyyaaaa."

Fear devoured every inch of my body. The voice was coming from behind the door.

My eyes wandered back to Lunette, silently pleading with her that she'd contradict what I heard. She didn't say anything, just looked at me with pitiful eyes.

Still, the voice continued. *"Zaya. Zaya. Zzzaaayyyaaa. Open the door."*

Terror rushed through me, so powerful it made me dizzy.

Morgomoth.

I stepped away. "How is he here?"

Something acidic curdled in my gut at the memory of his macabre, skull-like face. I recalled our encounter at Stazika Palace, his body blackened as though by fire, his flesh nothing more than shadows and darkness that folded around him like lost, wandering spectres. He had made me drink his blood and cursed me to this place. I still tasted it. My mouth felt thick with the metallic liquid. Each time he called my name, the sensation grew, so strong that I bent over and retched.

"Zaya. Open the door. Open the doooor."

His voice was a cruel taunt in my head. Agony drove through my skull.

Something slammed against the entry from the other side, making me jump. Cold sweat popped over my skin. My hands were deathly pale in front of me. I imagined my face must have been as bleached and grey as driftwood.

I shot a terrified glance at Lunette. "Why does Morgomoth need me to open the door? He'd been here for years. He should have done it when he took up residence in the Dark Divide."

She didn't answer.

"Zaya. Zaya. Zzzaaayyyaaa."

Morgomoth's voice was strained, yet somehow it grew deeper. Every time he called my name, pain flooded my scalp.

Lunette slapped a hand to my forehead. *"I'm sorry, Zaya. I have to do this. You're not strong enough to deny him. If you stay here... you will open that door, and I can't let you do that."*

Icy waves floated from her fingers. The cold sensation sank into the cells of my brain, the numbness a nice reprieve compared to the voice that split my skull like a sliced melon. The ground spun beneath me, but I couldn't move. I was paralysed, as pliable as concrete.

Lunette leaned her face very close to mine. *"You'll thank me for this. Opening that door would have cost everything. And... I'm sorry."*

The world went dark.

I WOKE ON MY ALTAR. The strangest sensation, like a dream I couldn't quite catch hold of, drifted through my mind.

This has happened before.

But when?

Have I lived this moment... earlier?

"Yes you have."

The voice was a dry whisper that encroached on the haze in my head. A ripple in the air flowed across the altar beside me, morphing into a familiar form. I wasn't surprised to see her. In fact, I was sure I'd seen her many times over the past few hours. Days? Maybe weeks? Time couldn't be measured in this place.

I shook off the dim fog of sleep that remained. "Lunette?"

"We've repeated this many, many times." The air sizzled around her with a negative charge. She closed her cold hand around my fingers. *"I'd hoped to spare you from the pain, but I can't hide it anymore. Each time I was able to stop you in the tunnel, but on this occasion, you ventured too far. Right to the door. He nearly succeeded."*

I wrenched my hand free. "Who nearly succeeded? What are you saying?"

She sighed. *"Here. It's time I return these to you."*

She pressed two cool fingers against my temples. That's all it took. The repressed memories returned with all the force and emotion they'd had when I first made them, demanding I take notice. I remembered venturing down the tunnel more than once. I recalled every cobweb I passed, every stone and cavity that steered me in the direction of the cavern. I remembered the door that looked like an entry to hell, and the voices that called to me with a haunting melody.

My throat choked with emotion. "You stole my memories?"

Lunette pinched her ashen lips. *"I'm not going to lie, nor will I apologise. I thought I was doing the right thing. Morgomoth wants you to open that door. Those wraiths you saw... those are his servants. They spy on you and report back to him. You have to stay here. You can't leave."*

"What?" I scrambled away from her, nearly toppling off the altar in the process.

"If you open that door, you merge the world of the living with the world of the dead. The Dark Divide will become a presence... an entity... a new element on the earth. It will consume everything."

The wave of disappointment that hit me was so strong I had to look away.

There's a way out of here. And Lunette took it from me... and not just once. Many times.

My jaw felt swollen from clenching my teeth so hard. "I can't stay in this place... in this... nothingness. I have to go back. To Jad. To Talina. To Marek. I have to return to all of them." I stood on shaky legs and made a beeline toward the tunnel, determined to find my way back to the door.

Lunette dissolved into vaporous mist and materialised in front of me, her face and eyes incensed. *"I can't let you do that."*

The stress of the situation had brought out a new side in her, one I wasn't entirely convinced I liked. "Get out of my way. I'm going home."

I attempted to walk right through her ghostly essence, but some-how, she'd become as compact as stone. Power emanated from her, the force catapulting me across the cavern. I hit the wall with a sickening thud and toppled onto the altar, a throbbing ache unfurling over my body.

"Hey, that wasn't nice," I complained.

A pained expression crossed Lunette's face. Her eyes flashed with sentiment. *"You think I don't want to return home? I do. Every waking second, which is all the time considering I'm dead. My life was stolen. It isn't fair, but that's how it played out. The same now goes for you. If you open that door, everything is destroyed. All the people you worked so hard to protect will die. Do you really want that?"*

I glared at the ground, anger simmering hot inside me, but it was too late. The tightness in my chest had turned into fire. I was stuck in limbo, and the only way out wasn't an option. I'd never see the people I cared about again.

I didn't want to cry. I wanted to scream.

Everything blurred around the edges. Yellow spots danced behind my eyes.

Am I having a panic attack?

My chest hitched up and down. I couldn't breathe.

I can't stay here. Not like this. Not forever.

Lunette sat on the altar. The fury that had annexed her was gone. *"Face the facts, Zaya. You can't leave through the door. We have to find another way out."*

Hope leapt through me. "There's another way?"

"I didn't say that. I said we have to find *another way."* She examined the altar room as though she expected a mysterious cavity to open and show us sunlit meadows and buttercups on the other side. She exhaled a sombre breath. "It will be hard."

"Just sugar-coat the facts for me, please. I really can't deal with any more bad news."

My entire body was taut from stress. I didn't think I'd ever be able to relax again.

Is this what Morgomoth experienced?

Morgomoth!

Why was the realisation only now coming to me?

"I need his blood."

Lunette narrowed her eyes. *"Whose blood?"*

"Morgomoth's. My blood is what got him out of this hellhole. What if his can do the same for me?"

My hope faltered at her blank stare. She brushed a wet strand of hair from her face. *"It was his blood that put you in the Dark Divide in the first place. It won't reverse the curse."*

I shook my head with bitterness. "You're just full of positivity today, aren't you?"

My spark of hardened resolution flicked out once more. Maybe I should have let Lunette take my memories again. Anything would have been preferable to sitting in this misery. I had an image of myself as an underground rat, little feet scampering from one dark nook to another, every recess an empty black hole that led to a dead end.

I can't be that. I have to get out.

Lunette's white lips pressed firmly together as she regarded me with equal parts curiosity and guardedness. *"I know that look. You're about to do something... impulsive."*

"Impulsive? I can't do shit in this place."

"There's no need for that sort of language."

Good thing she hadn't read my mind right then. She would have heard every curse word in existence.

I turned away. Lunette was right. Whenever I was angry or afraid, I became impulsive, and for the most part, that never led me anywhere good. I needed to clear my head and remain calm. I needed to be practical... and patient.

Looks like I'm going to have plenty of time to practise.

Pity gripped Lunette's face. This must have been equally hard for her too. To be in this place where there was nothing but endless tunnels and the lingering wail of lost and exiled wraiths.

Wait.

"Lunette, how are you here?"

Something troubled rose in her expression. She dragged her fingers down her cheeks, her nails scraping against the ice that was fixed upon her skin. She reminded me of a porcelain doll that had been discarded in a winter storm. *"I'm here for you. I'm not condemned to this place, but the longer I stay, the more I'll lose myself. Eventually, I'll end up like the other wraiths. Just a shadow. A flicker of movement."*

"Then leave. Don't stay here on my account."

"If I left, you would truly be alone." She looked down at her feet. *"And I don't trust you not to open that door."*

"Gee, thanks." I couldn't shake a nagging thought from my head. "Morgomoth was down here for years. Why didn't he open the door?"

Lunette shifted her shoulders. *"A necromancer can't open the door alone. For the two dimensions to merge, the door must be opened from each side. One necromancer to push the door, the other to open it in greeting."*

"And there never was a necromancer waiting on the other side for Morgomoth when he was trapped in here."

Lunette offered a weary nod in response. *"Now that he's returned to the world of the living, he's waiting to open the door with you. You mustn't, Zaya."*

I clapped a hand over my mouth. "Oh really. Why ever not?"

"There's no need for sarcasm."

She was right. My acerbic attitude wouldn't help either of us.

Calm, Zaya. Remain calm.

But it was a struggle to follow that ancient Zen wisdom. Despair had leaked into my soul, drowning everything that was positive.

Think, Zaya.

When our roles were reversed, Morgomoth had managed to communicate with me. I'd often felt a presence around me that I couldn't explain, a sensation that everything I was doing was being watched and calculated. If Morgomoth could achieve that from within the Dark Divide, why couldn't I? Why couldn't my spirit form return to the living like his had?

"There is a way," Lunette said.

This time I wasn't annoyed that she'd read my mind. If I was to survive this place, I was going to need my own personal shrink who could get up close and personal. "How?"

"You're a necromancer. Your spirit form has the ability to drift between dimensions. That's how Morgomoth did it. It will take practice… and patience. Can you do that?"

My chest shrank to the size of an acorn. I had been scared of necromancy. I'd been scared of what was inside me, demanding I pay it attention, demanding to be released. I feared that using my magic would make me like Morgomoth, that the power would strip me of

who I was and consume me. Instead of me controlling the darkness, the darkness would control me.

Was I ready to confront that possibility? Would necromancy take away who I was and replace me with a stranger? What if I ended up just like... Morgomoth?

I knew Lunette was reading my mind, but she didn't look dispirited at my lack of resolve. *"That is a real possibility if you let necromancy change you. It already has and will continue to do so, but it's up to you how you use your magic."*

She offered me her hand.

This time I knew there would be no going back. Lunette would show me what I was capable of. I'd accept my magic, and then I would be responsible for controlling it. A small part of me—a part that had always denied it—had known this was in the cards. Macaslan had suspected it. Darius knew it. If I wanted to put a stop to Morgomoth, I was going to have to stop denying my magic and use it.

It was time to learn necromancy.

I clutched Lunette's hand, hoping I wasn't about to make a huge mistake.

CHAPTER 4

I sat cross-legged at the altar, concentrating on... well, I wasn't sure exactly. Lunette insisted I had to keep my eyes shut for this to work; otherwise, I'd risk losing my concentration. She poked me whenever I snuck a peek at her.

This time, I purposely opened my eyes to glare. "It's a good thing you never became a teacher."

She shook her head. *"A student can never be taught if they're not willing to put the effort in."*

"Effort? I don't understand what I'm meant to be doing."

The more Lunette listened to my deliberations, the more frustrated she became, her shoulders shaking in exasperation.

"Fine. Theory never worked well on me either. Let's go practical." She took hold of my hands once more. *"I'm going to channel my energy with yours. Your spirit form is tied to the Dark Divide, but your body remains centred in the Earth's realm. Just as you conjure a wraith, you need to reach out for your body now."*

I bit my tongue to refrain from saying something I'd regret.

How the hell does one do that? Call your own body? It's not like it's a marionette on strings that I can pick up and play with.

Lunette bowed her head. Her eyes remained closed, but a twitch at the corner of her mouth indicated she wasn't impressed. *"I can read your mind, remember? Now concentrate. Call out for your body. Listen for it."*

Listen for it?

I closed my eyes. The altar room swelled with a deathly silence. Five long minutes passed with only the sound of my breathing.

I groaned inwardly. "I don't think this is working."

"That's because you're not thinking about your body. You're letting your mind wander to other things. Now concentrate."

I shut my eyes again with exaggerated annoyance.

Think about my body.

I'd like to know where my body is, that's for sure.

I forced all my energy into my magic, focusing on myself. My hair. My skin. My flesh.

Where am I?

A soothing, hypnotic hum, like cicadas singing in a breeze, rippled around me. There was a faint noise in the background that grew louder as I centred my concentration on it.

Breathing.

A restless energy thawed inside me, skittering through every vein like marbles. I called on that power, urging it to take me to my body. A heartbeat pulsed in my ears, ticking in time with my own. The breathing I heard became synchronised with my own. I had a sudden leg cramp, and my arms became as heavy as pillars by my sides. I wanted to move. The energy inside me demanded it, but there was something powerful and dark that had me captured in its embrace. It was a living nightmare. A living hell. My body wouldn't move.

"Lunette. This hurts."

Her voice called to me, far away. *"Your soul has returned to your body. If you want the pain to go, push through. Try to levitate your spirit form out of your body and into your surroundings."*

I didn't need further encouragement. My only scepticism was in my ability to achieve it. *"How do I do that?"*

"Focus on your breathing. Each time you exhale, send it farther. Imagine your soul is exiting with each breath."

That didn't sound promising, but I forced myself to concentrate through the agony that racked my body. The essence of life was time, space, and energy, and now that I thought about it, it made sense that it was measured by air. By breathing.

I focused on my inhales and exhales. A tightness formed in my chest. The sudden sensation that I'd been hit with a bulldozer slammed into my back. My breathing became muffled, and I couldn't hear it anymore.

And then I realised why. I had disconnected from my body.

I opened my eyes, embarrassed by the sight I was greeted with.

Oh geez. Seriously?

A shaft of moonlight descended from a small oculus in the ceiling, bathing my body in white light. I rested in a resplendent marble coffin that should have been reserved for queens. The twelve moons of the universe were carved into the stone, along with precious purple and white jewels arranged to depict the stars. Inside the coffin, my dark hair, long and wavy, spilled across my shoulders, my white dress embellished with roses that had been laid all around me. My hands were centred over my chest, my fingers and nails cleaner than they'd ever been in my waking life. I suspected I had Talina to thank for the manicure. I suspected I had her to thank for this entire charade. I wasn't a saint, a martyr, or a revered sovereign, and yet here I was, a sanctified object.

A voice whispered into my ear. *"Your friends care about you."*

Even in my spiritual form, I flinched. Lunette hovered beside me. She looked approvingly at my sleeping body.

I crossed my arms. "This is ridiculous."

"Is it? You're a necromancer. You're Morgomoth's equal and the only creature on this earth who has a chance of defeating him. This shows respect."

"It shows that they think I'm as good as dead."

"Only you can decide that."

I stepped back from my marble casket, suddenly cold. "I can't stay in this place."

I examined my surroundings. I'd been in this room only once before. It was a small memorial room for private services, a space to respect fallen soldiers whose bodies had never been retrieved from the battlefields. Trees and flowers were carved into the walls. The branches stretched across the ceiling and tapered into the oculus, as though reaching for the night sky. Nymphs and beautiful maidens were painted to depict scenes of harmony and peace. Real flowers were strung over marble statues that had their heads bowed and their hands joined in prayer.

I was both physically and spiritually present, yet my pulse pounded so violently that I felt sick.

I'm back.

In Tarahik.

This was the Midnight Garden Memorial Room. Night was always associated with death, and gardens with healing and recovery, which was what grieving family and friends needed in the face of losing a loved one. I'd never expected myself to end up here. Honestly, I wasn't dead. What was everyone thinking?

Everyone!

I darted out of the memorial room, straining to recall my way through this part of the castle. Memories surfaced like bubbles from a forgotten well. Tarahik was just as I remembered it. Arched Gothic windows revealed various shingles, roofs, and towers. Beyond that was the sea, which appeared deceptively calm amid the grey-and-purple clouds that coasted across the night sky. The hallways were large and airy, the oak doors adorned with the figures of the Founding Sovereigns. Every wall I passed was ornamented with portraits of decorated soldiers that seemed to watch me with curious interest.

I stopped at the threshold of a large hall, recalling a dinner party that had taken place there that I'd been reluctant to attend. Now that the hall was formidably dark and the mahogany tables were empty, I looked back on the memory with fondness. Life had been easy back then. Necromancy had been a part of me, yes, but my journey into the dark hadn't begun. I was looking back at a time of innocence that had been as delicate and fragile as dust, now swept aside as a distant memory.

I continued my exploration, scampering down passages that twisted and turned, sometimes a shortcut, sometimes a dead end. My heart gave a tug of regret when I passed the wonderful library, which was practically a city in itself of mezzanines, railings, and ladders, the walls stacked with books all the way up to the vaulted ceiling. Jad had sat in this room many times to escape the hustle of castle life, his nose in a volume. I was disappointed that he wasn't here now. It appeared no one had been in the library for a long time. Books had been strewn across the study tables, their covers coated in grime, even though the library had a staff of fifty to keep it maintained. A vase of wilting flowers stood sadly on a bench. The petals had reduced to shrivelled leaves.

"For death's sake, will you slow down?" Lunette tore up the passage, her hands on her hips. *"Even in spiritual form you're hard to keep up with."*

A lingering sense of alarm crept over me. "Where is everyone?"

The castle was empty and silent. Tarahik had undergone centuries of damage and deterioration—I was certain magic was the only thing holding it together—but it had always been packed with soldiers and cadets, their voices ringing up to the ceilings.

Is Tarahik... abandoned?

Lunette swept a hand over the head of a stone gargoyle. Her fingers come up coated in filth. *"I don't think anyone has been here for a long time."*

A ripple of terror turned my insides.

They left my body in this castle. Alone.

They really had thought I was a lost cause.

I sprinted in the direction of the underground base.

Lunette's voice trailed after me. *"Hey, wait. Didn't you hear what I said before? Slow down. Where are you going?"*

Tarahik's military base was deep in the mountain and consisted of levels upon levels of war rooms, control centres, armouries, weapons ranges, and hangars. It went right down to the sea caves that housed the naval port where warships were docked, restocked, or underwent repairs before their next deployment.

Please let everyone be in the base.

Please don't let Tarahik be abandoned.

I found the stairwell—one of many planted around the castle—that led to the base, my feet moving so fast it was amazing I didn't trip.

Can I even trip in my spiritual form?

"Of course you can't," Lunette called out to me. She appeared at my side, her ghostly manifestation a cold crackle in the air.

I glared. "Don't read my mind."

"Then don't make it so easy." She grabbed my hand. *"There's an easier way to do this."*

The metal stairway began to dissolve.

No. *We* dissolved.

We floated downward, as though we were on an invisible elevator reserved for ghosts. We descended through the concrete floor, something I never ever wanted to experience again. It felt like I was being squeezed through a funnel. Down and down we went, until we came to a knee-buckling stop. I was just grateful to feel the sensation of something solid beneath my feet again.

I blinked as our surroundings aligned into focus. We were in the base... where madness had taken over.

CHAPTER 5

The words were out of my mouth before I could stop them. "What the hell is going on?"

No wonder the castle had been deserted. Everyone was down here in the control rooms. I stared with confoundment, my insides revolving. Instead of the usual militaristic and organised conditions the underground base was renowned for, Haxsan Guard soldiers scrambled through the fluorescent-lit maze of hallways, their faces dampened by sweat. Cast-shooters were hoisted over their shoulders, and athame-sabres hung from their belts. They weaved in and out of the crowd with urgent strides.

A nervous, terrified energy saturated the air. Inhaling it made my own nerves shiver in response. The panic in this place caught like wildfire. Civilians flowed in a steady stream down the metal stairway that led to the level eight bunkers. Behind the glass walls of the control rooms, soldiers sat behind consoles, typing at keyboards and scanning holographic maps.

I recognised Tarahik's surrounding topography. Something dark shaped itself around Tarahik's celestial shield with frightening speed, causing a gasping chorus from onlookers.

What is that?

Was a nuclear missile on its way? An army of chak-lorks? A galactic storm?

Someone screamed, which elicited further cries. A siren wailed, which meant chaos ensued. People pushed and shoved, not caring who they trampled in the process. Soldiers shouted for order, but no one listened. I'd never liked it down here, and even in this form, the nagging thought that the ceiling might collapse at any moment still plagued me. The underground base was a crazy combination of natural rock and man-made concrete, reinforced with heavy steel beams and metal doors. I was positive that magic was the only thing holding this place together.

And if that fails?

Was it really wise to be this far underground?

Lunette made a sound that bordered on a disgusted scoff. *"The living never stop to think. Always panicking."*

I stared back at the darkness on the screen. It flowed and ebbed like blood, growing so large it was practically a moat surrounding Tarahik from the west, the sea shielding us from the east.

My trembling hands clasped my dress tight. "We need to find out what that is."

And why it has everyone so afraid.

I ran blindly down the shaft toward the metal door at the opposite end, doing my best to dodge the frightened mob, but they moved right through me. I flinched, the feeling intrusive. I didn't think that was something I would ever get used to.

Lunette drifted through the crowd like a ship slicing through water. *"What's the plan?"*

I let out a long breath through my nose. "Behind those doors is the war room."

The war room was the place where all decisions were made in secrecy. It was the most secure chamber in the entire Tarahik base. Many soldiers and cadets weren't allowed access.

I had been in there once. Scratch that—I had been *thrown* in there by my two least favourite guards, Pick-nose and Sneer-face. It was the first night I'd met Darius Kerr, a senator for the Council of Founding Sovereigns. It was the night revelations about my magic had been revealed. It was the night questions I had about myself were answered. It seemed so long ago now.

Lunette made a face. *"And we're going in there why?"*

"Because that's where we'll find the people with answers."

I hope.

My spirit form barrelled through the door. For a second, everything appeared pixelated, as though the war room were an image on a screen that hadn't quite rendered. When it cleared, I didn't understand what I was seeing. The last time I'd been in this underground chamber, the holographic screens projected images of distant topography, every steel surface in the room immaculate without so much as a speck of dust. It had been so clean I wouldn't have had a problem eating off the floor if I'd been ordered to.

Now, the war room was an unrecognisable mess. Desks were littered with papers and maps of distant lands marked with symbols and coordinates I didn't understand. Seven sleeping bags had been arranged sporadically on the floor, rucksacks open on five of the makeshift beds. I glimpsed clothes, weapons, and ammunition inside. Toys were scattered around the smaller two sleeping mats, a picture book bent so far back the spine had cracked.

What the hell is going on here?

The only thing that was familiar was the whir and hum of the holographic screens, but even they struggled to project clearly. Images flickered. Anxiety crawled through me at the sight of the darkness that surrounded Tarahik. It had stretched from the west and now barricaded the castle from the south and north. The way it moved on the screens reminded me of watercolours soaking into paper.

What is that?

Was it a fire poisoning the land outside, burning everything to a crisp? A toxic gas that could only be detected by Tarahik's sensory cameras? Even though I wasn't physically in the war room, just a ghostly spectator watching from the sidelines, fear seized me so tight that my head swam. I wondered if my body back in the castle was sweating and shivering as badly as my spirit form.

The war room was dimly lit, but I recognised the casters who sat around the circular conference table. Macaslan had been a thin woman to begin with, but she'd lost even more weight, her cheeks gaunt and her skin grey. She looked like a woman who survived on cigarettes and coffee. It was the first time I'd seen her wearing the traditional garb of a Haxsan Guard commander, and with her stormy-grey eyes staring everyone down, it was an intimidating visual.

Colonel Harper sat beside her with his usual perpetual scowl. His dark hair hadn't appeared to be washed in days and hung past his ears. He had his arms crossed and his ocean-blue eyes focused sternly ahead. Beside him, Darius leaned his elbows against the table, his head in his hands. His silver-white hair hadn't been brushed, and his grey suit was crinkled, as though he'd slept in it. When he peered up, his eyes stared fixedly at everyone. I wondered if he was hoping someone would burst out laughing and reveal the entire situation to be a bad joke.

My heart started to beat so fast, it was a wonder it didn't break my ribcage.

What has happened between them? Have I just walked into the aftermath of an argument?

The three of them were uncharacteristically quiet. I sensed grief in the room.

It must have something to do with this darkness surrounding Tarahik.

Which meant the situation was more dire than I'd first imagined.

A bird squawk resonated from the other end of the room. Macha stood with her palms pressed against the table, her pupil-less eyes roaming over a map. Her crow, Bartholomew, was perched on her stooped shoulder, examining the map and reporting back. He screeched into a ballad of unpleasant birdsong, only stopping when Macha scratched his tiny head affectionately. I was a little jealous of the unique bond they shared.

Macha was an obeahwoman, a caster capable of predicting the paths that different futures could take. She was a powerful caster and a damn scary one, but her obeah magic came at a price. Macha did not have eyes in the traditional sense. Bartholomew was her eyes; she saw everything through her bird.

I watched the pair, realising how much I'd come to miss them. Macha hadn't changed since I'd last seen her. Her black cloak—which I was convinced was a grave keeper robe—fell in dark ripples around her feet, her shockingly white hair an unbrushed mess. Perhaps she'd let Bartholomew make a bird's nest out of it.

Beside her sat Clorenzo, his arms wrapped around his twin children. Livel and Sarith wept, hiding their faces in their father's shirt.

Shame pounded through me. The last time I'd seen the Sujik
family, we'd been running for our lives from the Four Revenants. I'd
managed to summon Lunette, Adaline, and Violetta to get the twins
and their father out of Scarmouth and ordered that they be taken to
Macha's house, but honestly, that was the last time I had paid them a
thought. I'd been focused on finding Jad and saving my friends, too
occupied by fear and panic to reflect on anything else. Had I failed the
Sujiks? The queasy tap dance in my stomach said I had.

Livel and Sarith appeared pale and exhausted in the artificial light,
their apple-shaped cheeks plastered in reddish patches. It was further
proof that there was something very wrong with our world when even
children were stressed. Their fiery red hair had grown since I'd last
seen them but hadn't been brushed. Just above Livel's left shoulder, a
gigantic knot had twisted itself into her dry locks, which would need
Talina-healing attention right away. The children clung to their father
and watched the adults with apprehensive eyes.

Clorenzo sat on the edge of his chair, his dark hair wet and ruffled.
His beard—which he'd kept neat and trimmed when he'd been spying
on the ULD—now reminded me of a hedge, overgrown and
unshaped. He smelt of leather, metal, and sweat—that distinctive
odour we all achieved after hours of training. The athame-sabre at his
side was still warm, the rune markings illuminating colourful rays,
which meant he'd used the blade recently.

To train... or fight?

I scanned the other occupants around the table. They were casters
I recognised as officers and lieutenants, but I didn't know their names.

The hope inside me deflated.

No Jad.

Where is he?

Clorenzo's eyes seemed to devour everything in the room. I knew
that look. He was searching faces, demanding answers. "So that's it,
then? We're giving up?" His tone was full of scorn.

My breath shuddered out of my lungs.

Giving up?

Darius stood quickly. "Let's not jump to any assumptions." His voice was measured, but the crease in his brow betrayed him. "We are not giving up, but we must abandon Tarahik. Our celestial shield will not last much longer." He stared at everyone in the room. "Has anyone seen or heard from Zandor?"

No one spoke. Many people looked down at their feet.

Commander Macaslan's gaze was intent, as though she could pry the answer out of someone. "That's it, then. Zandor is gone. Another casualty."

"Or a deserter," someone cried.

The idea sparked outrage. Voices started rising. Arguments ensued. This Zandor, whoever he was, was a topic of hot discussion. Some believed he was a traitor. Others believed he was dead.

Macaslan stood, nearly knocking her chair over. "Quiet."

The chatter immediately died.

The commander continued to glare. "Zandor kept our celestial shield replenished for years. He went out two days ago to perform the spells. He hasn't come back. He is not a traitor. The ULD have him. I'm sure of it. Our shield is weak, but it hasn't failed yet, which means Zandor has told them nothing. He's buying us time to evacuate."

Clorenzo's face shifted into a dubious frown. "You own Tarahik. I thought no one could enter without your permission."

Macaslan stared stonily ahead at the projectors. "That was the case when the celestial shield was working properly. My magic is no match for Morgomoth's. The ULD will break the shield down. It's inevitable."

Darius's eyes shifted to the holographic screens. The darkness ebbed and flowed in a crescent shape around the castle. The colour drained from the senator's face. "Morgomoth tried once before to influence and reshape the magic in galactic storms. It looks like this time he's succeeded. He's able to bend these storms at his will. This is how he destroys celestial shields."

My hands trembled as my thoughts zeroed in on the one caster who had probably helped Morgomoth achieve it—Hadar. That heinous alchemist had tortured Jad and transformed him into a twisted monster. She had experimented on human bodies, using magic and science to transform them into chak-lorks. Now she'd given the power of storms to Morgomoth too.

As though to emphasise my point, thunder cracked in a menacing boom so loud the table and chairs shook. The holographic displays flickered once more. The cameras outside recorded lightning so bright that the screens lost visual for a moment.

Macaslan gasped, which startled me more than anything else so far. She'd always been calm and in control. She glanced back and forth between Darius and Harper.

If the effects of the storm were being felt this deep in the underground base, then that meant....

This is one hell of a storm.

Darius pressed his lips together, waiting for the rumble to cease. "Morgomoth destroyed the White Palace. He has decimated Free Zones and struck bases. Haxsan Guard soldiers are deserting their posts and fleeing to the ULD. I hate to admit it... I hate to see it, but Navask has fallen. The sovereigns and the Council have fled to Vukovar, and we must follow. If we want any hope of reforming the Haxsan Guard and defeating Morgomoth, then we must do it from Vukovar."

Clorenzo stared. I imagined the wheels turning in his head as he struggled to put everything Darius alluded to in place. His voice was sharp, and his brown eyes flashed like shards of black steel. "What about the people in Navask? You're just going to leave them here to... die?"

Darius's slender fingers traced the mesh fabric on the armrest. "Morgomoth will not kill casters. He wants casters to join the United League of Dissent. Most of them will swear allegiance to him out of fear. The humans...." He shut his eyes for a second, his voice full of regret. "There's simply nothing we can do for the humans in Navask. We don't have the means to save them."

It pained me to see Darius look so defeated. A senator in the Council of Founding Sovereigns, he had never agreed to the unjust system that had favoured humans and wealthy casters, leaving the rest of us to starve and fight for survival in the provinces. He didn't believe adolescent casters should be conscripted into the Haxsan Guard and forced to leave their families. Darius Kerr wanted change. He'd aimed to accomplish it through political means, not war.

And yet here we were. Smack in the middle of one.

Perhaps there really is no other way for change.

Whatever pretence of civility had been in the room evaporated. Arguments erupted into pandemonium. Some of the officers wanted to flee Tarahik immediately; others wanted to remain and fight. I admired their bravery, but I was with Darius on this one. I'd seen how powerful Morgomoth was as Stazika Palace, and that had been him at his weakest. If the galactic storm outside was his doing, then everyone in Tarahik had to run.

Macaslan stood again, hands curled into fists at her sides. "Quiet. Now."

Silence overtook the room.

Macaslan steered her way through the officers and took position beside a projector. She pointed at the dark mass of storm cloud on the screen, her voice powerful and amplified. "We have no way of defeating this. Fighting Morgomoth and the ULD forces would be suicide. If we want any hope of saving Navask, then we must do it from Vukovar. We need to convince the Council of Founding Sovereigns to rewrite the accords, to give both casters and humans equality and not favour one above the other. That's the only way we get casters back on our side. It's the only way to weaken the ULD."

Clorenzo threw a resigned look at the commander. "The sovereigns are human. They'll never grant casters from the provinces the same rights. Not when they're dependent on us to survive this world. We're their farmers, soldiers, merchants, and engineers. We do the hard work, and they reap the rewards. They're not going to give that up."

There were murmurs of agreement and more shouting.

Macaslan did not look deterred. Her voice came out way too rehearsed, and I knew she'd had this speech planned in her head for a long time. "Then we take over the Council of Founding Sovereigns. The people in this room become the new council, and *we* rewrite the accords. We restructure the Haxsan Guard in Vukovar, and we come back to defeat Morgomoth and liberate Navask."

My breathing was too fast and loud, my skin hot.

Am I having palpitations?

This plan was insane. It would take months, years to achieve. But it was also the only option.

Macaslan was right. Darius was right. Navask could no longer be saved from within. Our only hope was to flee to Vukovar and convince the sovereigns to rewrite the accords. And if they didn't? I shuddered to think what lengths Darius and Macaslan would go to overtake the Council.

Clorenzo winced, his arms tightening around his children. "Then it's decided? We abandon Tarahik?"

More voices rose in agreement and dispute. There were shouts to leave immediately and calls to fight, but never once were there any pleas to surrender. It didn't make me all warm and fuzzy, but it did make me glad to know that everyone in this room was determined to defeat Morgomoth and the United League of Dissent. There were no potential absconders in our ranks.

Up until now, Colonel Harper had sat still, casting withering looks at every person in the room. Judging from the way all the muscles in his face pulled into a glower, he'd had enough. His stern voice cut through the escalating argument. "We stay? We leave? You forget that what happens to us next is entirely dependent on whether Captain Arden and his crew return."

A sickening jolt rattled me.

Jad's not at Tarahik?

I focused on the holographic screens. The darkness bled into the landscape. If Jad was out there, his only way back was by sea. Jad had nothing to do with the navy. He was a pilot. If he was returning from some covert operation, it would be by carrier-hornet. The captain and his crew would need access to Tarahik through the runways. And those runways were obstructed by the galactic storm.

No.

No!

Something had to be done. Someone had to do something.

An officer whose name I didn't know scoffed. "That's as good as impossible. Forget him. The captain is dead, along with his crew."

I wanted to kick him. Maybe I'd been about to, because Lunette caught my arm.

Her voice was grim. *"You can't intervene. You can only watch."*

"You intervene all the time," I rebuked.

"Only in your business, and only because you're a necromancer and it's in your ability to communicate with the spirit world. These people can't."

I stared at the scene, trying to repress my mounting anxiety. I'd never felt more powerless in my life. My body was imprisoned in a sleeping curse, and my soul was floating around, useless and insubstantial.

This is what Morgomoth wanted.

A twinkle of confidence danced across Darius's face. "Captain Arden will be returning. And we will not be leaving Tarahik until he does."

A voice dripping with equanimity cut through the conversation. "I want to know what this mission is that Captain Arden volunteered for."

I spun around, surprised by the newcomer. She must have had a swipe card to enter the war room—and the correct authority—but I had never seen her at Tarahik before. Her smooth skin shone like an obsidian jewel in a sunset, her long hair braided in cornrows. She wore a knee-length doublet, dark leather pants, and a pair of boots so wickedly high in the heels it was amazing she didn't topple over. She was young, maybe a few years older than Jad, but her eyes conveyed a world of experience.

She crossed her arms, her coat moving an inch to reveal a very dangerous athame-sabre and cast-shooter holstered at her hips. She stared at Darius and Macaslan as though she were daring them to challenge her.

Her tone could not have been more caustic when she spoke. "I'm guessing the captain's mission has something to do with this secret you're hiding in the castle."

Everyone's eyes turned to the senator and the commander.

An officer with a white beard drew his heavy brows together. "Secret? There's nothing in the castle. No one is allowed to the surface."

His face lost colour when neither Darius nor Macaslan confirmed or denied it.

"Is it true?" another officer demanded.

"What do you have in the castle?" someone else shouted.

Darius raised his hands in a placating gesture. "It's nothing to be afraid of. We have in our possession a power that lies dormant. A backup plan should our negotiations with the sovereigns fail. I hope we don't have to use it. I hope we can defeat Morgomoth without it." He exchanged a tacit stare with the commander, a thousand words communicated at that moment. He turned back to the crowd. "Captain Arden's mission was to find the key to unlocking that power. To awaken it."

Lunette gasped and took my hand. *"Zaya, I think he means you."*

CHAPTER 6

A surge of helplessness swept through me.

If this great and incredible power Darius spoke of was, in fact, me, then we were eternally screwed. Even awake, I hadn't been strong enough to take on Morgomoth at Stazika Palace. He'd trapped me easily. I'd been a fish caught in his netting, flapping and flopping against his powerful binds. My necromancy was weak then. It was weak now. Even if I somehow did manage to return to the living world, I didn't stand a chance against Morgomoth. Darius had to know that, right?

Lunette's icy fingers sent a soothing chill through my skin, eliminating my sweaty panic. *"You're not strong enough now, but you can be. You just need to accept your magic. Let it become part of you."*

We'd had this conversation before, and it still frightened me.

My voice was so small, I almost didn't hear it. "Reading my mind again?"

She nodded. *"When you're this glum, I fear if I don't, you might do something stupid. At least this way I can stop you."*

I shrugged. It was a fair point. I had self-control over many things. I could withstand running with a stitch. I could turn glazed doughnuts away. I could fast for hours without so much as a sneaky run to the fridge. But when it came to my fear, my restraint dissipated like fog. My self-will became a rage I had no control over.

There was a collective flutter of nervous excitement in the room.

Darius had given these people hope—and me a bad case of the jitters. New voices rose. More shouts crossed the table. More demands. More doubt and scepticism.

"What is this power?"

"Why haven't you told us of this before?"

"How can we trust what you're saying when you keep secrets?"

All good questions.

Darius's face remained calm, but his lips had narrowed, betraying his tolerance for the situation. "We ourselves do not fully understand what this power is. Until we do, this information must remain confidential among us. No one else can know about it." He leaned forward, palms flattened on the table. "I'm not going to stop any of you from remaining behind. If you want to stay and fight, I will respect your decision. The ship we are to leave on is being loaded. Please help the civilians in bunker eight onto the vessel. When Captain Arden and his crew return, we'll be leaving. I hope you'll be with us. That will be all."

Darius had spoken like a preacher pronouncing an omen, and it had sucked the energy out of the room. Everyone seemed to understand that the briefing was over. The officers walked out with heavy shoulders. Only Darius, Macaslan, Harper, Macha, and the mysterious newcomer remained.

As soon as the shielded doors had closed, Darius jutted a finger at the young woman with the cornrows. "That little game you played back there was reckless and immature. Annaka, this is a war. There are casters depending on us to get them out of Tarahik. They're already afraid. They don't need you adding to their fears."

The young woman tilted her head, studying the senator with smug satisfaction. "No, they're relying on me and my crew to get them out." She slumped in a chair, rested her booted feet on the table, and took out a flask from her doublet. She swallowed a greedy mouthful. Even from this distance, a waft of syrupy alcohol drifted up my nose. Rum. It was so potent, she had to be drinking it straight.

That's both impressive and slightly terrifying.

Annaka put the bottle away and cracked her knuckles. "You're lying about this power you're hiding in the castle. I think you know exactly what it is. You're afraid of how people will react to it. You're afraid they'll want to destroy it."

Darius smiled, but it died on his face. "That is most people's reactions to anything they don't understand."

Annaka offered him a dry look. "I owe you a favour, Darius. It's the only reason I'm here, but if I'm to sneak out over six hundred casters on my ship, then I need to know what's really going on. Morgomoth is outside Tarahik's shields. He has you surrounded. You're a mouse caught in the cat's claws, and eventually, that cat is going to stop playing and make the kill. I believe you when you say you have a power in the castle capable of stopping him. It's the only reason Morgomoth would make such a dramatic entrance." She raised her flask, using the tip to point to the dark mass of cloud on the screens. "Morgomoth wants this power, too, doesn't he?"

Darius didn't back down or flinch. He would have made a formidable opponent in a battle. "Yes. I suspect it's why he hasn't directly attacked us. But you are right. Morgomoth will, and soon. I will not tell you what that power is, Annaka. You're here to take us to Vukovar, not to ask questions."

Annaka fixed everyone in the room with her smouldering gaze. "I want to know what kind of shit fight my crew and I have gotten ourselves into. The celestial shield on my ship is the only thing stopping that galactic storm from forming a complete circle around Tarahik. It's not going to take long for Morgomoth to realise his magic is being countered with another celestial shield."

"That's why we're leaving now," Macaslan stated after remaining silent for the duration of the conversation. The muscles in her jaw twitched. I sensed fear rolling off her in waves. She pointed to one of the radar screens. A red blip had manifested in the corner of the display. It moved at astounding speed toward Tarahik—toward the galactic storm. "Captain Arden has returned."

Colonel Harper stood up and cursed under his breath. "Not yet he hasn't. He needs to get through that storm."

"He will." Macaslan didn't sound confident, which made my legs feel as supple as spaghetti. She regarded Annaka with cool detachment. "Go down to the naval base and prepare your ship. Make sure everyone is safely aboard. We leave in thirty minutes."

Dizziness struck me. At first, I thought it was my panicked

response to Jad's predicament, but then I realised my spirit form was diluted. I was about as solid as a water bubble.

"Lunette, what's happening?"

I could no longer see her. Darkness closed in around the edges of my eyes.

Lunette's voice projected through my mind in a ghostly whisper. *"It's the Dark Divide. Your soul is bound to it. It's pulling you back. At least, I hope it's the Dark Divide."*

"What do you mean, you hope?"

"It could be him."

I reached for her, terrified by what she was suggesting, but it was too late. My hand evaporated, disappearing like water down a drainpipe. My entire essence was sucked away.

Into darkness.

Into emptiness.

Into the Dark Divide.

I woke up gasping for air. The cave's dank odour filled my nostrils, the scent permeating my hair, skin, and nails as though I were a corpse buried down here, slowly absorbed by the natural gases—if anything in the Dark Divide was natural. The mist had taken on viscous darkness. I caught glimpses of the tunnels shifting form. The earth walls groaned like a hungry beast as the labyrinth structured itself into a new intricate network.

This place is a maze on steroids.

Designed to trap me inside.

I hauled myself upright, my body still in shock from the maelstrom that had sucked me out of the living world like dust in a vacuum. Had that been the Dark Divide's doing? Or was Morgomoth behind it? It had to be for my soul to be dragged back at such a critical moment.

Jad.

He was surely flying to his doom right now. Carrier-hornets could withstand the dangers and hazards that came with galactic storms, but what Morgomoth had conjured was no ordinary storm. It was a monstrosity of darkness. I recalled the way Macaslan and Darius had exchanged terrified glances, their skin visibly sweating. Cold, hard terror made my head spin. Jad and his crew didn't stand a chance.

I wanted to scream at the world for being so unfair. How the hell had Morgomoth survived this crazy place for so many years? How was he controlling it now?

Realisation hit me like a submerged iceberg.

When Morgomoth had been trapped in the Dark Divide, he'd whispered threats and cruel comments in my ear, as though he'd been standing right beside me, watching and listening.

I can do the same.

I had to.

I focused my mind, mentally projecting. *"Lunette? Are you there?"*

Nothing.

Either the Dark Divide was blocking her... or Morgomoth was.

Lunette had told me that my spirit form had the ability to cross dimensions because it was technically still linked to my body. I wasn't dead. She'd told me to think about my body, to connect my soul through breathing, but what if I took that a step further? What if I applied the method to someone else?

Come on, Zaya. You've escaped chak-lorks, barghest hounds, and dissent rebels in the past. You can do this. It's simple. It's just like meditating.

I inhaled a deep breath and sat up straighter.

Think about the person you want to connect with.

Jad's face manifested in my mind, his tanned skin, his jet-black eyes, the dark hair that curled rebelliously around his jawline, his perfect lips which, even when he'd been furious with me, seemed to remain in a sedate line. Imagining him now, it struck me how young Jad was. His skin was smooth but blemished with faint scars from the countless fights and challenges he'd faced. He'd witnessed and experienced so much horror in his life, it had given him the wisdom of someone much older than his years, and that hardly seemed fair.

I sensed a familiar emotion inside me, something reckless and wild, something out of control that wrenched me like a magnet toward the image of Jad, only... I wasn't so sure if it was an image anymore. The steady beats of a pulse danced with mine. The air I breathed was shared with another, only their breaths were frantic and desperate. Excitement and fear washed over me, but these weren't my feelings. I sensed them coming from someone else.

I opened my eyes.

I was standing in the cockpit of a carrier-hornet that had seen better days. Sparks flew out of the controls. Compass needles spun in endless circles. The aircraft's metallic plates juddered and groaned as though the entire ship were about to tear apart. Heat that would blister a human's skin swept over me. I spun around to find the hornet was on fire. Something powerful, possibly a lightning bolt, had struck the plane. The plastic jump seats had melted into an oozy goop, and even the metal sheeting was warped and blackened.

My mouth tasted coppery. Sitting in the thinly padded pilot's seat, his arms and hands strained as he struggled to keep the carrier-hornet airbound, was Jad.

He was flying the craft toward the galactic storm.

CHAPTER 7

"Are you crazy?" a voice screamed behind me.

I spun around, startled to find Talina marching forward with her hands on her hips. Her honey-blonde hair had been pulled back into a braid, her green eyes wide and terrified. The entire plane throbbed. Even in my spirit form, I felt a tremendous pressure build inside the carrier-hornet. The energy from the storm filled every crevice and nook. Wispy strands escaped Talina's braid, as though she'd shoved a fork straight into an electrical socket. Even the hairs on my arms stood on end, my spirit form not immune to the charge in the air.

Talina leaned over Jad's chair. She stared at the writhing black mass of cloud ahead, so thick it was an impenetrable wall. Slate-grey thunderheads flashed with blistering light. The storm looked like a hot furnace, the panorama shockingly bright. Circles spotted behind my eyes. By the time they'd cleared, the roaring storm had started its routine again. This unnatural formation was like the tide: swirling, ebbing, flowing, each cloud powerfully crushing together.

Talina wiped sweat from her brow with the back of her sleeve. "We can't fly into this. This isn't a natural galactic storm. It's something else."

Jad's eyes swept across the scanners. "The carrier-hornet is largely intact. We'll make it."

"We're on fire," another voice cried.

Sitting beside Jad in the copilot's chair was Marek. Dirt and oil were smeared across his face, his brown clipped hair matted with blood. I hoped it wasn't his. All his muscles were strained, as though he were sitting in a firing line, waiting for the final shot. The gold flecks in his eyes flashed brightly. "Jad, did you hear me? Go around and make a crash landing in the sea."

Jad had been so focused on the storm, on the aircraft itself, that when he turned his dark eyes onto Marek, I couldn't prevent a horrified gasp. A cut along his hairline bled profusely. Blood spilled down the side of his face onto his clothes. There were burns on his dark flight suit. His hair was wet from both sweat and ichor.

"We won't make it to the sea." There was nothing kind in his voice. The words were blunt and direct.

What had happened to him? What dangerous mission had Darius sent him on?

Talina gripped the back of the captain's seat, digging her nails in to remain upright. "Then make a landing now. We'll have to walk around."

"We can't." Jad's voice was filled with desperation. "The storm spans kilometres to the north and south. Chak-lorks will find us and kill us. Our only option is to go into the storm."

Fear skittered up my neck. I knew Jad was forcing himself to moderate his voice. The knuckles on his fingers were white. Even the booms and ricochets of thunder couldn't deter his concentration.

He took a breath, perhaps to steady himself. "We're doing this. I can control the fire."

Marek bit his lip. I sensed an angry retort at the tip of his tongue. "You can't keep the flames at bay and land the hornet. It will exhaust you."

"I've been through worse." Jad angled the carrier-hornet downward, relying on the scanners to direct his way.

Talina hurried to a chair and strapped herself in. She exchanged an anxious glance with Marek. The copilot shrugged. Marek had utter faith in Jad, but this time I wondered if he believed that trust was misplaced.

The sky was ablaze with purple and white flashes. The moment the plane broke the cloud cover, gales battered the ship. Smoke made it hard to see, harder to breathe, but I was certain there were faces floating in the black clouds. Faces with hollow eyes, skin bleached out with bloodless veins, limp hair hanging off what was left of their skulls. Their grave-cold hands tore at the sides of the carrier-hornet, ripping metal.

Marek's hands froze on the controls. "The plane's falling apart."

He couldn't see what I could. He thought it was the natural effect of the galactic storm. He didn't realise what monsters were waiting to tear him apart. Maybe that was a small blessing.

A metallic groan roared above. I looked up to see the roof split apart, the fracture between the sheets of metal and broken wiring expanding. A gasping cry escaped me. The creatures that wriggled through moved like insects, crawling over and under, working in unison. Fire painted all their faces in its burned shades, reflecting off their chalky eyes. When they pulled their jaws back, stubbed teeth appeared from their gaping mouths. Their foul breath smelt of blood and meat.

It was another testament to Morgomoth's power. Chak-lorks were his ultimate vessels of destruction, but these creatures were something else. These were lost spirits under his control. Ghosts who should have been guided by a necromancer to the next world, not puppets to be manipulated.

I had to do something. My friends didn't stand a chance against this unseen enemy.

Think. What can be done?

The carrier-hornet had quickly progressed to the castle, but I doubted the aircraft would reach the mountain hangar before it was entirely gouged and ruptured.

The dead are part of the storm.

If Morgomoth can control the storm through the dead...

Is it possible I could do the same thing? Even in my incorporeal state?

I directed all my energy and strength into the ghostly faces that dipped and folded through the clouds, urging them to leave, demanding they depart this world and cross over to the next. Warmth spread through me; my body infused with magic. When I looked down at my hands, a white aura, lapping and gentle as smoke, curled around my fingers. It wrapped around my arms, looping over my body, expanding until it filled the entire cockpit. Rays of luminance, as strong as a rising sun, broke through the clouds ahead.

Marek's elated voice rose over the cacophony of splitting metal. "The storm is parting."

Jad pushed the centre stick forward, increasing the carrier-hornet's thrust. The plane sped through the clouds, the acceleration nearly giving me whiplash. Burning streaks of metal shot past the windows as pieces of the carrier-hornet broke apart. It wasn't just the dead destroying the plane now. The elements were helping.

Heinous laughter filled my ears.

"Did you think it would be that easy?"

A chill spread through me, dowsing everything warm inside.

"Your magic is nothing compared to mine. You are incompetent."

Morgomoth.

He was here somehow. In my head.

"You are weak."

He was right. My necromancy was no match for his. The silvery threads of light I'd conjured were swallowed by darkness. The storm clouds closed in. Scalding wind melted parts of the plane. The aperture ahead narrowed. Morgomoth had taken command. My power no longer had any authority here.

Marek gripped the control panel. "We're not going to make it."

Jad tugged the centre stick to a hard left. "We're going to make it."

The carrier-hornet rolled on its side. The sudden turn threw me off my feet, sliding me across the flight deck as the plane banked. Shoots of pain lashed through my body. Jad diverted the power again, flying the aircraft at rapid speed, trying to ride the waves of the storm. The ends of the wings clipped the clouds, and they ruptured and ignited. Flames licked the carrier-hornet, travelling over what was left of the hull.

For a horrifying second, I was convinced my friends would be joining the dead. Talina closed her eyes and gripped her seatbelt, as though it could save her from the wreckage the plane was about to become. Marek's lips parted without words. His reflection in the window showed sad acceptance across his face.

Jad's hands played over the controls, giving the carrier-hornet a final burst of power. The aircraft rose on the crest of a cloud. It reminded me of a choppy wave at the beach, violent and destructive, crashing over us. The plane tipped, the viewport revealing the mountain hangar below. Jad angled the carrier-hornet downward as much as he dared, then reluctantly let go of the controls. The dashboard flared bright with warning signs. We were at gravity's command now, and she wasn't merciful. Wind tore at the plane, spinning us into the hangar, my stomach stretching to parts of my body where it had no right to be.

The carrier-hornet struck the tarmac, its underbelly screaming violently as it skidded down the runway and deeper into the mountain. Soldiers dived out of the way, scrambling from the flames. Some were smart enough to grab extinguishers and douse the fires that spanned over the tarmac.

The aircraft lost traction and came to a screeching stop. For a moment, all Jad, Marek, and Talina could do was stare at each other, breathing hard.

Marek laughed in giddy joy.

Talina clutched her hand over her mouth. "I think I'm going to be sick."

The lieutenant gave her a thumbs up. "Better than dying."

Jad unbuckled his seatbelt. "Out now. I can't control these flames much longer."

The three of them clambered out of the plane, scrambling through the wreckage, waves of sparks skidding in all directions. They ran from the burning ruins, officers of various ranks joining them as the situation became clearer and the need to flee grew apparent.

The carrier-hornet exploded, a blast of powerful wind throwing everyone across the tarmac. Flames streaked through the hangar like a meteor shower. It struck me as incredible that none of the other aircraft ignited.

Is Jad doing that?

Safe in my incorporeal state, I stared back at the carrier-hornet. It was little more than an inferno of melted cogs, metal, and debris.

Talina got onto her feet. The fire's glow lit the shock in her eyes. "That could have been us."

Marek slumped against a large box of cargo and gripped onto an anchor strap to support his unsteady legs. His neck was saturated in sweat.

Jad's expression was bleak. Streaks of ash covered his hair and skin. He didn't say anything. The dark patches under his eyes became more pronounced, and I knew he'd put all his energy into making sure the fire remained contained and didn't spread through the hangar.

"I see you have destroyed another Haxsan Guard aircraft, Captain Arden. These planes don't grow on trees, you know."

The three of them turned around.

Darius Kerr appeared through the smoky air. He looked strangely out of place in his tailored suit. "Do you have it?"

Jad took out a small pendant from his flight suit, which hung on a chain from around his neck.

"Not here." Darius's voice was a low command.

Many of the officers were back on their feet and ran toward the burning aircraft with fire extinguishers and hoses. Darius took the opportunity to gesture my friends forward. They hurried across the hangar, using the smoke for cover. Dozens of air vessels appeared through the haze, and the senator led them around the ships until they came to a solid wall. Darius waved his hand. The stone ahead rippled like the surface of a lake and then morphed into a doorway. A hidden exit.

Trust Darius Kerr to know where a glamour was concealed.

"In here." His voice was a little too frantic for comfort.

My friends slipped through the exit. I followed, quiet and ghost-like. On the other side was a long tunnel, dark and littered with cobwebs. A spider scurried across the ground ahead. Talina cringed. She hated spiders. She had screamed so loudly in our apartment when she'd had the misfortune of seeing one.

Jad took a small flashlight out of his pocket. The light looked lonely in the dark, bleeding in the shadows ahead. "What is this place?"

Darius took out his own flashlight. The glamour reappeared behind him, the door now a wall of compact stone. "It's an escape passage. One of many that connects the castle with the base."

He rushed ahead, the sound of his feet amplifying through the narrow shaft. The walls and floor were a dull grey, broken up by the occasional tree root. Water trickled down the sides, creating puddles in the uneven stonework beneath my feet. It was a dank, miserable place and smelt of abandonment and fear. Parts of Tarahik hadn't been maintained in centuries. I wondered how long it had been since someone had ventured down this passage.

Darius swept nimbly down various twists and turns. "I was hoping we would never have to use these passages. Now it's our only choice. Our celestial shield is breaking. Morgomoth is outside the boundary. It's only a matter of time before he gets inside. Everyone has been instructed to head to the naval base. We have a ship waiting. It is not our ship."

Jad's face creased with confusion. "We're leaving Tarahik?"

Darius nodded as he ascended a flight of dusty stairs "He's here for her. He'll kill us all to find her."

Understanding weighed heavily in Jad's eyes. He quickened his stride.

Talina, struggling with the ascent, looked as small and innocent as a child in the shadows. "Where are you leading us?"

The senator smiled ruefully. "I need you to use these passages and transport Zaya's body down to the ship. Can the three of you do that?"

My friends nodded.

Marek swallowed, the sound loud in the lonely stairwell. "Why has Morgomoth come back now? It's been a month since Stazika Palace. If Zaya is what he's after, why didn't he steal her then? He had the opportunity."

I couldn't help but notice that the flashlight in Darius's hand trembled. "He was weak, only just awakened. He's had time to gain his strength now."

"What does he want with Zaya?" Talina's voice was so quiet, it was barely audible.

"I don't know," Darius confessed. "It is most infuriating. Morgomoth is playing a game with us."

Jad's black eyes glittered. He was wearing that look that I found both compelling and maddening. His brilliant mind had concluded something. Something big. Something that was a game-changer. "Perhaps Zaya knows what it is Morgomoth is after."

Darius's voice broke into a sarcastic chuckle. "She's in a coma. Not likely."

"She's hexed in the same sleeping curse Morgomoth was sentenced to. She always said she could feel a presence around her. It was Morgomoth. What if Zaya is now doing the same?"

The senator raised his eyes.

"She was in the carrier-hornet with us," Jad confirmed. "Why else did the storm part for us? She was there. She was fighting Morgomoth's dark magic with her own."

Hesitance flickered across Talina's face. "Zaya is powerful. What if that's why Morgomoth is here now? What if he wants to corrupt her? Bring her on his side? We'd never stand a chance against two necromancers."

"She wouldn't," Jad and Darius said in unison.

"I know she never would." Talina looked down at her feet. Regret darkened her features. I wondered if she was thinking about Lainie.

The group arrived at a dead end. Darius waved his hand again, and a second doorway appeared. They clambered out of the secret passage into a torchlit hallway. I recognised the long tapestries that hung from the walls. This was the passage that led to the Midnight Garden.

Conflict warred over Darius's face. "I dismissed the guards on duty. You'll have a clear run. Get her down to the ship. Do it quickly. This castle isn't going to be standing for much longer."

The senator tapped Jad on the shoulder. There was a sternness in his eyes as his gaze dropped to the captain's chest, where the pendant was concealed. "Keep it on you at all times, understand? We four and Commander Macaslan are the only people who know about this."

Before any of them could answer, Darius departed. I wondered if he would return to the base, giving orders and pretending he'd never seen Jad, Talina, or Marek.

What game is being played here?

Marek watched his retreating figure. "He's an unusual character, isn't he?"

Jad pushed the door open to the Midnight Garden. "We do as he said. In and out. No one sees us."

The three of them stood frozen in the doorway, surprised by the person who leaned casually against my marble casket, her arms folded.

"Who the hell are you?" Marek cried.

Talina's cheeks coloured with surprise.

Jad's hand instinctively gripped the cast-shooter holstered at his side.

The young woman, who wore a black tricorn hat, lifted her head. Her smile was wide and cunning. "My name is Annaka." She jutted her thumb at my sleeping body. "Now, can you tell me what the hell this is?"

CHAPTER 8

Jad stormed into the Midnight Garden. He stood by my casket and glared at Annaka, his eyes fuelled by suspicion. "Why are you here? No one is allowed in the castle."

Annaka grinned nastily. "And yet here you three are." She waved for Talina and Marek to enter, who stood awkwardly in the doorway. "Come on. Don't be shy. We're allies."

My friends stepped forward, distrust in their eyes.

"Are we? Allies?" Jad's voice was tight.

Annaka's smile dropped. "You tell me. My crew and I risked our lives to get my ship here. Morgomoth, a caster who everyone thought was dead, turns out to be alive and has taken over Navask, and now waits outside Tarahik on the brink of attack. We've had days to leave, but Senator Kerr insisted we stay until you three returned." She directed a finger at each of them. "What's so special about you three?"

My eyes darted to Jad's chest, where the pendant was concealed.

His hand never left his cast-shooter. "Your ship?" Recognition lit across his face. "You're Annaka Vandergriff. The pirate."

Annaka snorted. "I prefer raider, thank you."

"A romanticised version, I'm sure."

I shook my head.

Of course Senator Kerr has connections with raiders.

Marek stepped toward Annaka, an undertone of amazement in his voice. "I thought you were a myth. People say they see sightings of your ship, but then it just… disappears. No one can ever describe it. It's impossible that a vessel can vanish so fast, but people say it does."

Annaka winked at him. "It's possible, handsome."

The lieutenant's cheeks lit in a warm blush.

Annaka fixed her attention on Jad. "The senator said you had a weapon against Morgomoth. A last resort that needed to be taken to Vukovar. I've searched this castle, and all I can find is Sleeping Beauty here." She nudged my coffin. Her eyes met the captain's meaningfully. "*Your* Sleeping Beauty, judging by the speed you rushed to her."

Jad's lips remained pressed together.

Annaka examined my friends. "Would anyone care to explain?"

When no one did, she laughed. "Don't all speak at once."

Talina shifted her feet. Her eyes were heavy, and she looked like she'd been deprived of days of sleep. "Her name is Zaya."

Marek twisted his head around so fast I imagined I heard his neck crack. "Talina, what are you doing?"

"She's worked out enough. If we're relying on her to get us out of Tarahik, we might as well tell her the truth."

Annaka raised a finger. "I do have a name, you know."

"Shut up," all three of my friends said in unison.

"Zaya is a necromancer," Talina revealed. "She's a victim of a sleeping hex. We're not sure how to wake her."

Annaka crossed her arms, scepticism clouding her expression. "And who cursed her?" She looked down at my body as though she expected me to spring up like a corpse fresh out of the grave and tell her this was all a bad joke.

"Who do you think?" Jad's eyes had been bright, but now they were dull, overcome by exhaustion. He needed sleep. And a doctor. The cut on the side of his head still bled.

"Morgomoth." Annaka spoke quietly, but the name echoed through the memorial room, resonating across the walls and dancing like a ghost up my spine. "Why?"

My friends never had the chance to answer.

Explosions rippled outside. The walls and floor shook. Patches of plaster tumbled from the ceiling, coating the tiles around our feet in dust. It didn't bode well that the castle, which was protected by magic, felt the impact of the galactic storm outside. It was a testament that the celestial shields wouldn't hold. Our enemy's power was unlike anything any of us had faced.

I swallowed nervously, afraid of what this meant.

He's succeeding. Morgomoth and his rebellion will break our shields down. Tarahik will fall.

I knew it with certainty.

Annaka's confident smile vanished. "This is it, isn't it?"

Jad ran out of the chamber into the hall. My friends and Annaka were hot on his trail.

Talina gasped when they reached the nearest window, her already fair complexion turning a shade paler.

Marek's lower lip dropped. "Providence save us."

I stared out the window. The glass slowly fractured, unable to stand the pressure of the impending magic. A nasty twist stabbed my chest. Outside, the celestial shields were ignited. Fire licked the surface, sparks raining down, sending a blaze of hot fire through Shadow's Wood. The flames jumped from tree to tree. In seconds, the woods were reduced to a raging forest fire.

I stood back from the window. Large embers hit the glass like bullets, causing the window to fracture farther. I strained to see through the ash and smoke. I wished I could have grabbed Jad's hand in that moment. Anything to steady my pounding heart.

The galactic storm was like a volcanic ash cloud, incinerating everything as it approached Tarahik. Heavy swirls of fire crushed upon one another, blazing into much larger infernos. Lightning forked through the flames. The destruction was spurred on by the hungry cries of thunder.

Talina stepped away from the window. "There are faces in the fire. Dead faces. Can you see them?"

My friends' shocked expressions were momentarily radiant in the window's reflection.

Jad unsheathed his athame-sabre. "Chak-lorks! Get back. Now."

I narrowed my eyes, straining to see beyond the flames. He was right. Corpses, pale, pliant, and rotting, floated in eerie advancement through the fire. They reminded me of demons. The entire image was a scene straight from hell.

Marek laced his fingers with Talina's and forced her away from the window. "How is this possible? Chak-lorks travel through water. This... is fire."

Jad's demeanour remained calm, but there was panic in his eyes. "Get back to the memorial room. All of you."

None of them had to be told twice. I followed, but something wasn't right with my insubstantial form. My feet were sliding, the muscles in my legs immobile. Something had hold of me.

No.

Not again. Not now.

The power that emanated from the Dark Divide burned as cold as ice and as hot as fire. I screamed, my lungs spasming. The force threw me onto my side, dragging me by the legs down the hall, farther away from my friends, away from Jad. I cried out to him, but it was useless. I was disconnected from him in this spiritual form. He couldn't hear me.

The invisible force snaked up my body. It tossed me like a projectile into an aperture of black smoke. The wind was knocked out of me. Darkness greeted me in an embrace, blinding my eyes. I was falling, tumbling, plunging into the unknown.

The Dark Divide. It has me. It will never let me escape.

The despair, the loneliness, the isolation—it all became too much. I closed my eyes and surrendered.

I EXPECTED to wake up on my altar, to be greeted by tunnels and earthen walls, but the scene before me was unrecognisable. That's to say, I understood what was happening around me, but I didn't know where I was.

What is this place?

I was standing in a large military campsite. Smoke burned my eyes, my nose clogged with the scent of choking fumes. It would have been a chilly night, but the haze that surrounded the camp sent a sticky wash of heat across my skin. My eyes adjusted to the smoke. Black tents were propped around me as far as I could see. There were rolled logs positioned in circles, where soldiers sat and ate around campfires. No laughter. No merriment. Just strained, impassive faces as the soldiers ate and waited.

But for what?

I risked a step to my right. A branch cracked beneath my foot, and I stilled. The sound rolled into the night, but no one noticed.

Thank Providence. I'm still in my spiritual form.

The soldiers couldn't hear or see me, which meant I could snoop around without being detected. I drew closer to the campfire, recognising the soldiers' dark uniforms and the insignia on their armour—a circle with a dissent swastika in the centre, held by an eagle and griffin.

I leapt back.

No.

Not soldiers.

Dissent rebels.

I stared ahead beyond the camp, to the maelstrom of shadows and flame. The galactic storm had destroyed the celestial shield. Tarahik was on fire. The blaze leapt from one tower to the next, which broke from their foundations to tumble like cut trees. Shadow's Wood, which surrounded Tarahik from the west, was one large firestorm. Even here in the camp, small animals—rabbits, squirrels, even deer and creatures I neither knew the names of nor recognised—scampered around the tents to flee.

I was watching the destruction of Tarahik from the other side. From Morgomoth's camp.

I need to get away. I need to disappear.

The Dark Divide was a more appealing option over this.

One of the rebels spoke, her voice dripping with uncertainty. "Why didn't he give them a chance to surrender?"

The voice cemented my feet to the ground.

No. Surely not.

I nudged forward, wishing my ears were mistaken, but they were not.

Lainie's eyes were swollen and red, her face streaked with sweat and ash. She swallowed her meat, but I could tell by the way she flinched that she didn't enjoy it. What strength was left inside me broke seeing her dressed in dissent armour. The red-lacquered insignia was as dark and vibrant as blood against her chest. For all I knew, it could truly have been made from blood.

One of the rebels around the campfire grunted. He wiped the crumbs from his unkempt beard and glared at Lainie. "Thinking about your friends?"

Lainie rubbed at her arms. "If my friends could just see what we're trying to do, if they could see reason, I know they'll join the ULD."

Some of the soldiers leered and laughed.

The dissent rebel with the beard shook his head, disgust clouding his dirty face. "They've had a month to surrender. They ain't interested in joining our cause. They'd rather serve humans and continue to be brainwashed by the Council of Founding Sovereigns." He beckoned with his fork to Tarahik. "Those casters in that castle have betrayed their own kind. There is no mercy now. They've no place in the new world. Morgomoth is right to let them burn."

Another rebel slapped Lainie on the shoulder. "Harden up, little girl. Those friends are dead. They chose their path. You chose yours. Forget them." He lifted his bowl and slurped his meat and broth. Some of the liquid trickled down his neck, amalgamating with the dirt and blood on his skin.

I wondered how many battles this group had seen. How many Free Zones they had watched implode. How many times they had delighted in hearing the screams as entire civilisations were burned by radiation. These rebels had desecrated cities and erased them from history. They'd scavenged the provinces, intimidating casters into joining their rebellion or killing them if they refused. It both saddened and infuriated me.

I stared at my friend—or the girl I thought was my friend. Lainie wasn't blind. How could she do this? How could she be a part of something this evil?

"Girl."

Lainie twisted around, her eyes reflecting relief at the welcome distraction.

A woman stood before the group. Her chalk-white skin appeared ghostly amid the smoke, her sleek bob, streaked black-and-white, straightened to such perfection, I wondered if it was a wig. The ends of her white lab coat were caught in the gale, revealing the deformity that jutted out from her side. A broken hip, never properly healed. Or the devastating result of a hex bomb. Whatever it was, it had to have caused her years of pain.

Hadar.

The name was poison in my mind.

She was Morgomoth's creepy scientist. The creator of chak-lorks. The mother of horror. Just looking at her made my insides struggle to keep the sickness at bay.

She hobbled closer, using a cane to guide her step. She smiled at Lainie, but it lacked warmth. "Your magic is required, girl. Come with me."

She shuffled back in the direction of what was presumably her tent. Lainie dropped her plate and scrambled onto her feet. I sped after her, keen to keep the pair in my sight.

What does Hadar want with Lainie's magic?

Lainie followed Hadar around the tents, some placed so close that the space between them was barely wider than an arm span. Lainie had to shove her way past dissent rebels who stood and gaped at the sky, watching the galactic storm smash down on Tarahik like a hulking beast. If I hadn't known any better, I would have said they stared in amazement, as though enraptured by a fireworks display.

Lainie struggled to keep up with Hadar's quick pace. It seemed absurd that the woman could move so fast with such a profound limp.

"Come on, girl." Hadar's voice was thick with impatience. "Time is of the essence."

Hadar entered a large tent pavilion covered in fine black silk, pennants with the ULD's insignia flying high above. Lainie stopped walking and frowned in confusion. This was no mere soldier's tent. Behind this pavilion was something important. Something perhaps Lainie did not want to get involved in.

Inhaling a deep breath, she drew back the tent flap and entered. I scampered in after her, my insubstantial form causing little more than a soft breeze.

It took a moment for my eyes to adjust. Torches cast flickering rays of light and shadow through the pavilion, revealing the horrible scene. Long wooden tables ran the length of the tent. Human bodies were stripped naked on top of them. Bloodstained knives and machinery I didn't want to know the names of had been left haphazardly on the tables.

A wave of nausea swept through me. This was a makeshift morgue. The humans had been burned by radiation, but it had been Hadar who'd butchered and experimented on what remained of them.

"Don't be afraid." The scientist smiled at Lainie. "Magic and science serve a purpose."

Lainie was pale. She trembled, appearing as though she wanted to run the other way. "What do you need me for?"

Hadar stepped aside to reveal a male caster tied to a chair. Chains had been secured tight around him, cutting into his wrists and ankles. His naked feet were scratched and bleeding, his arms so bruised, they barely resembled skin. At first, I didn't think he was alive. His head was down, his tangled hair a curtain that hid his face. Then he groaned. It was the sound of someone begging for death.

Hadar scrunched her thin fingers into his hair and forced his head up. I gasped, shocked by the brutality that had been unleashed on him. Both his eyes were swollen from too many punches. His nose was misaligned, his lower lip cut so severely that it hung across his chin, exposing the broken teeth behind it. His ears had also been slashed, but his blood-soaked hair prevented me from seeing how badly.

Fury ripped through me. No one deserved this, no matter who or what they were, or what they had done. I wished I'd had healing abilities. I would have poured every ounce of that magic into this broken man's body.

Lainie was breathing hard. Her ashen cheeks had nothing to do with her pale make-up.

"I need you to fix him," Hadar revealed.

Lainie cast a sad glance at the man. "I'm not a healer."

"I'm quite aware of what you are, Miss Binx. You're a harmonist. I need you to fix his mind. Relax him. Deep in that brain is information the ULD needs. Torture couldn't shake it out of him. Now I need you to find a way into his mind and extract that information. Do you understand?"

Lainie nodded and squared her shoulders, trying to appear brave. "I need to know his name."

Hadar let go of the prisoner's hair. His head dropped, lolling to the side on his shoulders.

"Zandor."

CHAPTER 9

*Z**andor*

The name was familiar.

But from where?

The dots connected. He'd been the caster tasked with replenishing the celestial shield. He'd disappeared, suspected of desertion or of being taken prisoner. Now I knew it was the latter.

Lainie took a hesitant step forward. "What is it I'm trying to find?"

Hadar's face shone ghoulishly in the half-lit tent. "The answer to the celestial shield."

"But it's destroyed. It's falling as we speak."

"It's *nearly* destroyed. When it's finally obliterated, our troops will be able to enter Tarahik, but Morgomoth senses something else in the base. Something hidden deep. Another shield of some kind. I've tried to get it out of Zandor through more... traditional methods." She motioned to her array of scalpels and knives, which were still wet with blood. "It seems he's willing to take this secret to the grave. Get in his head. Find what he's hiding."

Lainie didn't say anything. Anxiety flared across her face.

Hadar placed a hand on Lainie's shoulder. Her voice flowed smoothly like honey. "You are a powerful harmonist. I have seen how you've worked with our injured soldiers, removing their panic and calming their minds. Use that strength to save us all now. Tarahik is the last opposing stronghold in Navask. Once it's gone, all of Navask is ours. Its name on the accords vanishes. The Council of Founding Sovereigns, even the Haxsan Guard, will no longer have any claim on this continent. It will be the start of a new world. A new age reigned by casters."

"My friends—"

"Are in the castle. I know." Hadar stooped forward, her eyes level with Lainie's. "You do this, and I promise your friends will have the chance to surrender. You can even talk to them if you like. Try to make them see that what we're doing is not evil."

Lainie nodded. A single tear streaked past her cheek.

"Good girl."

Hadar limped back to the captive and tugged his head back. Zandor moaned. He tried to speak, but his damaged mouth prevented anything besides blood from spilling out. His eyes, at least what could be seen of them through the swollen lids and puffy cheeks, were glazed.

Lainie pressed her middle and index finger onto his forehead and shut her eyes. Her facial muscles stiffened, and her lips pressed together in stern concentration. I had experienced my mind being meddled with once. Back when I'd first met Lainie, she'd been suspicious of my arrival at Tarahik and had worked her way into my mind without my consent. I remembered the intrusive sensation, my thoughts and memories sifted through, pulled apart, and scrambled as she searched for answers. It wasn't a pleasant experience.

Judging by the way Zandor grimaced, he wasn't fond of it either. The rise and fall of his chest stopped. His face turned a shade that matched the ash that rained down on Tarahik.

He's holding his breath. He wants to die.

"I'm losing him," Lainie cried. "He's resisting."

Hadar watched her with a hawklike gaze. "You're not trying hard enough, girl. Dig deeper. Convince him to tell you."

This time when Lainie pushed into the prisoner's mind, her own eyes and nose started to bleed. Crimson liquid ran in little rivulets past her cheeks and down her lips. Zandor screamed, his mouth open so wide I saw the congealed blood on his tonsils. Something white came up his throat. It fizzed, foamy and thick like ocean bubbles. He began spasming.

He's having a seizure. Lainie, stop!

But she didn't. She was digging so deep into Zandor's mind that the tips of her fingers pierced his forehead.

She'll kill him.

She'll kill herself.

The entire scene repelled me. My spiritual form felt cold and clammy with sweat. Anger built pinpricks of fire behind my eyes.

This was not my friend. This was not the Lainie I knew. I needed to remind her of that.

I sped forward, slamming my body into hers. She fell back in an ungainly heap on the ground, her eyes bursting open with surprise.

Zandor's head lolled to the side, his hair flung back. The centre of his forehead had a hole about an inch deep. He looked like he'd been struck with a bullet.

"What happened?" Hadar hobbled around, her gloved hand tightening on her cane.

Lainie stared up at her as if woken from a dream. "I don't know. Something pushed me. Something intervened and broke my connection."

I stepped back, alarmed by my own ability.

I can move and touch things in the earthly realm?

Lainie was glancing around the tent, in search of the force that had knocked her over like a bowling pin.

"Get up, girl," Hadar spat. "Your task isn't finished."

No, Lainie. Please don't do it. I'll stop you again.

She climbed onto her feet, but before I could intervene, heavy wind whipped my body, pulling me back.

No.

The Dark Divide.

I had no idea why the mysterious dimension had brought me here in the first place, and I was terrified of where it was taking me now. The maelstrom of nightmare clouds rushed toward me. I was no match for it. The hideous, formless darkness tangled around my arms and legs. Wind screamed in my ears, sounding like the mournful cries of a thousand lost souls. I tried to slap the shadows away, to break free of the suffocating darkness, but it only grew in strength and intensity. When I no longer thought my ears could handle the pressure, the black-ridden storm vanished.

One thing was evident: the Dark Divide had transported me somewhere new. It was another tent, decorated with elaborate furnishings. Torches shaped into wolf heads had fire blazing from their gaping jaws.

I'm still in the ULD's military camp. But where?

"Hello, Zaya."

The voice sent a cold shiver through my veins, spiking ice into my heart.

I turned around to face the last person I wanted to see.

He sat in a large chair, extravagant enough to have come from a throne room. His bones were blackened by fire. Trapped souls ebbed in the smoke that made up his body. He wasn't dead, but he wasn't alive either. He was something else. Unnatural. Monstrous. Evil. Magic always came at a price, and I was seeing first-hand what the price was for choosing darkness.

Morgomoth.

His cruel eyes had me pinned like a butterfly to a board. I scanned my surroundings, seeking an escape, but thick folds of clouds closed around me again, trapping me in a merciless ring. Trapping me with *him*.

"Are you enjoying the Dark Divide?" His insufferable grin was vicious, his tone dripping with derision.

I swallowed, wishing I could erase the sickly taste of fear from my mouth. "Why did you bring me here? This is all you, isn't it? You control the Dark Divide. You brought me to this camp. You made me watch…."

I couldn't get the words out. It was too distressing to acknowledge.

You made me watch Lainie hurt Zandor.

You made me watch my friend become a monster.

Morgomoth's black teeth gleamed in the torchlight. "I did nothing of the sort… in relation to your friend, that is." He lifted a skeletal hand to his chin, pondering theatrically. "Lainie? That is her name, correct?"

I pressed my lips together, afraid of what I might say otherwise.

He doesn't even know her name.

Morgomoth let out a throaty laugh. "Your friend chose her path, but of late, she has been distracted, doubting her choice. Extracting information from Zandor is a test of her commitment to me and the ULD. So far, Lainie is passing."

"I stopped her," I fired back.

"You interrupted. It's why I conjured your soul here. I can't have you intervening in my affairs."

"Intervening? You sent me there. You wanted me to witness Lainie do that. You've been controlling the Dark Divide this entire time."

"I learnt to control the Dark Divide." Morgomoth stood, his burnt bones creaking, the wraiths around him hissing as he moved. He began to circle like a shark in the water, or an eagle hovering for attack. The shadows closed around us, the torchlight fluttering out, the space claustrophobic. I stood my ground, despite my legs teetering down to my toes.

I lifted my eyes to his face to find his gaze no longer derisive or scornful but curious. "I am the conqueror of this continent, Zaya. Navask belongs to the United League of Dissent. Tarahik will fall. The celestial shields have failed, and yet I know there is something in the base that's protecting everyone inside." He shut his eyes, as though his mind might be wandering the castle now, searching for answers.

The rush of blood to my brain made me tremble. "It's not me, if that's what you're alluding to."

A toxic smile spread over his face. "No, but you are part of it. I wonder what magic Darius Kerr and Commander Macaslan have involved themselves in now. Their plans are surely to flee. They do not have the strength or the caster power to fight."

I raised my eyebrows defiantly. "There's no point talking to me about it. I won't help you."

Morgomoth's black eyes glimmered, but he was looking beyond me.

I spun around, straining to see against the fluttering shadows.

Three figures appeared, their forms taking shape. I recognised Hadar's limp and wished I could break her other hip. Beside her was Lainie, holding her arms as though she were cold, all the muscles in her body tight. The third figure made my gut curdle. He was much thinner since I'd last seen him, his jaw and cheeks hollow, eyes sunken and skin pallid. His black hair was greasy, hanging in tangles around his face. Dark magic must have been poisoning his body, because his eyes were red and blotchy.

Vulcan.

He was a shadow of his former self. Since he was psychically linked to Morgomoth, I wondered if the connection was what drained Vulcan's appearance, his energy and magic transferred to his master.

Good. After what he's done to Jad, he deserves this.

But I couldn't help but feel a little sorry for the wasted life in front of me.

If only Vulcan had chosen a different path.

If only he'd chosen his son. Not Morgomoth.

Triumph shone in Hadar's green eyes. "The girl did it. She broke Zandor."

Lainie flinched, her lips parting in surprise. She'd seen Morgomoth at Stazika Palace, but judging by her face, this must have been the first time she'd been close to his charred form. She glanced between Hadar and Vulcan, as though one of them might help her.

Vulcan's eyes flashed with violence. "Don't waste time, girl. Tell your master what you discovered."

Morgomoth raised a silencing hand at his lieutenant, then swept his attention on Lainie. "Do not be afraid. I know you fear for your friends in that castle. I do not wish for their deaths. The deaths of any casters are a terrible waste. But your friends' time is running out. The reward Hadar offered still stands. Tell me what you learnt from Zandor, and I will give your friends a chance to surrender."

Bitter laughter erupted from me. "And kill them when they refuse to join your side. Isn't that right, Morgomoth the *Just*?" I spit sarcasm into that last word.

It sucked that no one could hear or see me except for Morgomoth.

Lainie stared at the blood caked under her nails. Zandor's blood. "There's a caster in Tarahik. A powerful witch. Annaka Vandergriff."

Morgomoth made a sound that sent all the hairs on my arms erect. Responding to his anger, the darkness around us crackled with energy. "So, Darius hopes to flee Tarahik on the *Velorosa*."

Vulcan stepped forward, speaking in a low, urgent voice. "We must advance quickly. By now they'll have everyone on board that ship. Darius and Macaslan waited for my son to return with the key. They've no reason to remain at Tarahik."

The key?

I recalled the mysterious pendant concealed beneath Jad's flight suit.

It's a key? To what?

Morgomoth spun on Vulcan, his eyes furious and glowing. "And whose fault was it that the captain made it back?"

Dark power radiated off Morgomoth in waves. A strange pressure built in my head. It wasn't just me suffering from it. Lainie winced and covered her ears. Hadar squeezed her eyes shut. Even Vulcan trembled at the terrible surge of magic that escalated in the tent.

Fear stabbed me, a reminder of just how dangerous Morgomoth was.

A glimmer of regret flashed across Vulcan's face. I didn't think he'd been scolded by anyone in his life before. "I take full responsibility for that."

Morgomoth snarled. "Get that pup of yours back into our ranks, with the key; otherwise, I'll be feeding the pair of you to the lycan-thors. Now get outside. Rally the troops. Destroy Tarahik, and sink that ship. I want to hear that the *Velorosa* is lying on the seabed by the end of the night."

Vulcan nodded at the command. He snapped at Lainie and Hadar to move, steering them out of the tent.

Morgomoth's snake eyes turned on me.

I arched my neck, determined to not be afraid, but in reality, fear ate everything that was brave inside. "Was that sad display for me?"

"That display was to show you that you have lost. But I am true to my word. Your friends and everyone in the castle will be given a chance to surrender. Even Darius and Macaslan."

"They won't do it."

"I am aware. That's why I'm proposing a trade."

My tongue felt paper dry.

Morgomoth stepped closer, smirking down his nose at me. "I left you at Stazika Palace because I needed you to be at Tarahik. What I have planned for that castle... it requires the both of us."

I tried to step away, but the shadows pressed closer, preventing me from distancing myself. "I won't help you. Ever."

"You will if it means your friends will be permitted to live."

I barked out a laugh. "You mean they'll be prisoners."

Morgomoth's voice was a whisper, a sickening caress that built layers of revulsion within me. "All you have to do is open that door."

Before I could answer with a very firm *no*, a gust of wind slammed into me. The shadows coalesced, tugging on my arms and hair, dragging me closer to the yawning abyss that had opened behind me.

The Dark Divide was here. It refused to let me out of its grip.

No. That wasn't true.

Morgomoth was sending me back.

My heart was racing in my chest, pounding against my ribs like a mallet. The last thing I saw was Morgomoth's smiling face before I was enveloped in the darkness again.

CHAPTER 10

"*All you have to do is open that door.*"

The words were a mocking echo in my head.

I bolted upright, as though waking from a nightmare. The stone altar was cool beneath me. Murky shapes filtered in and out of the cave's mist, the tunnels reforming once again into a new maze, throwing dust as they moved. Rock grated against rock, defying physics. The sound was so loud it felt like it was scratching against my bones.

I felt the urge to slip past the slabs of shifting rock and find the door. Glimmers of eerie light shone through the new tunnels, a beacon lighting the way. My mind burned with the haunted image of Tarahik blackened to a crisp, my friends' bodies reduced to ash. I couldn't let that happen. If I didn't open the door, Morgomoth would ensure that it would.

I scrambled off the altar.

"*Don't,*" a voice snapped, right at my ear.

Lunette materialised beside me.

"You're back." A spark of relief soothed some of my anxiety away.

"*He's distracted. Otherwise, I'm sure Morgomoth would have barricaded my access to the Dark Divide.*" Her thin hand, much stronger than it appeared, gripped my arm. Her eyelids fluttered briefly, pain and regret dancing behind them. "*You can't open the door.*"

I shoved her hand away. "I have no choice. Morgomoth will kill everyone in the castle if I don't."

"Opening that door will destroy them anyway. This is Morgomoth. Nothing he says can be trusted. When he cursed you to this place, he knew that by leaving your body at Stazika Palace, Darius and Macaslan would bring you to Tarahik. This is all part of his plan."

I lifted my head up to the cavernous ceiling and let out a frustrated scream.

Open the door. Don't open the door.

I was filled with terror at what the consequences would be for both.

I dabbed at the watery haze that filled my eyes. "What does he want with Tarahik?"

A shade of doubt crossed Lunette's face. *"I don't know with certainty. I can only guess."*

"Then tell me what your *guess* is," I demanded through clenched teeth.

Her incorporeal form flickered as her expression darkened, wounded by my harsh tone. *"The ULD forces have taken every stronghold on the coast. My guess is Morgomoth wants to establish control over the entire coastline. He'll do it from Tarahik."*

Understanding struck me. "He'll re-establish the celestial shields. He'll link them in a network... a sort of defensive wall right along the coast. Meaning no one can flee Navask."

"Or get in." Lunette's voice was grim, echoing mournfully through the tunnels. *"If he links all the celestial shields together, controlling them from Tarahik, the ULD impedes Vukovar forces from the east. No one will be able to get in and help. Navask will be entirely cut off."*

My stomach felt full of broken glass. The continent had fallen. Morgomoth's meticulous plan had been followed with precision. Did Darius and Macaslan suspect? Judging from their attitudes in the war room, my guess was that they did. The senator and the commander were right. There would be no aid coming from Vukovar if we didn't act soon.

"I have to help my friends flee Tarahik." My voice sounded quiet, distant.

Lunette watched me for a long time, her expression difficult to define. *"I saw what you did with the galactic storm in the carrier-hornet. It was impressive, but it took a great amount of power on your part. It nearly drained you. This could—"*

I laughed. "What? Trap me in here for all eternity? It sounds like I'm stuck with that ending anyway."

"You are an untrained necromancer. Just remember what you're capable of."

And with that cheery wisdom of advice, Lunette's ghostly form disappeared in a fold of mist. I wondered if she'd returned to the otherworld or if Morgomoth had sent her away.

I closed my eyes, trying to evoke a level of calm. I focused on my breathing, my inhales and exhales. My soul might have been trapped in the Dark Divide, but I was starting to understand that my spirit form was still linked to my body. I could tap into it. Draw myself to it. I just needed the self-belief to achieve my goal.

That same soothing, hypnotic hum reached my ears, as gentle as lapping waves on a beach. The breathing in my head, loud and melodic in its rhythm, moved to my chest, my pulse no longer a trailing echo that felt too distant to be real but now beating lively inside me.

And that's when the pain started. My spirit form had connected with my body. My immobile, sleep-cursed body. I desperately wanted to open my eyes. Wanted to move. Anything that would drive sensation into me rather than the endless pain of paralysis.

Lunette's advice surfaced to memory.

"Focus on your breathing. Each time you exhale, send it farther. Imagine your soul is exiting with each breath."

I mentally summoned an image of my soul being extracted through my breathing, a little bit each time, becoming a disembodied entity on the other side. I understood now what Lunette had been trying to tell me during that first lesson. My body was the gateway. A connection between the Dark Divide and the earthly realm. I just had to cross through it.

I exhaled a final breath.

My eyelids fluttered open.

I was standing in the Midnight Garden Memorial Chamber, but my elation quickly fell. Jad stood by the large bronze door. He had his hands raised, using his magic to barricade the entry with fire. All the veins in his neck bulged from his skin. Sweat ran down his face. It was taking an immense amount of his energy to keep the door obstructed as something heavy pummelled the other side. The impact nearly drove the doors open, but Jad forced more magic into the fire, and the doors slammed shut with an epic boom. The flames leapt, embers glowing throughout the chamber. Horrible shrieks cried beyond the door, mad, incensed screams that combined into one chilling war cry.

Chak-lorks.

The celestial shields are down. They've broken through the castle.

They're outside.

"Hey, fire wielder?" a voice yelled.

Jad managed to level his gaze at Annaka.

She stood by my casket. "I appreciate the defence you're putting up, but we need to get the hell out of here."

"That *is* the only door out of here," Talina piped up. "We're trapped." Soot and ash lined her face. Her lovely long braid now resembled tattered rope.

Annaka stared up at the ceiling. "Darius Kerr, what the hell did you get me into?" she muttered under her breath.

Amid the fear, the confusion, and the screeching, tormenting wails from beyond the door, Marek's eyebrows creased in stern concentration. "This makes no sense. Why would Darius have Zaya brought up here? Why not keep her secure in the base? Or on board your ship?"

Annaka watched him with impatient eyes. "By all means, if you have the answer, do tell."

The lieutenant gazed around the memorial room, taking in the angel effigies, the stone plaques, and all the flowers and candles placed in ceremonial flair around the chamber. "This place is a connection to the dead."

Annaka's narrow lips shifted into a bitter smile. "So, Darius wanted her to feel at home. Who cares? It doesn't change our situation."

Talina watched Marek, the fear ebbing away from her face as she caught on to what he was saying. "Zaya can connect with the dead. This place would draw power to her."

Marek smiled, his teeth white against the ash that lined his face. "Darius was giving her a chance to make a connection."

Talina practically danced on her feet. "She did. Back on the carrier-hornet. Remember how the galactic storm parted? Jad was right. It was Zaya."

A rumble ripped through the air. The doors opened a few inches, pried with skeletal fingers, the flesh burnt away into glowing cinders. Twisted, half-decayed faces with hollow eyes stared through the gap, leering with blackened teeth. It looked like the doors to hell were about to burst open, the underworld ready to unleash destruction on the earth.

Destruction on us.

"I can't hold this much longer," Jad cried.

The doors shuddered.

Annaka contracted her hands into fists. "We can't be trapped in here. Darius wouldn't be so foolish." She crossed the chamber and began searching the walls. She threw a hostile glare over her shoulder at Marek and Talina. "There has to be another way out. Help me find it."

"A trap door, you mean?" Talina joined the search, combing the stones with her fingers. Marek did the same at the opposite wall.

Hopelessness rained down on me. They were running out of time and sloppy with panic. I knew Annaka was right. Darius would never have housed my body in a chamber where there was only one door in and out. There had to be another exit.

I studied the memorial room. The statues of weeping angels stared back at me. Sculptures of fallen soldiers, depicted with brave, courageous expressions, all had their faces angled toward the large shrine at the end of the chamber. The shrine was an impressive monument. The Tree of Life, made out of solid gold, had its enormous branches splayed out across the wall, the tips intricately laced with the night stars that had been moulded with accurate detail into the ceiling. The tree was lit with candles and incense burners. Bells with long ropes hung from the branches. On any other occasion, it would have encouraged peace and serenity, but now the fire and smoke that burned around the castle reflected off the tree's gold surface, making it appear as though it were in a forest fire.

I knew from my studies that the Tree of Life was an ancient symbol, so old that even humans had once worshipped it. It was also meant to express enlightenment at the end of the journey. The branches represented the other side, while the roots symbolised earth and mortality.

Symbolising death.

My skin tingled.

Why would a monument that embodies the bridge between life and death be here?

Anything related to the other side, even a hint of necromancy, was forbidden and punishable by death, yet here was a symbol staring me plainly in the face.

But only if you know what it means.

The journey to enlightenment.

A tiny burst of excitement rippled inside me. I approached the golden tree. There was a shape in its centre, a hand mark carved into the surface. The tapestries that hung off the branches swayed slightly, as though the softest breeze had made them dance.

A breeze blowing out?

Could it be?

I pressed my hand into the carved symbol, surprised when it moved back. The entire tree slid along the ground, throwing sparks and dust as it moved inside the wall.

A dark passage loomed before me.

Cold wind whipped gently at my face in a ghostly caress. Cobwebs danced in the draughty air, as though beckoning me in greeting.

Annaka's cynical voice ran out behind me. "Fancy that. A door just appears."

I detected a little surprise in her tone.

"No." Talina's eyes were bright. "That was Zaya. She's here."

"Well, whoever or whatever the hell it is, let's not keep it waiting." Annaka tossed an impatient glance over her shoulder. "Hey, Captain. There's a way out. Ditch those burning carcasses because I'm not waiting."

Marek crossed the chamber back to my coffin. He lifted me out of the casket, my body limp but safe in his arms, and took me through the trap door into the passage. I found it offensive that he grunted and strained. I knew I was a dead weight, but geez, I wasn't that heavy.

Annaka took up two torches from the wall and handed one to Talina. They ran into the passage, the glow from the flames fading fast. I stood by the trap door in my spiritual form, unable to pursue my friends. Jad was still fending off the chak-lorks. A dark cloud of dismay swept over me. This was no time for him to be a hero or self-sacrificing. He needed to run. Flames shot from his fingers, forming into a sphere of fire so bright it was like looking into sunlight. Even from this distance, heat licked my skin, making my upper lip damp from sweat.

Jad raised the fireball he'd conjured and sent it like a meteorite into the doors just as they burst apart. Flames erupted in a multitude of directions, bouncing off the castle walls, igniting everything in their path. It was incredible magic, burning brighter than any natural fire. Grisly, snarling howls filled the hall outside. Chak-lorks raised their arms to ward off the inevitable, only to be engulfed in the destructive fire. Some of them, the stronger ones, managed to evade the inferno and spilled into the memorial chamber.

Jad turned and ran. Apprehension scuttled up my spine. Despite my attempt to keep my breathing steady, my legs nearly buckled beneath me. Jad had spent his magic, and his progress was slow—slow for Jad, that was—to the trap door. I feared watching him being gained upon and ripped apart.

The creatures leapt onto the walls and ceiling, swinging from statues and effigies. They pursued Jad like a swift and reckless tribe of apes through trees.

A grinding shudder shook the hidden passage. I gasped, startled that the tree was sliding back into the wall.

Jad.

He isn't going to make it.

The tree had to weigh tonnes and was on a safety timer to prevent invaders from finding it. Even in my spiritual form, there was no way I'd be able to hinder weight like that.

There was no panic in Jad's eyes, just sheer determination and vigour. And that's when I saw the colour change in them. Black bled into red, as vibrant and dramatic as a red moon at night.

He's using his lycanthor strength.

His speed increased, his stride longer. He was nearly at the door.

A guttural howl swept through the memorial room. A chak-lork had swung from a chandelier, pivoting toward the captain. Its taloned claws, larger than any bird of prey's, were aimed at the back of Jad's head. I had an image of the captain split in two before me, a vision that would surely haunt me for life should the premonition have proved fruitful. At the last second, Jad raised his athame-sabre and plunged the weapon through the chak-lork in one fell swoop. Both halves fell to the floor, the legs skittering for a few seconds. Then they broke out into flames, scattering into ash.

Jad leapt for the trap door.

Panic made my blood pound, which circled through my body with a dizzying effect.

He isn't going to make it.

CHAPTER 11

The door was closing. Fast. And yet it felt like the world had frozen in place, every second slowed down, playing out the terror a little longer. Jad had two metres to go. One and a half. Half. A last impulse of determination shone in his red eyes, and he squeezed through the diminutive gap before the door closed with a resounding boom. It was such a sudden, final sound that the silence and darkness that encompassed us in the passage became alien, as though we'd been transported into an unknown world.

And we had. Who knew how long ago it was that the last person had entered this passage? The air was cold and dry, with just enough hint of dust to make my nose itch.

Jad leant forward, catching his breath.

A frustrated voice sped out from the darkness. "That was cutting it fine."

Annaka appeared with a torch, the light bouncing off her smooth brown skin. She raised an eyebrow at him. "Do you always do that, or do you just like showing off?"

Jad smiled, but it was tight and didn't contain warmth.

Annaka stepped back, shocked by the red fire in his eyes. "You're going to have to explain that one to me later, but for now, we need to find our way out of here."

She scanned the walls, possibly searching for any markings or engravings, but was greeted with only stone. She caught the captain looking at her. "Pray tell, what's so amusing?"

Jad wiped sweat from his nose. "Nothing. You just remind me of someone."

He pushed away from the door and moved down the passage, his shuffling steps the only sound in the darkness. "Where are Marek and Talina?"

"They're ahead. Not too far. I told them to keep going. They wanted to wait for you. They're kinder than me. I would have just left you."

"And yet here you are."

"So it would appear. I must be getting soft." Annaka hurried after him. "This person I remind you of is that girl, right? Beautiful, radiant, and charming, I suppose."

Jad squared his shoulders. "She's rash, headstrong, doesn't listen, and disobeys orders."

Ouch.

"Sounds like she and I would get along."

Jad turned around. Sincerity softened the hard lines that edged his face. "She's also determined, brave, smart, and honest. And she's very persuasive."

Annaka's lips twisted into a teasing smile. "Sounds like you've got it bad for the sleeping girl currently being held in another man's arms."

"Lieutenant Spiers is her friend."

"Lieutenant Spiers. So that's his name. He looks... interesting?"

There was a hint of a question in her tone. She wanted to know more about Marek, but Jad either didn't catch on or chose to ignore it. For someone who had been out of breath only moments before, his gait was astonishingly quick. It made me fret that he was using too much of his lycanthor strength. It could tip the balance that he'd worked so hard to control. It could bring back the monster—the assassin and the weapon—Hadar had created through cruel torture and wicked experimentation. Trajan Stormouth was someone I never wanted to see again, and yet traces of him were now shining through.

Don't turn to the darkness, Jad. Hold on a little longer.

I convinced myself that once he was on Annaka's ship and sailing away from Tarahik, he'd be able to rest. He'd be able to suppress the demon inside.

But they have to make it to the ship first.

The galactic storm had been the first attack, the chak-lorks the second. Morgomoth's ULD forces were outside just beyond Shadow's Wood. It wouldn't be long until Morgomoth and his rebels swarmed the base in a third and vicious attack. My friends had to get down to that ship. The alternative was… death.

Annaka quickened her pace. "How are you moving so fast?"

Jad was spared answering. Up ahead, two figures emerged as soundlessly as smoke. The captain's fingers traced the hilt along his athame-sabre, ready to unsheathe it at any moment. Annaka cocked her cast-shooter and pointed the barrel forward. The faint swell of hissing, distorted murmurs became audible.

"Get ready," Jad whispered.

Annaka nodded. Her finger was poised on the trigger.

The figures emerged from the darkness. Jad lifted his blade, ready to swing it down.

"It's us," a pair of startled voices cried.

Marek and Talina stepped into the light. The lieutenant was looking right at the tip of Jad's sword. He gulped.

Annaka let out a frustrated sigh. "What the hell? Do you two want to end up killed? I told you to keep going. And where's your torch?"

Talina swallowed heavily. "I dropped it, and the flames went out."

Annaka raised her cast-shooter again, worked up by anger. "I can't even trust you to be a light bearer."

Talina's cheeks reddened, but it wasn't with embarrassment. I could tell it was resentment coursing through her taut body. Even her hands had formed into fists at her sides.

Jad sheathed his athame-sabre. "We don't have time for this. We need to keep moving."

Marek was still carrying my body. I looked dead in the torchlight, my face and arms pale. Marek shifted from foot to foot, my weight apparently a heavy discomfort. I scowled at the insult.

"We couldn't leave you both." Talina's voice was tinged with disgust. She glared at Annaka. "Did you think we were chak-lorks?"

"You sounded like chak-lorks," she pointed out.

"The passage plays havoc with the acoustics."

"Yeah, no shit. You disobeyed my command."

Talina shoved her hands onto her hips and stared Annaka down. "I'm not a raider. I don't take orders from a pirate."

I paused at that, surprised by my friend's hostility.

Where the hell did this come from?

Annaka stepped toward her, leaving only the smallest trace of air between them. "On my ship, you will."

"We're not on your ship," Talina fired back.

"Yet." Annaka's lips curved into a nasty smile.

The air sizzled with feminine challenge. I'd witnessed catfights before in the base and wasn't in the mood to see an episode of hair-pulling, shoving, slapping, and scratching. I didn't understand Talina's antagonistic behaviour, but it had to stop. Didn't these girls understand that Tarahik was a ticking time bomb?

I pressed between them, relieved my spiritual form was strong enough to push them apart. I don't think I would ever understand why my incorporeal abilities could have an effect on some things in the earthly realm but not on others. I suspected it had something to do with how strong my emotions were. There was only one caster who could offer an explanation, who'd experienced it before, but I wasn't willing to find the answers from him.

Both Annaka's and Talina's eyes widened at the mysterious gust of wind that forced them apart, but their body language still resembled feral dogs sizing each other up for round two.

Marek shook his head at the pair. "Let's keep moving. *Together*," he emphasised. "We can't have chak-lorks crawling in here to find us already fighting each other."

Jad took the lead, walking with aggravated steps down the passage. "We don't have time for this. If we can get into this passage, chak-lorks can too."

In a cruel twist of fate, as though Jad had spoken magic words, a shudder tore through the secret tunnel. Annaka spun around, staring back the way we'd come. The darkness was complete, her torch's rays unable to light anything beyond a few metres. Vertigo gripped me.

My gut warned that something very dangerous was about to occur. The raised hairs on my arms guaranteed it.

Light pierced the inky black ahead. The secret door at the entrance of the passage crept open, grinding across the ground as though mocking us, extending the terror just a little further. A figure stepped into the tunnel, followed by several more. Grunts, shrieks, and hideous giggles resonated down the passage.

Chak-lorks.

Their stalking gaits lurched forward, fire still rippling across their bodies. The smell of flesh cooking permeated the air. Their eyes locked onto my friends, an animalistic hunger lighting up the glassy orbs. Repulsive snuffling and sniffing sounds worked down the passage. Even from this distance, I saw the chak-lorks' nostrils flare, lips pulled back, jaws snapping at the scent of prey.

"Run," Jad demanded. "Run now."

My friends sped down the passage, kicking up dust and casting a thick cloud of grime around them. The chak-lorks raced forward, their horrible screeches a constant reminder of the horror that awaited my friends if they didn't move faster.

I forced myself to look over my shoulder, gasping at the sight. The chak-lorks were gaining. Their speed, their strength—it was unlike anything I'd seen.

The tunnel twisted up ahead. Marek followed the sharp curve, my limp body bouncing in his arms. I was slowing him down. I was slowing them all down.

"Give her to me." Jad took my body in his arms and crushed me against him. He sped forward, everyone else in tow.

There didn't seem to be any sense to the layout of the tunnel. It turned abruptly left, then right. Sometimes ascending, other times the descent so steep I wondered how no one toppled.

"This is madness," Annaka cried.

She was at the back, but I barely heard her over the hyena-like howls that reverberated down the tunnel. A chak-lork appeared behind her shoulder, clawed talons raised for her neck. Fiery tendrils radiated from its long fingers, about to clasp her in a burning strangle. She couldn't see the danger behind her—but Marek could. He unsheathed his athame-sabre, leapt forward with a war cry, and drove the blade into the chak-lork's abdomen. Fuelled by battle frenzy or a desire to protect, I didn't know which, Marek raised the weapon, slicing the creature's torso clean through. What was left of its body burst into flames before any of its gory features became apparent, which was something to be grateful for. That was an image I'd prefer to do without.

Annaka gasped. Surprise sprang across her eyes, and something else. Admiration. "Thanks."

Marek nodded. "You're welcome."

He swallowed, perhaps amazed by his own daring.

Talina watched the pair, and that's when I understood why she'd verbally attacked Annaka. I'd been aware of Marek's feelings for Talina, but I had thought she was oblivious or indifferent to him. Turned out I was wrong. She did like Marek; the hurt and jealousy that flickered in her eyes was all the evidence I needed. She turned away before either Marek or Annaka saw.

"We need to keep moving," Jad urged again, his voice determined. "There's a lift up ahead."

Relief rained over me. I knew Darius wouldn't have led my friends on a wild-goose chase. There was a reason why he'd hidden my body in the memorial chamber. It was a secure room, and it was equipped with an escape passage that led to an elevator.

Well, it had *been a secure room. I guess Darius didn't foresee everything.*

The cries of approaching chak-lorks spurred my friends on. The elevator ahead was old. Inside was a single platform. Outside, intricate scrollwork ensured passengers remained inside, though it had rusted so drastically that I wondered how the lift managed to still be intact.

I hope it's still in operation.

Something large, darker than the surrounding shadows, appeared from around a bend, barricading the lift. Everyone halted. The creature ahead shrieked, the sound a menacing threat down the tunnel. It was met with more sinister cries. Another chak-lork appeared. Then another. Three and four and five. More and more kept coming, creating a barrier between us and the elevator.

I strained to see beyond the mass of twisting, writhing limbs. The tunnel ahead divided at a fork. It made sense that multiple escape passages would lead to one elevator. The mountain rock was hard and thick, and judging by the age of this tunnel, it had been created with pickaxes and pales. Magic had come far later, after Tarahik was built.

I remembered what Darius said. No one knew about these tunnels. Only him… and Macaslan.

Then how do the chak-lorks know?

How does Morgomoth know?

"Jad." Marek's voice was high-pitched.

My friends were trapped from either side.

Tension lines cut deep into Jad's face. I could tell he was weighing up an assessment. His eyes took on a sinister shade, the deep midnight colour leeching out until it was consumed in a hue that reminded me of blood.

No.

He could absolutely not use any more of his lycanthor strength. He couldn't risk becoming Trajan Stormouth again, but judging from the power pulsing off him, he had every intention of doing that to save his friends. And he would do it. He'd destroy the chak-lorks. He'd break bones and rip off heads. The monster in the tunnel would no longer be the chak-lorks. It would be Jad.

"In here." Annaka darted into a small alcove with a deep drain. It must have been designed as a culvert to prevent flooding.

Marek shook his head, his eyes hooded. "We'll be trapped in there."

Annaka smiled. It was a grin full of secrets. "No we won't. Get in. Press up against the wall."

The lieutenant scrambled through the stale water that had accumulated over the years and flattened himself against the wall. "This is a terrible idea."

"This is suicide," Talina corrected, stepping into the culvert. "And this place smells like a sewer." She directed a hostile glare toward Annaka.

Marek looked down at his feet, barely stifling his cry of disgust. "I think this does connect to a sewer."

He moved his leg, sending ripples across the surface of the water. Something rather large, brown, and slimy floated past his foot.

Talina's cheeks turned a shade green.

Jad appeared, fear and urgency pushing through his voice. "Get back. As far to the wall as you can."

They scooted to the end of the alcove, which really wasn't that far from the passage. Jad held my body in his arms, silent in the dark, listening for telltale signs of the chak-lorks' approach. I didn't think any of my friends even breathed. Annaka's torch sent flickering rays of light across the alcove's walls.

There's no way we won't be seen.

Talina levelled the pirate with a stern frown. "Put it out. Throw it in the water. Otherwise, they'll see."

Annaka's impish grin reached from ear to ear. "No they won't."

I wondered what devious measures Annaka had in place, but the thought scuttered from my mind at the wheezy breath just outside the alcove. I whipped my head around. A chak-lork stood there, on the edge of the light's range. The creature's nostrils flared, inhaling the rotting stench of sewerage. The chak-lork turned, his eyes on my friends.

CHAPTER 12

They stood frozen. The chak-lork sniffed the air, the creature's chunky nostrils flaring. He might have looked burnt and horribly injured, but I knew there was strength in those decrepit muscles. Saliva dripped from the large stubbed fangs that jutted from his jaws.

Another creature appeared, dragging himself out of the darkness into the torchlight. This one was of slimmer build but equally grotesque. Something that resembled wet tar oozed between his crooked skin.

He looks like he's been baked in an oven for too long.

Fear forced its way into my chest, the seriousness of the situation closing in on me.

The newcomer widened his mouth and flicked his tongue like a snake. It was a hideous, mutilated purple thing. "Where are they?"

Little embers fell off the creature's arms as it leant forward to inspect the alcove. "It's empty. Thought you said you saw them enter in here."

The other chak-lork grunted, the mess that was his face pinching into a disgruntled frown. He gave the walls a thorough stare-down. "They did. This is witchcraft. Caster magic. They're in here."

The chak-lork's voice held hints of once being human, but now there was a metallic hitch in the tone.

For all I knew, Hadar could have ripped his voice box out and replaced it with an electrolarynx.

Marek and Talina stared incredulously at Annaka. She raised a finger to her lips, urging them to remain quiet. Jad continued to hold me tight, my head cradled under his jaw. Had I been present in my body, I could have imagined hearing his heartbeat, ticking faster and faster. Jad was studying the chak-lorks with venom in his eyes. His entire posture told me he wanted to grab his athame-sabre and slice them in two, or shoot them apart with a cast-shooter.

It probably wasn't a bad idea, if it wouldn't have attracted other chak-lorks to the scene.

No. Jad and my friends had to remain silent.

This time, both chak-lorks stepped forward to sniff the damp air.

"I can smell them. They're close," the burly one drawled, mouth salivating.

"Well, I can't," the slighter one protested, flicking his long tongue again. "All I smell is caster faeces. Admit it. You lost them."

The larger chak-lork didn't like that. He unsheathed his athame-sabre, faster than I'd ever seen the most agile casters accomplish, and, with a clean swipe, sliced the other creature's head right off. It landed in a gory mess at Talina's feet. She opened her mouth, about to scream, but Annaka slapped a hand over her lips.

The chak-lork wasn't finished. It stepped over its companion's decapitated body and entered the alcove, its gait startlingly bearlike. It roared a battle cry that iced me to the core, then flung the sword forward. Marek dived to his left, but he wasn't fast enough. The weapon sliced his cheek and ear. Blood pooled from the cuts. The lieutenant squeezed his eyes shut, his face contorted into an agonised grimace. I imagined he had a slew of angry curse words he wanted to shout, but he kept silent.

My insides toppled. If Talina didn't get to Marek's wounds right away, there would be serious risk of infection.

Go away. Please go away.

But the chak-lork wasn't done with his search yet.

Annaka, perhaps guessing what the creature was about to do, frantically signalled for everyone to duck. Everyone dropped, narrowly avoiding the second swing. The blade sliced through the air, the tip scraping across the stone, sending out sparks. The creature snarled, foul breath steaming from his mouth. Grunting, he kicked the wall, the impact causing some of the stones to crumble. Spitting into the water, he retreated, heavy footsteps lumbering back down the tunnel.

His voice echoed from the passage. "No one's here. They got away. Must have taken the fork farther ahead. Find them."

His command was met with a cacophony of hideous shrieks and wails that slowly faded. Their thunderous footsteps disappeared.

Marek made a beeline out of the alcove. He held his ear, his lips straining from the pain that no doubt throbbed in his face. Blood streamed from the cuts, running down the side of his neck and soaking his collar. "How bad is it?"

Talina carefully inspected the wound, apologising when Marek flinched. "It's not deep. I'll be able to heal it, but I need to apply an antiseptic potion on it first. Who knows where that creature's blade has been? If I heal it now, we risk bacteria being trapped under the skin."

Marek's face was the picture of misery.

Talina turned furiously on Annaka. "What the hell was that back there?"

The pirate glared. "That was me saving all your lives. Perhaps you should try being grateful."

"No, that was you nearly getting us all killed."

Jad intervened before Annaka could get another word in—or throttle Talina. "You made us invisible. It's the reason why Darius insisted you come to Tarahik, isn't?" He watched Annaka, evaluating her face, as though if he concentrated hard enough, he could bore right into her mind and retrieve the answer. "It's why you're infamous for being an escape artist and why your ship is never seen. You have the power of invisibility."

I wished I'd guessed it earlier, because now it was startingly obvious. It explained how Annaka had slipped through the castle unnoticed by the guards. She wasn't just a pirate, thief, or spy in the night. She was an *invisible* pirate, thief, and spy in the night. The gift of invisibility was almost as rare as necromancy, but unlike us, casters with the power of invisibility weren't hunted, captured, and killed. They were brainwashed into becoming spies for the Council of the

Founding Sovereigns—or so the history books had told me. I'd never really taken much interest in them. I never actually expected to meet one.

Talina didn't look remotely impressed. She held her head high. Both girls' gazes were riveted on each other in a squinty-eyed stare-down.

Jad stepped between them. His broad hands tensed as he clutched my body tight to his, my long hair running down his arm. A flash of red appeared in the captain's eyes but disappeared so quickly that I couldn't be sure if I imagined it. He focused on Annaka. "Why didn't you make us invisible from the beginning? We could have avoided danger. We could have avoided hiding in the first place."

Annaka's signature grin materialised. It was a smile full of challenge, capable of disarming the most dangerous caster. Darius had requested her help for a reason. Now I knew why. Her magic made Annaka one lethal woman. I certainly wouldn't want to get on the wrong side of her.

She placed her cast-shooter back into the holster at her hip. "I can only use my magic sparingly, and I need to save all my energy for what's coming next."

She moved to Marek and pulled his hand away from his face. "You need to stop touching it, handsome. Otherwise, you'll infect it. Here, use this."

She took out a handkerchief from her pocket, but rather than handing it to him, she applied it to his cuts. "Use pressure. Trust me, it'll help."

Talina's eyeballs looked like they were about to burst from her head.

Marek grabbed the handkerchief, his fingers touching Annaka's as she pulled away. Appreciation, maybe even fondness, lit the lieutenant's face. "What happens to you if you use too much invisibility magic?"

"I become weak. I get headaches."

Talina's face twisted in annoyance. "You *are* the headache."

Annaka winked at Marek. "You do not want to see me with a migraine. If you think I'm feisty now, wait until you—"

"Point taken," Jad intervened. "We need to move."

I watched the frustration form in the lines around Jad's mouth whenever the group stalled, the sheer drive to get them moving again, and some sort of inner battle with himself.

It worried me that he was losing his cool. Whenever he spoke, his voice was sharp and bordering on snappish.

It reminded me of Trajan.

He's using too much of his lycanthor strength.

The captain moved down the passage. At the elevator, he unlatched the iron handle and kicked the door aside. My body still wrapped firmly in his arms, he stepped inside and tossed the rest of the group an impatient stare. "The chak-lorks are gone for now, but they'll be back."

Annaka, Marek, and Talina were nearly in the lift when hideous shrieks echoed down the tunnel, proving Jad right. The cries escalated from multiple directions, meeting at the fork to reverberate along the walls in sinister harmony.

"Inside, Now," Jad cried.

Despite how quiet my friends had been, they hadn't been cautious enough. Swarms of chak-lorks approached from either direction of the tunnels, crawling over each other, snarling and biting, ripping through one another's limbs with their horrible sharp teeth. They didn't care how they captured their quarry, only that they did.

I felt as though I'd been thrown headlong into a whirlpool of fear. I remembered what had happened to Tusk when a chak-lork had merged with his body, erupting from the inside. The result had reduced Tusk to a bloody mess. That was horrible, unnatural magic. These chak-lorks didn't operate with water but fire. I fretted that all these creatures would have to do is spit fire, and everyone would be doomed.

Talina and Marek leapt into the elevator. Annaka just missed the fiery tendrils that stretched out from one of the chak-lork's burning arms and tumbled into the lift, her body hitting the metal floor with a loud whack. Marek closed the cage door and pushed the lever. There was a jolt, followed by a screeching whir of the cables clicking into motion after so many years, maybe decades, of disuse. But we couldn't breathe easily yet. The chak-lorks appeared, arms reaching through the metal cage, determined to rip bone from limb and flesh from bone.

Everyone pressed against the wall. I wished I could do something, but I was inadequate for any task in my spiritual form. The chak-lorks hissed and screeched, rattling the bars in an endeavour to tear them from their hinges. They reminded me of sharks attacking a cage.

Another sporadic jolt, followed by a shuddering lurch, swept across the cage. Talina stumbled forward, but Marek caught her before she could fall into the chak-lorks death grip. The cage descended, deeper and deeper, the darkness growing around us. The chak-lorks' screams disappeared, cut off by the mountain. Annaka had long lost her torch. There was no light in the mountain, just the whir and groan of chains and cables, and our intense breathing as we dropped lower into the dark.

CHAPTER 13

The farther we descended through the mountain, the smokier the air became. Marek began coughing, his gasps achingly loud. I fretted that maybe the chak-lork's blade had been dabbed in a silvex potion, and now there was poison running through the lieutenant's veins. The first symptom was violent coughing.

Talina's voice escalated with panic. "Marek! Marek, are you okay?"

The coughs sounded like they were ripping his throat raw.

"Does he sound okay?" Annaka snapped.

It was a horrible sensation, slipping farther into the dark, unable to help a friend who desperately needed it.

"He's been poisoned," Talina screamed, confirming my worst fear.

"Crying about it isn't going to help," Annaka yelled. "We need to get him to my ship."

Jad's voice sliced through the dark. "You both need to stay calm. Listen to the lift."

I stilled, every fibre in me frozen as I detected the strange sound between Marek's incessant coughing. A tinny whine, like cables screeching under too much pressure, shook the fine hairs in my ears. Anxiety spread through me, crackling with an energy all its own.

No. Not this again.

I had experienced an elevator drop once before, and I didn't fancy a replay.

Talina's voice was panic-stricken in the dark. "What's happening?"

The lift dropped.

I was detached from my body, but sensation really did come from the mind. My spiritual form underwent every maddening sense of terror. My legs felt about as supple as water, my gut cramming into my chest. Talina screamed; her cry shattered my ears. Annaka shouted at her to shut up. Marek said nothing. I wondered if he'd passed out. Jad encouraged everyone to hold on.

I was hit with a wave of confusion. Shouts. Cries. Screeching chains. Screaming pulleys. It all spun in my mind, making nothing coherent.

The elevator halted, jolting me across the floor. Light leaked into the metal cage. After so long in darkness, the brightness lanced my eyes. My friends gingerly peeled themselves from the floor, groaning and rubbing at pain that would no doubt turn into bruises.

Orange light reflected off Annaka's dark eyes as she lifted her gaze, the terror radiant in them. "Run! Get out of the lift."

She attempted to pull the metal doors back, her knuckles losing colour from the strain. "They're damaged. Wedged together. We can't get out."

I realised why she was so scared.

Fire.

Whatever place this was where we'd landed, it was burning. Flames licked the grill gate, blackening the iron. Heat wafted through the elevator, black smoke rolling into the confined space.

Jad picked up my body, which had fallen at some point onto the floor in all the chaos, and hoisted me over his shoulder. "Out of the way."

Annaka leapt back as he kicked the door down. It fell in a mangled heap on the ground, a great hole in its centre where Jad's boot had made contact. Impossible for an average caster.

Annaka turned her gaze on him with surprise. "When we're safe on my ship, I want to know exactly what your magic is." She stared up at the ceiling. "Providence help me. What diabolic crazy has Darius Kerr gotten me into?"

"Help Marek," Jad demanded.

My fear was confirmed. Marek had passed out on the floor. The smoke swirled over him like eddying waves across a stone. Blood pooled around his face.

Talina had been standing by the wall, silently crying. As soon as her eyes settled on Marek, her healing instincts kicked in. Coughing, she took three quick strides toward him and, with Annaka's help, lifted him from the floor. The girls draped the lieutenant's arms over their shoulders, securing him between them. His limp body must have been heavy, because Talina and Annaka both winced. At least they were working together and no longer fighting. If they survived this, I hoped their shared aim to save Marek would wipe out their ridiculous rivalry.

If we survive this.

The words were a nasty slap in the face.

What will happen to me if my body burns here? Will I remain like this forever?

If Annaka and my friends didn't escape, would I see them in the world beyond?

Or will I be stuck here?

A spirit?

Just a lonely essence haunting the world?

The dismal thought vanished from my mind as the crackling hiss of the fire matured to a roar. Survival became the only goal—for me and my friends.

Jad stepped out of the elevator. "Follow. Quickly."

The lift had taken us to Tarahik's navy dockyard, deep in the mountain where the sea met the caves. As an infantry cadet, I'd had nothing much to do with the navy base and had been down here only once. It looked different from what I remembered. The massive cave walls, once glimmering like obsidian, were now scorched and inundated with flames. Rocks and stalactites plunged from the ceiling, coming down upon us like a monster's sharp teeth.

Jad squeezed past the fires and sidestepped the shattering stalactites. Molten stone rained down on him. Talina and Annaka struggled behind the captain, coughing violently. Their faces were covered in black soot, their features hazy through the thickening veil of smoke. They lugged Marek between them, his feet dragging on the ground. One of his boots came off, but no one went back to claim it.

"This way," Jad shouted.

I wondered how he could possibly know where he was going.

Up ahead, the pier appeared through fleeting glimpses in the smoke. Warships, barges, and troop transports burned beside their wharves. Explosions blasted from the ships' hulls, and the water shifted from dark ripples into waves. Sparks shot through the air, as beautiful and magnificent as fireworks in the night sky.

Crackling, sputtering, popping sounds bounced off the cavern walls like heinous laughter, but it was nothing compared to the vicious shrieks that escalated. It was worse than the buzzing of hostile bees, worse than wolves howling together as a stalking pack. This was a war cry. A chant taken up to rally an attack.

I turned around, wishing I could unsee what burned my eyes. Chak-lorks. Hundreds of them. Maybe even thousands. An army moving in from every direction. They even came from the ceiling, crawling down like some kind of twisted version of spiders, weapons brandished.

I had witnessed Morgomoth's forces invade the castle, but now they had accessed the base, right into the heart of Tarahik.

"Keep going," Annaka cried. "Get to my ship."

Through the smoke, an immense warship appeared at the end of the pier. It was unlike any vessel I'd seen that belonged to the Haxsan Guard. Weirdly futuristic, it was both a ship and aircraft carrier, painted with a camo pattern but in darker colours. It was a black-and-grey beast that would have blended with the ocean waves at night, making it impossible to see. It must have been at least two hundred and fifty metres, maybe more, equipped with three large radar sets that were mounted on five rangefinders. I counted six gun turrets along the bow and seven facing the stern.

It had definitely been a Haxsan Guard warship at some point, likely attacked and stolen by pirates. How the ship came into Annaka's possession was a story I longed to hear. She was strategic and possessed a ruthless attitude, but even a ship of this scale would not have been an easy thing to commandeer.

Figures appeared on the ship. Haxsan Guard soldiers. Survivors. Refugees. Anyone who lived or had been housed in Tarahik was on the vessel. They screamed out to our incoming group, urging them to get on board, their voices filled with panic.

The flames ahead dissipated, providing us with a clear path to the ship. Jad's eyes shone arterial red. He was using his magic again to impede the fires, fuelling his power with his lycanthor strength. I wished he hadn't, but unless I wanted my body and my friends to be burned alive, it was the only way we were getting onto the *Velorosa*.

A horn blasted from somewhere on the vessel, a long, aching bellow that hinted at one thing: the ship was about to leave. The water turned choppy as the propellers deep below spun into motion.

The shrieks behind us grew even louder. The army of chak-lorks assailed. We ran, pivoting around the blazes of caster-fire that exploded from the creatures' weapons, bullets whizzing past us. I gasped when a projectile flew by the pier like a shooting star, pulsing with burning light. Purifying ripples emanated from the ship. The celestial shield flung the projectile back onto the pier. It smashed, hurling rock fragments into the sea, spraying us with hot, briny water. The last remaining gangplank to the ship was lopsided, hanging by a few threadbare ropes. I imagined the plank's scorched handrail would melt flesh from bone if anyone touched it.

Jad reached the gangway and stilled for moment, the tight lines on his face hinting that he was looking for any possible footholds. "Step where I do," he instructed over his shoulder.

He took one anxious step onto the gangplank. Then another. The plank was at a forty-five-degree angle. Anyone with half a brain could manage it, as long as they were careful.

So long as they're calm.

And my friends were far from calm.

I shot an anxious glance behind me.

Annaka and Talina reached the end of the pier, their cheeks smudged with tears and ash. Marek had regained consciousness, but he was slow and still relied heavily on the girls to keep him upright.

Sweat glistened along Annaka's brow. She spat blood onto the pier, her teeth stained in red. "How are we supposed to get up there?"

Whether out of fear or wanting to prove she was more capable than Annaka, Talina stepped onto the gangplank. She wrapped her arm around Marek, urging him to step where Jad trod. Annaka went next. It was painful to watch them test their footing while an army of chak-lorks came for them. I feared that at any minute, the ship would depart and they'd all end in the water, left to drown or be burned.

The gangplank groaned, metal slowly ripping away.

What if the gangway collapses?

My friends dragged themselves upward. I wondered how they could concentrate. How they didn't break down in fear at hearing the relentless cries of the chak-lorks, at the buzz of bullets flying past, or at the rippling explosions that inundated the cavern.

Jad reached the deck. Two soldiers leant forward and collected my body from him. Jad turned back, climbing his way down the gangplank, disappearing and reappearing through the smoky haze. He reached Talina. Even from this distance, it was evident by the tension in her upper body that the muscles in her overtaxed shoulders strained to support Marek. Jad effortlessly lifted Marek onto his shoulders, evenly distributing the lieutenant's weight like he was a rolled-up carpet, and continued his journey up the gangplank.

Talina dragged herself up the twisted, dangling walkway in pursuit. She'd had some combat training, but as she was an appointed healer in the Haxsan Guard, the majority of her coaching had been on medical education. She was nowhere near as fast as Jad. Annaka swiftly caught up with her, yelling when Talina didn't move fast enough. I understood the urgency. The chak-lorks were approaching fast. Fifteen metres away. Fourteen. Thirteen. I didn't hear exactly what Talina shouted back, but judging from the tone, it hadn't been nice.

More soldiers appeared on deck, quick to take Marek off Jad's shoulders. They laid the lieutenant next to me. We were both pale, our skin as ashen as snow. Mine was caused by lack of movement and sunlight, but Marek's was far more serious. For a terrifying moment, I thought he was dead. Only the very shallow rise and fall of his chest indicated life.

"Talina," he moaned, his voice barely audible.

His head lolled to the side. He'd passed out again.

Please let him be okay.

I turned my gaze back to the gangway, gripped by fear. Jad had returned to help Talina and Annaka. The smoke had thickened, and through it, I heard my friends' whimpering breaths as they emerged. Jad shoved Talina onto the deck. Annaka scrambled off the gangplank. She stormed through the soldiers, pushing men and women aside with her elbows, not caring who she bruised in the process. "Who's in command of my ship?" she screamed at the top of her lungs.

"Cryton," a man yelled. He was wearing combat gear I didn't recognise as belonging to the Haxsan Guard, and his arms were heavily loaded with two submachine cast-shooters. Now that I was aware of him, I spotted more men and women dressed in similar gear and regalia, each holding powerful cast-shooters or athame-sabres.

Annaka made her way to a ladder and climbed two steps at a time, likely heading toward the bridge. "I will kill my first mate."

The ship began to shake, vibrations rippling through my feet. Another motion pulled at my legs. It was a powerful surge forward. I realised the propellers had set to full rotation, the propulsion driving the ship away from the pier.

Jad!

He was still on the gangplank.

Of course, Jad would make sure Talina and Annaka were on board first. Others' safety was always his priority, which was one of the reasons I loved and cared about him so much, but sometimes his self-less attitude irked me. He'd thrown himself in danger. Again.

Ripping metal filled my ears. The gangplank was falling away from the ship. A nightmare image of Jad plunging into the water filled my mind. The ruined gangway would fall on top of him, its heavy weight sinking him farther into the deep.

I had watched him fall to the dark in Galvac Tower, and it had been like throwing my own soul into an abyss. I could not let that happen again.

Before I knew what I was doing, my feet were running toward the gangway.

CHAPTER 14

When I say running, what I meant was that somehow, I ended up at the gangplank in a blink of an eye. Another discovered necromancy skill, or power borrowed from the Dark Divide? I didn't know which. I was just grateful that my essence was capable of moving in time to grab Jad's hand and haul him from the plummeting walkway.

Gasps ran across the deck. Jaws dropped. Eyes bulged. I supposed it must have been a sight, seeing the captain appear on the deck so suddenly, as though projected straight from a catapult. He landed hard on the steel surface, shaking his head to clear what must have been vertigo. A small smile tugged the corners of his mouth. He knew it was me. At first, I was surprised by my own strength before happy relief settled through me. He was safe.

"What the hell was that?" a soldier cried.

The young man examined the area where I stood, but of course, he stared right through me, unable to see my spiritual form.

A deafening blast hit the port side, just below where I stood. The gangplank had been hit. Water rose like geysers, sloshing over the side, salt spray falling in a hypnotic mist over the deck.

Talina was bent over, cradling Marek's body and yelling at anyone who came close to trampling mine. Four medics rushed forward, lifting both myself and Marek into stretchers.

"Stay with them," Jad ordered.

Talina nodded. On either side of her face, wispy strands of hair had escaped her long braid, which was flattened to her temples by either sweat or seawater.

Jad hurried for the ladder that Annaka had taken only minutes before. Soldiers were firing their own cast-shooters now. Caster-fire sliced through the celestial shield, bullets hitting targets below on the pier. Chak-lorks fell, their hideous shrieks silenced by the treacherous water. Their reinforcements came by tens and twenties, swarming and regrouping. The creatures weren't only using cast-shooters now—they'd upgraded to cannons.

It was an impressive celestial shield that protected the ship. Explosions rattled the port side, but the only thing that managed to penetrate the shield was water.

How does Annaka's ship have such a high-tech barrier?

A buffer like this, where forces could shoot their enemy down and remain protected behind the shield, were exclusive to the imperial palaces and Free Zones. Or so I'd thought.

So long as the chak-lorks are kept back, we stand a chance.

I didn't what to imagine the devastation that would occur should even one of the creatures manage to cross the shield.

The air smelt of ash and salt. I spied Jad at the top of the ladder.

He's going after Annaka.

Which meant I had to go after him.

I dashed through the battle, weaving my way through the throng, gunfire and explosions rippling through my ears.

"Pull back," someone barked. "Get inside."

I reached the ladder and climbed two steps at a time, wild with impatience not to lose sight of Jad. My sea legs did little to help me, the *Velorosa* rocking each time explosions rippled across the celestial shield. I smashed into the rail more than once, still surprised that the world had such an impact on my essence. Did all ghosts go through this? I didn't think so. I wasn't dead, just detached from body, so it made sense that my mind and soul continued to experience reality, but this was one situation I would have been happy to skip.

When I looked back at the deck far below, it was empty. Everyone was inside. Panic flared within me like warning beacons. Each time a projectile bounced off the shield, it was followed by a deafening explosion in the water. Shock waves tipped the ship on its starboard side before crashing back down. Water shot through the air, showering me in a deluge, making my climb slippery and difficult.

I passed various viewing platforms and bridgewings, each new ladder testing the muscles in my legs. I wished I could perform that neat trick again and appear by Jad's side, but no matter how much I concentrated and thought about it, the magic didn't work. For now, I had to follow him the old-fashioned way—with my feet.

Jad was fast, despite the ups and down of the ship. He burst through the door into the wheelhouse, where I imagined the helm was located. I climbed the last rungs of the ladder, nearly slipping on the wet metal, and was surprised by what I saw when I entered the bridge. It was like stepping into an aeroplane cockpit, only ten times larger. My eyes roamed across the radars, navigational instruments, electronic equipment, and compasses. There were many switches and buttons, none of which I had a clue about what did what. Navigation equipment and charts were arranged haphazardly on a metal bench, as though someone had pulled them from cupboards in a hurry.

There were more people in the wheelhouse than was comfortable. Annaka was by the wheel, steering the ship, wincing each time an explosion flashed ahead in the glass screens. Everything on the bridge rattled. Darius, Colonel Harper, and Commander Macaslan stood by one of the navigation stations, lips bloodless. Red lights from the controls reflected on their pale cheeks. Plenty of able seamen were on watch, some staring through binoculars. I wondered how they managed to stand.

Darius's eyes swept across the bridge to Jad. "Is she safe?"

Jad clambered toward the navigation station, holding on to the edge. He was a capable pilot, but a seaman he was not. "There were complications."

If by complications he meant I was now in an infirmary somewhere on the ship, then yes, I could see how that would be a problem.

Macaslan grimaced. She and Darius had wanted me to remain a secret. But surely anyone who didn't know me would think I was merely a girl. What reason would they have to suspect I was a necromancer?

"We've got bigger problems than that," Annaka shouted.

The ship was approaching the mouth of the cave. We were heading out to sea, the dips and rises more violent. My gut felt like it had soured into curdled milk. We were facing monster waves. For a few horrifying moments, the entire bow was underwater, then up in the air, as though the entire vessel was about to be thrown onto its back.

"What's happening out there?" Macaslan's voice had a pitch of alarm.

"What do you think?" Annaka cried back. "I might be able to make the ship invisible, but Morgomoth's galactic storm will be impossible to outsail."

The vessel rode the waves out of the cave into the ocean, the water depthless, dark, and rising around the ship in heights only a hurricane could conjure. Annaka hadn't been exaggerating, but judging by the way everyone's jaws dropped, no one had expected Morgomoth's galactic storm to have built in such intensity. Churning black clouds swept across the sea from either side, fire and lightning sending flickering bolts down into the water, further infuriating the waves.

We may have escaped the navy base...

But would we escape the storm?

"THEY CAN'T SEE US?" Jad's voice rang across the bridge, tinged with anxiety.

Jad always knew what to do. He was always calm, always enduring and courageous in the face of danger, but the dubious look he passed to Annaka made my legs weak.

Annaka shot him an aggravated glare. "I made the *Velorosa* invisible the moment I stepped foot onto her deck. Morgomoth and his forces can't see us. We just need to pray to providence that we get through this storm."

Annaka stroked the wheel like an owner affectionately petting a cat. "We're going to get through this, girl. I have faith in you."

But she didn't sound certain.

I moved closer to the navigation station where Darius and

Macaslan stood—or at least tried to stand. They held on to the inbuilt handrails beside the controls, each lurch and drop of the *Velorosa* sending them off balance. Colonel Harper was behind them, legs positioned wide, arms spread to maintain stability.

Macaslan's voice was a harsh whisper. "This is madness. We waited too long."

"We couldn't leave without the key." Darius eyes rested on Jad's chest, right where the pendant would have been under the captain's flight suit.

Macaslan swallowed hard. She levelled her gaze at Jad. "Can you do something about the storm? Control the fires?"

Jad sucked on his lower lip for a moment, then shook his head.

She inhaled a shuddering breath.

"This is not a natural galactic storm," Darius revealed. "It's tainted with necromancy."

Jad squeezed his eyes shut as the *Velorosa* dived, the smooth contours of his face now taut. Even his hand by his side had curled into a rigid fist. He was no longer pale—his face was green. "There are chak-lorks in the storms. Not like the ones that attacked Stazika Palace. These were imbued with flames."

Macaslan's storm-grey eyes reflected the fires outside. "Hadar has taken her experiment to the next level. First water, now fire."

"She'll target earth next." Darius tossed his head back and chuckled darkly. "Why did I not see it before? Morgomoth and Hadar are combining necromancy and elemental magic with human DNA to make the ultimate army."

My jaw clenched so hard that if I were in my body, I would have made my gums bleed. I could almost hear Morgomoth's sinful laughter echo through my skull, overjoyed with contentment by his wicked plan. Water. Fire. Earth. Not only would Morgomoth have control over the dead but the elements too. His chak-lorks could literally form into water and fire. What would happen when they merged with earth?

A terrible scene played in my head. Chak-lorks burrowing down into filth and mud, breaking through the trenches from underground, sinking armies into sludge and bogs. If you couldn't escape water, fire, or earth, what chance was there of defeating the monsters?

Morgomoth would be an unstoppable force.

Correction. He already is an unstoppable force.

"And Zaya?" The sound of Jad's strangled words snapped me away from the nightmare. He glanced between Macaslan and Darius, desperate for someone to answer him. "What does Morgomoth want from her?"

He wants me to open the door.

I wished I could shout the words out, but no one would hear me.

Morgomoth wants me to unleash the Dark Divide.

And I can't.

The reality of my situation lowered my already dark mood into an even more dangerous temperament. I would be stuck this way. Forever. An essence, trapped between this world and the Dark Divide. I wondered how I would ever be happy again.

Lunette had warned me that opening the door would be the end of the world as we knew it.

But what does that mean?

Is there another way?

Could Lunette be wrong?

The thought vanished from my mind as the *Velorosa* plunged downward again. No one had expected the massive rogue wave that smashed onto the bow. Everyone on the bridge was flung from their feet. Many sailors hit the ceiling, slamming back down in tangled messes of limbs and screaming. Jad was tossed to the ground. The relentless waves tipped the ship, sliding him across the bridge. Darius and Macaslan clung to each other, holding the handrail for dear life.

Another wave pummelled the ship. Then another. Each was higher than the last.

How much longer can the Velorosa *take this?*

An image of the ship split in two flashed in my mind, bow and stern consumed by the sea, forever an underwater graveyard.

Each wave that rose was like the hungry jaws of a monster, the creamy froth its teeth, ready to swallow us into its depths.

Everyone in the bridge was airborne, then on the ground, then airborne again. They reminded me of swirling snow caught in fierce gales. Annaka was screaming. She and another man who I assumed was her first mate were struggling to get back to the wheel. Each time they crawled closer, another plunge dragged them away.

Despite the cool, refrigerated air in the bridge, drops of sweat beaded on Annaka's forehead. "We can't let the *Velorosa* turn parallel with the waves."

I had no sea training, but even I knew that navigating large waves parallel was dangerous. The *Velorosa* could roll and become an upside-down vessel in the water—or worse, sink.

Flashes of fire filled the windows.

This isn't a natural galactic storm.

This is controlled by Morgomoth.

He's trying to sink us.

I could not let him destroy everything and everyone.

Another wave crashed against the ship, this one so high that the windows revealed an underwater world. My hands turned clammy with nervous sweat. Faces floated in the water. Hundreds of them.

Chak-lorks.

Their skin was puckered and grey, hair swirling like reeds. Unctuous fingers tapped the glass, then began pounding it. Some of the creatures smiled at me, teeth scalpel sharp. Just as it had been on the carrier-hornet, no one could see them. This was a secret army. Worse than sirens, serpents, or krakens. That was an enemy I would have preferred.

The wave crashed back into the sea, leaving me shaken.

The dead are part of the storm. Part of the sea.

If Morgomoth can control the skies and the sea through the dead, then... can I?

Granted, it hadn't worked so well the first time, but I wasn't one to give up.

Focusing on my breathing, I summoned my magic—and courage. Warmth spread through me. When I looked down, a glow had formed around my hands, as wispy and gentle as smoke at first but growing into something as strong and magnificent as an aura. The magic flowed around me, filling the bridge with rays of light.

When I looked out to the sea, the storm started to part.

CHAPTER 15

I just had to believe I could hold on. To the magic, that was. Last time, I'd exhausted myself, using too much necromancy too fast. I was convinced that was the reason Morgomoth had been able to slip into my mind, tormenting and teasing, until I could no longer control the magic.

The galactic storm ahead was dissipating. Even the ocean was calming down. But boy, did it zap energy from me. I sensed death, sadness, and longing for life in the water and clouds. The chak-lorks might have been animated and under Morgomoth's every whim and command, but there were real souls in those bodies, trapped and hurting. I reached out to them, hearing their whispers and their cries, and tried to console them. I was radiating warmth, forgiveness, and sincerity, and I keenly felt how each chak-lork responded, their souls craving to escape the darkness Morgomoth had bound them in.

A heinous chuckle brushed my ear.

For a terrifying moment, I thought Morgomoth was standing right beside me, but the prickling sensation across my scalp told me he was only projecting his voice, linking our minds.

"You cannot save the dead. Or the Velorosa.*"*

I shivered. The cruelty of his voice washed over me.

"Go away," I snapped. *"You are not welcome here."*

His laughter escalated.

"The dead belong to me, Zaya."

I was getting tired of these mind talks.

I focused on my magic, imagining it like a white orb spreading farther and wider, taking on the sea and the storm. My chest pinched, then tightened. Shooting aches spread all through my essence. I was using too much magic too fast. My lungs felt like they were being squeezed into a pulp.

"You are not strong enough," Morgomoth mocked. *"You are untrained. Hopeless. Weak."*

I refused to acknowledge him, but I couldn't ignore what he said. He was right. My magic was dwindling. The light was leaving me.

I pressed my eyes tighter, refusing to give in.

Concentrate. Focus on the warmth. The kindness that comes with necromancy.

I had come to learn that necromancy wasn't dark magic as everyone feared. Like everything powerful, there were two sides. Two choices—one for good and one for evil.

Silver folds of light flashed behind my eyes. They were blinding at first, then softer, like the balmy rays in a sunrise.

"It's going," I heard one of the sailors exclaim.

Gasps of amazement filled the bridge.

I peeled my eyes open.

The galactic storm was rolling back across the sea, the waves calming.

Annaka dragged in a ragged breath and ran to the wheel, shouting orders at her crew. The seamen dashed to the controls, flicking switches and turning dials. Beneath my feet, I felt pulsations through the steel floor. It must have been the vibrations caused by the engines and propellers.

Under Annaka's command, the *Velorosa* sliced through the water, making quick progress out to sea.

Jad climbed to his feet and ran out to the viewing platform, his cast-shooter slung over his shoulder. I raced after him, nearly staggering when I saw what was left of Tarahik behind us. Ash rained down from a sky ablaze with lightning and fire. Tarahik's keeps had collapsed, falling like a set of dominos. The roar of the castle's death echoed across the sea. I imagined each level beneath the underground base dropping into the mountain, falling deeper until it met the sea, and even then sinking into a part of the world where no one would ever find it.

Macaslan and Darius appeared. The commander gasped and grabbed the handrail, wincing like she'd been struck by a blow. Our relationship couldn't be classed as friendly—most of the time, the commander infuriated me—but at that moment, I couldn't have felt more sympathy. She was watching her home burn. Everything she had fought for was being ripped apart by flames.

Darius wrapped a comforting arm around Macaslan's shoulders. He whispered something into her ear, and she silently nodded. I watched the pair slip back into the bridge, disappearing in the throng of sailors hard at work.

I focused back on Jad. This couldn't have been easy on him either. His eyes were the same colour as the flame-filled sky, his face beautiful but covered in sweat. A bruise had formed on his cheek, and blood had crusted on the cut in his hairline. I really hoped the flames in his eyes were the reflection from the sky, but I worried that what I was seeing was lycanthor magic taking possession again. The shadows under his eyes became more apparent as I drew closer. I reached forward, touching his shoulder, wishing I could comfort him.

He flinched, then slowly turned around. "Zaya?"

He was looking right at me, but he wasn't seeing me.

"I'm here." I cupped his face in my hands.

The fire in his eyes softened a little. He'd heard me.

He touched his cheek, his hand slipping right through mine.

"Zaya." His head moved like a satellite, searching for an echo.

I opened my mouth, wanting to offer more words of comfort, but my voice had disappeared.

I tried again.

Nothing.

What is happening?

The smile around the corner of Jad's lips started to fade, doubt creeping in. He pulled away, probably chastising himself for thinking he could sense me.

I'm right here. Please. I'm here.

But whatever connection I'd made had been as fragile as glass and was shattered.

Agony wrenched my spine. My wraithlike form was tugged from behind.

No.

The smell of death and decay flared in my nostrils. I risked a glance over my shoulder. The Dark Divide had ripped a void through reality, opening like a black hole. Harsh gusts of freezing air dropped me to my knees. It was as powerful as a fighter crusader's backwash, sliding me over the platform's edge, sucking me in like a huge vacuum.

Jad!

But my voice was a silent scream in my head.

My eyes stung with smoke and tears. Then the darkness closed around me, and I saw nothing at all.

Drip.

Drip.

Drip.

I imagined cool waters splashing my face. What felt like sea spray gently rained on my skin, soothing away the tension in my muscles. I opened my eyes, expecting to see a turquoise sea, or a beach with golden-white sands, but that was only a lovely dream. Instead, a drop of filthy water smacked onto my forehead. It trailed down my nose, where it dipped over my lips, taking a circuitous path down my chin.

Another drop fell.

I sat up, my breath taking long moments to calm. The familiar scent of damp earth floated into my nose. Wet, cavernous walls bordered me, large globules of what I hoped was water dropping down. I was in the Dark Divide, but this time the strange world had delivered me not to the stone altar but somewhere else. A tunnel. The walls were distant enough that I could comfortably stand, but I still had to be careful of the stalactites that adorned the cave ceiling, which hung like icicles off a frozen tree.

Where am I now?

I wanted to kick something. I'd been so close to Jad. I'd nearly convinced him I was there. It was so unfair. The Dark Divide had stolen the opportunity from me.

A breeze swirled around me. I listened, certain there was a voice calling my name. A familiar voice.

A smile played on my lips. "Lunette?"

She materialised in front of me. Her skin was as white and translucent as ice, her lips a shade of periwinkle, as though she'd applied glossy lipstick over them, but really, I knew it was postmortem hypostasis. I'd learnt about it in my first-aid training at Tarahik. If I looked close enough, I could just detect small veins of black around the corners of Lunette's lips, a sign of the decomposing process. I was grateful there were no mirrors or reflections in the Dark Divide. Lunette would hate seeing herself that way.

She floated several centimetres off the ground, hands on hips. *"You're back, I see."*

I wished she didn't have to say it like a chiding mother scolding her child for running away.

"Unfortunately, yes. Morgomoth must have sent me here."

I hated that he was so good at interfering. It made me feel so useless.

Lunette shook her head. *"It wasn't him."*

"What do you mean?" I waited for her to elaborate.

"I warned you what would happen if you used too much necromancy too soon. You exhausted yourself, and your soul couldn't hold on to the earthly realm. That's why the Dark Divide sucked you back in."

"Morgomoth controls the Dark Divide."

"No. Not always. The Dark Divide is magic. It has a mind of its own." She sat beside me, wrapping her arms around her knees. *"You cannot intervene with the outside world again. Not as an essence. Your place is here, finding a way out of the Dark Divide. Without opening that door,"* she added when I opened my mouth to complain.

"What if there is no other way out?"

She didn't answer, and I knew that meant it was a real possibility.

Lunette raised her hands in a consoling gesture. *"Listen. There are rules. You can be an essence. You can be around people. You can watch them. But you can't intervene. What are the people on the Velorosa going to think about the strange phenomena that just occurred?"*

"They're going to be damn grateful their lives were saved."

"*They're going to question what magic interfered,*" she argued. "*They're going to question if another necromancer is present.*"

"Is that such a bad thing?"

"*Yes.*" The tone in her voice was icy. "*Casters and humans are inherently stupid. They think all necromancy is bad. They will kill what frightens them before they let themselves or anyone else have a chance to understand. Do you want them to go on a witch hunt? Your body is protected for now, but if anyone learns the truth....*"

She let her words slip away.

Lunette didn't have to explain it. I knew the dangers from the history books. If casters learnt of my necromancy, they would either kill me right there and then or send me to the Council of Founding Sovereigns to claim their reward.

"I couldn't let everyone die," I protested. Even thinking about it made my eyes haze. I looked up at the ceiling, the rocky terrain staring back at me with mock indifference. "I need to get out of here. I need to wake up."

I was so tempted to head to the door—if I could find it. I actually had no idea which part of the Dark Divide I was in.

"*You need to rest,*" Lunette advised. "*Sit down and sleep. Let your magic build its strength again.*"

A mad impulse took hold of me. I got to my feet and walked away.

"*Where are you going?*" she cried.

I didn't know. I didn't care.

I just had to get away.

I wandered a long time, aimless, energised only by my pent-up fury. The maze of tunnels that made up the Dark Divide moved again, the rock walls rumbling as they shifted into new paths. If I hadn't been so mad, I would have been frightened. In hindsight, storming away from Lunette probably hadn't been such a great idea.

She'll turn up like she always does. She's just letting me cool off.

That's what I hoped, anyway. I didn't want to comprehend the notion that I might be lost.

Damn my anger and rashness.

Many times, I shut my eyes, focusing on my breathing, trying to reach out for my body again, but every attempt came back blank. Lunette had been right. I'd used up too much magic saving the *Velorosa.*

How long am I going to be stuck here, waiting for my strength to return?

The despairing thought vanished from my mind at the sudden crunching sound that reverberated down the tunnel. A shocking jolt tore through the cave, lifting the rocks up and down. I fell, my hip hitting the ground hard. A stalactite plunged from the ceiling, barely missing me. I leapt out of its path, crying when rock fragments shattered on the ground, shooting back up at me like missiles. The entire world was shaking.

It's an earthquake!

In the Dark Divide?

I supposed anything was possible.

I crawled, rocks raining down on me, dust stinging the cuts on my hands and arms.

Find something steady.

There was a large rock pillar ahead. Biting my lip, I wriggled through the deluge of falling earth and stone, framing my body against the secure column, hoping it was strong enough to shelter me. The tremors continued. Even the marrow in my bones felt like it was being tossed around. I sank to the ground, curling into a foetal ball. The rocks that hit the back of my neck were painful, but a sore neck was preferable to a broken skull.

The quake stopped.

I lifted my head.

Everything was still.

I barely trusted my eyes and ears, expecting the world to come crushing down again.

Something glistened ahead through the dust. It looked like... light.

Daylight.

I scrambled through the rocks, not caring that their jagged edges tore my dress or scratched my knees.

Ahead, a silver-white glow emanated from behind a smooth round boulder.

No.

Not a boulder.

A door.

CHAPTER 16

I touched the door, expecting it to disappear the moment my fingers connected with its smooth surface. It wasn't gold or bronze, rather a metallic colour that resembled sunlight rays in the early morning. It was a material not natural to the world, something that belonged to the Dark Divide.

Another door.

Which leads to where?

I was convinced its mysterious appearance had caused the earth-quake but was unsure whether I could trust it. It could be exactly like the one Lunette feared and was determined I would not set foot near again.

Beautiful, intricate latticework lined its exterior. The tunnel was still dark, but there was enough light glowing behind the entry to show that the latticework was a depiction of serpents. Their eyes were golden-green and slitted. Each creature had its reptilian head raised, fangs sinking down into the end of another serpent's tail. They were one long connecting loop—a symmetrical knot.

I inhaled musty air, unsure whether I could trust this entry.

Why did it just... appear?

Rule number one: Never trust anything that just happens to come by chance. If it's too good to be true, that's because it is.

And yet I couldn't help but feel propelled to open the door.

Soft, otherworldly voices came from behind the entry, their words insubstantial. Were they saying a warning to stay away? Or a beckoning to come forward?

The pull spread deeper, curiosity circulating through my blood. I nudged closer. I touched the handle, the briefest contact of skin, but it was enough to make the serpents come alive. The reptiles circumnavigated the surface, sliding around and over each other, scales shimmering emerald and gold. They slipped through the crack, disappearing into the blinding light.

I blinked back at the burn in my eyes. Its radiance was increasing.

A groan, as though emitting straight from infinite space, shook the door. The slab of rock fell backward. Defying every known law of physics, it became a ramp to another world.

I waited, expecting something dangerous to occur, like the Dark Divide leaking into the world and destroying everything as Lunette feared. But nothing happened.

A cool breeze touched my face. As the light settled and my eyes adjusted, swirling flakes of snow drifted through the opening. It wasn't quite a winter wonderland out there, as the snow hadn't been falling for long; there was still grass and earth visible on the ground. A line of trees appeared through the cold mist, their branches already starting to bow from the build-up of ice.

I wouldn't last long out there in my flimsy white dress, and Lunette would hate me for it, but inquisitiveness spurred me on. I crawled down the ramp, my dirty ballet flats sinking into the slush when I reached the ground. This was beyond anything I had ever experienced before. And I'd experienced some strange things.

Everything felt... real. The feel of air against my skin. The way my breath clouded as I exhaled. The sun was weak behind the cloud cover, casting a blue haze across the land. The mountains beyond the trees stood with tall white peaks, reminding me of the ranges that surrounded Tarahik. But I was far from the base. I had never seen natural beauty like this before. The only thing off about this place was the light. It seemed just a bit too dazzling, as though someone had scaled the brightness and contrast in a photo.

The glittering white snow started to fall harder. I should have returned to the Dark Divide, but when I stared back at the opening, which stood like a slash in the air, I couldn't bring myself to go back.

Lunette is going to kill me.

I shielded my eyes from the glare of swirling snow and moved through the trees. There were no animals. No tiny footprints in the snow. No chirping birds. They must have all been hibernating.

Is it winter?

It must have been.

The ground descended, and as I reached the basin of the slope, a structure appeared through the trees. It was a small cabin with a low roof and a tiny porch. Bitterly cold wind now lashed at my face, sinking right through my dress. Wet, heavy snow tumbled from the sky, soaking me. There was no time to turn back and trek my way to the Dark Divide. I'd freeze before I got there.

Feeling diminutive compared to the enormity of the forest, I hiked to the cabin. Light emanated from the windows. Not electricity but warm, toasty firelight. I stepped up onto the porch and knocked on the front door, admiring the way the wind chimes danced in the breeze. Someone had put a lot of work into making the porch look relaxing and homely. There was a little folding table and two sunchairs at the side, covered in dust, further proof that the weather was in the beginnings of a seasonal change and heading for a long winter.

The door opened. A middle-aged woman with a mop of messy brown hair appeared. She stared at me but didn't seem to take me in. She popped her head out and peered around the porch.

"Damn door," she muttered. "It's creaking and groaning again. I swear I heard someone knocking."

The hope that had accumulated inside me dwindled. I was still an essence, just a waiflike girl invisible to the world.

The woman turned back to close the door. Not wanting to risk the cold, I slipped inside, barely missing the handle as it neared my elbow.

"Isgrad. Willieth," the woman called. "Come to the kitchen and eat your dinner."

She rubbed at her tired eyes.

I examined the small cabin, grateful to feel the warmth that radiated from the fire. From what I could tell, there were only four rooms: a large living area with beat-up, antique-looking furniture, an adjoining kitchen, two doors that must have led to the bedrooms, and another that must have been the bathroom. The entire place could have fit into my apartment back at Tarahik three times, with a little room left over.

Two boys stepped out from one of the bedrooms and wandered to the rickety table, where three bowls of steaming soup waited. It smelt delicious. It was ironic that even in this disembodied form, I could still feel. Was my body hungry at this moment? It had to be for my insides to be rioting with uncontrollable cravings.

"Eat up," the woman, who I now believed was their mother, encouraged. She sat down beside them. "You don't want your food to get cold."

The youngest boy looked up, his blond hair falling over his face. He had blue eyes like his mother's. He couldn't have been any older than five. "Where's the bread?"

"No bread today." His mother picked up her spoon, blowing onto her soup.

"But we always have bread."

"Well… today we don't."

"We can't afford it," the other boy snapped.

He was older, maybe fourteen, with white-blond hair that appeared silver in the firelight. The only thing the boys had in common was their hair and blue eyes. The latter was like looking into the depths of a frozen sea.

The youngest sibling scrunched his face. "Bread, please, Mummy."

His mother dropped her spoon and leaned forward, elbows on the table, face in her hands.

Is she… crying?

"Willieth. No bread. We don't have any," the older boy yelled. His eyes burned with sapphire flames.

Willieth stared, his mouth open.

I wasn't sure whether he finally understood or if what his brother was saying to him was still unclear.

His mother lifted her head and wiped her tears away. She grabbed Willieth's hand. "Listen, sweetheart. The Haxsan Guard have taken all our coin. We have enough food to get us through the winter, but we don't have bread. We won't for a long time."

"But why?" Willieth's inquisitive gaze shifted from his mother to his brother.

The older boy, who I assumed was Isgrad, gave him a long, sneering glare. "Because the Haxsan Guard need children for their armies. Their numbers are dwindling. Too many of them have died. And now the Council is desperate."

Willieth continued to stare.

His mother squeezed his fingers kindly. "It'll be all right. You're much too young to be taken by the Haxsan Guard."

She passed a glance at her older son, her brow creased in worry lines. Isgrad evidently did not have the same luxury.

But he's too young.

Teenagers were conscripted into the Haxsan Guard at nineteen. That was the way it had always been.

My mind sifted through a deeper knowledge in my head. I'd read many books on the history of the continents. There had been one period in time when the Council of Founding Sovereigns had grown desperate and conscripted teenagers far too young for the Haxsan Guard. It had lasted for ten years. The ten-year winter had destroyed crops and frozen resources in the provinces. The Haxsan Guard forces had slowly died of starvation, or frozen to death. That's why, in the end, desperate to keep the Free Zones working and prosperous, children as young as twelve had been handed over to the Haxsan Guard. And if they weren't surrendered, they were taken.

But that happened decades ago.

I tried to recall the exact dates from the history books.

Maybe even a century and a half ago.

I swallowed, tasting bile in the back of my throat. I had either travelled back in time or I'd stepped into a memory.

I stared, my body tight with emotion. Panicky thoughts bombarded my mind.

If I was in a memory, then I had to be in either Isgrad's, Willieth's, or their mother's. If I'd time-travelled, then that was a bigger problem, because as far as I knew, that was a skill and magic no caster possessed. The Dark Divide had once again proved to be infuriatingly mysterious and all-powerful.

I'm an essence. They can't see me. The Dark Divide led me here for a reason.

Because I did not believe for a second that this was Morgomoth's work.

But even as I tried to console myself with those words, I fretted that the Dark Divide couldn't be trusted. What if I became stuck here? What if that was what the Dark Divide's intention had been all along? To trap me in this place?

Lunette will be furious.

I wish she was here.

"I want to go home," Isgrad announced suddenly.

His mother stilled, her thumb and forefinger tense on her spoon. She set it gently beside the bowl. "You know we can't." She smoothed out the apron on her lap. "They're searching the village every day now. We're lucky we got away when we did. They won't find you here."

Isgrad shook his head, unconvinced. His young face creased with frustration. "You think you can outsmart the Haxsan Guard? What a joke. They'll find us here eventually. And then you'll be executed, and Willieth will be the youngest child in history to be conscripted into the Haxsan Guard."

Willieth began to cry.

"Hush," his mother snapped, but it wasn't directed at the youngest boy. A spark of emotion flickered across her face when she looked at Isgrad. "You're frightening your brother."

Isgrad deliberately dropped his spoon. It hit the table with a heavy clang. He looked like he wanted to toss the entire table onto its side and storm out of the cabin, but he remained seated, his shoulders trembling. "We're going to run out of food, despite how much you lie and tell us otherwise. The weather is strange. Who knows how long this winter is going to last? We need to go back."

His mother pressed her lips together, perhaps biting back a retort. "Florian will be here in a few days. He's bringing food and supplies. Blankets. Candles. Talismans to keep us safe."

Isgrad scoffed. "You're an idiot, Mother. How many times has Florian left us before? Too many for me to count. Your boyfriend is a flake. He only comes back when he's run out of money. He's probably halfway to Thronesbore by now."

"Daddy's not coming?" Willieth's little voice radiated with despair.

Isgrad shot him a sour look. "Your dad is not coming. Mine's dead. Killed by the very people who want to take us."

Willieth dropped his spoon in terror. It landed heavily in his soup, which splashed onto his jumper, joining the already copious food marks on his clothes.

The boys' mother stood now, her slight hands on her hips. She looked like she was trying hard not to cry again. "Why are you being such a brat?"

Isgrad flinched.

"I'm trying to protect you," she continued.

Now Isgrad stood, knocking his chair over in the process. "You can't save me. Or Willieth. We're from the provinces. We have nothing. We belong to the Council. All you're doing is prolonging the inevitable."

Willieth was bawling his eyes out now. Even as an essence, his cries pierced my ears, sending sharp vibrations through my skull.

Isgrad's mother aimed a stormy glare at him. "Now look what you've done. Why do you insist on upsetting your brother? You know he idolises you."

She bent down and wiped away Willieth's tears with her apron, trying to console him. "It'll be all right. Your brother is just in one of his moods."

"Half-brother," Isgrad snapped, his voice filled with loathing.

He left the table.

"Where are you going?" The rosy colour in his mother's cheeks paled as she watched her son move to the door. "You can't go out there. The snow is coming down heavily. You'll freeze."

"Better than being surrounded by all this falseness."

Her lips twitched with uncertainty. "Don't wander too far. If there are Haxsan Guard soldiers out in the woods and they test you...."

She let her voice drop, the implications silent.

"Thought we were hiding in a place where they'll never find us?" Isgrad stepped out onto the porch, pulling the collar of his coat over his ears.

"Just be careful," his mother warned. "If you're tested, and they realise you haven't specialised...."

She didn't have to finish for me to understand the repercussions. In the past, a teenager's magic became apparent the moment they struck puberty. Today, there were late bloomers. I'd lied when I'd been a prisoner in Gosheniene, pretending I hadn't specialised in a magic in order to hide my necromancy. It hadn't been a big deal. The Council and Haxsan Guard couldn't afford to be picky and were willing to recruit what they called inferior casters, so long as that caster specialised in a magic before their twenty-first birthday, when it really mattered and they graduated from being cadets. No caster could go into the armed forces without a magic. If you never specialised, you were thrown back into the provinces, outcast and ridiculed for the remainder of your life. Most of those casters died from neglect, starvation, or sickness.

It was a grim fate not to specialise in my time, but it was far worse during the ten-year winter. If Isgrad was caught and tested, and no magic made itself apparent, he'd be taken to trial, sentenced, and executed. In the eyes of the Council, an inferior caster was a lazy caster. They had no place in the world.

No wonder Isgrad's mother is terrified.

Reluctant to leave the cabin's warmth but needing to quench my curiosity, I slipped through the door before it closed and followed Isgrad down the steps into the snow.

Bad idea.

The cold air bit into my skin like needle-sharp teeth, and I didn't have a warm coat like Isgrad. I stepped back up to the porch, deciding it was better to return inside than chase him into what was promising to become a snowstorm. Hopefully, Isgrad's mother would answer my knock on the door again.

Isgrad gazed back at the cabin, eyes burning with hatred.

There was a familiarity in that dark gaze, something that made the blood freeze in my veins. But then the moment passed, and I couldn't be certain if what I saw had been real or if my overactive imagination had created it.

Isgrad walked into the forest. Mist and snow swirled around his withdrawing figure until I could no longer see him.

CHAPTER 17

I woke on my stone altar, the cavern ceiling looming over me. Fog ebbed around the stalactites, so thick at times that I could have mistaken it for the white breakers in a river. I sat up, taking a moment to assemble my thoughts. I didn't know how long I'd been here. One minute, I'd been in the memory, or the past—I still didn't know which—watching Isgrad fade away into the snow, and in the next, I was here.

Sleep clouded my eyes, the grogginess tugging at my lids. It was like I'd woken from some deep, anaesthetic dream. Maybe I had.

Can I even be sure what I saw was real?

For all I knew, I could have been hit on the head by a rock, falling into an unconscious haze.

But I didn't think so.

It was real.

I could still smell the earthy scent of the woods and feel the blistering cold snow.

Where is Lunette?

She knew enough about the Dark Divide that she might have answers.

I examined my hands and arms, expecting my skin to be bruised or bleeding. The earthquake hadn't been kind, nor had the rocks and stones that had fallen on me, squeezing my airways. But there wasn't a scratch on me. It startled me out of my paralysis. I slipped off the altar, raised my skirt up to my knees, and inspected my legs. Not a blemish, which I knew shouldn't have been possible—I'd seen them marked with abrasions. My dress was dirty but dry, the fabric stiff where the grime had hardened. The material was no longer white; it looked like it had been buried in the earth, left to disintegrate.

I'd healed.

Which meant....

How much time has passed?

Can I get back to the Velorosa?

A longing to see Jad and my friends swept through me.

Could I?

Lunette said I'd used too much magic and needed time to heal, but now that the grogginess had faded away, I really did feel as though I were capable of anything.

Concentrate. You need to get back to Jad.

To all of them.

I feared what Darius had my friends doing next.

I shut my eyes, focusing on my breathing again, listening to the way it flowed in and out of my nose, my chest rising and expanding. The cavern was deathly still. For once, the ghostly wails from the tunnels didn't reach out to me. Or maybe, somehow, I'd managed to block them. Something else matched my breathing now.

Found you.

Or should I say, found myself?

Buzzing filled my ears. It wasn't the soothing hum that reminded me of cicadas during a sunset but rather a swarm of aggressive bees, hellbent on stinging someone who dared to approach their hive. Through it, I detected the sound of my own body inhaling and exhaling, becoming synchronised with my soul. Cramps drove through every muscle in my arms and legs. Pain radiated down my spine, stiff from lack of movement.

I'd done it. My essence had returned to my comatose body.

Now for the hard bit.

I had to levitate my soul from my body and into the environment. This was where my concentration often failed. Astral projection wasn't a great talent of mine.

I set aside the discouraging thought. This time, I imagined my soul attached to a string, extracting me away from my body. It took immense focus, but I wouldn't let the image slip away. I visualised my spirit form floating above my body, the string now taut where it held me.

When I opened my eyes, I had projected. I wanted to scream a whoop of joy, but then I took note of my surroundings, and any delight I'd felt over my success vanished.

I stood in the ship's infirmary. I'd seen some gruesome images in my time—burnt bodies, amputated limbs, lacerations. The ship's hospital was designed for trauma, but all I saw were casters lying on beds, bent over buckets and vomiting. I was grateful no one was severely hurt, but even with proper ventilation, the stench of sick was overwhelming. It made me want to barf myself.

Seasickness. The scourge of the ocean.

A soldier inhaled a shuddering breath, his ashen skin dampened in a cold sweat. "When is this intolerable rocking going to stop?"

A nurse with blonde hair passed him a paper bag. "I can't say. The captain says the sea is uneasy. She says the ocean senses evil on the surface." Her shoulders sagged. "It's a sign. Morgomoth and his forces are in pursuit."

The soldier wiped the dry crusts at the corners of his lips. Repulsion flitted across his face. "Captain? That woman is no more a captain than I am pretty. She's a pirate. A deserter from her duty to the Haxsan Guard. It's a disgrace that the senator and the commander asked her for help."

"Not so loud." The nurse's eyes were as large as platters. "They're just beyond that door. You don't want them to come out and hear you, do you?"

"What does it matter?" He grinned a nasty smile, revealing stained teeth. "The *Velorosa* is a cursed ship. It was the moment it fell into pirate hands. What I don't understand is how they're so confident Morgomoth won't find us. We're a floating duck on the sea. We'll never be able to escape—"

Before he could voice his complaint, he bent over and threw up into his paper bag.

Even in my spiritual form, my own insides were in a spin. Each time the ship dipped and rose, my gut jammed into my ribs, then plunged into my intestines. Up and down, up and down, my insides like a ball on a slippery court.

We must be sailing in a storm.

Or a hurricane.

I spied the door the nurse had mentioned. It was shut, probably locked from the inside. There were no noises or loud voices from the other side. The door was soundproof.

I'm practically a ghost. I should be able to walk straight through.

My head hit the door hard when I tried. I winced, surprised by the wretched tenderness that struck my body. I tried again, but each attempt was thwarted by the steel door.

What the hell is the point of being this way if I still have physical limitations?

I searched my memory, trying to recall if Lunette had taught me how to manifest in and out of solid barriers. Back at Tarahik, when I'd wanted to move quickly through the base, she had made our essences dissolve. Our spiritual forms had floated down each level of Tarahik until we arrived next to the war room, none the wiser.

Lunette had made it look so easy.

I focused on the door, which seemed to have grown larger in the space of a moment, or maybe my nerves were making me feel smaller. I imagined myself like the petals on a flower, tugged free by a fierce wind, each part of me drifting away. Holding the image, I ran to the door, giving myself extra oomph to get through.

The latch unlocked at the last second. Someone opened the door, and I fell right through them, smacking the concrete floor hard on the other side.

"What in the name of providence?" the person muttered.

I climbed onto my feet.

Darius wasn't looking at me but right through me. He turned and stuck his head out the entry, shouting into the infirmary. "Who keeps banging on this door?"

No one responded. From what I could glean, everyone in the infirmary was much too sick to take notice of the riled senator. He shut the door and bolted the latch.

"Perhaps it was a ghost," a voice suggested.

I spun around. Annaka was leaning against the wall, lips pressed into a smirk. I glanced around the private sick room. There were two hospital beds, one where my sleeping body had been placed, wrapped in warm blankets and IV tubes, and the other for Marek. He was sitting up, grimacing. Talina stood by his side, gingerly applying stitches to the large cut on his cheek and ear. She held her breath, the slightest tremble in her fingers hinting that she didn't want to mess this up. Marek's eyes were bloodshot and dull. Full-blown nausea racked me, and I questioned how he could sit so still. The blade that had sliced him had been laced with poison. His wound would heal, but it was going to leave him with a hideous scar. Already I could tell his confidence had shattered. His shoulders were heavy, and his head drooped. He wouldn't look at Talina, focusing on the wall instead. A part of me shattered seeing it.

He loves her. He needs to confide in her.

Talina had done the right thing not healing Marek's face in the tunnel. If she had, she would have closed the poison beneath his skin, and then it would have spread like cancer, consuming Marek in a slow and painful death. Cleaning the wound was the right call, but I doubted Talina saw it that way. Guilt flashed across her face. I wished the two would just confess their feelings rather than skirting around each other and making it awkward for everyone else.

A brief smile pulled at my lips.

I suppose that was how Jad and I were at first.

Captain Arden was standing in the far corner, his dark eyes shadowed with concern. I was grateful they weren't red. He fisted his hands, nails digging into his palms. I knew what was happening inside his head. Jad didn't like feeling helpless. He was fiercely protective of his friends. He'd see Marek's injury as his own failure. I wished I could hug him or say something to console him. I felt so useless in this pathetic form.

Beside Jad, Macaslan was perched on a faded black saddle stool, her cheeks a tinge of green. I didn't think anything could unsettle the commander, but apparently, the choppy sea was her undoing. Colonel Harper remained close to her, staring at the floor with an unsympathetic frown. At first, I wondered if he couldn't abide watching Talina stitch Marek up. Beads of sweat ran down his face, or perhaps it was seawater. He was drenched. A chill spread through me that had nothing to do with the cool air-conditioning. There was more happening here than met the eye. Colonel Harper was in some kind of posttraumatic daze.

What has happened?

Annaka's almond-coloured eyes seemed to sparkle in the harsh fluorescent light. The sway and movement of the ship didn't bother her, her feet firm as though she were anchored to the ground. She wet her lips and blew out a breath before meeting Darius's eyes. "Senator, we have to go back to the bridge. You need to tell me and my crew our destination. We need time to prepare our course."

Darius shook his head. "No. The only people I trust on board are in this room."

Annaka spat out a bitter laugh. "You might have trust issues, but my crew are my family. I can't sail this ship on my own. Once we're out of the galactic storm's range, I need to rest. I can't keep the *Velorosa* invisible when I'm asleep. You have no choice but to trust my crew."

Darius started to pace around the room like a caged lion. "It's safer that we keep our destination between us for as long as possible."

"Us? You haven't even told me our destination." She flicked some of her long cornrows over her shoulder. "How long do you think it will be before people start asking? People don't like uncertainty. They might be grateful to have escaped Tarahik for now, but the sea does strange things to people. Another day or two, and everyone is going to get restless. A destination is the only thing that will be on their minds."

Darius rubbed the short stubble on his chin. "They know we're headed to Vukovar."

"Vukovar is a large continent. They're going to want specifics. *I* need specifics."

"The only thing everyone on board seems to be occupied by at present is being sick. We have time."

"We do not." The certainty in Annaka's voice made everyone look up. "We're making good headway. Another hour or so and we'll be away from the galactic storm. The sea will settle. That's when people are going to start asking questions."

The senator's words fell harshly from his lips. "There are spies everywhere. I can guarantee there will be one on this ship. My instinct is always right," he added with a sharp undertone.

I stiffened, the revelation stunning me, though it shouldn't have. I'd wondered what Darius Kerr's magic was. He was so secretive. A mystery. Always right and five steps ahead of everyone else.

Annaka's unsettled laugh rang through the room. "You're a sensitive, aren't you?"

I turned to Darius, waiting for an answer.

He pushed up his sleeves, his muscles strained. His silence was answer enough.

How had I not seen this before? A sensitive was a caster who had premonitions. Their instincts and intuition were, for the most, 99 percent accurate. It was a rare magic, and heavily desired by the Council of Founding Sovereigns. Sensitives were wonderful interrogators, negotiators, and advisers. They could also use their premonitions for personal gain. I'd heard that all known sensitives were banned from the Free Zones' casinos and gambling halls on the basis that they had an unfair advantage.

I studied Darius in a new light. A chill settled over me. If he suspected someone on board was a traitor or a spy, he was probably right.

Annaka glared at everyone in the room. "This is my ship. I'm doing you a favour here. I'm in charge. Tell me our destination."

"A favour?" Darius spoke the word as though it left a sour taste in his mouth. "You're paying back a debt."

My curiosity was piqued. Annaka didn't appear to be the sort of caster who owed anyone a favour. She was confident, independent, and full of self-belief. I wondered what her story was. What did she owe Darius? And how on earth did she become a pirate?

The captain of the *Velorosa* stepped toward the senator with quick strides, but the uneven hitch in her breath told me she was rattled. "My ship, my rules."

Macaslan stood, snapping at the pair like a teacher admonishing two troublemaking children. "For providence's sake, our destination is Helms Point."

The tension in Annaka's shoulders rose. "A naval base? Seriously?

You think a pirate ship can just sail up to Helms Point without there being consequences?"

I imagined she meant the *Velorosa* would be rained down upon by caster-fire the moment the ship appeared in the base's early-warning radars.

When no one answered, she turned to leave, a curse under her breath.

Darius grabbed her wrist, his fingers pressing deep into her skin.

She scowled. "Senator, unless you want everyone in the room to see you toppled to the ground in a one-arm shoulder throw, and in the most undignified way possible, I suggest you let go."

If Annaka's eyes had been lasers, Darius would be reduced to tiny embers by now.

They stared at each other like two cats with their hackles raised. It made my toes curl with anxiety.

Darius let go and made an audibly defeated sound. "Forgive me. I am... not myself."

Jad had been silent this entire time. He looked like he'd prefer to do nothing more than roll into a bed and get a few hours of sleep, but he moved across the room and stepped between the pair. "We all need our rest. It's been a long day." His eyes settled on Annaka. "I'll come with you to the bridge. We can chart our course."

Annaka scoffed. "You have experience?"

"No," he said, making his way out of the sick bay. "But I'm a fast learner."

CHAPTER 18

*H*elms Point.

We're headed for Helms Point.

From memory, though it was foggy at best, Helms Point was a navy base north of the Black Palace. The palace was situated in the capital, Muiren, the most protected Free Zone in all of Vukovar. Helms Point had to be at least 150 kilometres away from Muiren, but it had been a long time since I'd looked at a map of Vukovar, so it could have been closer. Or farther.

Why Helms Point?

We were all fugitives. The Council of Founding Sovereigns wanted Macaslan, Harper, and I suspected Darius, too, dead. If there was one thing the Council hated, it was troublemakers. The Haxsan Guard at Helms Point would never accept us with welcoming arms.

Does Darius know someone in the base who's willing to take us in and hide us?

An entire ship of outlaws, refugees, and pirates?

It didn't seem like the sort of thing one could easily hide.

What is Darius playing at?

A blast of sea air hit me, specks of water swirling in a frenzied dance in the hallway's light. Jad had opened a hatch to the deck, revealing the world outside. I had followed him and Annaka through the infirmary, wanting to see them chart a course for Helms Point, but mostly because I wanted to remain close to Jad. I'd missed him. Our time had been… interrupted. I didn't know what we were. Not a couple. We'd never reached that point. Or had we? Everything was so up in the air. This sleeping curse had ruined everything.

It was night outside, the horizon lit by lightning forks, the clouds churning too fast to be natural. Rain fell in a torrent across the sea. The waves roared like monsters that wanted to devour the ship. It brought on a grim thought.

I suppose there really are creatures in the deep that would eat us if they had half a chance.

"Hey there, Mr Moody and Brooding." Annaka slapped Jad's shoulder. She shut the hatch and turned the locking wheel, securing the exit. "No one is to go out on deck. That's an order. The celestial shield might stop projectiles from hitting us, but it won't prevent you from being thrown overboard if you go out into that madness." She pointed down the passage. "This way is much safer."

I followed them down various passages, forcing myself to scramble fast when they climbed the steep ladders, and crept into the bridge behind the pair before the door shut. Three crewmen were present. The man at the wheel, who must have been Annaka's first mate, and two pirates on lookout, though I doubted they could see much through the rain and haze. They turned when Annaka and Jad entered the bridge.

A violent crash of thunder tore through the night sky, forcing Annaka to shout her order. "Helms Point. That's our destination."

Her first mate blinked, as though unsure he'd heard correctly. He was bald, had a bulky build from years of training, his muscles practically bursting out of his shirt, and a long scar that started from the corner of his lip all the way up to his right cheek, like someone had put a hook in his mouth and tugged upward. It was rude to stare, but I found myself struggling to look away. There were cruel casters in the world, but a scar of that magnitude? I honestly found myself wanting to know his story.

"Helms Point?" He was red-faced and breathing hard. Driving a ship through this weather couldn't have been easy.

"You heard me." Annaka shouted instructions and coordinates I didn't understand. Then she motioned for Jad to follow her into an adjoining room at the back of the bridge.

She flicked on the light. "Welcome to the chart room. We call this the ancient library of the sea."

She wasn't joking. There didn't seem to be any logical order to the way the *Velorosa*'s inventory of charts was stowed. Graphs, maps, and plans were strewn across the table, the drawers beneath half open, containing so many diagrams and records, they looked incapable of being shut.

Jad kept his face neutral, but I knew from the slight twitch on his lips that he was unimpressed by the mess. "How do you work like this?"

Annaka cleared the chart table by sweeping all its contents to the floor. "Calm down, Captain Arden. I'm a collector of old and ancient maps. I like to study them in my spare time."

"Collect or steal?"

She waved his question away. "Same difference."

Annaka dug into one of the drawers and took out a large scroll. She flattened it onto the table across a glass display, though I wasn't entirely sure if that was what it was. There were buttons along the screen. She pressed one, and a sizeable holographic appeared, a projected image of the map. I stepped forward, amazed by the intricate, hand-drawn detail. The map might have been made thousands of years ago, but there was no denying that it was fused with magic. This was a map that updated itself on its own. It was a perfect visualisation of the oceans and geographic regions, with legend, scale, and orientation indicators.

Annaka's shout made me jump. "Cryton. Get in here."

The first mate appeared at the door.

"Get Ansell to take over at the wheel. I need you to be present for this."

Cryton left, then reappeared a few moments later.

Annaka shut the door and switched the light off. The holographic display, now the only light source, shone blue radiance through the chart room.

Annaka pointed to a red dot on the holographic screen. "That's us. We're still too close to the Navask coastline for my liking, but we're progressing well."

Jad studied the screen with curious interest. "Those dark smudges, that's the galactic storm?"

She nodded. "The very one we just escaped. It's travelling east after us, but it's slowing down. I'm confident we can put at least fifty kilometres between us by dawn."

"That's comforting."

I knew from the tone in Jad's voice that he thought that was still too close. Galactic storms were unpredictable in their strength and speed. The storm might have been slowing down for now, but it only took one change in the wind and they could advance with alarming celerity—and this was no ordinary storm. It was controlled by Morgomoth. Who knew what this galactic monstrosity was really capable of?

"Helms Point." Cryton said the name like it was a dirty word. "Is the senator mad? It's a secure naval base. Even if the *Velorosa* is invisible, they'd still pick us up on their thermal imaging radars. Going there is reckless. And stupid." He shot a nasty look in Jad's direction. "Why is he here? He's not a crew member. He's not even a seaman."

Annaka crossed her arms. "I couldn't agree more."

"Then why'd you bring him?" Cryton spat. "This is your ship. We don't have time for Haxsan Guards who think they're superior to everyone else. Especially amateurs like him. He knows nothing about the ship. Or the sea. You're in charge here, not him."

I stole an anxious glance at Jad, terrified he'd have the barrel of his cast-shooter aimed at the first mate, but instead, his face was cold with indifference, hands loose by his sides.

I swallowed, hoping Cryton wouldn't suddenly take a swing at Jad. He looked like he wanted to do nothing more than punch Jad's teeth out.

Annaka slapped a hand over the first mate's chest, forcing him to step back. "Calm down, Cryton. Save your testosterone for the taverns when we make land." She turned a smile on Jad. "Apologies. Cryton is a little adverse to the Haxsan Guard."

A little adverse?

Cryton was breathing like a madman in a boxing ring.

"He lost his hand to a soldier," Annaka explained. "They tried to take his sister away by force. She had been conscripted but refused to go."

My eyes travelled down Cryton's long arm. I'd never have guessed his hand was fake. It was so lifelike. The only indication it wasn't real was the way the light reflected off the skin. It was too glossy, too smooth, like plastic. His little finger was replaced with a hook. Something about that gave me the heebie-jeebies.

Annaka nudged Jad's elbow. "Cryton does have a point, though. Care to explain why we're heading to a secure naval base?"

Jad rubbed a hand across his tired eyes. "Can you zoom in to Helms Point?"

Annaka leant forward and pressed buttons on the flashing consoles. The holographic screen changed, displaying a closer view of the topography around Helms Point.

"There." Jad pointed to a series of curved lines just north of where Helms Point was marked. It was maybe five kilometres away from the navy base. "They're sea caves. Darius has a contact in the base who's going to meet us there and hide us in the caves. He'll have supplies, food, and weapons for us. He'll take the refugees back to Helms Point."

The beads in Annaka's cornrows glittered in the screen's luminance. "And who is this contact?" There was baiting in her voice.

Jad took a moment to answer. "I do not have the privilege of knowing."

She rolled her eyes. "Sure you don't."

I didn't believe Jad either. What Darius and Macaslan knew, Jad knew. They were a trio of secrets, all trusting one another and no one else.

Jad steepled his hands on the table, his jaw set hard. It was something he always did when he was thinking and had a million strategies running through his mind—at least, that's what I imagined was happening in his head. He pointed to the screen. "Could you anchor a short distance away and use the tenders to take us to the caves?"

Cryton grimaced with pure distaste. "How do you know about the tenders?"

I detected a trace of a smile at the corners of Jad's mouth, but he kept his face impassive. "All warships have them on a secure level above the engines."

"Warship?" The first mate's eyebrows drew together, his face forming into an irritated frown. "This is the *Velorosa*. Fastest and most feared pirate ship in the twelve seas."

Jad didn't flinch away from Cryton's hostile glare. "This is one of the Haxsan Guard's warships," he corrected. It wasn't a question. Jad was raising a fact. His eyes travelled between the pair. "You've made impressive modifications to it. Fitted it out with new navigational equipment. Painted it. Gave it a new name. But I've been on ships like this before. I recognise the layout. I'd love to hear the story about how you commandeered it."

Annaka's cheerful smile was false politeness, because underneath the jaunty façade was a threat. "I didn't think you had any experience on ships, Captain Arden."

"I lied."

"Clearly." Her taunting smile dried up. "What makes you think my crew and I commandeered it?"

Jad stared. "Because you're all pirates."

"I didn't steal it. It was a gift."

"Truly?" Jad didn't sound like he believed her. He focused back on the screen.

"Yes. A gift from Darius Kerr."

He whipped his head around.

I blinked in surprise.

"I wish I'd stolen it," she admitted. "That would definitely have raised my name on the most-wanted list, but alas...."

She said it like it was something to be ashamed of. Maybe it was in the pirate world.

Jad studied her quizzically. "That's why you're doing this for us? Because of a gift? That's what you owe Darius?"

Something dark churned across Annaka's face. "Yes. My father was a captain in the Haxsan Guard. This was his ship. When he died, the vessel was so old, the Council ordered it to be reduced to scrap metal and sunk in the ocean. As far as they know, it was. I'd been on the ship many times as a girl. I loved the sea. I couldn't bear the thought of this beauty being in the water, rusting into a forgotten tomb. Darius knew my father. I begged him to give me the ship. He answered."

I watched Annaka the entire time she told the story, studying the way her lips moved, the way her eyes flicked back to Cryton, a silent secret shared between the pair. She was mixing the truth with half-facts and eliminating others. I knew it. Jad knew it. There was more to the story.

Jad retuned his gaze to the holograph. "So, can you get us to shore with the tenders or not?"

Annaka laughed, but I detected alarm in the sound. "The entire Vukovar coastline is monitored. The Haxsan Guard are on the lookout for refugees fleeing from Navask—if there are still refugees out there —not to mention they're on constant watch for ULD forces attempting to infiltrate Vukovar. We'd have to be at least ten kilometres from the caves to keep the *Velorosa* from being seen."

Jad's firm jaw clenched. "But you can make the ship invisible."

"Yes, but I can't stop the thermal radars from picking up our location if we approach too close to the shore. There are protection spells all along the coast. They pick up everything from nine kilometres away."

"What's the sea like in that region? Could we make it on the tenders from that distance?"

I understood what Jad was asking. The sea was unpredictable. Galactic storms formed sporadically across the twelve seas and eight oceans. Just because it was sunny and fine one moment didn't mean it would be the next.

The captain of the *Velorosa* gritted her teeth. She analysed the screen with dark eyes. "It would take the tenders two trips. But yes, it's possible, so long as the weather behaves."

My internal temperature rose, sweat breaking out everywhere. That didn't sound promising.

Cryton's nose crinkled. "So, we drop them off ten kilometres from shore, take the tenders out, and leave them at the sea caves. Is that what you're saying? Then we're done and we can go back to normalcy?"

I wondered if "normalcy" meant raiding ships and stealing magic loot.

Annaka was silent for a moment. "Yes."

Jad stretched his hand out. "I want your word. Swear it on your magic."

I flinched, hating the aggressive tone in his voice. Jad's suspicions worried me. Swearing on your magic was an unbreakable promise. It meant you had to deliver. If you didn't, bad luck would return twenty-fold. In some provinces and towns, it was illegal to swear on your magic, though how the authorities found out was a miracle to me. I doubted the Council of Founding Sovereigns cared. They probably made casters swear on their magic all the time.

Annaka bit her lip as fierceness darkened her face. "You don't trust me?"

"I don't trust anyone."

"You trust the girl who's sleeping in my infirmary."

"Because she earned my trust."

"She earned something else, too, I see."

The briefest hint of colour rose in Jad's cheeks, but it disappeared so quickly, it could have been a trick of the light.

He wasn't backing down.

Annaka exhaled a dramatic sigh, then clasped Jad's hand. "I swear on my magic that I and my crew will get you to the sea caves near Helms Point. There. You trust me now?"

"Not in the slightest. But now I have your promise." Jad faced the screen. "Let's chart that course."

CHAPTER 19

Annaka was a sore loser. She didn't like Jad getting the better of her. Neither did Cryton. Most of the *Velorosa*'s crew were now in the chart room, watching with large eyes. It was a tight fit in the small room. The movement of dozens of bodies had me pancaked to the wall, fretting what the sensation would be like if someone stepped through my essence. I hadn't enjoyed it when I'd stumbled right through Darius in the infirmary. Feeling someone else's insides in you was a nauseating experience.

The crew grunted dismissively whenever Jad raised an idea, argued his reasoning, and flat-out refused to acknowledge any of his navy experience.

"We can't go that way. That's suicide."

"We'd never make it."

"You're a madman. You know nothing about the sea."

"Get him out of here."

Whenever Jad spoke, the arguing began anew. If it wasn't Morgomoth, his chak-lorks, his army of dissent rebels, or the galactic storm that killed us, it would be this crew's pride and bigotry.

We're screwed.

"Enough." Annaka's shout tore through the room, silencing everyone. "I'm the captain. I make the final decision."

At that moment, she reminded me of a younger version of Macaslan—alert, assertive, and confident. Most of Annaka's crew were twice her age. I knew her father was a respected captain in the Haxsan Guard's navy, but how on earth did this girl, who was only a few years older than Jad, earn these pirates' respect and trust? There was so much more to Annaka's story, and it worried me that we weren't being given the full truth.

She stepped up to the screen, her eyes raised at Jad. "Do you know why the Haxsan Guard's navy vessels and merchant ships take the Baruda ocean lane?" She pointed to the holograph, tracing her finger down the Navask coast, across the equator, and up to the Vukovar seaboard. A thin blue line trailed after her finger, creating a curved U-turn across the North and South Alanric Oceans.

Jad stared, chin high and back straight, but his face revealed a hint of reluctance. "Because the North and South Alanric Oceans are too dangerous."

"Dangerous and unpredictable." She slapped her hand on the western region of the South Alanric Ocean, causing the holographic's sapphire light to flicker. "Here, in this section, this is where rogue waves capsize, disable, and sink ships. Avoid it at all costs. Here—"her hand travelled to a region in the North Alanric Ocean—"ships face the sirens. I wish sirens really were merpeople who sing to lure sailors into the sea. But no, they're large sea serpents with teeth like piranhas. And they can eat through vessels," she added with thinly disguised fear. "Here." The Northeast Alanric Ocean. "If we go this way, we face the oceanic blackholes, which span kilometres. They're maelstroms that suck ships down and bury them in the sea. Here." A region in the Southeast Alanric Ocean. "This is the Devil's Square. Celestial shields cease to work. Navigational equipment goes haywire. Crew members start behaving strangely. Anyone who's ever attempted to research the phenomenal craziness of the Devil's Square has never come back. You want to know why?"

Jad aimed a patient glance at her. "I assume they met a merciless end."

"Damn right, they did. Do you understand now why every suggestion you've made has been complete insanity?"

I wondered how Jad put up with her snarky attitude.

Months of dealing with me, probably.

Before Jad could answer, Cryton stepped in. "Don't forget the decemkrus. This time of year, they migrate south to warmer waters. They'll have babies, which means they'll be protective… and fierce if we get in their way. I've seen one twelve metres in length. Bigger than any octopus. All its ten legs had terrible suckers. And its mouth. I've never smelt anything like—"

"Thank you, Cryton." Annaka gave him a terse glare that said *shut up*.

Her crew were restless with the jitters, men and women whispering their superstitions and objections in hushed voices.

Jad raised his dark eyebrows. "Then what do you suggest?"

Annaka swivelled a dial on the controls. The holographic display refocused, zooming in to the Sargrossio Sea. "This is the safest option."

Jad looked like he was repressing the urge to throw something at them all. "The frozen sea. You're kidding. We'd be facing icebergs and glaciers."

"My crew and I travel through those waters all the time. Yes, it can be dangerous, but we know what we're doing. We cannot travel through the Baruda ocean lane. Haxsan Guard naval ships would catch us. The Sargrossio Sea is the only option."

"It's too far north. We'd never make it in time."

Annaka twisted around, her face aglow with suspicion. "I was under the impression we were running from Morgomoth and his ULD forces. What is this 'making it in time' situation about?"

There was no change in Jad's stoic expression. He wasn't offering up anything.

Providence help us all.

This was never going to work if no one in this room could trust one another.

"There is one other way." Cryton's timid voice sounded ridiculous coming from his bulky frame. "The Bone Towers."

The name sent chills across my skin.

The Bone Towers. That doesn't sound good.

Annaka turned on her first mate, eyes burning with anger.

Jad homed in on them like a missile. "What are the Bone Towers?"

The captain of the *Velorosa* squeezed her eyes shut. Averseness seeped from her voice. "It's in a part of the North Alanric Ocean called the Bassinger Strait." She fiddled with the controls. The screen changed, revealing a new region. "The Bone Towers are monolithic rocks that rise from the sea. On the surface, they're around forty-five metres in height. It's a tight fit, but we can navigate through the towers… in certain places," she added with a hint of doubt.

"And you've done it before?"

"Once. Cryton and me. We swore we'd never do it again. We had to be constantly alert. The towers travel deep underwater. Just because you miss the surface doesn't mean rock won't scrape the hull. If you don't know what you're doing, the Bone Towers could easily gut the ship."

"How long would it take if we took the Bassinger Strait?"

"A few days."

"Then that's what we do." Jad jutted a stern finger at Annaka when she opened her mouth to protest. "You promised on your magic. Chart a course."

"Yes, Your *Highness*," she retorted with bitter enthusiasm.

"Why are they called the Bone Towers?" a crew member yelled, raising his voice to be heard over the din.

I would have liked to have heard the answer, but a tug yanked at my body. My legs gave out beneath me, causing me to hit the floor hard.

No. Not now.

The Dark Divide was back. It was a tear in reality, like a seam ripped in an item of clothing, the hole growing larger. My chest constricted, my lungs forgetting how to breathe as the unfathomable force jerked me to the opening, dragging me across the chart room floor like a rag doll.

"Jad!" I screamed, barely hearing my voice over the gale of bitter wind as the Dark Divide's suction engulfed me.

Tears sprang to my eyes when Jad turned around, his eyes searching for the source of my voice. He looked right at me, but he didn't see me.

I don't want to leave.

I don't want to leave Jad.

It was my last thought before the darkness enveloped me again.

THE AIR that rushed through my hair was cold, almost freezing. Frost crept over my skin, my dress damp and clinging to me. Darkness greeted my sight everywhere I looked, but something bright attempted to penetrate the shadows, as though the morning sun's rays were breaking through the night. It gave me hope that perhaps I wasn't entirely lost to the Dark Divide.

Am I standing?

I didn't think so. The lack of pressure in my legs hinted that I was lying on something. But what? It wasn't my stone altar. The surface beneath me was too cold and wet for stone. It was almost watery around my body. And the air? It was too fresh for the musty scent of the Dark Divide. This air smelt of winter, of woodsy pines and a lingering scent of grass.

My pulse thrummed, strong and steady. My pupils forced themselves to find their way through the dark, to wander closer to the burning light.

I jolted out of sleep.

The light was no longer bright but a silver coin in a hazy sky. Heavy snow fell, sometimes looking like the soft, icy flakes in a snow globe, other times falling so hard it provided low visibility through the trees. I awkwardly inched up to sitting. I'd been lying in the snow, my arms almost resembling Lunette's frosty skin tone. The tips of my fingers were wrinkled from the dampness. I always loved it when my long hair shielded my neck from the cold, but out here, my curls were wet and heavy, the ends dripping cold water down my back.

It was a relief not to be back in the Dark Divide.

But honestly, this wasn't much better.

Gingerly, I stood, my eyes sweeping across the landscape. Wind and snow buffeted my skin. I didn't think the whiteout would have an impact on my disembodied form—it couldn't kill me—but I still felt every aching chill that accompanied the brutal cold.

Where am I now?

A light appeared in the distance ahead, bobbing spottily through the trees, reminding me of the haunting tales of the will-o'-the-wisps. I lunged for the cluster of thick trees, using them to hide for a moment and assess the situation. I didn't know who—or *what*—was travelling through the woods. Could they help me? Could they be a threat?

I squeezed my eyes shut against the gusting snow. Counting down from five, I made a hesitant dash through the trees, using the trunks to keep myself hidden. The light grew. There were voices ahead, faint at first in the gale, the wind distorting the words, but gradually becoming clearer as I approached. And familiar.

I came out at the edge of a gorge. Below, probably where a walking trail was buried beneath snow, two boys were carrying lanterns. The knot of anxiety in my chest loosened, but it wasn't enough slack to break it entirely.

"Why can't we use the wood around here?" Little Willieth rubbed at his eyes, trying to shield his face from the snow. He followed his older brother, who moved much too fast for his small legs to keep up.

Isgrad spun around. "I've already told you. For the hundredth time, everything around here is wet. We need to find dry wood. Go back to the cabin. I don't need you making this any harder than it already is."

He wheeled around and plodded heavily back up the snowed-in path.

Willieth's back jerked ramrod straight. "Wait for me." He struggled through the teeming flurry, his lantern nearly flickering out.

I've gone back in time again.

Or was it a memory?

I still wasn't certain.

But one thing I did know: last time, Willieth, Isgrad, and their mother hadn't been able to see me.

Was this my own magic bringing me here to this time and place? Or was this the Dark Divide? Whatever it was, I had to trust that it wanted me to know more about these two boys.

I hurried down the wooded slope, my feet sliding on the ice, nearly causing me to topple. The strain of moving through the snow made my muscles tense with exhaustion. Even in this form, I fancied I could feel balls of pressure building in my lower back. My shoulders felt heavy and sore, as though I'd been slouching all day in front of a monitor.

I made it onto the snow-buried path, and, even though it wasn't necessary, I couldn't help but sneak up toward the siblings. I worried the faintest snap of a twig beneath my foot would give me away, but the boys didn't sense anything. I really was as visible as... a ghost.

"Go back to the cabin," Isgrad yelled at his brother again when he realised the young boy was still following him.

"I don't want to be left alone in there," Willieth cried. "It's scary."

Alone? In the cabin? What happened to their mother?

Much time must have passed since I'd last been in this world, because both boys' hair had grown, curly strands hanging out beneath their knit caps, which would have been cute if they didn't look so scrawny. They were noticeably thinner, their cheeks hollow, their eyes appearing to bulge from their thin faces. It gave them the permanent expression of surprise.

Isgrad swivelled around. The flamelight from his lantern cast severe shadows across his face. "Do you know why Mother doesn't like you coming out into the woods?"

Willieth shook his head, looking immensely afraid as his brother stepped forward to loom over him.

"It's because of the silver-thorned witch," Isgrad continued with overly dramatic alarm. "These are her woods. Everyone knows her story. She eats lost, wandering children. She boils them alive. Peels their tender flesh, sucks on their bones, and smears what's left of them on toast."

Willieth gasped.

"But that's not even the worst part. The silver-thorned witch always offers her victim a chance for an escape, though it comes at a cost. You have to make her an offer she can't refuse. Magic. Coin. Maybe even an annoying little brother who she can cook in a broth."

Willieth was breathing hard. "Then why are you allowed out in the woods?"

"Because I'm not little. She only goes after people who are little."

I shivered, wondering how much of Isgrad's story was true. I remembered reading about the cruelty that came with the ten-year winter. Caster men and women considered too old and worthless to help with the running of the provinces were often banished by their own people to live out the rest of their lives in solitude, somewhere deep in the mountains or forests, where no one could find them. People feared that the Council of Founding Sovereigns would see the older casters' weakness as a reflection on their entire village, and that the Haxsan Guard would penalise them all by halving their food rations.

Over time, it became a witch hunt. Not only were the old targeted, but anyone who wanted to settle a score, eliminate a threat, or simply satisfy their jealousy could accuse another of using dark magic to fulfil their own ends. With food shortages so slow, panic everywhere, and casters dying from the severity of the winter, it was no wonder everyone in the provinces turned against one another for their own survival.

Was the silver-thorned witch one of these casters? Or was Isgrad's story something more sinister?

"Now go." Isgrad pointed down the path. "Leave me alone. Mother will be back soon. Get lost, you little freak."

He kicked snow. Icy whiteness soared into the air, cresting over Willieth and causing the little boy to yell in despair. The snow probably fell down the back of his jacket and into his gloves. Willieth turned and ran, his boots struggling to find traction.

This poor little boy, who clearly idolised his brother, had experienced his first taste of animosity.

Maybe not.

Judging by the way Isgrad's eyes watched him, narrowed to abhorred slits, Willieth had been bullied and humiliated before.

I stepped back, again recognising something familiar about Isgrad. The pent-up tension. The hostile glare. The way his fists were pressed together at his sides. It was all so damn familiar.

I stepped away, my arm hitting something solid behind me. It was cold and fleshy, definitely not a tree. Surprised, I turned. Repulsion fluttered all through my insides. A woman stood before me—looking straight at me. Her long brown hair whipped around her face, her dark eyes hooded and unblinking. She slowly bent her neck to the side to get a closer look at me. I gulped. The jutted angle reminded me of a long neck that had met the end of a noose. When the wind tossed her hair back, swollen bruises appeared on her pale skin, confirming my suspicion.

She didn't say anything, just continued to watch me with her dull, milky eyes.

Stay calm.

It was the first time I had encountered a ghost, besides Lunette or the aimless wraiths in the Dark Divide, and the entire situation felt... wrong. Threatening.

I licked my lips, forcing my voice to come out assured and strong, but confidence failed me. "What do you want?"

The woman tilted her chin. Wispy snow landed on her ashen lips. Her long hair was blown across her face, but somehow, she still managed to see me as she stepped forward and raised her hand. I moved back, slipping in the snow in my panic, waving my arms for balance. Her dead fingers touched my face, and coldness rushed through me. Screams ricocheted across my scalp. I didn't know if they were mine... or someone else's.

CHAPTER 20

I gasped for air. My cheeks were flushed, not from warmth but from the impossible, burning cold that had come with the ghost's touch. Stiff and uncomfortable, I examined my new environment, wondering where the ghost was.

Where have I been transported to this time?

But my surroundings weren't so strange. I was in the *Velorosa's* private infirmary, likely once reserved for the captain and other prestigious crew members of the Haxsan Guard, not just mere sailors. Those crew members recovered in the large, open hospital ward, where the smell of illness, infection, and death would have spread from one bed to the next like wildfire. Even with all the medical supplies, healing herbs, ointments, and potions on board, the sea was relentless with who she took. People went crazy out at sea. Compared to the mainland, the injured or sick took longer to recover, if they even did recover. I wondered if Annaka was right about the sea being a mysterious force on the earth. Did the ocean enjoy claiming souls?

My unconscious body rested on the hospital bed like some kind of ethereal sleeping beauty from a fairy tale. Had it not been for the nasogastric tube, the IV lines, and the heart monitor beating in time with my steady yet slow pulse, I would have looked at home on a bed of flowers.

Raised voices caught my attention.

On the opposite side of the room, Darius was talking animatedly with Jad, Marek, and Colonel Harper. Some sort of meeting was taking place. The men stood around a portable bed table, which was covered in maps similar to those I'd seen in the *Velorosa*'s chart room.

On no. Don't tell me they've stolen Annaka's maps.

They wanted the captain of the *Velorosa* to trust them. This definitely was not the way to earn her confidence. Annaka promised to get them to the sea caves, but she never pledged that she would deliver them alive. And knowing Annaka, she'd make them pay for this if she ever found out, which seemed probable.

Darius fixed Jad and Marek with a calm look, but his voice betrayed his nervous anticipation. "We need to plan the logistics now. While there's time. Once we reach the caves, you'll have a day's journey by foot to the barge. It's another three days across the Golden Ocean."

The Golden Ocean?

I'd never heard of such a place.

I inched closer, staring at the region Darius pointed to on the map. It was a large expanse of swirling lines that had been drawn to resemble a lake. A surprisingly big lake. No wonder they called it an ocean. This had to be the biggest lake in the world. I examined it closer, not liking the massive serpent that dipped in and out of the waves, jaws open in a cunning smile.

What has Darius got Jad and Marek doing now?

Indecision shone on Jad's face. He stared at the map, probably calculating other options. "We can't go around the ocean?"

The senator frowned, considering Jad's question. "No," he said at length. "It's too risky. Legend says that the Isla Necropolis only appears during the course of a full moon. If that's true, then that means it's only accessible for three days. The full moon is six evenings away. We can't risk waiting till the next month cycle. Morgomoth won't wait."

"Morgomoth doesn't have the key," another voice chimed in.

I hadn't realised Commander Macaslan was in the room. She sat in a patient chair, regal as a queen as she watched the debate. She pressed her fingers together, forming a steeple with her hands. "Morgomoth's focus will be on his pursuit of us. Without that key, he will never access the necropolis."

My eyes roamed to the pendant hidden beneath Jad's shirt.

The key.

Finally. I'm going to get some answers.

But that led to more questions. Why did Jad have a key to a necropolis? And why had he, Marek, and Talina risked their lives to find it?

Necropolis.

I raked my brain, trying to remember what the word meant. I was fairly certain it translated to "city of the dead."

Colonel Harper's gaze lingered on the map. "I do not think this is a good idea. The Isla Necropolis is not something we can just enter and leave like that." He snapped his fingers to emphasise his point.

"I'm sorry," Marek interrupted. He scratched his eyebrow. "What is the Isla Necropolis?"

"It's an island in the Golden Ocean," Darius answered. He inhaled deeply, as if it were the first real breath he'd taken since boarding the *Velorosa*. "It's where the first casters of Vukovar's Haxsan Guard were buried. Legend says they guard the necropolis, protecting a powerful secret."

Jad's lips twisted to the side. "And we all know that legends contain an element of truth."

"Precisely," Darius agreed.

Marek fiddled with the bandage attached to his face. He looked at the map and gave a one-shouldered shrug. "So why does Morgomoth need the necropolis?"

Darius massaged what must have been an ache at his temple. "Not the necropolis. It's what's *inside* the dead city that he seeks."

"And how do you know?" Colonel Harper stared at the senator with hard resolve.

"My intuition. A premonition. My instincts have never been wrong before. This time, the feeling is so strong, the veins in my body are throbbing. Morgomoth is going after the Bone Grimoire."

Silence settled through the room. The name sent chills along my naked arms. Grimoires were spell books. Spell books were rare. What was left of them in the world were locked away in secure libraries in the Free Zones. I'd even heard rumours that they'd all been collected over time and kept in a dungeon beneath the White Palace. The dangerous ones were burned.

The Bone Grimoire didn't exactly sound like a friendly spell book. And if it was hidden somewhere in the Isla Necropolis and guarded by the dead, well... that didn't bode well for any of us.

Colonel Harper leaned forward. His voice dropped to a whisper. "Morgomoth is after Zaya."

"He's going after both her and the book," Darius cut in vociferously. "That's why it's paramount that we hide Zaya and the key."

The door creaked, causing everyone to turn anxiously.

Talina entered the private infirmary and closed the hatch with a firm shove. "There are no patients outside, but you should keep your voices down. I could hear yelling from the passage."

The slope of Macaslan's eyebrows drew together. "I thought there were spells in place to make this room soundproof."

"Not anymore," Darius confirmed. He rubbed at his eyes. The time on the clock was late. "The spells on this ship answer to the captain. It seems Annaka's charity has ended."

Talina stepped around the group and spoke timidly to Marek. "I need to change the bandage."

Marek touched his cheek absentmindedly, then flinched at what must have been sudden pain in the wound. "Soon," he told her. He smiled, but it didn't reach his eyes.

Jad watched the pair like they were some kind of weird carnival exhibit. Marek noticed. He stepped away, leaving Talina looking stricken and unsure of herself. She stared down at her hands. The expression on her face said she wanted to sink into the floor.

I didn't understand how Jad's stern gaze could make Marek wither away from her like that.

What am I missing?

Jad raised his brows at the senator. "What's inside the Bone Grimoire?"

Darius answered in a measured voice. "The book contains numerous spells of the dead. Necromancy. Resurrection. Conjuring."

"I thought everything pertaining to necromancy had been destroyed."

"The Bone Grimoire remains to be the last magical reference to necromancy. At least, that's what the Council will have us believe. The grimoire is hidden in the Isla Necropolis. Throughout the centuries, there were expeditions to recover it, but most of the brave souls who volunteered to find the grimoire died trying. Others gave up. Eventually, the Bone Grimoire and the dead who guarded it became a myth. When it became forbidden to even speak of necromancy, the Bone Grimoire was forgotten entirely."

Jad's jaw tightened. "But not by you?"

"I thought it was a myth," Darius confessed. "Until Chauvelin told me the truth."

I fidgeted with a loose thread that hung from my grimy dress. Whenever someone mentioned Clarence Chauvelin, it always filled me with guilt. It was because he refused to give up my location when I was a child that Melvina killed him. Chauvelin was a scientist who discovered magical properties in human blood. Humans were evolving into casters. A century and a half into the future, if Chauvelin's calculations were correct, the transformation would be complete. There would be no more Free Zones. No more subjugation. No more war. The Council hadn't been interested, which had forced Chauvelin to take his research to Morgomoth. It had been a mistake that had cost Chauvelin his life. He'd stolen me away from the ULD forces, hidden me in Brendlash Orphanage, and made Darius and Commander Macaslan swear on their magic to become my legal guardians. To always look after me and protect me from Morgomoth and the United League of Dissent, because one day they would come after me for my magic.

I watched Darius, questioning what other secrets he and Chauvelin had shared.

There were shadows under the senator's eyes. He looked dishevelled from lack of sleep. "Before Morgomoth fell, Chauvelin revealed that he sought the Bone Grimoire. Morgomoth found the Isla Necropolis. He was on a mission to recover the book."

Every eye in the room turned to the senator with confoundment.

"He didn't have the key," Darius explained. "He couldn't open the temple that housed the Bone Grimoire. Now he wants to complete the task." His gaze met Jad's and Marek's. "That's why it was imperative that you retrieved the key before Vulcan did."

Jad flinched at the mention of his father. The cut in his hairline had healed, nothing remaining now but a raised abrasion and a bruise. I recalled the state of the captain's carrier-hornet as it soared through the night sky, the galactic storm burning its wings and hull. Jad, Marek, and Talina had arrived with seconds to spare. Where had they been? What dangerous region had they been deployed to in search of this tiny key?

A key the world was now dependent on.

Colonel Harper snorted, a hint of challenge in his voice. "What is this spell that Morgomoth is after from the Bone Grimoire? Or did Chauvelin not tell you that?"

I sensed by the way Darius curled his fingers that he didn't appreciate the colonel's scepticism.

Why is Colonel Harper being so argumentative?

I'd never describe the colonel as being pleasant, but this continual questioning and mistrust were out of character, especially when Commander Macaslan, the caster he trusted most, was on board with the senator's plan.

Again, what am I missing?

Darius fixed him with a penetrating glare. "It is to do with the Larthalgule and Neathror blades. He wants to combine them, make them become one ultimate necromancer weapon."

My knees began to tremble. Larthalgule was the athame-sabre powerful enough to bring back life. Neathror did the opposite. It brought death. If the two athame-sabres became one, I didn't want to imagine what a weapon of that magnitude would look like or be capable of. Total destruction and annihilation were my guess. If Morgomoth achieved his plan to unite the weapons, we wouldn't stand a chance. We were barely scraping by as it was.

"Are we agreed?" Darius searched the faces around the room. "Jad and Marek take the barge across the Golden Ocean to the Isla Necropolis."

Commander Macaslan sat up straighter. "It's their decision to make, not ours."

"I'll do it," Jad answered without hesitation.

Of course he would.

Always throwing himself into danger.

Uncertainty flickered across Marek's expression. His eyes travelled to the corner where Talina stood beside a medical cabinet, her arms wrapped around herself, watching the scene with tired eyes.

"I'll go," he said at last.

I detected the faintest trace of reluctance in his voice.

Talina looked up right at the moment the lieutenant glanced away. The worry and hesitance on her face was an expression I was seeing too often. She looked like she wanted to stop Marek, but instead, her eyes drifted to the map, as though she found that more interesting.

I could have strangled the pair of these lovesick puppies. Why couldn't they just confess their feelings to each other?

"Then it's settled." Darius's voice was like steel. "Once we land at the sea caves, Jad and Marek will travel through Vukovar to the Golden Ocean and retrieve the Bone Grimoire from the Isla Necropolis. Commander Macaslan, Colonel Harper, and I are wanted fugitives. If the Haxsan Guard find us, our heads will roll. We will remain in the caves until Jad and Marek return with the Bone Grimoire. My contact will meet us there. They will guide what's left of our Haxsan Guard soldiers and the refugees to Helms Point. Talina, you will go with them. They'll need a healer."

She nodded, then took a tentative step closer to the medical cabinet, as though she were hoping to blend in and remain inconspicuous.

"And what happens once the Bone Grimoire is retrieved? *If* it's retrieved?" Colonel Harper's voice, deep and raspy, was filled with a nasty undertone.

The senator pressed his lips together, maybe to stop himself from saying something he'd regret. "Then we will endeavour to find a spell that will break the sleeping hex Zaya is bound in. After that, the real assignment begins."

Assignment?

That did not sound good.

What does Darius want me to do? Fight Morgomoth in hand-to-hand combat?

My spine tightened with dread.

Darius's lip curled up in a weak smile. "Now, we just have to keep our plan from the *Velorosa*'s nosy captain. No easy feat." From the tone of his voice, some of his confidence had deserted him. "That concludes the meeting."

Jad and Marek moved in tandem out the door. I followed, curious to know why they'd departed so fast. It was a struggle to keep up, as their long legs trekked through the infirmary at a swift pace.

"What is it you wanted to tell me?" Marek whispered.

"Not here." Jad focused ahead, not once looking behind him. "Up on deck, where we're away from prying ears."

"Darius's plan. It doesn't feel foolproof to me."

"That's because it's not."

Marek didn't answer.

The pair turned into a passageway.

I trailed behind, trying to repress my mounting anxiety.

CHAPTER 21

The sea was deceptively calm. The waxing crescent of the moon lit the gentle waves in silver. It was picture-perfect, like something on a postcard, but I knew it was just an illusion. The sea had two faces. Tonight, it chose to display calm emotion on the surface, but below, it was depthless, dark, and wrathful. The sea was not to be trusted; it could change its attitude at any moment.

Jad and Marek stood on a private viewing platform above the deck. I lingered close, wishing they could see me, that I could be physically present. It hurt to be so near and yet so distant.

The wind made a mournful whistling sound. Jad's hair blew fiercely in the squall. His dark eyes were drooped. He was clearly exhausted. He looked capable of climbing over the rail and ending it all.

I could have so easily wrapped my arms around him at that moment, but it would have been in vain. I wanted to comfort him, but Jad didn't know I was there, and even though there'd been times when I thought he'd heard me, they had ended in disappointment. The Dark Divide had sucked me away, thwarting any progress I'd made to connect to this world. My entire essence was racked with sorrow by the knowledge that I wasn't able to help.

Marek blew warm air onto his hands. "Are you going to tell me now? Or do I have to guess?"

Jad looked up. On the horizon, streaks of light lit the plum-shaded clouds. There was a storm, probably too distant to have an impact on the *Velorosa,* but Jad's white-knuckled hands gripped the rail regardless, the hard line of his jaw tense. His gaze turned to Marek. "Did you bring the mapographic?"

The lieutenant hastily took out a device from his carrier bag. The mapographic came to life with silvery light. It was a hologram display that projected out of a tablet. It had saved us more than once on our failed journey to Port Serres, before I had become this essence. Before Morgomoth had cursed me and any of this mess had started.

I inched closer. Mapographics scanned and exhibited the geography around them, but the only terrain it displayed now was an endless expanse of water. This was the first time I'd been on a ship this far out to sea. Now I understood why people feared the vast emptiness of the ocean. It was isolating.

"Can you zoom in to the coast of Vukovar?" The tightness in Jad's voice had me worried.

Marek skimmed his fingers across the screen. "Do you have coordinates?"

Jad listed them.

The lieutenant typed, and the hologram's display changed. It now resembled the region I had seen on Annaka's chart map.

"Are those the sea caves Darius wants us to hide in?" Marek sounded a little breathless. "They look difficult to get to."

Jad gritted his teeth. "It can't be done. I've thought long and hard about it. Even if the *Velorosa* did remain ten kilometres away from the coast, the thermal radar images would trace the tenders. We'd be caught. The Haxsan Guard would not be lenient on us. We'd be captured, sentenced, and put to death."

I didn't like this sullen, depressing conclusion, but Jad did have a point. Unauthorised boats arriving in Vukovar's waters would raise alarm bells in every navy base along the coast. My friends would never make it to the sea caves.

A weighty silence settled between the pair.

Marek wrinkled his nose. "I know you have an alternative plan, so let's hear it."

Jad pushed back from the rail and straightened his shoulders. "There's a carrier-hornet on this ship. It's on the same level as the tenders, a floor above the engines. From what I could see, it hasn't been used in years. We'd have to service it, but we could do it in a day. The carrier-hornet isn't in bad condition."

Marek chuckled drily. "The only reason we would need a carrier-hornet is if we were flying somewhere. Are you suggesting we leave the *Velorosa*?"

"Yes. We depart tomorrow night. We'll fly to Vukovar and across the desert to the Golden Ocean. We'll land near the Isla Necropolis. We'd have to wait till the full moon. That will give us time to hide the carrier-hornet and rest. The journey will take a few days, but we'll reach the Isla Necropolis sooner than if we were to follow Darius's plan. Everything is dependent on us finding the Bone Grimoire."

The lieutenant stared with stunned silence.

"We'll take Zaya, of course," Jad resumed. "And Talina. If you wish." He eyed his friend meaningfully.

Marek didn't answer right away. I didn't know if that was because he found the plan crazy or because the very mention of Talina had unsettled him. He stared up at the sky, as though the stars had the answers.

"There's one problem with your plan," he said at last. "The thermal radars along Vukovar's coast would detect a carrier-hornet."

Jad passed his friend an exasperated look. "They wouldn't be suspicious of a Haxsan Guard carrier-hornet, especially if we made it look like we were heading to Helms Point first. They'd think we were returning from a routine mission, monitoring the coastline."

He really had thought of everything.

Marek let out a laugh riddled with disbelief. "They wouldn't fall for that. They'd have every mission logged. There would be access codes to enter Vukovar. We'd never be able to report a code. The base would know we were impostors, and they'd shoot us out of the sky."

A half-smile tugged at Jad's lip.

Marek's shoulders visibly tightened. "What have you done?" He sounded like a father reprimanding a naughty child.

"I have the access codes."

Marek's eyes widened with guarded scepticism. "How?"

My blood thrummed in my veins.

Yes, how?

I wished I could pull the answer out of Jad's mind. He was resourceful, inventive, quick-witted, and a badass, but even I'd be surprised if he'd managed to learn the technical know-how to break into computer systems and access data. It wasn't exactly something you could learn in an evening.

"Renith." Jad kept his voice so low that the name was almost lost to the wind.

"Renith," Marek repeated, his tone hinging on disbelief. "The kid who barely graduated from being a cadet? He failed all his physical training and his exams. I don't even know how he graduated."

"I passed him."

"Why?"

Jad's lips broke into a small smile. "Renith is a shy, nervous kid who would probably faint if an athame-sabre was pointed at him, but he has useful qualities. He's brilliant with mathematics, and he has a talent for exploiting vulnerabilities in magic networks."

Marek exhaled a heavy sigh. "So, what you're telling me is... you encouraged and passed a hacker into the Haxsan Guard forces."

"Yes, and it's a good thing I did. I've had Renith working in the carrier-hornet. He's been hacking into Helms Point's security network. He's gained access and has retrieved various authorisation codes. We'll be able to fly past Vukovar's coast. It won't be an issue."

"So why not tell Darius?"

Jad's confidence faltered. "Darius's intuition is usually right, but this time, I think his plan is wrong. The *Velorosa* will be sunk before it makes it anywhere near the Vukovar coastline."

I knew it pained him to say it.

His voice was heavy. "I've made Annaka swear on her magic that she'll get the passengers to the sea caves."

Marek stared with surprise.

"Annaka doesn't know it yet, but I've already released her from that oath. So long as she thinks she's still bound to her promise, she'll get the *Velorosa* as close to the coast as possible. Helms Point's coast guard will capture the passengers on the tenders, but at least they'll be safe and away from Morgomoth."

"Safe?" Marek echoed. "They'll be imprisoned or put in a detention centre."

"If what's left of our forces swear allegiance to the Haxsan Guard in Vukovar, they'll be granted clemency. The refugees will be sent to work in the provinces. It's a far better solution than being killed."

"And what about Darius and the commander? The colonel?" Total shock filled Marek's voice. "They'll be tried and executed."

Jad tilted his head and stared at the sea. I detected another confession at the tip of his tongue. "Annaka made a second promise on her magic. Well... I made her."

The lieutenant waited.

"Darius, Macaslan, and Harper will not be getting off this ship."

I stared at Jad, cold all over. For the first time, I doubted him.

Have faith. Jad always has a reason for what he does.

But Darius did too.

I trusted both of them.

A game of tug-of-war played inside me. I did not like that our little group was divided.

Marek bit down on his lip. "Why are you suggesting this, Jad? Why not tell Darius your concern with his plan?"

"Because Darius believes his intuition. He's convinced he's right, but for the first time, I'm not. He's putting too much trust in his contact at Helms Point. We can't trust anyone outside our circle." His dark eyes filled with an emotion I didn't understand. He swallowed heavily. "Darius, Macaslan, and Harper are no good to us if they're captured or killed. It's safer, and smarter, if they remain on the *Velorosa*. Once we've retrieved the Bone Grimoire, we'll return to the *Velorosa*. Reunited, we'll attempt to find a spell that can break Zaya's curse. The *Velorosa* will become our new headquarters."

"A pirate's life. Great."

Jad's lips teetered into a smile. "What do you say, Lieutenant? Are you joining me on this mission?"

"Are you going to make me promise on my magic?"

"No. I trust you."

Marek frowned as he considered the astounding idea. "You know I wouldn't let you do this on your own."

"Do what on your own?"

The voice startled them both.

Jad drew himself almost regally, immediately on guard.

Marek flinched. His good cheek flushed with warmth. At first, I thought it was because he was afraid their entire plan had been overheard, but then I realised it was the deep, abashed colour of attraction.

Annaka stood with her arms crossed near the open hatch. "You two are whispering like a pair of schoolgirls." Her eyes roamed between the pair, reading their faces. Her gaze settled on Jad. "Good, so you told him about your intended betrayal."

Marek turned on his friend. "You told her?"

Jad's expression clouded. "There is no betrayal. Just a diversion in the plan that Darius doesn't know about."

Annaka laughed. "I hate to break it to you, but that's called a betrayal."

Jad raised his head to the sky, the way he so often did when I did or said something that infuriated him. It brought on a painful bout of homesickness.

"Call it what you want," he said. "It's happening. We're leaving tomorrow night."

"Sooner." Annaka leaned on the hatch, a wolfish smile on her beautiful face. "You'd better start working on that carrier-hornet, Captain Arden. The sea favours us. We've reached the Bone Towers." She nodded toward the bow.

Ahead, the *Velorosa* steadily approached clouds of white-and-grey fog. It rolled across the sea, as far as the eye could see in both directions. There was something almost hypnotic in the way it moved, hiding a churning mystery beyond its thick haze. The fog danced across the bow, wispy threads reaching out to slowly wrap around the deck and viewing platforms. Jad and Marek leaned against the rail, straining to see beyond the roiling mist. I stepped forward. When the haze settled over my skin, it sent goose bumps down my arms. The sensation was similar to being doused in fine spots of rain. Not entirely unpleasant, but I wouldn't like to have remained out in it for long.

My ears detected Marek's short gasp.

I peeled forward, grabbing the handrail in surprise. Incredible limestone monuments appeared through the fog. They jutted out of the sea like knives, the points ending in spires. No wonder these megalith rocks were called the Bone Towers. Skulls had been elaborately painted and decorated with seashells and pearls, placed in the stone among the bones of other aquatic creatures. The skull's empty eye sockets watched us as the *Velorosa* sailed past.

This was a sea graveyard. An ancient site. But who had put these skulls and bones here? I tried to recall a history lesson about the sea and the ancient funeral rites that the earliest sea casters had followed, but my mind came up blank.

A howl broke through the eerie stillness of the fog, overpowering even the waves. The deck suddenly felt unsteady beneath my feet. That roar had been the sound of a—

The realisation closed my airway.

Oh no.

Annaka's lips tipped into a smile. "Stagma," she explained. "They live in the Bone Towers farther north."

"Stagma," Marek repeated, incredulous. "That howl sounded close."

Annaka shrugged. "They do fly, and this is *their* home, after all." She stretched her arms and arched her shoulders like an unperturbed cat. "I better return to the bridge and take over from Cryton. He gets nervous."

She left.

I stared at one of the monolithic columns that broke through the sea like a crooked headstone. The skulls that smiled back at me were smooth from centuries of seawater and briny winds. I couldn't help but think there was a secret behind their grins. Normally, I sensed when wraiths were present, but the Bone Towers were an empty graveyard. No matter how strange or eerie the burial site, the souls had moved on to the otherworld and found peace. It should have made me calm, but my pulse was erratic. Something didn't feel right about the stillness of the towers, or the waves that gently lapped around them.

Jad and Marek left the viewing platform. I moved to follow and nearly screamed. The woman with the long brown hair stood before me again, eyes staring but unblinking, almost as dark and sunken as the skulls in the Bone Towers. She was so close that, if she were alive, I would have felt her breath on my skin. Her posture was straight, strapped in a bodice. The intricate pearl beading and cream lace of her white dress shone in the deck's lights, the rays floating through her translucent skin. It wasn't a wedding dress, but maybe something worn to a girl's debutante. That meant this girl, woman—whoever or whatever she was—was originally from the Free Zones. Casters from the provinces weren't granted the honour of being debuted to society.

The heavy wind swept her hair across her face. There was something weirdly familiar about her, but I couldn't place it.

It occurred to me then that we were just... staring at each other. Peculiar behaviour even for a ghost. By now, she should have at least shattered my eardrums with a scream, manipulated my surroundings into something nightmarish, or morphed her own appearance into a gruesome display of rotting flesh and blood. That's normally how these things worked. But all she did was... stare.

"Who are you?" My voice sounded clipped.

Her lips, thin and pale, didn't move.

Great. A ghost who's mute.

I didn't like it when people who were breathing stared at me for too long, let alone a dead person.

A new thought popped into my mind.

Maybe she can't speak.

My eyes instinctively wandered to the markings on her neck. The skin above the collar of her white dress was bruised. Abrasions caused by rope had left a nasty redness across her throat. It was blistered and bleeding, one side swollen where her neck protruded at an off angle.

Where the rope broke her neck.

She turned in a slow rotation, as though she was carefully keeping her head balanced on her neck, and floated gracefully down the deck. The movement was almost regal, except for the continuous twitching of her feet. She raised her hand, signalling for me to follow, the same way a queen would summon a handmaiden.

My adrenaline spiked. She led me down the deck toward the stern, sometimes drifting so fast through the wind that at times she became nothing more than vapour and smoke. Whenever I struggled to keep up, she turned to look at me, or at least I thought she did. Each time, her long brown hair was swept across her face like a mourning veil.

She glided around a large cabin-like structure that I thought might have been the docking bridge. I pressed forward, wishing my feet could take longer strides. When I reached the stern, I glanced around and took a deep breath. She was gone.

This part of the *Velorosa* was the flight deck for the takeoff and landing of aircraft. Once, the landing pads would have been the home to fire-crusaders and carrier-hornets, resting here at night after a long day of launching attacks at land and sea. In a strange way, I could still smell the combination of exhaust, oil, and hydraulic fluids. It made me long for Tarahik, which was ironic. I'd hated that place when I'd first arrived, and now that the base was in ruins, I thought of it as home.

A raw, fleeting cough caught my attention. Colonel Harper was standing at the end of the stern by the rail. He stared at the storm on the horizon, his hands tight on the rail. I moved toward him, finding the appearance of the colonel out here alone at night... strange. His shoulders were slumped, his skin so pale he would have looked at home in a morgue. He took out a glass vial from his pocket, something that had an unpleasant black texture inside it, and brought it shakily to his lips.

I stilled.

The air no longer carried the briny scent of the sea. Around Colonel Harper, the wind was tainted with the unmistakable whiff of decay. It was the stench I imagined assaulted a plague house, infection and illness festering in the humid day, becoming unbearable during the evening.

Colonel Harper swallowed most of the bottle and returned it secretively to his pocket. Sweat ran down his face in beads. He shut his eyes for a moment, and when he gripped the rail again to steady himself, I saw how bone-thin his fingers were.

Something was very, very wrong with Colonel Harper.

He coughed again, only this time it was long and wheezy, and he couldn't stop. It was awful to listen to the desperate gasps of air and violent hacking.

I have to help.

But how could I?

Colonel Harper spat blood out into the sea. And then the worst thing happened. He collapsed onto the deck and began to convulse, a sticky white foam frothing from his mouth.

My mind felt foggy. I didn't know what to do.

I was certain of only one thing.

Colonel Harper was dying.

CHAPTER 22

*D*o *something, Zaya. Find a way to get help.*

I knew from my first-aid training that all Haxsan Guard navy vessels were equipped with emergency stations. Searching frantically, I found it beside the docking bridge and prayed my essence was strong enough to hit the button with EMERGENCY written in red across the front. Then I prayed Annaka and her crew had kept this network serviced. It would just be my luck if it had been neglected in the pirates' care.

Long, escalating beeps echoed across the deck. They sounded like the alarms during a muster drill. It wasn't what I would deem a pleasant sound, but at that moment, the incessant *woop, woop, woop* spurred my relief.

Colonel Harper just has to hold on.

He can do that.

He had to do that.

I dared a peek over my shoulder. The colonel was still convulsing, only now his head thrashed wildly, sometimes in such violent twists that I wondered if his neck had snapped off his body. His eyes were open, but they were empty and unseeing.

This isn't a normal seizure.

I'd witnessed some horrible images in my time, but this would go down in my history book as one of the worst. And eeriest.

What was that black potion he drank?

Could it have done this to the colonel?

The more I pondered on it, the more I didn't think so.

Colonel Harper wasn't dumb. He wouldn't drink something that could harm him, and he wasn't the type to willingly harm himself.

No, there was something bigger happening here. This wasn't a medical emergency. This was a hex.

Colonel Harper has been cursed.

"Over there!" a voice shouted.

Two men I recognised as belonging to Annaka's crew appeared from around the docking bridge and sprinted toward the colonel. Colonel Harper was someone who I... semi-cared about—because I had to be honest, the pair of us never really got along. Despite this, I would have liked to remain close until he recovered from medical aid for my own ease of my mind, but that was a kindness not granted.

An aggressive, hungry wind ripped me off my feet. I landed hard, barely having time to register the pain before the next gale spun me across the deck like a hockey puck on ice. My eyes watered, the briny air gusting at my face and hair, disorientating my direction till I could no longer see clearly. Only one image remained firmly imprinted in my mind: a deep, jagged crack in the centre of the empty flight deck that widened into a cavernous black mouth.

The Dark Divide.

It had returned.

And I was heading straight toward it.

My body toppled half over the edge. Refusing to give up without a fight, I clawed at the deck's surface, my upper half prostrate, my legs bicycling through the air. Agony wrenched my spine. I couldn't hold on. My fingers were bending, about to snap. The Dark Divide had captured me as its prize, and it wouldn't let go.

I can't go back to the tunnels.

I can't go back to that endless... nothing.

But fate didn't give a damn about what I wanted.

My strength failed, and I plummeted into the void. Air as cold as an Arctic night tormented me with its icy gusts. The aperture closed above me, shutting out the deck, the *Velorosa*, and the night. All I heard was the endless whistling of the cruel wind and my own ragged screams.

I OPENED MY EYES, fighting to clear the shock of fog that clouded my brain.

Where am I?

I wasn't hurting, so that was a promising start, but disorientation left me confused and panic-stricken, my chest constricting to the point where I couldn't breathe.

Calm down. Try to think. What was the last thing that happened?

Thick and sluggish, my memory slowly surfaced.

The Dark Divide.

I remembered falling, being ripped away from the *Velorosa* and claimed back. Tossed and thrown into the Dark Divide's bleak, hollow world.

But where are the tunnels? The altar?

There was a rumble in the distance, like a peal of thunder. Perhaps I'd hit my head when I'd fallen, because all I could see around me was a white fog that ebbed in and out like ripples across a lake. Something soft landed on my cheek, a gentle sensation at first, then burning cold. It was all around me. I was lying in it. It came from above, falling on me as though it were a downpour of rain, only it hit like bullets.

I found strength in my upper body and crawled up to sitting. Everything was blurry and lacked detail, but gradually my vision settled into focus. The whitewash that had obstructed my sight became apparent for what it really was—snow. Thick and heavy and falling fast. Fog swirled through a sea of trees, making them appear haunted in the eddying flurries.

I had returned to the woods. To the memory.

The cabin. Where is it?

The elements couldn't hurt my essence, but that didn't stop me from feeling the frigid wind that whipped through the thin fabric of my dress, or the acute chill that sucked the warmth from my soul.

The cabin can't be far. The Dark Divide wouldn't have brought me to this world of ice and snow just to torment me.

Or would it?

I had no idea how the Dark Divide operated when it wasn't under Morgomoth's control.

Clearing the negative thought away, I struggled through the snow. Wind tore at my face and skin, causing my eyes to water. Every time I bowed my head and closed my eyes, I worried I'd never be able to open them again. My tears were freezing. I imagined my eyelids frozen shut, sealed together like glue. It felt like they were being ripped apart when I opened them.

The temperature plummeted. My hands and feet were numb, my movements uncoordinated and slow.

Can my essence… freeze?

The horrifying thought startled me from my stupor.

Find the cabin. Find the cabin.

I slogged through the trees, cresting up one wooden slope, disappointed to discover I was only met by another.

What if I'm heading away from the cabin? What if it's in the opposite direction?

I couldn't turn back. I couldn't let panicked thoughts cloud my judgement. I remembered the cabin stood at the bottom of a sharp slope. If I started second-guessing myself, I would remain lost in the woods forever, always wandering, always feeling the cold and the bitter bite of winter's sting. I would become like the wraiths in the tunnels. Trapped.

I had just reached the peak of another hill when I saw chimney smoke through the trees below. I plodded heavily through the snow, stumbling and half crawling my way down the slope. I could no longer tell if the howl that echoed around me was thunder from an approaching storm, the wind playing tricks, or the hungry cry of a wolf who'd just found his next meal.

Keep moving. Don't look back.

I did not want to learn if a wolf could harm or feast on an essence. I was starting to think anything was possible in the Dark Divide.

The cabin was dark. Isgrad, Willieth, and their mother were in hiding. It made sense that they would have the curtains closed, concealing the light, but I knew from the chimney smoke that they had a delicious fire inside.

I scrambled up the stairs onto the derelict porch and pounded on the door. My numb fists were ineffectual against the thick wood.

No. Please no.

In the real world, I'd had to concentrate to be able to move things or make a sound, and I no longer had the mental energy it took to focus. I was weak. The cold and the ice and the snow were winning. My lips teetered into a sad smile. How ironic that I had reached this far only to freeze on the porch because I couldn't open a door.

A long, grisly howl resonated through the snow-capped land. It was greeted by a much louder, more voracious cry that sucked away whatever warmth was left in my body. This was a different kind of cold. This was a chill triggered by fear.

I focused on the woods, trying to discern where the sounds had come from. Low, guttural snarls escalated from the trees. They were coupled with shrieks and giggles that increased in volume, reminding me of a pack of hyenas' hideous laughter.

Lycanthors.

The creatures could shapeshift back into caster form, but from the sound of this nightmarish duet that sprang from various directions around the cabin, these monsters had long ago given in to their predator instincts. They were wolves now. The caster inside them was gone. They were nothing more than hungry, volatile beasts.

The heavy pounding of their paws met my ears. All around me, lupine forms appeared through the trees. Red-blooded eyes, hulking black muscles, shaggy fur matted with blood. I gulped. The blood was probably from their last victim.

The creatures zeroed in on something in the trees, hunting as a pack, snarling viciously. Long strings of saliva dripped from their fangs, and when the wind blew in my direction, I smelt the foul odour of decaying meat.

A form materialised from the woods, the lycanthors hot on their heels in pursuit.

Isgrad.

I gasped in a strangled breath.

What has he been doing out in the woods?

In the middle of a snowstorm?

Isgrad sprinted across the snow. Unlike me, he wore proper boots, giving him traction in the ice and snow, but the wolves still gained on him. He was nearly at the porch when one of the wolves snapped at his ankle, its nasty muzzle barely missing Isgrad's flesh as it chopped down on thin air.

Isgrad raced up the stairs.

This was it. My chance to get inside the cabin. I had to be quick.

He flung the door open and was inside within seconds. I dashed in after him, having to squeeze through the narrowing gap. I just made it, feeling the swish of wind behind me as the door slammed shut. Isgrad bolted the latch, some sort of heavy-duty brass-looking contraption, and stepped back as a violent force shoved at the door again and again. Savage growls rose from outside and all around the cabin.

My insides quivered.

Is the door strong enough to hold them back? Can the lycanthors get in through the windows?

Isgrad's face was flushed with panic, his eyes alight with fiery aggression. He looked like he was capable of walking outside and taking the dogs on one by one. He bent down and rested his hands on his knees, breathing loudly, either to catch his breath or to calm down.

At last, the lycanthors gave up. Their howling cries resonated from the steep incline above the cabin, becoming more distant.

I recalled a story I'd heard at Brendlash Orphanage. One evening, I and the other wayward youths had gathered around a fireplace to hear the tale of the Erlking and his Wild Hunt. At the time, I'd thought having a pack of hungry, blood-feasting wolves was cool, but now I'd seen what lycanthors were capable of when they'd given in to their animalistic natures. They were demented, malicious, and primitive. There was nothing caster left in them.

Loud coughing escalated from one of the bedrooms.

"Isgrad, are you back? Did you get it?"

His mother's voice was wheezy and rasping. It sounded like she was on her deathbed.

Before Isgrad could answer, another fit of violent hacking broke through the cabin.

Groaning, he moved to the small fireplace, where a large pot was nearly boiling over. He stirred the strange liquid, the contents settling back into a smooth black surface.

This was a cauldron. Isgrad was making a spell.

He reached into his trouser pocket and took out three purple flowers, their petals wilted and crushed. He squeezed them in his fist and tossed them into the cauldron. Sparks flew, the potion taking on vibrant swirling hues of lavender, lilac, and plum. I racked my brains, trying to remember if I had ever heard of a spell that used flowers like these. Flowers, herbs, and fungus were often used for healing potions. Macha would have known. Even Talina would have spelled the name out right in front of me, her hands on her hips as she looked at me with disappointment. But neither of them was here to help.

Isgrad took up the ladle, spooned some of the potion into a cup, and hurried to the bedroom where his mother's incessant coughing erupted.

I followed, shocked by what I saw when I walked through the door. Isgrad's mother was lying in her bed, the sheets wrapped around her. She was shivering, though large pearls of sweat dripped down her ashen face. Her pillow was damp from the sweat. I held my nose. The room smelt of illness, faeces, and vomit.

"Did you find it?" she gasped. Simply talking triggered another round of relentless coughing. She tried to force her body into a seated position, then gave up and dropped back against her pillow. Her chest looked like it might rip apart right there to relieve the stress in her lungs.

"Yes." Isgrad handed her the cup.

She tilted her head and swallowed greedily. Some of the potion spilled down the side of her chin, trailing in a long line down her neck. I doubted she'd be able to differentiate the sensation from her sweat.

She finished drinking and settled back into the pillow, closing her eyes. "Did I hear wolves out there?"

Isgrad watched her. His voice was flat when he answered. "No, just the wind. When it picks up it sounds like a lycanthor's howl."

"You mustn't take risks," his mother cautioned, but she didn't sound especially worried about him.

She drifted off to sleep, light snores wheezing from her parted lips.

A little voice carried from the door. "Isgrad?"

He turned, his face changing into piqued lines when he saw his small brother. "What do you want? You should be asleep."

Willieth awkwardly clung to the architrave at his side. His eyes watered, his face very pale in the dim light. "I wet the bed."

Isgrad tossed a frustrated groan to the ceiling. "For providence's sake, Willieth. You're five years old. What the hell is wrong with you?"

"I'm scared."

"Of what? The snowstorm? Mum's illness? Grow up and act your age."

Willieth looked down at his feet. A tear dropped to the floor.

Isgrad balled his hands into fists. Exhaustion tugged at the hard lines on his face. "You'll have to sleep on the couch. I can't wash your sheets until the morning. It'll take days for them to dry in this weather."

He moved across the room, grabbed his brother's small arms, and forced him into the cabin's living area. The room was overly hot and stuffy, but it was a nice reprieve from the cold outside.

"Wait here." Isgrad disappeared into the second bedroom and came back with a pair of pyjama pants. He threw them at Willieth. "Get changed."

Poor Willieth slipped out of his wet pyjamas, his face flaring with embarrassment.

"What the hell made you so scared anyway? Did you have a bad dream?"

Willieth looked up, his eyes big and wide. "No. She was standing in the corner of my room again... just watching me."

Isgrad squeezed the bridge of his nose, as though he had a headache building at the back of his skull. "What are you talking about?"

Willieth's lower lip trembled. "The silver-thorned witch."

CHAPTER 23

"Don't be ridiculous. The silver-thorned witch doesn't exist—" Isgrad stopped himself. The glint of hesitance in his eyes shone bright, then dimmed into dark fury. "You had a nightmare. Now, go sleep on the couch. You won't need a blanket. The fire will be warm enough."

I wondered if Isgrad regretted telling Willieth the story about the silver-thorned witch. At the time, I'd hoped it was just a nasty story created by a provoked older brother intent on scaring his little sibling, but now I suspected there was truth to the legend.

Scrunching his face in disgust, Isgrad picked up Willieth's pyjama bottoms and found a bucket in the kitchen cupboard, where he promptly discarded the soiled trousers. He crossed into the bedroom, which had two single beds too narrow in size for anyone to sleep comfortably, and took up the sheets and pillow. He returned to the living area. Willieth was already settled on the couch, staring into the fire.

"You'll go blind if you keep doing that." Isgrad dropped his bedding in a grumpy huff on the floor, took off his shoes, and lay down.

"Are you sleeping here?" Uncertainty filled Willieth's voice.

"Well, I can't sleep in the bedroom, can I? It stinks of urine."

Isgrad's tone was sharp, but I think deep inside he was using it as an excuse. Willieth was scared, and he felt responsible. He wasn't going to let his little brother suffer alone at night, frightened and jumping at the shadows.

"Do you think I was really dreaming?"

Isgrad didn't answer for a while. "Sometimes our dreams, especially nightmares, can feel very real."

"What if the silver-thorned witch was visiting me in my dream? I've heard of dream walkers."

"Dream walkers are dead. They were all rounded up centuries ago and executed by the Council's decree."

"How do you know?"

"I read it. In a history book."

"What if the book was wrong?"

In the fire's flickering rays, I saw exhaustion pull at Isgrad's eyelids. He'd been out most of the night, searching the woods for the elusive purple flowers, had been chased by bloodthirsty lycanthors, which he'd barely escaped, only to come home and find his five-year-old brother had wet the bed and was in desperate need of comfort.

Exhausted was an understatement. Isgrad looked like he needed to drop into a coma to catch up on some much-needed sleep.

He smoothed his pillow, perhaps trying to flatten the big chunks beneath the yellow-stained fabric, and settled his head on the side to stare up at his little brother. "Nothing can hurt you here. It's why Mum brought us to the cabin."

"I don't think that's true." Willieth looked far too young to have such a troubled look in his eyes. "The silver-thorned witch told me something bad would happen." He breathed in and out rapidly, his upper lip dampened with sweat. "She said you would hurt me... and that it would change everything."

"I'm not going to hurt you. It was a bad dream."

"You get so angry at times."

"Willieth, what did I just say? You're not the only one who needs sleep."

Isgrad turned on his side, staring into the fire, glaring with a sour expression.

Willieth sniffled. He sobbed softly, but in the quiet cabin, with only the crackling fire for comfort, the sound was audible.

Isgrad groaned. "I'm not going to hurt you, Willieth. The silver-thorned witch can't get into the cabin, and she can't wander into your dreams. You want to know why?"

Willieth wiped tears from his eyes and nodded.

"Because there's a celestial shield around this cabin. It's protecting us."

"Really?" Willieth sounded hopeful.

"Yes. You've seen the celestial shield around the Free Zone near home, haven't you? Well, we have the exact same magic around us. Now, go to sleep."

It worked. Willieth closed his eyes. A few minutes later, his breathing deepened, his face relaxed. He was blissfully asleep.

Isgrad continued to stare at the ceiling for a long time.

I wondered if his lie about the celestial shield would keep him up all night.

A LONG CREAK startled me out of sleep. I flinched. The cabin was overly warm and stuffy, my skin damp. Stabs of pain shot through every muscle in my back. The rocking chair screeched again as I attempted to shift out of my uncomfortable position. It annoyed me that even as an essence, I still felt every raw sensation and was limited by the physical world. I couldn't float through walls unless I concentrated really hard, and even then, it left me drained and exhausted. On a positive note, being able to feel meant I wasn't dead.

The walls flickered with shadows. The fire, which had died down, still gave off heat, but it would need more wood soon. Imagining the cold now felt like a distant dream, but I knew once the fire was extinguished, that cold would return with an unforgiving vengeance.

On the couch, Willieth stirred. Isgrad remained on the floor, the skin around his eyes dark from lack of sleep. I wondered if he'd managed to drift off even once. He sat up when the early morning light crept beneath the curtain, dust mites drifting through the soft beam.

Isgrad climbed onto his feet and slipped around to the kitchen to grab a glass of water. Nothing came out of the tap. It had frozen during the night.

"Shit," he muttered under his breath.

"What's wrong?"

Willieth was sitting up on the couch, rubbing his eyes.

Isgrad bit his lip, holding back frustration. "Nothing. Go to sleep."

"But it's daylight."

"It's still early. And you need more rest. Otherwise, you'll be cranky all day."

"Like you are?"

Isgrad didn't say anything. He moved to the second bedroom, opening the door very slightly to peer inside. "Mum?"

No answer.

He shut the door.

"Is Mummy awake? Is she better?"

"No." Isgrad returned to his muddled bedding on the floor and shoved on his boots. "I need to go find more wood. The fire is nearly out, and I need to warm the tank outside or we'll have no water."

My eyes bugged. I didn't like Isgrad's chance of finding any dry wood out there. He had the same odds as finding a hotly roasted meal waiting to be discovered.

He tossed on his coat and knit cap and headed to the front door. Unlatching the bolt, he breathed warm air into his hands and braced himself for the outside elements. A bitterly cold wind sent swirling snow through the entry. Maybe it was because I'd been in the warm cabin all night, but the cold seemed to have doubled in intensity, shocking me out of my sleepy stupor.

"I don't think you should go out there." Willieth's tiny voice was laced with hesitance.

Isgrad's nostrils flared. "Do you want to freeze to death?"

"No, but the silver-thorned witch is out there. She was here all night, watching us sleep."

Icy fear fluttered through my body. I really hoped Willieth's belief in the silver-thorned witch was childish fear, just a nightmare that warped his reality, making him think it was real. Because that's what it had to be. The alternative was far too frightening.

I would have sensed it if someone else was in the cabin last night.

But would I?

Necromancy alerted me when a wraith was present, but the silver-thorned witch, if she was real, wasn't a ghost. Was it possible someone could have stood over us all night, watching us sleep? No. The door was bolted.

Another disturbing thought overwhelmed me.

What if she doesn't need a door to enter?

The nerve-racking thought left me feeling vulnerable.

A clouded, uneasy look formed on Isgrad's face, but he shook it off. "I was awake for most of the night. I didn't see her. You were dreaming, Willieth."

"You were asleep at one stage." There was no emotion in Willieth's voice. He was stating a fact, which made what he was saying more alarming. "She said it was going to happen soon. Something bad. Something you would regret."

"Well, I regret a lot of things," Isgrad fired back with furious intensity. "One of them being moving to this cabin."

Before Isgrad could slam the door behind him, I slipped through the entry out to the porch, regretting my decision as soon as snow bit into my feet like sharp needles.

Isgrad plodded heavily down the steps. I followed closely, feeling the urge to understand him and know what he was about.

Is this the Dark Divide? Is it controlling me somehow? Does it want me to see something I'd otherwise miss if I remained in the cabin?

Because in all honesty, I would have preferred to stay inside, out of the elements.

I didn't know if Isgrad had a destination in mind. He wandered among the trees, cresting up the wooded slopes, only to be greeted by another. The sun had barely risen, and shadows were still prevalent through the foliage. I doubted the sun would have much influence even at noon. The snowstorm had cast an impenetrable cloud across the sky. From the woods, the sun would look like nothing more than a distant star seen through a telescope, barely bright, barely memorable.

After ten minutes of trekking through what seemed to be an endless, churning white landscape, Isgrad arrived at a fallen tree, the trunk hollow. Over time, the tree's roots and branches had clumped together and were now frozen in a twisted mesh, creating a cosy nook inside. Isgrad climbed into the tree. Several large pebbles, each the size of my hand, had been arranged in what appeared to be a makeshift tomb. Isgrad grabbed the first three stones and dropped them into the snow. Now, with the absence of the top layer, the piled stones no longer resembled a tomb but a badly made water well. Isgrad dug his hand down the centre and took out a rusted tin. My muscles tensed when I saw what was inside. Cigarettes. He must have hidden them here some time ago and had built a rock wall to secure his secret treasure.

He settled among the tree roots, sitting tall, as though his new surroundings were as grand as a throne room. He took out a lighter from his pocket, lit a cigarette, and inhaled. Out in the snow and icy wind, it hurt to draw breath, but I preferred the cold, clean air of the forest any day over the greasy scent of tobacco. The smell made my insides crawl.

Isgrad lost his usual look of scornful detachment as he shut his eyes, his facial muscles going from strained to relaxed. It saddened me that this was how he escaped the demanding responsibility of caring for a sick mother and looking after a dependent child. Isgrad was truly alone.

"You shouldn't smoke those. Bad for your health."

The voice startled me.

A woman—if she was, in fact, a woman—stood outside the tree trunk. She had skin the colour of a pale moon. Her silver hair fell past her knees, her eyes unnaturally bright. The irises were green with flecks of blue. Staring into them was like looking into the depths of a teal ocean. It was her clothes that stunned me the most. A dress made of white feathers, white flowers, and—I gulped—silver thorns. Spines and prickles encircled her entire body like barbed wire, running up the back of her neck and over her scalp to form a silver crown on the top of her head. The crown was so radiant with tiny speckled snowflakes that anyone could have mistaken them for diamonds.

The silver-thorned witch.

Willieth hadn't been dreaming.

Isgrad hadn't made up the story.

She was real.

Isgrad stared with his mouth open.

"Did you believe me to be a myth?" she asked with mock civility.

Disbelief fluttered across Isgrad's face. His jugular vein looked as though it might pop right out from his neck. "You! You've been frightening my brother."

The silver-thorned witch flicked her long hair over her shoulder and gave a flippant laugh. "He's more afraid of you than he is of me."

"What do you want? Do you want us off your land? Do you want us to promise you something in exchange for living in that cabin? That derelict, worthless dump? Do you? That's how you work, isn't it? The silver-thorned witch demands payment with promises."

When she didn't immediately answer, Isgrad's face contorted with rage. "Come on. Tell me."

She answered with coolness and eloquence, the dialect of winter. "That is one of the popular beliefs, yes. But that's not why I'm here."

"Then why?" Isgrad's fingers shook, and he dropped his cigarette in the snow. It turned into a soggy paper roll, but he didn't seem to care. His attention was fixed on the mysterious queenlike figure.

Her lips curled into a soft smile, but the way her fine eyebrows dipped over her belittling eyes told me she had no patience for insolence or crassness. I couldn't be certain how old she was. Sometimes her beauty was youthful and vibrant; other times she looked as wise and cunning as the ancients I'd read about in human fairy tales. That made me nervous. There was always an element of truth to the myths and the stories.

The silver-thorned witch watched Isgrad keenly, as though she were looking right into his soul, reading his past, present, and future. "I'm here to offer my help."

"I don't need your help. If you won't tell me what you're really after, what interests you have with my brother, then go away and leave me be."

He crossed his arms and glared, as though this would somehow prove he was not someone to be toyed with.

A hint of amusement sparkled in the witch's eyes, but her face remained stoic. "Your anger is a weapon working against you. Learn to control it; otherwise, you will regret it. Both you and Willieth will pay the price." She pointed a slender finger toward the trees in the east. "Follow the silver moon to the black mouth. That's where you'll find me."

"And why the hell do I need to find you?"

Her perfect posture radiated superiority. "You will know soon enough."

She disappeared. One second there, and the next, gone.

My spine tightened with dread.

No one in the history of casters could teleport. Or had that been another lie told by the Council?

Isgrad's eyes flashed with unsettled fear. "If you want to help me," he shouted, his voice a lonely echo through the snow, "let me know where there's some frigging dry wood for a fire."

Up in a tree, a bird squawked, flapping away with displeasure at the loud interruption.

"Crazy bitch," Isgrad muttered under his breath. He lit a new cigarette and inhaled greedily.

I moved closer, assessing whether I could fit into the tree trunk to shield myself from the snow. Something fleshy and cold touched my shoulder. I twisted around. A rush of blood pounded in my ears, quickening with my pulse. She was back. The ghost with the long brown hair and bent neck. The corners of her lips were tipped in that unsettling smile, her eyes hidden by her windswept hair. For a moment, I smelt lavender shampoo and lilies before it was overpowered by the earthy scent of an open grave. Rot assaulted my nose, fear seeming to stab into my ears like needles.

"What do you want?" I managed with trembling diction.

She didn't answer.

Her fingers dug deeper into my shoulder, so hard that I wondered if her nails had pierced into my flesh. Before I could dare to take a look, the world dissolved around me. The snow and ice and frozen trees faded like a half-finished oil painting, altering into something new and dark. My feet were unsteady on the angled surface beneath me. Whatever I stood on suddenly rolled to the left, then the right, and back again.

What the hell?

Lights blinked. Shouts broke out. Cries of panic escalated around me. An alarm was ringing somewhere, its incessant *boop, boop, boop* splitting my ears.

My eyes caught up. I gasped, now understanding why I felt like I'd been transported onto a slippery dip and merry-go-round all in one.

I was on the *Velorosa*'s bridge. Annaka was at the wheel, madly turning the instrument as she navigated the ship through the powerful waves that crested over the vessel's sides. For a few horrifying seconds, the *Velorosa*'s bow was completely underwater before she floated back up like a bobbing apple. In the disjointed flashes of lightning, I saw grinning skulls in the salt spray and haze.

The Bone Towers.

Not only were Annaka and her crew facing a storm but also the monolithic structures that travelled deep into the sea. All it would take was for one rogue wave to smash the *Velorosa* against the colossal rocks, and the helm would be gutted like a fish.

The waves grew in intensity and height, their roar sounding as though they were trying to outmatch the menacing thunder.

This is no ordinary sea storm.

I felt the negative charge in the air, sinking right into my skin to scrape across my bones.

Galactic storm.

Morgomoth had found the *Velorosa*.

CHAPTER 24

I sped out of the bridge onto the viewing deck, daring to risk the pummelling waves that smashed against the *Velorosa*'s hull. I had to know what we were up against, what new nightmare we were facing. I clung to the rail, my hair blown in multiple directions, as though the wind didn't know which way it wanted to turn. The sky was pulsing with fire, the churning smoke as dark and violent as a volcanic ash cloud. It became almost difficult to see what was happening through the dense sea spray and thickening smoulder, but whenever the lightning flashed, grisly forms appeared in the sky. Skeletal figures and wasting bodies, torn flesh and festering wounds. The creatures' muffled cries rang in my ears, lusting for blood and carnage.

Chak-lorks.

The same creatures who'd attacked Tarahik.

The monsters Hadar had imbued with fire.

We're surrounded by water. We'll be okay.

My relief was short-lived, because in that terrifying moment, an enormous wave rose over the *Velorosa*, towering like a growing giant. Just as it crested, thousands of puckered grey faces emerged in the water, the deep grooves in their skin covered by sea slime. They must have been decomposing an eternity in the ocean. I imagined their flesh had become as squishy and wrinkled as rotting prunes.

These chak-lorks were infused with water magic.

Have they been following us this entire time through the sea?

Fear seeped through my body.

Chak-lorks can pass through celestial shields.

I'd barely comprehended the thought when the wave struck the *Velorosa*. An unfathomable rumble tore through the vessel. The ship shuddered and groaned, the force of the impact tossing me off my feet, sending me sprawling across the viewing platform. I landed hard by the door to the bridge and scrambled for traction on the wet surface, fighting to shake my dizziness.

Whatever hope I had faded away like a photograph left out in the sun when I looked over the rail. The deck was swarmed by chak-lorks. The creatures had easily infiltrated the celestial shield and were now crawling over each other like skittering bugs and burrowing worms. More of the foul monsters appeared as another wave crested, smashing down onto the *Velorosa* like a pounding fist. Then another wave from the left. Another at the right. The deck became a swirling mass of hungry, carnivorous dead.

I stumbled back onto the bridge, panicking at what the next step was.

There is no next step.

We were on a ship in the middle of the sea, surrounded by a galactic storm and an army of the swimming dead.

We're screwed.

One of the commanding pirates shouted to be heard over the cacophony that had swept through the cabin. "They're on board."

I blinked, barely recognising the burly man. Cryton's shaved head was bleeding, his collar and shoulder soaked through with blood. He must have hit his head.

All the pirates were in states of terror, faces dampened by sweat and lips white. Lights flickered. Alarms blared. Many of the crew, me included, were thrown from their feet, reaching out for anything to keep them upright. Somehow in all the upheaval, Annaka remained by the wheel, furiously navigating through the tumultuous waves.

Cryton fought his way to reach her.

A reproachful glare darkened her gaze "Is everyone secure in the dining hall?"

"Yes, but those creatures... it won't take them long to get inside the *Velorosa*. We need to abandon ship while we still can."

The air in the bridge smelt of fear. Annaka's crew knew they'd met their match and had become sloppy. One of the men, maybe a couple of years older than me, had ducked into a corner, breathing hard, as though at any minute it would be his last. Another man bolted from the bridge onto the viewing deck, only to be swept away by a wave, lost forever in the sea. He hadn't even had a chance to scream.

Annaka gritted her teeth. "I am not abandoning my ship."

Cryton's tight muscles shifted into a threatening stance. "The *Velorosa*'s headed for the bottom of the sea. It's not *us* he wants. Abandon ship. We can use one of the tenders."

"You'd leave the rest of them behind?"

Cryton's silence was answer enough.

Annaka shook her head with a snide laugh. "I made a promise to get these people to the cliffs."

His face split into a nasty grimace. "It was an empty promise. One you should never have made. Now, what will it be, Captain?"

When Annaka didn't immediately reply, Cryton shouted across the bridge. "Abandon ship. Get to the tenders."

The crew didn't have to be told twice. They hightailed it out of the bridge, taking one of the ladders down to the levels below. Annaka watched them leave with thinly disguised regret. I couldn't be sure if it was because in a matter of seconds, Cryton, her first mate, and probably the crew member she'd trusted the most, had pulled a mutiny, or because she knew deep inside that the *Velorosa* was doomed. I doubted anyone would be getting onto a tender. Not with a galactic storm raging down and the sea inundated by chak-lorks.

Cryton paused on the ladder. "Annaka, don't waste your life for this. Come with us."

She waved him away. "Someone needs to make sure the *Velorosa* doesn't collide with a Bone Tower. We hit one of those, and we'll all be swimming with the fish. It should give you time to get to the tenders."

"Annak—"

"The *Velorosa* is my ship," she interrupted. "Captains go down with their ship."

Cryton didn't say anything, only nodded his understanding and descended the remainder of the rungs. He was gone, forsaking his captain and his home.

Annaka focused on the wheel. I didn't think she was the type of girl to cry. Offended? Yes. But she was tied emotionally to her ship. She would never leave it, even when remaining meant certain death.

Certain death.

Fear surged through my veins.

I had to find Jad.

Talina.

Marek.

All of them.

Morgomoth wouldn't let them die. Not right away. He'd give everyone on board a choice first, to join him and the United League of Dissent. If they refused... then they would die.

My friends would never do it. Macaslan, Harper, and Darius would welcome death over siding with Morgomoth. They were all going to end up bloated corpses in the sea.

I barrelled down the ladder and pushed my way through the lower passage, but fear had made my feet numb, and I was so consumed by dread that my head was weak and dizzy. I dashed down the various halls, thrown into walls and stumbling past sharp corners whenever the *Velorosa* was hit by another violent wave.

Where's the dining hall?

I wasn't familiar with the layout of the ship. I felt like I was going around in circles. Everything looked the same, the passages identical.

Wait.

My friends wouldn't be in the dining hall. They'd be at my side, protecting me in the infirmary or whatever new hidey-hole they'd placed me in.

Close your eyes. Think about your body.

I focused on my breathing, on my sharp inhales and exhales, annoyed by the heavy swaying that rocked me. Meditating was difficult when the floor beneath you was rolling.

Concentrate.

I could imagine Lunette's chastising voice, disappointment heavy in her tone, which fuelled me to stay focused.

My breathing soon matched another. I not only heard the heart-beat of my essence but the heart that pulsed in my body, too, growing louder and urging me to find it, as though the beat from my essence and the beat from my body had joined in a dance. My arms felt heavy, the muscles sore from lack of movement. My legs were itchy, desperate to move.

Found you.

I was in my body, a silent prison where I couldn't move, see, or speak, only remain asleep.

I exhaled, imagining my soul floating out with my breath, the numbness fading.

I opened my eyes, staring down at my body, expecting my sleeping form to be surrounded by my protective friends.

But I was alone.

REALISING my friends were absent was initially upsetting, until I heard the stinging bolts of caster-fire behind the door. Even here, secure in this private sick bay, I still felt the resonant boom of the cast-shooters in my teeth. I grabbed the handle, desperate to get into the infirmary, but my fingers went straight through the metal.

Really? Now my spirit form is too weak to move physical objects.

Balls of pent-up frustration sidled through me. This couldn't have come at a worse time. There was a battle happening in the infirmary —my friends could have been dying—and I was trapped in here, unable to do anything because I was stuck behind a damn door.

Or am I?

I can float through the door. I know I can.

Granted, I had ballsed it up last time, but there was nothing like pressure to make you do something right. At least, I hoped.

Anxious about the precious seconds I was wasting, I shut my eyes, imagined myself as a swirling ball of energy, and ran to the door.

Please let this work. Please let this work.

Expecting a collision, I braced myself for the impact. I opened my eyes, surprised to find myself in the infirmary. I squealed with triumph, but my elation dropped the moment I saw the chaos I'd walked into.

My friends had the steel hatch to the infirmary locked and barricaded. Darius and Colonel Harper pushed beds and chairs against it. Talina was scrambling through medical cabinets, grabbing scalpels and anything else that could be used as a weapon. Jad, Marek, and Commander Macaslan fired their cast-shooters, waves of sparks skidding in all directions through the smoky air. The sight of it churned wildly in my brain.

At first, I didn't understand why they were shooting at the hatch, until I saw the deluge of seawater slipping through the seams.

So much for being watertight.

Chak-lorks rose from the bubbling dark surface. Their skin was waterlogged and pliant. Soppy drops fell from their flesh, probably where small crabs and fish had feasted.

I stepped away, nearly wanting to turn and run back into the private sick bay. The air no longer smelt of smoke and burnt metal but the rotting, fishy scent of putrefaction at sea. The chak-lorks approached with graceless steps. My friends fired their weapons. The wave of caster-fire caused the chak-lorks to explode into bloody splatters, but the moment the pieces hit the water, the creatures reformed, rising again. Their grisly snarls reminded me of wild dogs hunting in the dead of night, but it was their eyes that were truly terrifying. They were white globules. If you poked one, I imagined the eyeball would rupture into a gooey mess on your finger.

Marek dodged one of the creatures' outstretched arms. He shot the chak-lork down, cringing as he stepped away from its soggy remains, which were already morphing back together. "This is impossible," he cried. "There are too many of them."

Jad fired three rounds, a rapid volley of caster-fire toppling the creatures like ducks in a carnival game. I knew from the determination on his face that Jad would fight to the end. I also knew the odds of my friends surviving this were slim. They were trapped. The infirmary was filling with water, and more chak-lorks were appearing by the second.

Jad slung his cast-shooter over his shoulder and summoned balls of fire into his hands. For a moment, the infirmary was ablaze with red energy as he flung the fire at the chak-lorks. As impressive as the stunt was, it was useless. Fire couldn't outmatch water. The flames hit the chak-lorks and sizzled out.

The creatures had my friends surrounded, forcing them back into the far wall. The chak-lorks drew closer, the repetition of their succinct steps making them appear as though animated by a single transmitter. Awful yellow blobs dripped off their soaked bodies, splashing across the water.

"Master wants the girl," one of the chak-lorks hissed, its voice creepy and mechanic. "Master wants Zaya."

The creature's large nostrils flared.

A sickening swell rose in my chest.

It can smell me beyond the door.

Jad was breathing hard. His sweat glistened down the side of his face. Talina was chalk-white, the tendons standing out in her neck. She grabbed Marek's tight hand, squeezing his fingers. I didn't think she was even aware she did it. Macaslan, Darius, and Harper, soaked through by the water, exchanged fretful glances. I knew each of them was ruminating about how this could have happened.

The leader's white cataract eyes examined my friends. His lips split into a pitiless smile. "Bring the girl. Morgomoth waits for you on deck."

CHAPTER 25

Outside the *Velorosa*, the world had erupted in thunder and lightning. Gigantic forks streaked overhead like meteors. The thunder's ominous boom ricocheted off the Bone Towers, as though the monoliths were part of a pipe organ in a hellish symphony. A torrent of hot rainwater fell on the deck, reminding me of gushing blood.

The chak-lorks shepherded my friends onto the deck, forcing them on their knees. My eyes raked over Jad, and I knew from the fury on his face that he didn't have a plan. Beside him, Marek, Talina, Macaslan, Darius, and Harper looked like prisoners lined up to be beheaded. At least Colonel Harper seemed healthier now. His skin had more colour than the previous night. I wondered what the strange hex had been, and who had cursed him.

The leader of the chak-lorks dropped my sleeping body before my friends like some sort of sacrificial lamb. For a moment, all I could do was stand there, numb with penetrating dread.

After everything we'd done, how had it come to this?

I moved across the deck and kneeled beside Jad, wishing I was strong enough to make him sense me, but my essence had grown weak. I didn't think I'd be able to levitate, let alone make contact with the living. Jad stared at the sky, eyes wide with disbelief. Next to him, Talina's face reflected shock, and Marek's jaw dropped. I looked up, overwhelmed by the blinding incandescence that built in the clouds above. The light swirled like a maelstrom, faster and brighter. A tremendous pressure grew in my ears, reverberating right through my brain. I wanted to look away, but my eyes were fixed on the blistering radiance.

A bolt of pristine lightning erupted from the clouds. For a moment, it lit the sea as far as I could see. It was impossible to not be awestruck. The jagged bolt exploded on the deck. Harsh gusts and hot ash rained over me, the static in the air causing all the hairs on my body to stand on end. Every joint and muscle felt like it had come loose, but that sensation was nothing compared to the next horror. The *Velorosa's* celestial shield crumbled, reduced to fiery debris. It reminded me of a broken snowglobe, left shattered in pieces.

Talina's startled gasp drew my attention.

A hideous rising form appeared from the blackened deck where the lightning had struck. Morgomoth's tall figure was so far from caster or human that even Commander Macaslan, who I didn't think would yield even in the face of a tornado, gave a small moan of terror. The ruler of the ULD was charred bones and fire, his flesh and muscles replaced by flames and smoke. Faces ebbed in and out of the embers, their mouths agape in silent screams. They were wraiths trapped in his body. I wondered if Morgomoth had collected them in the Dark Divide, sewing them together to make his unnatural body complete.

He drew himself upright, and I got the feeling that with just a blink of his eye he could turn us all to dust. His fearsome face scanned my friends. When his listless gaze met mine, he smiled in cunning greeting.

MORGOMOTH WASN'T ALONE. Vulcan and Hadar had joined their master in the lightning descent, remaining a respectful distance behind him. Vulcan had lost more weight. His cheeks were hollow, his skin sickly and sallow. He looked like a skeleton in the rain. His long hair cast shadows across his face, making his hooded eyes appear eternally dark. His gaze found Jad's. There was no fatherly love in Vulcan's expression, only disappointment. Jad's glare was full of loathing.

Hadar watched my friends with boredom. It was my body, lying asleep on the deck, that piqued her interest. I shivered, imagining what she would do to me on an operating table, visualising how deep she'd let the scalpel cut.

There were other members of the ULD on board too. Male and female dissent rebels.

Recognition sent a wave of sadness through me when my eyes landed on one of the women. Lainie. She stood uncertain at the edge of the group, as though she had half a mind to join us and kneel by our side. Part of me crumbled inside seeing her so thin. She had misunderstood what she'd signed up for, but to back out now would be suicide. To join the ULD was like dying. There was no going back to your old life. The heavy lines around her eyes, which were damp and red, suggested she was aware of that now.

Morgomoth watched us all with a hunter's stare. "Foolish casters."

His voice was like a knife to the skin.

When he moved, his shadow expanded, spanning unnaturally across the deck. He circled around us, giving the impression of an executioner about to swing the axe and behead us all at once. "Did you think you could escape me?"

"You're the fool," someone spat.

Annaka appeared around the corner of the deck bridge. She wasn't alone. Two chak-lorks, twice her size, dragged her toward Morgomoth, but she didn't go without a fight. She kicked at the creatures' shins and struggled in their hold, twisting to flee. I smiled when the sweet crunch of bone resonated across the deck. One of the chak-lorks went down, his foot broken clean off. The creature didn't howl or scream. Pain didn't come to the undead. The chak-lork rose on its one good leg and limped forward on its new stump, tugging Annaka with him.

Morgomoth looked at the captain of the *Velorosa* with an exaggerated sigh. "Bind this child's impertinent mouth."

"You are a fool," Annaka repeated. She sounded confident, but her shoulders were tight, and her pulse beat visibly in her neck. "No one is navigating the ship. We could collide with a Bone Tower any minute. Do you want us to end up at the bottom of the sea?"

Morgomoth evaluated her slowly. "So, you are Annaka Vandergriff. Once the captain of the *Velorosa*."

Her eyes flashed resentfully. "I am the captain," she fired back with fierce animosity.

"You are a prisoner."

At his command, Annaka's captors dragged her to my friends. She gasped in pain when they hit her spine, the force knocking her to her knees, but like the rest of the group, a moment later, she was still and weirdly compliant. It was chilling to see them conforming.

They've been spelled.

My eyes roamed the rebel's faces, trying to find the one with cerebrokinesis. One of the dissidents had to be using mind control to keep everyone so... obedient, but before I could work out which rebel it was, chak-lorks appeared to take positions behind their prisoners. They raised their weapons, ready to use them at Morgomoth's command. In the formidable lightning, silvery luminance gleamed off their weapons. There was even an implement that resembled a meat cleaver, still fresh with blood, which dripped in the heavy rain.

All it would take was one wrong move, one slip-up to annoy Morgomoth, and my friends would be dead.

Hatred for Morgomoth burned in my eyes. Struggling against the rising panic in my chest, I dared to look at the skeletal horror that was his face.

"Please," I begged to his mind. *"My body is there. You've won. You don't need them."*

His disconnected gaze lingered on my friends. *"And what will you offer in exchange for their lives?"*

I didn't have an answer. I knew *exactly* what Morgomoth wanted. For me to open the door to the Dark Divide. To unleash that dead wasteland onto the earth.

But why?

Lunette's melancholy words rose from my memory. *"If you open that door, you merge the world of the living with the world of the dead. The Dark Divide will become a presence... an entity... a new element on the earth. It will consume everything."*

Choked tears worked their way down my cheeks. All this time, I'd been wondering what the Dark Divide was when I should have been trying to figure out what Morgomoth wanted with it.

His greedy eyes sought the key around Jad's neck. At some point, either during the siege in the infirmary or in the time it took to reach the deck, it had slipped from his shirt, now exposed against his chest. Lightning reflected off its gold surface, making it shine like a beacon.

"Trajan Stormouth." Morgomoth called his name in a voice that sounded like victory. "You have slighted and brought shame to your father and the Stormouth name. I am not a cruel leader. I am giving you an opportunity to allege yourself to me and the United League of Dissent." He moved forward and wrapped his long, bony fingers around Jad's jaw, forcing the captain to look at him. "Give me the key," he demanded, his tone eerily controlled.

Jad's tone was laden with icy aversion. "You're right there. You take it."

Morgomoth sneered, reminding me of a rabid dog.

Jad raised a good point. Why didn't Morgomoth just take the key?

The captain drew his lips together in a satisfied smirk. "The key can only be possessed by those it deems honourable. And you are not honourable."

The leader of the ULD slapped him, hard enough to knock Jad's head to the side. I bit back a cry. I was surprised Jad didn't spit out a few teeth.

The key decides who takes it.

No wonder Morgomoth was furious.

He laughed sharply, but the tone sounded livid. "You may want to reconsider your loyalty, Trajan, especially now that we have Zaya. I kill you, and the key is free to choose another *honourable* subject." He motioned to my sleeping body. "Together, she and I will be an unstoppable force."

"She won't help you."

"She won't have a choice."

Up until that moment, Jad had remained remarkably calm, but now his irises burned scarlet. He looked capable of ripping all the dissent rebels apart with his bare hands. Lucky for them, he was under someone's mind control.

Seeing Jad's silent rage chilled me to the core, filling me with defeat. Morgomoth was taunting him, provoking the lycanthor inside. And it was working.

Morgomoth swept his gaze over my friends, watching them like a hawk over mice. "And what about the rest of you? Are you willing to follow in Captain Arden's footsteps and die? Or will you join the United League of Dissent? Will you become the makers of a new beginning?"

I was proud that everyone remained silent, even though I knew it would cost them their lives.

My ribs felt tight, my airways blocked.

There has to be some way I can stop this.

Lainie took a cautious step forward to catch Talina's eye. *Please,* her expression seemed to beg.

I didn't know whether Lainie couldn't stand the thought of witnessing her best friend's death or didn't want to be alone among the ULD forces any longer. Whatever it was, she didn't get an answer. Talina averted her eyes, her expression a combination of pity and disgust.

"How disappointing," Morgomoth said, not sounding the least bit disheartened.

His voice drifted into my mind, a vibration that made me feel like I'd been doused in poison. *"I will kill them all, Zaya. I will have them bludgeoned and sliced and fed to the chak-lorks, unless…."*

"Unless what?" I mind-snapped, knowing full well what the answer would be.

Morgomoth pulsed with dark energy. Flames, smoke, and shadows surged around his bones. The wraiths that were trapped in his disfigured form wailed, their cries chilling. The angrier Morgomoth became, the more the spirits writhed. It was like staring at and listening to a medieval depiction of hell.

"Unless you open the door."

It was what I'd expected, but it still made me flinch as though I'd been struck by a blow.

Morgomoth signalled for the chak-lorks to raise their weapons. The implements' sharp tips looked wicked in the lightning.

My essence had gone cold with fright.

"What will it be, Zaya? Time is running out."

I couldn't grovel, couldn't bargain, couldn't come up with an alternative offer.

There was nothing else Morgomoth wanted. He would kill my friends. He would use me to take possession of the key and enter the Isla Necropolis. He'd find the Bone Grimoire. If I did what he asked and opened the door to unleash the Dark Divide, what surety did I have that he wouldn't double-cross me and kill my friends anyway? Either way, he'd take the key. All that hard work Jad, Marek, and Talina had achieved to find the key would be undone. Macaslan's, Harper's, and Darius's plans would be undone.

I couldn't let that happen.

Morgomoth grinned nastily. *"Should I make it easier for you?"*

He clicked his fingers.

It was truly frightening to see his necromancy at work. A seam of darkness split the air before me, expanding into a yawning gap. He'd opened a doorway to the Dark Divide.

If Morgomoth could do that, what would he be capable of if the Dark Divide was unleashed?

But I never had a chance to think about the consequences. The howling wind tossed me across the deck. Rivers of black cloud clutched my arms and legs, dragging me into the Dark Divide.

Now I understood how a mouse felt right before it was devoured by a snake. The heavy jaws snapped closed, leaving me in the monster's mouth.

I BLINKED, peeling back the grogginess from my eyes. Silver-blue radiance played havoc with my sight at first, my vision taking a moment to adjust. I was back in the Dark Divide, but instead of being returned to my altar and the never-ending expanse of gloomy tunnels, I stood in the underground canal—in front of the door.

The gilded panels that depicted war scenes of a long-ago battle were striking in their detail, horrific but elaborate. In the centre of the door was the demonic-shaped head with the circular handle in its gaping jaws, just waiting to be turned. The blue light, luminous and glowing, made it tempting to see what was on the other side.

No. I can't afford to think like that.

A claw of ice struck my ribcage. I knew what was on the other side.

Morgomoth.

I had not forgotten where I'd come from or what had happened. Being tossed and thrown from one plane to another had left my skin feeling raw and my muscles screaming, but that was nothing compared to the silent agony of not knowing what had become of my friends.

"They are alive... for now," Morgomoth's voice chided in my mind.

His tone sent ripples of terror across my skin.

I turned my head in a slow arc, expecting Morgomoth to be right behind me, but the cavern was empty except for the canal, the water mirroring the darkness of the cavern.

Morgomoth's laugh was full of mockery. *"You know where I am, Zaya. Open the door. Save your friends."*

He was on the other side, waiting. Once I opened the door, he would tug it back. Lunette had told me it took two necromancers to unleash the Dark Divide. The very idea that I was even contemplating it made me feel ashamed and traitorous. A weighty silence settled around me, my thoughts between what was right and what was devotion to my friends spinning in an undying circle in my head.

"Time is of the essence. The clock is ticking. What will it be?"

I didn't answer.

I couldn't speak.

I couldn't breathe.

"That is your answer, is it?"

I struggled to suck in whatever wisps of air was in the canal.

"Then you have made your decision. You are doomed eternally to the Dark Divide, Zaya. Not a wraith but not alive. An essence. Cursed to loneliness and darkness."

And then, in a voice that was a ruthless command, he spoke the order that would seal the deal. *"Kill them."*

He'd deliberately let me hear it. He wanted me to feel the guilt of my decision for all eternity.

I thought about Jad closing his eyes before the deadly blow met his head. Talina's delicate swanlike neck cleaved in two. Marek lying in a pool of his own blood on the *Velorosa*'s deck. Macaslan's, Harper's, and Darius's heads lopped clean off.

I can't let that happen.

I grabbed the handle and pushed. At the same time, I felt the wrenching of someone yanking it back.

CHAPTER 26

I gasped, my nose assaulted by burning air, my body battered by wind and sea spray.

My body.

For weeks, I'd been an essence. Every tormented sensation, every painful experience, couldn't really hurt me. It couldn't inflict real damage. Being tossed back into my body was like waking from a vivid dream, tumbling headlong into a whirlpool, and being thrown back by a shock wave combined. My brain struggled to keep up with the senses that assailed me. My arms and legs were stiff from lack of movement, or maybe my brain wasn't very good at recalling how my muscles were meant to work. Brightness played havoc with my vision, dots of burning yellow bleeding across my sight.

Pins and needles. Fatigue. Sweat. Palpitations.

I was aware that I was lying on the *Velorosa*'s deck, my white dress soaked by sea and blistering hot rain. Cries and tortured screams wailed around me, but the sound was so distant, it was like listening to everything underwater.

What is happening?

My disorientated mind took a moment to catch up.

The door.

I'd opened it.

Now I understood why my vision was attacked with severe brightness. The sky was filled with incandescent bursts of light, the clouds a roiling maelstrom. Bolts of white light zigzagged down to the sea, sending waves the size of mountains across the already treacherous surface.

My ears ringing and my muscles protesting, I slowly peeled myself off the deck. Agony wrenched my spine, but I forced myself onto my feet. There was smoke, ash, and fire everywhere. It was incredible that the *Velorosa* could be burning in the middle of a storm. Magic was at hand in this. Fire magic.

Jad.

No. He wouldn't do this.

If anything, Jad would be using his power to put the flames out.

People ran in and out of the smoke. Dissent rebels or chak-lorks? I couldn't tell anymore. From the brief glimpses I caught, they were all too badly covered in burns and ash for me to differentiate.

My foot hit something hard. I looked down, my insides contracting. It was a charred body, too blackened and bloody to identify.

What have I done?

Did opening the door do this?

Have I killed everyone on board?

A tremendous, unearthly quake ripped through the night, separate from the rumbling, cracking thunder. Ahead, the horizon glowed as if a new sun were rising.

No. Not the sun. Explosions.

Fire and black clouds rose from the sea, followed by masses of upturned earth. For a moment, I wondered whether the seabed had lifted or if the Bone Towers were rising. My body gave a shudder of protest, my eyes refusing to believe what they were witnessing. Volcanoes. Hundreds of them rose out of the sea like ant mounds. Lightning volleys leapt from one crater to the next. The volcanoes were conjoining. They were forming an island.

I recognised the black rocks and their jagged surfaces.

It was the Dark Divide.

Morgomoth had achieved what he wanted. A deadland. A wasteland in the middle of the sea. A kingdom where he was on the throne.

And I helped him.

"Zaya." Morgomoth's scalding voice broke me out of my shocked trance.

He stood behind me, his hand stretched out as though he were about to escort me onto a dance floor. But I knew what he had planned was much worse. This was a final chance to join his side.

Dissent rebels, those who were still alive or capable of standing, had paused behind him, watching me with vindictive glee. Vulcan, Hadar, and Lainie were among them. I was relieved to see Lainie wasn't injured, but I was also disappointed. She had betrayed us. She had chosen the United League of Dissent over us. She had chosen to use her magic to break Zandor's mind. I didn't recognise her anymore. Perhaps I never really knew the real Lainie.

She dropped her gaze from me and stared at the *Velorosa*'s bloody deck.

Good. Her guilt should be endless.

Morgomoth shared a bemused look with his followers. "I had hoped to unleash the Dark Divide at Tarahik, but perhaps the Bone Towers will turn out to be more fortuitous. It will make it difficult for our enemies to find us here. We're protected by violent seas and, from this vantage point, capable of projecting airpower worldwide." He turned to me. "Thank you, Zaya. I could never have accomplished it without your help."

"Where are my friends?" I wanted my voice to sound ruthless, but it came out like a modest squeak.

"With any luck, they're dead." He turned and barked an order at one of his men. "Find Trajan Stormouth's body. I want that key."

Dead?

I didn't know whether it was the unimaginably painful thought of Jad being reduced to an empty, dead body or if it was because maddening rage had seized me, but suddenly I wanted nothing more than to destroy the monster who stood in my way. Something firm materialised in my hand, hidden from view by my long skirt. It was the Neathror blade. The familiar onyx dagger glistened like black snake scales. It was narrower in width than most blades, and strange runes marked the weapon. The language of the dead.

Somehow, my anger had summoned the athame-sabre. I never knew where the blade went when it wasn't required. Where had it been hiding all this time when I'd been trapped in the Dark Divide?

I clung to it tightly, some of my fear ebbing away now that I wasn't entirely vulnerable.

A deep groan came from the bowels of the *Velorosa*. Cracks split the deck, multiplying in hundreds of directions. Shattering metal assailed my ears. The cracks had stretched into fissures. I was already unsteady on my sea legs, and I didn't have the strength to run yet. I clutched the handrail, feeling like a caged animal with nowhere to go. Some of the rebels lost their footing and were swallowed by the apertures, their screams silenced as they disappeared into the dark levels below.

Are those levels on fire? Underwater?

My bruised head was swimming. The *Velorosa* was sinking.

A crack, heavier than thunder, ricocheted across the deck. Morgomoth had conjured a portal. The rift expanded, stretching across what was left of the *Velorosa*'s deck. It was a gateway to the new land that was forming behind me at astonishing speed.

Morgomoth stretched his hand toward me again "Come with us, Zaya. Your place is beside me, ruling the new world. We'll find Jad's body and resurrect him."

"That's a lie," I roared with sudden savagery. "All you want is the key."

"Zaya." Morgomoth hissed my name like a serpent. His eyes glistened with ire. "There is nowhere to go. The *Velorosa* is sinking. The sea will have no mercy on you. This is fate. Do not cross it. Join the ULD. You have incredible necromancy. I can train you. You could be a queen of the new world. Ruler of both the living and the dead. This is where you're meant to be. By my side."

A union of power was what he wanted. I did not agree with the Council of Founding Sovereigns, or with the way the world operated now—humans and ruling casters living in the Free Zones while lesser casters were made to slave in the dangerous, unpredictable provinces —but I would never agree with Morgomoth's extremist, racial ideologies.

My face must have expressed my repugnance because his lips cracked into a thin smile, and he shook with a humourless laugh. It sounded defeated. It sounded angry. He marched toward me, reaching out to wrap his bony fingers around my wrist and wrench me through the portal.

I lashed out with Neathror, slashing it across his abdomen. He leapt back, smoke and black liquid pooling from the wound, his cry of anguish splitting my head. Smoke and shadows wrapped around him, already healing the injury. Neathror couldn't kill him, but it gave me the distraction I needed.

I ran to the handrail, climbing over. The water below me was a swirling flurry of darkness.

Please don't let it take long.

Don't make me suffer.

"Zaya." Morgomoth's voice was a twisted scream. I didn't understand how he'd managed to move so quickly to the rail. He lunged for me, a storm of shadows and smoke, his eyes a threat of violence.

My foot slipped, but I managed to catch myself on the rail just in time.

That was stupid. It would have been far easier if I'd tumbled into the sea. Now I had to find the courage to jump all over again.

I didn't see who threw the first hex-grenade, but I heard the explosion and the screams that followed. Dissent rebels dived and ducked for cover. Another grenade rolled across the deck, erupting into flames and smoke, sending steel fragments into the air. My ears rattled. The sounds of burning, ripping metal pummelled my chest. In the haze, I made out rebels running in the direction of the portal. Morgomoth had disappeared. I didn't know if he'd been hurt by the hex-grenade. It didn't seem likely.

Someone screamed orders to return fire. I think it might have been Vulcan, but there was so much smoke, so much hot rain, ash, and sludge, so much noise and chaos, I couldn't be certain.

Another hex-grenade landed not far from me. The deck was suddenly brighter than daylight before it was engulfed in a second volley of flames. A face appeared through the smoke. My fingers curled into a fist, ready to punch the dissent rebel who dared to capture me.

"Zaya, no. It's me."

My eyes stung with smoke and tears, but no matter how badly I hurt, no matter how great the assault around me was, that voice would always calm me.

Jad.

I'd never fail to recognise his voice.

Summoning what was the last of my strength, I climbed over the rail and wrapped my arms around him, relishing the comforting deception of security, because we were far from safe.

Jad crushed me to him in an embrace, but only for a moment. "We need to go." He stared into my eyes, cupping my face in his hands. "Those hex-grenades won't stop Morgomoth."

We picked our way around the fires and gaping holes in the deck. It haunted me, the dead faces my eyes came across, the charred bodies we had to step over, the blackened arms and legs that had been ripped from bodies. It was such a tragic, despicable waste.

Jad used the smoke and fire to shield us from sight. I suspected his magic was what kept the flames burning; otherwise, the sea and rain would surely have doused every spark. He led me below deck.

"The ship's sinking," I cried.

Surely he knows that.

Jad offered me a weak smile. "We have a way out."

We?

Does he mean…?

I didn't want to dare hope for fear of disappointment.

We descended deeper into the *Velorosa*. Each time we came to a ladder, it seemed to be tilted on a sharper angle.

The bow must be underwater.

Jad's gaze lingered on me for a moment, his eyes stricken. "I'm sorry I had to leave you on deck, but Morgomoth and his rebels had you surrounded. I had to get the others out."

I waved his excuse away. "I would have done the same thing."

I wished I could have kissed him then, and privately scolded myself for it. What a ridiculous thing to want when we were facing the possibility of being trapped and drowned.

"Where are we going?"

"To the tenders." Jad's voice was far too panicked for my liking.

A moment later, I understood why. We descended into a level filled with water. It was up to my knees and getting higher. The angle of the *Velorosa* made wading through it treacherous, and all I could achieve were awkward, plodding strides. My weeks in a sleeping curse were finally taking their toll on my awakened body. Jad wrapped his arm around me, letting me rest my weight against his. It helped... a little.

He led me into a large expanse of a room, something that must have once been the cargo hold. The large hatch was open, water spilling in, causing everything that wasn't locked down to float. A tender boat was just beyond the hatch, floating on the sea. It must have been anchored to remain so close to the *Velorosa*'s side.

My head whirled so badly that I nearly went into a faint. We waded through the water, pushing and kicking through the obstacles that floated past us: crates, boxes, barrels. There were other tenders, still secure inside the hold.

"Jad, what about everyone else on board?"

The passengers had been secured for their own safety in the dining room, hidden away from the chak-lorks. Where were they now?

Jad's face changed into an expression reserved for people in mourning. "It's too late. The dining room is underwater. I couldn't get there in time."

The news made me freeze up for a second. "They're all...."

I couldn't bear to finish the sentence.

"Drowned," Jad confirmed.

I went into a daze, where my instincts took over but my mind froze, still trapped in the horror of what he'd revealed.

The water swept up to our waists, then our chests. Jad's lycanthor strength was the only thing that got us out of the cargo hold. A rope drifted from the tender. Jad grabbed it, his other arm secure around my waist. I couldn't see through the haze and rain, but people on the tender tugged the rope, pulling us up. Hands grabbed me, settling me onto the deck. I recognised Annaka's almond-coloured eyes. Talina's flustered gaze. Marek's parted lips, open in shock. They were all looking down on me. Beyond them, I saw Macaslan and Darius, sopping wet in the downfall. Macha was also on board, Bartholomew quiet on her shoulder. The crow's feathers were flattened, the rain sliding down his sleek wings. Clorenzo waited behind the obeah-woman with his twin children, Livel and Sarith. I was relieved to see them, but that made me wonder how many other children aboard the *Velorosa* hadn't been so lucky.

Where's Colonel Harper?

He wasn't here.

My vision went hazy, my mind tilting toward vertigo.

Ripples and vibrations shuddered beneath me. The tender's motor had started. We were sailing away.

Someone had lifted me from the deck and taken me inside. They settled me beside a window. Outside, the flames from the *Velorosa* flickered once, twice, and then, like a light bulb gone out, were doused by the rain. In the lightning, I watched the ship's silhouette dip beneath the waves, sinking into the ocean's secretive depths.

Screaming started in my ears. I didn't know whether it was my own or if I could hear the echo of hundreds of souls forever lost in a watery grave.

I was grateful when the glass fogged up.

CHAPTER 27

I woke to hot sunlight, the sea air doing nothing to prevent the heat from climbing. The tender was a people mover, a refueler, and a cargo supplier, designed to support a much larger ship. She was not a luxury yacht by any stretch of the imagination. The vessel was no larger than ten by three metres. The cabin had no walls, just expansive windows that allowed full sunlight to access the interior.

I sat up, my thighs peeling off the plastic seat. My dress stuck to me, and my scalp was itchy from sweat. The ends of my hair felt like straw. The ocean was meant to do a world of good for the complexion, but all I experienced was the ache of sunburn. My tongue was dry. I desperately needed water. Judging by how high the sun was in the sky, I must have been out of it for several hours. I buried my face in my hands, taking a moment to collect myself.

The Velorosa *sank. The Dark Divide was unleashed. I survived. My friends saved me. We're on a tender. We're safe.*

"You're awake."

The voice startled me.

Talina dropped onto the chair next to me. Her lips were cracked, and the skin around her nose was dry, but her emerald eyes still shone with relief. She swept me into a hug and didn't let go for a long time. From her perspective, she hadn't seen me alive in weeks.

I swept my eyes around the tender. Macha and Bartholomew were asleep in a corner, lightly snoring. Next to them, wrapped in sheets, were Livel and Sarith. They slept soundly but didn't look comfortable on the hard floor. Through the window, I saw Macaslan and Darius sitting by the stern, quietly whispering to each other. I wondered what they were plotting now.

Talina began catching me up on everything I'd missed.

I raised a hand, interrupting. "I know. I've seen and heard everything. I've kind of been a... for lack of a better word, a ghost. There's no need to explain. I know."

"That isn't creepy at all, is it?" Marek appeared, or maybe he'd already been there. He settled on the seat opposite, staring studiously at the mapographic in his hands.

Talina gave me a sideways glance. "So, when you say you've seen everything, do you mean you already know about Colonel Harper?"

I rubbed my arms, bracing myself for bad news. "What happened to the colonel?"

Talina pressed a shaky hand to her lips. "It all happened so fast. When we were launching the tender, Colonel Harper got swept away by a wave. There was nothing we could do. He was just... gone."

I squeezed my eyes shut, forcing the sorrowful tears away. Colonel Harper and I hadn't had a warm relationship. We couldn't have been more different if we tried, but he'd protected me and remained loyal. He'd put me first, risking his own life to save me. Once in Shadow's Wood, right after I'd discovered Lunette's frozen body, and again when he'd retrieved me from Tarahik's infirmary and sent me through the portal. He was Macaslan's friend. He hadn't deserved to die. Not like that—just swept away like a piece of dust.

"Zaya, are you okay?"

I turned away so Talina couldn't see the rebellious tear that streaked down my cheek. "I'm fine."

But I was far from it.

"Where's Jad?" I asked.

Marek tapped his finger nervously on his mapographic.

I knew from his tight frown that something troubled him. "What's wrong?"

The lieutenant peered up, but his eyes were focused on the floor. "He's inside the hull, trying to fix the inboard engine with Clorenzo."

Talina's sunburnt cheeks lost colour. "What do you mean 'fix the engine'?"

Something had been amiss since the moment I woke up. Now I understood what it was. The soft groan and whir of an engine was missing.

Marek straightened in his seat, but his expression remained awkward. "We're drifting. Southeast by the look of it. It appears Annaka and her crew may not have entirely serviced the tenders as well as they should have. The motor stopped working about an hour ago."

A bead of perspiration trickled down the side of Talina's face. "You mean Annaka didn't have them serviced at all, did she?"

He nodded. "Most likely."

I did not want to comprehend what this meant for us now. If we were drifting, then we were at the mercy of the sea. Today she was calm, but she was temperamental and could change without a moment's notice. Remembering the waves from last night made anxiety rattle my bones.

The worry on Marek's face deepened. "Hopefully, Jad and Clorenzo can get the engine working."

"And if they can't?" My voice came out more hysterical than I would have liked.

He leant forward, showing me the mapographic's screen. "We're here right now." He pointed at a red dot that marked our location. "These lines here indicate the ocean's current. I've calculated how long it will take us to reach land if we drift. Two days. We should end up here." He pointed to a new spot on the map. "Vukovar's coastline. South by the Beccstrait region."

Talina stared vacantly ahead through the window. "That's assuming nothing gets in our way and we do just drift."

I did not like the hidden meaning in her words. "Talina's right. The currents could change. We could be swept away in another galactic storm. There are sea creatures, too, some of them capable of eating this vessel in one mouthful. And then there's Morgomoth."

"You think he's still out there?" Marek slumped in his chair again, desolation in his eyes. I wondered when he'd last slept.

I nodded, wishing I wasn't the bearer of such grim news. "He opened a portal. Morgomoth and his rebels escaped the *Velorosa* before it sank."

I hadn't actually seen what had happened to Morgomoth, but I knew it was true.

"Then we have to assume he's coming after us." The lieutenant's voice sounded weak. "That means more chak-lorks."

I didn't want to imagine those slimy, decrepit forms boarding this little tender. It caused a shiver to run across my bones. My friends had defied Morgomoth and rejected his offer. When he found us, he would order his chak-lorks to kill. There'd be no second chance this time. He'd just kill them. He'd take Jad and the key... and this time he would take me as a prisoner.

When *he finds us?*

Why was I so certain he would?

Talina rubbed the bridge of her nose. "If Jad can't get the engine to work, and the current does float us around in circles, let's hope we die of starvation before any of those horrible alternatives can occur."

"There's no food?" I looked at them both, hoping one of them would contradict me.

Marek shook his head with disappointment. "This is a tender, not a lifeboat. It's not designed to be out in seas like this. There're a few dry biscuits, but that's it."

"There isn't even a first-aid kit on board," Talina added with heavy scorn. "Some captain Annaka is."

"But that's totally against protocol," I argued.

Marek shrugged. "Pirate, remember."

Talina's face scrunched into a scowl. "Honestly, that girl and her crew are the worst pirates ever."

"*Were* the worst pirates ever," an unappreciative voice interrupted.

Annaka stood in the narrow entrance of the cabin. She had pulled her hair back, her braided cornrows swept into a long pony down her back, allowing us to see the hard lines that had taken form on her unimpressed face. She was soaked, water dripping onto the ladder as she stepped down into the cabin.

"Where have you been?" Talina's voice was uncomfortably snarky. "Why are you wet?"

Annaka dropped into the vacant seat next to me and crossed her legs. Her toes were pruned and wrinkled. "I've been trying to fix the propeller blade. And before you throw any more insults at my crew, let me warn you that at sea, it's a long-held belief that talking unfavourably about the dead leads to ill fortune. So shut your mouth."

Talina flinched but didn't apologise. Marek focused on his mapographic, avoiding eye contact with everyone.

Uneasiness coursed through me. I studied Annaka's face. "Sorry, did I miss something? Your crew escaped?"

She hitched her shoulders back, but her eyes betrayed her, filling with grief. "We found them dead a few hours ago. Their tender drifted past us. They'd been... damaged by those things."

"You mean chak-lorks?"

She nodded silently.

Her crew were her family, and even though they'd abandoned her, seeing them dead must have been devastating.

"I'm sorry."

She looked at me for a long time, her eyes evaluating mine. "It's good to see Sleeping Beauty is finally awake, even if your resurrection did annihilate my ship."

"Sorry again."

Now it was my turn to look away uncomfortably.

Nobody said anything for a long time. We were probably all trying not to think about the events that had occurred on the *Velorosa*. The only noise was the constant lapping waves against the tender.

Talina fidgeted with a tress of hair. Her voice held a hint of uncertainty when she looked at me. "What happened back there? When we were trapped on the *Velorosa*'s deck, there was just this... bright light, like an explosion... and then these masses of stone and land came up from the sea. They were volcanoes, right?" She glanced at Marek and Annaka for validation.

They nodded.

Talina stared at me with bated breath. "Volcanoes? In the middle of the sea? And Morgomoth... he looked thrilled. He kept saying you had finally done it. What did he mean?"

The air felt like it was being squeezed from my lungs.

"Zaya?" Marek's voice was soft. "Were you responsible? Did you do that to the sea?"

"That," a voice interrupted, "is an excellent question."

We all looked up to see Commander Macaslan standing in the entry, her eyes darker than storm clouds.

THE GROUP GATHERED in a semicircle around me. Darius had joined us. His trousers were oil-stained, and his silver-white hair, which I'd only ever seen neat, was now a tangled mess around his ears. He must have been helping Jad and Clorenzo with the engine at some point, because his sleeves were covered in grease, and his nose was sunburnt, the peeling skin paper-thin. Jad and Clorenzo had been excused from attending the meeting. Someone needed to continue working on the engine. Our lives depended on it.

I explained where I'd been and what my soul had been reduced to. I told them about the Dark Divide and the door, and why Morgomoth had cursed me to a sleeping hex in the first place. I spoke too softly one minute, too loudly the next. Guilt and disappointment caused a dull headache at the back of my skull. I finished by telling them what had really transpired on the *Velorosa*. I had opened the door to save their lives. It was my fault the Dark Divide was here on earth. My fault the *Velorosa* had sunk. My fault that so many casters were dead.

"I don't understand to what end Morgomoth wanted the Dark Divide unleashed," I admitted. My husky voice stopped me from saying anything further.

"Foolish girl," Macaslan snapped, her gaze dark with ire. "You should have let us die. You should have remained an essence in the Dark Divide. You've doomed the world."

I was shouting before I realised it. "Apologies that I wanted to save your lives. Next time I'll take all your death wishes into account."

"I'm not sorry," Annaka pointed out. "Just saying, I'm happy to be alive."

Macaslan whirled on her. "You won't be when Morgomoth commences stage two of his plan."

I slid onto the edge of my chair. "You know what he's planning?

You know what the Dark Divide is?"

She fumbled to reply. I had never seen her so rattled and uncertain. I wondered if the commander's rage had less to do with me and more to do with Colonel Harper's death. She was grieving. She wasn't herself.

She dropped into a seat, shielding her face in her hands. Her shoulders shook as she silently wept.

I was unsure what to do or say. Everyone looked so haggard, eyes red and faces heavy with worry.

Darius watched me with an expression I couldn't translate. His voice was low when he spoke. "When Morgomoth was last at large, before he was captured and bound in a sleeping curse, he had the desire to raise a new world capital. A place where he would rule."

I sank my teeth into my lower lip. "Morgomoth has never said he wants to rule. Only to eradicate humans and the Free Zones."

"Yes, he's a Good Samaritan who just wants equality for us all. That's naive and gullible thinking, and you know it. Morgomoth wants to create a new empire. He wants to crown himself and sit on the throne."

"And now I've helped him achieve it."

I'd gifted Morgomoth the Dark Divide. Morgomoth had a kingdom in the sea, a new land of fire, shadow, and darkness. A wasteland protected by the dead.

How can any army defeat that?

"He wanted it to happen at Tarahik," I revealed in a small voice.

Darius laughed harshly. "Yes, I imagine he would have. Tarahik was built in a strategic geographic location, but the Bone Towers will prove just as favourable for him."

The reality of the situation dawned on me. An island kingdom meant Morgomoth would see every threat and assault coming for him. He'd have unconquerable naval power and would have control of the sea between Navask and Vukovar.

I drew a sharp breath, the air seeming to dry out my mouth. "What do you suppose he's capable of now that he's made the Dark Divide his kingdom?"

Darius's upper lip shone with sweat. "I have no experience with the Dark Divide. Only you can answer that."

CHAPTER 28

There wasn't a hell of a lot any of us could do but pray that Jad and Clorenzo got that engine working. But even if they did, and we somehow managed to reach Vukovar without being detected by the coastal guard, what waited for us next? None of us had been to Vukovar except Darius, and he warned that the regions that made up the entire west coast were desert lands, hostile for most plant and animal life. The provinces were dangerous and battered by violent sandstorms. Galactic storms were also known to bury entire towns and villages in sand. We were out of luck and out of hope.

Later in the afternoon, Marek grudgingly returned to the cabin and announced that the tender was low on fuel.

Talina yawned in a sleepy daze. "Can't we use the solar panels?" She'd been lying across the bright orange seats, trying to rest, but the plastic was about as comfortable as sleeping on hot coals. There were no curtains, the sun making our little cabin unbearably warm, but the alternative was to sit outside on the deck and suffer heatstroke and sunburn.

Forget a first-aid kit. We needed sun lotion and aloe vera. Fresh water would have been nice too.

Marek scratched at the bandage that concealed the nasty gash on his cheek. "I've cleaned the dust from the solar panels, but the tender has been sitting so long in the *Velorosa*'s cargo hold, the panels haven't attracted enough energy. Even if the engine worked, we'd only get maybe a few kilometres out of the solar panels."

Talina dropped back across the seats and stared ruthlessly at the ceiling. "Then I best go back to sleep. And pray I die in my sleep," she added with bitter sarcasm.

I remained silent. All afternoon, my hunger and thirst had increased. I wanted to help Jad and the others with the engine, or Annaka with the propeller, but Macaslan insisted that I needed to remain in the cabin and rest. Coma patients recovered slowly after they woke up. Even though I wasn't a coma victim, I understood where Macaslan was coming from. My muscles were slow to adjust to waking life. I barely had the strength to stand, let alone help rebuild an engine.

Talina was excused from assisting too. If someone was injured, her healing abilities were the only chance we had of helping that caster. She had to conserve her magic. And someone had to stay with Livel and Sarith. The twins slept most of the time, which I was grateful for. They were crabby and complained of hunger when they were awake, and it took both Talina and me to calm them.

Macha and Bartholomew continued to sleep. The obeahwoman looked like she'd aged another hundred years. I fretted that she was sick and poked her a few times just to make sure she was alive. She'd slit her eyes open at me, unseeing, then nodded off again.

The sun made a slow trail across the sky and settled to the west. A beautiful tangerine glow lit the horizon, the clouds painted in shades of pink and purple, but all too soon the night closed in, and the only light we had to rely on were the stars.

Marek, Darius, Clorenzo, and Macaslan returned shortly after. The four of them, smelling of engine oil and grease, settled on the plastic seats. They told me Jad had remained in the hull to work on the engine. Annaka was still trying to fix the propeller. That didn't seem safe to me, working at night with no source of light except for the stars. Maybe Jad was using his fire magic. And why hadn't he come to see me at all? Surely he had to take a break at some point.

I fidgeted, rolled over, and tried to get comfortable. Even though I had no energy, I was itching to move. I needed to do something besides sitting around and waiting.

Silently, I slipped away from the group and stepped out of the cabin onto the deck. Cool night air gently danced across my skin, a nice reprieve from the humid air that circulated in the cabin. It was incredible how the stars lit the sky. Without light pollution, they had a chance to burn bright and show the majesty of the heavens. I now understood why the ancients thought there was magic in the stars, and how they saw animals and people in the constellations. It reminded me of Professor Gemmell's astrology lessons, a class I'd been keen to take back at Tarahik.

The happy memory deflated.

I suppose he's dead now.

Professor Gemmell had likely been one of the refugees on the *Velorosa*, trapped in the dining room.

Another life I'm responsible for taking.

I sat on the deck, wrapping my arms around my legs and leaning my chin against my knees. The sea stretched far and wide, deep, depthless, and eternal. Tonight, it was crowned with foamy waves, almost hypnotic in the way it moved.

I jumped at the sound of someone treading up the ladder from the hull. Jad paled and went perfectly still when he saw me. It hurt that he hadn't come to see me at all during the day, and then I understood why. The real reason why he'd been preoccupied in the hull.

He'd been avoiding me.

THE LONGER WE STARED, the more my heart beat uncontrollably. Worry made my confidence deflate.

Have I done something wrong?

Does Jad regret the moment we shared on the carrier-hornet before I'd been hexed to the sleeping curse?

Has too much time passed and he's now indifferent?

There was so much I wanted to say, so much I wanted to ask, but all I managed was a weak "Hi."

He nodded but didn't say anything.

The tender wasn't a large boat, but at that moment, there was a world of distance between us. A mix of emotions churned in me. Sadness. Anger. Disappointment.

"How's the engine going?" I forced levity into my voice, but it came out sounding bitter.

Jad wiped his hands on his trousers. "There's a failure in the battery isolator. The spark plugs are broken. The fuel lines are kinked. And the batteries are drained. We don't have any of the right tools on board to fix it."

I didn't know what any of that meant, and to be honest, all I wanted to know was whether whatever it was that was happening between us could be fixed.

A heavy uncertainty pressed down on me. "You knew that right from the beginning, though, didn't you? You knew the engine was beyond repair."

He fixed me with a disquieting look.

"Why?" I hated that my voice sounded pleading. "Are you... avoiding me?"

His dark eyes held mine, but he didn't say anything.

I turned away before he could see how much his silence upset me. I focused on the sea. Its gentle, calming waves mocked me.

This isn't the best time to discuss this anyway.

Hunger pangs made my stomach feel like it was on fire. A nasty throb at the back of my skull threatened to form into a migraine if I didn't get food soon. I needed to be sensible. I needed to put survival first. Not my on-again, off-again boy troubles.

I'd wanted to appear confident, but my shoulders sank. I felt like crap both physically and mentally. "Are there any fishing rods or netting on board?"

Surprise flittered across his face. "You don't strike me as the sort who likes to fish. In fact, I distinctly remember you hate fish."

"We're trapped on a boat with an engine that doesn't work in the middle of the sea. We have no food. If I can catch a fish or two, and you're willing to conjure some fire magic, we'll at least have a meal to keep us going for a while."

His eyebrows furrowed. "There's no need. Annaka's already a few steps ahead. She's at the stern, gutting fish as we speak."

I had resolved to be strong, but a spark of jealousy doused that doggedness. "Oh, so you're happy to talk to Annaka but not me?"

He didn't say anything.

I was over this. I had come out to the deck for air, to try and clear my head, and I'd ended up with more complicated feelings than I'd begun with.

If Jad wants to be unfriendly and aloof, fine with me.

I was a mistake to him. A regretful choice. That was clear now.

My face coloured. I felt so humiliated and exposed and... so, so stupid.

This serves as a reminder to never rely on anyone else. To never get close.

I moved to stand, preferring the insufferable heat in the cabin to being in Jad's presence a moment longer. Fingers lightly touched my arm, and I jumped at the soft feel of skin against my own. Jad was sitting next to me. I hadn't even realised he'd moved. That was lycanthor stealth for you.

His face was close to my own. In the fiercely briny sea air, I could also smell burnt oil and exhaust—not the most pleasant of scents, but on him, it was amazing. "I have been avoiding you," he confessed. His voice was ragged. "I wanted to give you space."

"Space?" Wind whipped my hair. I annoyingly swatted it behind my ear. "From what?"

He looked so defeated as his shoulders sagged. "You've been asleep for weeks. Practically in a coma. I did my research. Coma patients wake disorientated and confused. Most of the time, their memories take time to return. I worried that you had forgotten... about us... or regretted it. I just wanted to give you some time to catch up and figure everything out."

The saddest expression crossed his face.

I stared at him, my brain taking a moment to compute what he'd said. He'd been worried about the same thing I'd been concerned about? My chest became heavy with guilt, and at the same time, I wanted to melt away with happiness. I didn't think I'd ever truly understand love and the hundreds of complicated emotions it dealt when you were under its spell.

A shadow of a smile flickered across my face. I took his hand with a mix of fear and eagerness. "I don't regret anything. I thought that, maybe, you did."

"Never."

The word filled me with hope.

I nudged closer. "It's difficult to explain, but my soul has been present for everything. My body was asleep, but I was... there."

"Darius filled me in. Creeps me out, actually, to know you've been watching and listening to us all this time."

I shoved my shoulder playfully into his. "That wasn't what I was intending."

"I know." He brushed some unruly hair from my face.

I hesitated, my doubt still lingering. "So, are we okay?"

His lips crept into a smile. "More than okay."

He leaned forward, his mouth meeting mine. The kiss was gentle at first, his lips warm and soft. My stomach exploded into fireworks. Not even a blazing sun in the middle of midday could have compared to the heat of that touch.

I wrapped my arms around his neck and pulled him closer. The kiss grew powerful and fierce. His fingers slid down my back. The sensation was electric; it felt sweet, intoxicating, dangerous. I didn't stop Jad when he drew me closer so I was nearly on his lap. His hands explored my body. I started to worry how far things would go, if I even wanted it to go there, but then I was swept up in the hunger of our kiss again, and my mind could only focus on me and Jad and how perfect we were for each other.

"Sorry to interrupt," a voice said behind us.

I broke away, my lips still burning from the kiss. I was mortified, but mostly I was annoyed that someone had interfered.

Annaka stood on the deck. She had a cast net draped over her shoulder, full of fish. Her lips were tipped in a brazen smile. "I'd tell you both to go get a room, but we're out at sea, so please, could you kindly respect everyone on board and control yourselves? We don't want to see you two sucking tongue and teeth... and whatever else it was you were about to do. The last thing we need is this boat tipping over."

She winked at me. "Come help me prep dinner. I need fire magic to get this feast started, by the way."

Jad's lips twitched into a half-smile, not at all embarrassed. He was more amused by how discomforted I'd become.

I got up and followed Annaka, feeling like a schoolgirl who'd just been caught kissing her crush… or in this case, her much older, hotter tutor.

THE KISS BOTHERED me all night. Well, not bothered me. I'd happily do it all over again. But thinking about it did keep me up. I tossed and turned across my sorry excuse for a bed, the edges of the plastic chairs digging into my back. I could still smell our horrible fish dinner hours after we'd eaten it, the cabin flooded with its aroma. I wasn't a seafood girl, but I'd been so hungry, I would have eaten fried slugs if it was handed to me.

At least I'm not hungry anymore.

Not for food, anyway.

I was hot all over, and not just because of the humid air in the cabin.

Stop thinking about the kiss.

At this rate, I was going to have to go sleep on the deck to cool down.

I examined my fellow cabinmates to distract me. Commander Macaslan was asleep in a chair with her arms crossed. Even in her sleep, her pale face was pinched, making her look ill-tempered and grouchy. Darius was curled up on the floor, his mouth slightly open. Marek rested below the seats Talina lay on. Her arm was drooped over the chair, her fingers only a few inches away from his, as though the pair had been reaching out for each other in their sleep. Clorenzo had both his children curled up with him. Macha and Bartholomew hadn't moved since the afternoon.

I didn't dare let my eyes cross to the corner where Jad rested. I was worried what I might do if he was awake. My body had been deprived of so much in the Dark Divide, but I didn't realise just how much it had missed *him*.

"Can't sleep?" a voice whispered.

Annaka sat up. She had a blanket on the floor, but it didn't look like it made the wooden surface any comfier.

I shook my head.

"Still thinking about that kiss, huh?"

"No."

"Yeah you were. I can tell from the dreamy smile on your face."

I made a point of biting the inside of my mouth to hinder any further smiling.

"It looked epic. The kiss, I mean. I'm jealous."

This did catch my attention.

Annaka leaned back onto her elbows. "He cares about you. And you care about him. Anyone can tell that the two of you would go to the ends of the world for each other. You're lucky. Some people in life... they never find that."

Sadness seeped from her voice.

A cloud must have passed across the sky because I had to strain to see her through the dark. "Did you have that... once?"

"I did." Her shoulders drooped. "It didn't last."

"What happened?"

Annaka looked at me in silence for a moment. "He died."

I'd lost Jad once, and it had ripped me apart. I understood what Annaka suffered. "I'm sorry."

She shrugged. "It was four years ago. Time moves on. Heals all wounds, or whatever the saying is."

I questioned if it really had moved on for Annaka. Something told me that she was just going through the motions, not really enjoying life.

She pointed at Marek and Talina. "Those two... there's something going on between them, isn't there?" She sounded almost afraid to hear the answer.

I hated to disappoint her, but I couldn't lie. "I believe so."

Her eyes settled on Talina's honey-blonde hair, which was splayed around her face, the ends dangling off the seat. She looked like a fairy-tale princess asleep.

"Lucky girl." Annaka dropped back onto her blanket. She fluffed the ends to make a misshapen heap that would serve as a pillow. "Goodnight, Zaya."

"Goodnight."

It seemed like such a stupid, trivial thing to say after Annaka had revealed a huge, soul-crushing episode of her life.

"Annaka?"

"Mmm?"

"You can have more than one love in your life. I'm sure there's someone else out there for you."

She snorted. "Have you seen the world we live in? Hope only leads to disappointment."

I didn't have an answer for that.

CHAPTER 29

For a long time, I stared at the tender's ceiling, listening to everyone else's soft breathing, wishing I could drop off to sleep. The boat swayed and tilted, and I worried that something was out there in the water, circling us. A shark? A sea monster? Chak-lorks? Morgomoth himself? All of them were terrifying possibilities.

Shut your eyes.

It was a neat trick I'd learnt. If you just kept your eyes closed, eventually, no matter what was going on in your head, you would fall asleep.

On this occasion, it worked a little too well, because I woke suddenly, disorientated by where I was. Icy snow pelted the environment around me, the trees an endless whitewash in the landscape. Icicles hung off their branches, shining like crystals. It was almost pretty.

Am I dreaming?

To the west through the trees, I could just make out the setting sun on the horizon. It was a bleak orb, a milky coin that descended too fast. Night closed in through the woods.

Iciness rushed through my veins.

No.

How is this possible?

I had escaped the Dark Divide.

Had my soul somehow left my body again? Was this astral projection? Into a memory?

I'd never heard of such a thing, but then, necromancy wasn't a commonly understood magic. Nobody was certain what necromancy was capable of. No one except for Morgomoth.

"Isgrad," a tiny voice called, almost washed away by the gusting wind.

I whirled around.

Through the dense fog, little Willieth appeared. He was wrapped in a coat far too big for his small body and wore a knit cap, his blond curls poking out beneath the edges. "Wait for me, Isgrad. Wait."

He started running, but it was a struggle for him in the thick snow. I wanted to warn him about rocks and loose branches that could have been concealed beneath it, but to do that would have been useless. I was nothing more than a ghost in this memory, just watching. I now understood why wraiths were always vexed and frustrated.

Someone stepped out through the mist, catching Willieth before he tripped on a barely exposed tree stump, its bark fragments looking as sharp as blades.

Isgrad shook his brother firmly. "What are you doing out here? Did you follow me? All the way from the cabin? Does Mum know you're out here?"

Willieth shook his head with a big smile, proud of what must have been a meticulous escape plan. "You're always sneaking away. I wanted to know where you were going." His eyes widened with elation. "Is it a magic place? Are there fairies, and goblins, and ogres? I've always wanted to see an ogre."

"Don't be a baby. There's no such thing as ogres." Isgrad pointed a threatening finger at his brother. "Go back to the cabin. Understand?"

"But I want to go with you."

"You can't. It's dangerous where I'm headed."

Willieth's face became alight with the possibility of danger and adventure. "Really? Please, can I go? Are you fighting Haxsan Guard soldiers? I can help."

His childish naivety was adorable but annoying. Willieth was probably imagining swordplay and knights in shining armour.

The veins in Isgrad's neck threatened to pop. "I'm collecting wood to keep our fire going. Now go back home."

Willieth paused, his small eyebrows scrunching in puzzlement. "But we have enough dry wood."

Isgrad kneeled to face his brother, still managing to loom over him. "For the love of providence, go home. I don't want you here. Understand?"

The boy's eyes teared up. He ran back the way he'd come, disappearing into the mist.

I had no idea how far away we were from the cabin, but I didn't think it was a good idea for Willieth to return on his own. There were hidden dangers in the woods. Hungry animals and birds. Lycanthors. Even snatchers—male and female casters who banded together to steal lone travellers or small groups. They enslaved their captives or sold them to anyone willing to buy. I'd read about the enslavement movement in the history texts. It did a roaring trade during the ten-year winter.

How could Isgrad let his little sibling go by himself? It didn't strike me as being overly brotherly or protective.

Isgrad was shivering, but I didn't think it was because he was cold. Sweat ran down his face. His eyes were bloodshot, and his skin became blotchier the longer he stood in the snow and wind. Shadows lined his eyes. He looked like he hadn't slept in weeks.

He stuffed his hands in his pockets and continued his trek through the woods. I followed, unsure if it was my own curiosity that led my feet to move in pursuit or if the Dark Divide was playing the cards, showing me something I needed to see. Either way, wherever Isgrad was going, I knew in my gut it was not something I could miss.

The night closed in quickly, making the woods hauntingly bleak. Gloomy vapour played tricks with my eyes. Every time we slogged over another crest, I saw ghostly faces among the trees, watching us with seemingly macabre intentions. The chilling wail of the wind only heightened my anxiety. Were these wraiths from the Dark Divide? Just shadows of former people who had, like me, wandered into this memory? Or did they belong here in the woods and I was seeing them because I was a necromancer?

Isgrad plodded heavily ahead, oblivious to the ghastly faces. He couldn't see their flowing hair, or the way their clothes billowed around them as though suspended in water, or the way they opened their mouths in pitiful screams, revealing dark holes framed by stubbed teeth. I hurried past, ignoring the way the wraiths turned their gazes on me.

We came to a parting in the trees that looked vaguely familiar. I recognised the fallen tree with the hollow trunk, roots and branches clumped together by mud and ice. I couldn't be certain how much time had passed since we'd last been here, but judging by the way Isgrad had to brush snow out of the trunk to crawl inside, there had been another heavy snowstorm during that time. He found his rusted tin and took out a cigarette to light it, then settled back into the tree roots with his eyes closed, inhaling the wafting smoke. Relaxed bliss took hold of his face. It couldn't be said for the rest of his body. His neck was blotchy with sweat. His skin was grotesquely sallow, his cheeks sunken. The tips of his fingers were stained yellow. When he coughed, the sound was raspy and dry. He sounded dehydrated. He sounded ill.

I snuck forward, taking a closer look at the rolled-up papers in the rusted tin. They weren't cigarettes, not in the literal sense. These were spellrock herbs. I'd never actually seen the herbs before because the Haxsan Guard confiscated all traces of the drug during raids, but I'd heard rumours when I was at Brendlash Orphanage that it could still be bought if you knew the right people. Spellrock was a psychoactive drug from the spellrockabis plant.

Now Isgrad's erratic and secretive behaviour made sense. He was an addict. I was divided by both empathy and disappointment. The problem with smoking spellrock was that it was a lifetime addiction. It was a curse that never let you go. Going cold turkey wasn't an option. Withdrawal would kill you. The only option was to continue smoking the drug in smaller increments.

Isgrad, you foolish, stupid boy.

What could possibly have made him want to use the drug?

And where was he getting it from? Was there an abundance of spellrockabis plants in the woods somewhere, and he was grinding the leaves himself? Or was he buying it from someone? It had to be the latter. There wasn't exactly any thin rolling paper available out in the woods.

"What is that?" a tiny voice asked. "Can I have one?"

I turned around, astonished to find Willieth. He must have followed his brother, pursuing in secret.

Oh no.

Isgrad opened his eyes. High on the drug, his rage seethed. "What are you doing here?"

Before Willieth could answer, Isgrad crawled out of the trunk and stormed toward his brother.

He grabbed Willieth by the collar and shook him. "I don't want anything to do with you. Why can't you understand that? Why can't you just leave me alone?"

Isgrad pushed his brother away with more force than was necessary. Willieth cried out, his foot hitting a twisted tree root that curved up from the ground. He fell into the snow with a loud thwack, his cry suddenly silenced. He was utterly still.

I scrambled forward, throwing a hand over my mouth. The back of Willieth's head had collided with a rock. Thick, dark blood had pooled from a large split in the back of his scalp, staining the snow. Willieth's eyes were open, unseeing. He was dead.

The world went silent, almost as though the memory had been set on pause.

There was a shuffle behind me. "Willieth?"

Isgrad looked down at his brother's body. He blinked rapidly, his pale face whiter than the snow around him. "Willieth. Stop faking. Get up."

He kicked Willieth's leg. The little boy's booted foot rolled lifelessly to the side with no resistance and was still.

"Willieth, get up." Isgrad's voice sounded choked, as though his lungs had turned to ice. He dropped beside his brother's body and cried. He screamed and howled, glaring up into the sky. I didn't know if the tears were from shock and grief or disgust with himself.

The scene made my heart ache like it would burst.

The muscles in Isgrad's jaw twitched. I wondered if he was having trouble breathing. He searched the snow-capped ground, then examined the trees, looking for something. He pressed his hands into the earth, then began to dig, flinging damp dirt, grass, and sludge into the air. His knuckles bled where the cold burned. The soil was shockingly dark against the snow.

All my nerve endings iced over when I realised what he was doing.

He's going to bury his brother in a shallow grave.

I could not witness this. This couldn't have been the real Isgrad. This was the drug making him behave irrationally.

His face wet from snow and tears, Isgrad collapsed onto the ground next to Willieth. Whatever madness had taken over him had vanished. He reached down to close his brother's eyes, but Willieth's lids were still, frozen by the plummeting temperature.

It became agonisingly cold in the woods. I ran my tongue over my teeth, the chill playing with my sinuses and causing my gums to ache.

Somewhere, a howl escalated into the night.

It was either a wolf, wolverine, or... a lycanthor.

None of the options were good.

Yaps and yelps resonated through the trees. There was more than one, and they sounded hungry. Could they smell a recent kill?

Isgrad listened to the prowling animals that were closing in through the trees. For a horrifying moment, I thought he was going to leave his brother's little body for the wolves, but then he curled one arm beneath Willieth's legs and one arm under his upper back and lifted him from the ground.

He started walking to the east, the opposite direction from the cabin.

What are you doing, Isgrad?

I really hoped he wasn't finding a new place to get rid of his brother's body.

Heavy snow swirled down from the sky. It grew thicker, making the path through the trees ahead difficult to trek. The moon rose like a new sun on the horizon, commencing its circular route across the night sky. Silver rays shone down into the surrounding woodland, imbuing everything with an eerie, otherworldly glow. I could no longer tell if Willieth's knit cap was dark because of the shadows that stretched between the trees or if it was because it was damp from blood.

We hiked for a long time. The wind bore down on us, causing ice to lick over my skin. The snow accumulated so quickly that I could no longer see Isgrad's feet.

Where are you going, Isgrad?

Where are you taking Willieth?

We must have struggled through the snow for at least an hour before something large loomed through the endless white landscape ahead. A cave that was by no means a natural erosion in the earth. It had been created with magic. The cave's entrance was artistically sculpted to resemble the jaws of a wolf, the stalactites carved into incisors.

I could tell from Isgrad's quick breathing that he was excited. He stepped into the cave.

How does he know about this place?

Is this where his dealer lives?

I grudgingly followed. Inside the cave, a torch spurred to life with flames, revealing a spiral stairwell that led deep into the earth.

This is a really bad idea.

All I could do was follow and watch the memory play out, praying nothing bad happened.

Isgrad descended the steps, straining to hold on to Willieth's limp body. Flames sparked to life as we passed, the torches becoming a beacon to light our way. The earthen walls were covered with cave paintings that depicted scenes of wolves and birds hunting people. I'd only seen cave drawings in the reverse, tribes hunting animals, so seeing the opposite was disturbing, to say the least.

Isgrad's eyebrows furrowed. It made my skin prickle with terror. If the drawings were strange to him, too, then that meant he'd never been here before.

We must have been at least four levels underground when we arrived at a cavern that resembled an open living area, everything made of stone or wood. I dabbed my tongue over my cracked lips, wanting to walk right back up the stairs. We had entered a witch's house. A cauldron bubbled over a fireplace. On top of a working benchtop were knives, herbs, potions, and animal parts that had been dissected and cut up.

In the corner, sitting in a rocking chair, was the silver-thorned witch.

Now I remembered.

"Follow the silver moon to the black mouth. That's where you'll find me."

We had followed the moon. The black mouth was the cave.

The witch stood, the chair creaking behind her, reminding me of the sounds a noose made when it swung in the wind. Her silver lips shifted into an unsettling smile as she gazed upon the lifeless form in Isgrad's arms. "I warned you."

"You did not warn me of this," he spat.

"I told you to come to me for aid. Do you accept my help?"

She watched him with her cool, insightful eyes.

Isgrad's voice was hoarse. "Yes. Can you do something? Can you... bring him back? Is that in your ability?"

I stiffened. Isgrad was asking for necromancy.

A hungry pleasure seemed to light up the witch's face. "I can. But it will come at a price."

CHAPTER 30

"Anything, please," Isgrad begged.

The witch cleared space on her workbench. "Put him down here."

Willieth's body was laid carefully beside the herbs and potions. His head lolled to the side, his eyes seeming to stare at his brother with a condemned glare. His skin and lips were already an unnatural shade of blue. Willieth looked like he should have been lying on a silver table in a morgue.

Isgrad flinched. "What are you going to do?"

The silver-thorned witch seized his hand and dragged him over to the hearth. The cauldron bubbled and hissed, the liquid inside a shade of poisonous black. She grabbed one of the thorns from her barbed crown and pricked Isgrad's thumb.

His eyes widened. "What was that for?"

"Put your hand over the cauldron. The spell needs three drops of your blood."

"Spell?" Isgrad scrunched his face in confusion. "Wait. You had this potion ready? Did you know this would happen?"

The witch's tone was short. "I know everything that happens in my woods. Past. Present. Future. I witnessed what you did to your brother in a dream three moons ago."

Isgrad stared, stunned. Then he leaned forward, allowing three drops of his blood to roll down the tip of his thumb. The potion smoothed into a silvery surface as the blood was absorbed.

The witch grabbed a ladle and spooned the potion into a goblet. "Come. We have no time to waste."

They hurried back to the workbench. Isgrad looked down at his brother, uncertainty clouding his face. "What's in this potion?"

The silver-thorned witch gently parted Willieth's mouth with her long fingernails and poured the spell down his throat. Grabbing his cold hand, she pricked Willieth's thumb with the same thorn she'd used on Isgrad, squeezing the fleshy tip to let three drops of blood land in the potion. She raised the goblet to Isgrad.

He stepped away, the colour draining from his cheeks. "I can't drink that. It's unhygienic."

"You will if you want your brother to live."

"I... I don't understand any of this." Isgrad raked his fingers through his hair. He looked capable of pulling it from the roots. The drug high was long gone. Now, he was agitated, tense, and fidgety. He needed another fix.

"Drink the potion, and your life force will be connected to your brother's. You will share the same energy."

Isgrad started to cry. "Why are you doing this? You don't owe me anything."

The witch remained impassive, but I detected a powerful delight in her silver eyes. "There is a magic long banished from this world that needs to be reborn to set the balance."

"Balance?"

"Yes. The Council and the Haxsan Guard have done everything they can to remove it, but the magic must always be equal. The scales have been tipped too far. It needs to be realigned. Your brother's death is a chance for that to happen."

Isgrad rubbed a grimy hand across his nose, smearing dirt along his tear-stained cheeks. "What does the balance have to do with us?"

The silver-thorned witch lifted her gaze. Her voice was as cold and piercing as an icicle. "You have no magic."

Anger and mounting anxiety chased each other across his face. "How dare you. You don't know a thing about me."

The witch gave a hollow chuckle. "Isn't that why you turned to spellrock? To lessen the pain of not belonging? Neither caster nor human. You are a loner. An outsider. An undercast."

Isgrad visibly shook. His cheeks were no longer pale but flushed and mottled with fury. I was afraid that at any moment he would lash out.

The witch's tone softened. "You can change that. Drink the potion, and you will be granted a magic far more powerful than any caster could dream of possessing on this earth. You will have control over death."

"Control over death?" Isgrad swept his eyebrows up, frowning at her as though she were insane. "What you speak is lunacy."

"What I speak is the truth." She offered him the goblet again. "Drink. Save your brother. You will no longer fear the Haxsan Guard or the Council. The magic will ignite inside you. Everyone will fear you."

"I don't want people to fear me. I just want...." Isgrad swallowed, unable to finish his sentence.

I suspected what Isgrad really wanted was to just be accepted the way he was.

"Very well," the silver-thorned witch answered in a low, measured voice. "You don't have to accept the magic, but you must drink if you wish for your brother's life to be returned."

Isgrad snatched the goblet from her. He held it, poised near his lips. "How do I not accept the magic?"

"It's simple. As you drink, in your mind, say the words *I renounce this power.*"

"That's it?"

He didn't look like he believed her.

I didn't believe her.

The witch gave an imperceptible nod. "You have my word. Drink the potion, speak the words, and your brother's life will be returned. But you must hurry. His soul is quickly crossing to the otherworld. If you don't do this now, he will not return the same."

Indecision flickered across Isgrad's face.

"Remember," she persevered, the warning prevalent in her voice, "the trade for life from death will come with a price."

Isgrad took his brother's lifeless hand in his own. I imagined hundreds of uncertainties firing through every cell in Isgrad's mind. He brought the goblet to his mouth, his eyes never leaving the witch's.

She silently nodded. "I swear on my magic."

Isgrad drank the potion, closing his eyes as he greedily downed it like a man about to die of thirst.

He did not see the shadows, black as night, rise from the earth. He did not see the wraiths who screamed and swatted at him with their wispy fingers as they materialised from the cave walls. He did not see Willieth open his eyes, glassy at first but slowly coming alive with colour.

I drew away, my fear mingling with horror. The wraiths circled around Isgrad, closing in tighter. They were latching onto his skin, biting him, digging into his flesh, sinking inside him like parasites. He dropped the goblet. It fell with a heavy clung to the floor, empty. Isgrad's jaw dropped in a silent scream, his eyes glazed over. The wind became a powerful roar, the storm of souls now grabbing Willieth, consuming the little boy in the twisted magic.

I covered my ears. The wind felt capable of ripping my eardrums right out of my head. The torches went out, casting us into suffocating darkness.

I had always questioned why the Dark Divide showed me these memories.

Now I understood why.

Now I knew whose memories these belonged to.

Isgrad had been tricked into accepting necromancy.

Isgrad is Morgomoth.

I'd barely had time to comprehend the realisation when something cold grabbed me in the dark.

I OPENED MY EYES, groggy from the sudden pull out of the memory. It took me a moment to recollect where I was. Muted light bled through the windows. The tender was not quite lit by the new dawn, shadows still prevalent.

A hand crushed my mouth, restricting my breathing. "Shhh."

I stilled.

I felt Annaka's tense breathing in my ear.

I twisted my neck to see fear in her eyes. She lifted a finger to her lips, urging me to be silent. Behind her, Clorenzo was kneeling on the floor, his hands wrapped around Liezel and Sarith. Marek and Talina were crouched beneath the seat, reminding me of the way rabbits burrowed in the ground to hide from a predator. Darius's and Macaslan's faces were gleaming with sweat, the panicked kind. Macha sat rigid with her bird on her shoulder. Bartholomew, usually boisterous with birdsong in the mornings, was silent.

What really drove it home that we were in danger was Jad. He sat by the entry in the cabin, cast-shooter in one hand, athame-sabre drawn in the other.

I followed his line of sight to the window next to me, jumping when something slimy hit the glass. It was a long tentacle. Powerful suctions scaled the surface, leaving behind a trail of milky gunk. I gasped when the tender groaned. The ceiling caved like crushed metal. The creature outside, whatever it was, had its tentacles wrapped around the boat. It was squeezing.

Another tentacle snaked its way across the opposite window, right above where Talina and Marek were hidden beneath the bench seat. Hundreds, maybe even thousands, of tiny eyes stared at us from each sucker. This was not simply a giant squid. This was a decemkrus. I knew they lived in the deep waters of the ocean, rising for food at dawn and hunting with all ten tentacles. Seals, sharks, and whales ranked among their favourite foods.

"Decemkrus are blind," a voice said in my head, causing me to jump for a second time.

Bartholomew's bright yellow eyes were aimed at me. Macha affectionately brushed a finger across the bird's wings. Her own eyes, which were colourless orbs, though unseeing, were facing me too.

I blinked a few times, wondering how she could be so calm. *"If they're blind, why do they have so many eyes?"*

Macha's voice effortlessly reached me in mind speak. *"They see in the dark, but in daylight, their eyes do not see. Instead, they smell and feel."*

Which was what the creature was doing right now.

"What does it want?"

"It wants to eat."

Again, Macha seemed far too composed. Had she foreseen this event? Did that mean we were going to be okay? I had come close to some very terrible ends. I'd imagined various painful ways to die and expected it on most occasions, but to be eaten alive and slowly digested by a decemkrus had to be one of the worst ways to go.

"We must remain quiet," Macha instructed. *"Decemkrus can detect the slightest sound."*

Did that include raging heartbeats? Because my chest was about to explode. And on another terrifying matter, we could be still all we wanted and not make a sound, but what about smell? Most of us had at least two days' body odour and were in desperate need of showers. We'd smell delicious to the decemkrus.

Bartholomew must have seen the hesitation race across my face because Macha tipped her head ever so slightly to get my attention. *"Be still. If it thinks the tender is empty, it will move on. Calm your heartbeat. I can hear it ticking from here."*

"Oh sure. It's not like I have a switch to turn it off."

A tremendous, unearthly roar ripped through the dawn, the air overwhelmed by the stale stench of fish and rotting scales.

It's found us.

"Oh providence," Annaka muttered under her breath, forgetting the rule not to speak.

Several scaly tentacles rose up from either side of the tender. Grating metal reverberated beneath us, then above us. The boat was being squeezed from every direction. I had an image of us caught like flies in the mouth of a Venus flytrap, slowly being swallowed.

A lurching shudder shook the boat, and we all went flying across the floor. The creature had the tender wrapped in its scaly arms. It shook us up and down like a saltshaker. We were all thrown onto our hands and knees, then slammed onto our backs as we hit the ceiling, all of us trying desperately not to cry or scream.

The decemkrus's large tentacles dropped the tender into the water, tipping us on our side. I slid across the floor and crashed into the bench seat, every muscle and bone in my body aching. At first, I didn't understand the wet surface beneath me, until I realised what it was.

The decemkrus had torn a hole through the hull.

We're taking on water.

The creature would drown us, then eat us. Or maybe it would eat the entire boat.

Either way, we were screwed.

Little Livel, who'd been so brave and deserved a medal, could no longer take it anymore. She screamed.

I spun around, having half a mind to cry out to. The entry door had been ripped away, and in its place was a gigantic mouth, teeth the size of knives.

A long tongue, wrapped in viscous mucus, shot out like a chameleon's and tangled around Talina's ankle. She screamed as she was dragged across the floor, her fingers desperately scraping for hold on anything sturdy. Marek raced for her, but he'd never reach her in time.

Blinding red light flared to my right. A ball of flames struck the decemkrus's tongue. Jad shot another, and another, until the creature let go. Talina scrambled away, running into Marek's arms.

We're not going to be able to fight this creature off with Jad's fire magic for long.

Especially when we were sinking.

Water lapped around my knees, quickly rising to my thighs. Even if we did somehow manage to kill the creature, that still left us out at sea with no boat and no lifebuoy ring. We'd soon become a meal for the sharks.

What are we going to do?

But there was no time to come up with an alternative plan, or to even grab a life jacket, because at that moment, the entire tender was ripped in two. I was seized by the current, which turned and twisted me as though it wasn't sure what direction it wanted to go. I rose to the surface, managing to gasp one lungful of air before a wave pulled me back under. Tentacles appeared through the hazy water. The decemkrus thrashed and beat what remained of the tender, tearing it to shreds.

The surge pushed me upward again. I swallowed another

mouthful of air, my lungs burning.

That's when the screams started.

The decemkrus had seen us.

"Swim," Jad yelled, right at my ear.

I hadn't realised he was even next to me.

I forced my sore arms and legs into a freestyle, battling the current, my mouth filling with more water than air every time I twisted my head to breathe. Talina wasn't far, swimming for her life. Marek was behind her. I remembered him telling me once that he was out of practice when it came to swimming and would struggle to make it even fifty metres in a pool. The others were nowhere to be seen. I feared the decemkrus had already made a meal of them.

I dared to look behind my shoulder, half expecting a long tentacle to wrap around my legs, but the image that greeted my eyes was far worse. The decemkrus had opened its mouth like a large sea serpent. The creature charged toward us, the current changing direction, sucking us in toward the decemkrus and its chomping teeth. It was going to slurp us up like noodle soup.

Jad caught my hand, thrashing in the water to keep us both above the surface. Even his lycanthor strength was no match for this beast of the sea.

I stared at him. If I was going to die, then I wanted the last thing I saw to be his face. Fate owed me that, at least.

A roar unlike anything I'd heard before shattered my ears. A hex-harpoon had wedged into the decemkrus's head, exploding in the creature's brains. I dived away from a massive tentacle that came plunging down. The huge wave that resulted knocked me sideways.

The decemkrus was dead.

Where did the harpoon come from?

Something large eclipsed the morning sun. It was a warship, much like the *Velorosa*, only this one was in pristine condition and had the Haxsan Guard flag raised. Silhouetted figures appeared along the guardrail.

"What do we have here?" one of the men called down. "Drifters? Or deserters?"

I bobbed in the water, shivering.

The Haxsan Guard had found us.

CHAPTER 31

"I would get out of that water if I were you," the man continued from the upper deck. "Lots of blood. The sharks will arrive soon."

He signalled to one of his men. A moment later, a rope ladder was lowered from the ship.

I had no intention of arguing with his logic, and neither did my friends. We swam to the ladder and climbed. The horizon's faint pink was now a beautiful sunrise with a tangerine glow, allowing me to glimpse the name on the side of the ship: VMS *Vanquisher*. The name was familiar. I recalled soldiers at Tarahik having mentioned that it was a ship that monitored the southern trade route, searching for people smugglers and slavers.

What are they doing so far north?

Or had we drifted farther south than we realised?

I clambered onto the deck, standing in my sodden white dress, shivering so hard that my teeth chattered. My friends stood beside me, arms wrapped around themselves, sopping wet. I ran my eyes over them, checking that we hadn't lost anyone. We were all on board.

The breeze wasn't cold, but in my damp gear, it felt icy to the bone. It made my head feel too heavy for my body. Maybe I had blacked out for a moment, because suddenly Jad's hand was latched around my elbow, keeping me upright. I'd been struck, hit, and tossed about in the tender. I hadn't had a proper meal in weeks, and my sleep most evenings was interrupted with memories from the Dark Divide.

Nausea overwhelmed me, but I managed to swallow it back and stare into the arrogant faces of our rescuers... or maybe they were captors.

The man who I assumed was the captain of the ship stepped forward to take a closer look at us. His long hair was tinged with grey, his salt-and-pepper stubble a few days old. His face was heavily lined and lacked the elasticity of youth. I couldn't determine how old he was; he was withered and aged by the sea. Even his Haxsan Guard uniform, which was meant to be kept pristine, was discoloured by the sun. There was a large gap between his teeth when he smiled, and I realised he was missing a front tooth. It wasn't a friendly smile.

His eyes roamed over each of us, widening in recognition as they came across Darius and Macaslan. "Well, well, well. Look what providence has gifted us on this fine morning. Senator Kerr and Commander Macaslan. Traitors to the Council."

Neither the commander nor the senator spoke.

The captain's lips curled into a smug grin when he saw Annaka. "The renowned pirate Vandergriff, I assume? The Council will have your head."

It unnerved me that Annaka didn't say anything, not even when the Haxsan Guard sailors laughed. Even she knew we were outmatched. Her cold eyes burned like fire, but she remained silent.

"The hag with the bird... and the others?" The captain shot a look at Macaslan, waiting for an answer.

Her cheeks reddened. "They are no one. Just lowly soldiers we found on our way across the sea who we decided to help. The man and his two children, and the woman with the bird, are refugees fleeing Navask."

The captain sneered. "A likely story. More like fugitives."

His eyes settled on me. "And who is this?"

He advanced and gripped my jaw, moving my head from side to side to examine my face. "She looks familiar. I've seen you on wanted posters."

"She is no one." Darius lumbered forward, but a sailor stepped in his way. "She's a refugee. No one."

The captain of the *Vanquisher* smiled down at me, his breath a foul combination of alcohol and egg, last night's indulgence mixed with his morning breakfast. "General Kravis is searching for a girl with your exact appearance. A girl said to be travelling with Senator Kerr and Commander Macaslan." His gap-toothed smile widened. "I think I've found her."

Dizziness swept over me. I was going to lose consciousness.

"She is no one," I heard Jad cry, but the words were distant, almost sounding as though they were spoken underwater.

"Chart a course to Muiren," the captain ordered his Haxsan Guard sailors. "And make sure our new friends are comfortable belowdecks."

Firm hands grasped me.

I wondered if "comfortable belowdecks" was subtext for a prison cell.

It turned out I was right. I woke in a cell. I couldn't be certain if I'd fallen asleep from exhaustion or if I'd passed out. Whatever it was, I did not feel refreshed. I craved a warm shower, a hot meal, and a comfortable bed.

My head screamed at me to stay focused, but my eyes kept drooping until I was out again. It could have been twenty minutes; it could have been an hour. Time couldn't be assessed in this cage—and that's what it was, just a square room with three walls and solid metal bars for an entrance. I suppose I should have been grateful there was a toilet, but it lacked privacy.

The *Vanquisher* was a modern warship, but it was evident the prison cells hadn't been upgraded in years. At least it wasn't like Gosheniene, which had been medieval and barbaric in the rusty chain sense. No, these cells were cold, sterile, and spotless. The tiled floor was cool on my feet, perhaps a little too cold.

I dropped back onto my steel sleeping bench, hundreds of thoughts spinning in my mind. Where were Jad and the others? If they were in this cell block, I couldn't see them.

It's probably designed that way.

Gosheniene had been a panopticon prison, which meant the guards could monitor the inmates without being seen, and no prisoner could see another. This cell block was no panopticon, but I guessed it had been constructed with the same intention. I wondered if there was a camera somewhere, and if someone on the ship was monitoring my every move.

I didn't know how long I sat there, just thinking. After everything that had occurred, my mind hadn't had the time to process what the Dark Divide had revealed.

Isgrad is Morgomoth.

He'd been a broken and desperate teenage boy, tricked into accepting necromancy. I didn't know how to feel about any of it. Morgomoth was the embodiment of evil. He was dark, twisted, and murderous. And yet he hadn't always been that way. Isgrad hated the Haxsan Guard, but he wasn't a killer. Had necromancy made him into the monster that became Morgomoth? Had necromancy changed him?

Could it change me?

"Hello."

I jumped, startled that I wasn't alone. All my senses sprang to action, trying to ascertain whether the voice belonged to someone alive or dead.

Someone, or something, moved in the cell opposite. The darkness on that side of the prison block gave me that disorientating feeling that the walls, floor, and ceiling were closing in.

Something detached itself from the dark. I leapt up from where I'd been sitting and pressed against the bars, straining to see. Cold spots and frigid air always announced the arrival of a ghost, but the air remained warm and stuffy.

Not a ghost.

A face emerged, and a relieved breath worked its way into my lungs. He was young, maybe midtwenties, with a short crew cut and olive skin. A few purple marks around his left eye showed that he'd met someone's fist more than once. It was difficult to define at first, but as my eyes adjusted, I realised he was wearing a Haxsan Guard uniform, ruffled and in disrepair. The hexagonal eye on his shoulder was embroidered in blue. He was a soldier.

In a cell?

What had he done?

"You're the girl, then." His voice was croaky, as though his vocal cords hadn't been used in weeks.

"I'm sorry?"

"The girl?" he repeated. "The one General Kravis has been searching for. I saw them bring in Senator Kerr and Commander Macaslan. They were protecting you, right? At least, that's what General Kravis told me."

I stepped away from the bars. "You work for General Kravis?"

After the event at Galvac Tower, General Kravis had worked out that I was a necromancer, or at least he'd put the pieces together and just needed the final evidence. Macaslan and Harper had helped me escape through a portal. I'd only just made it.

The man in the cell ahead passed me a droll look. "Would I be locked away if I did work for him?"

I ignored his sarcasm. "Where are the commander and the senator?"

And the rest of my friends?

His eyes carefully assessed me. "Probably down in the cells below. This block is only for prized prisoners."

"And you're a prized prisoner, are you?"

"I'm a prisoner General Kravis doesn't want anyone else talking to."

"And why's that?"

"Because I know what he and the Council of Founding Sovereigns did at the White Palace."

I had heard about the destruction of the White Palace. A sneak ambush by Morgomoth's forces had resulted in the celestial shield coming down, every human destroyed by radiation and fire. The sovereigns and the Council had only just escaped, though I somehow doubted whether that last part was true. I imagined they would have had prior notice and left hours before the initial attack.

I pressed against the bars again, determined the strange prisoner would answer truthfully. "Who are you?"

There was exhaustion all over him—I saw it in the way his shoulders slouched—but in that moment, his eyes were alert, as serious as a fighter on the battlefield. "My name is Bronislav Olski."

"I SURVIVED the attack on the White Palace," Bronislav explained.

I settled down on the cold tiles, listening to his story. He told me the truth about the attack on the White Palace, that it had been left unguarded and unprepared. The Council and the sovereigns had saved themselves. I suppose it said General Kravis did have some semblance of decency if he sent Bronislav to warn the advisers of what was coming, but it wasn't nearly enough to redeem him. The general, the Council, and the sovereigns had left their people to die.

I licked the dryness from my lips, unsure what to say. "How did you end up on the *Vanquisher*?"

Bronislav grimaced in the dark. "After the attack, I had nowhere else to go. I heard my unit had been destroyed by dissent rebels. There was nothing left for me in Navask. I found a smuggler who I paid to take me to Vukovar. I thought I might be able to join the Haxsan Guard there, or flee, make a new life for myself, whichever option presented itself when I arrived. The *Vanquisher* captured us. Captain Forsythe is responsible for finding smugglers along the trading coast. He detains anyone fleeing Navask and makes sure they never arrive in Vukovar. Not freely, anyway."

"And what happens to the detainees?"

Imprisonment was my guess.

"For now, they're in cells on this ship, but once we arrive in Vukovar, they'll be put in detention camps and made to work."

"And that includes you?"

"I thought so. Now I'm not so sure." The tip of a sly smile appeared along his lips.

A strange sensation spread over me, one that told me to remain alert. "What's that supposed to mean?"

His voice was low and held a hint of scepticism. "We were headed for Askivna, but something happened north. An event of the… magic kind. At least, that's what I heard the guards say. They were afraid. Whatever it was that occurred, it changed the tides. Caused a king tide right across the Navask and Vukovar coastlines. Flooding in low-lying areas too."

My fingers twitched, but I kept my panic in check. "My company and I have been adrift for days at sea. We never experienced or saw anything strange in the water."

Bronislav didn't look like he believed me. "Captain Forsythe received orders to investigate and changed course."

"And you picked all this up from the guards?" My suspicion rose. Bronislav was a little too knowledgeable for a prisoner.

It's possible he's an informant.

He could have been ordered to pretend he was a captive to gain my trust and obtain information from me. I breathed in deeply, trying to keep my cool.

He smiled, but it looked rehearsed. "The guards talk. I listen. I'm good at it."

"Clearly. I've been a prisoner before," I revealed. "I know guards are discreet. They're trained that way. For you to be able to hear them from your cell... well, you must have supersensitive hearing."

This time, the smile that grazed his lips was genuine. "General Kravis said you were smart. That is my magic." He raised a finger to his lips. "Don't tell anyone on board. They don't know."

"Wait. You have supersensitive hearing?"

He nodded.

"How far can you hear?"

"I can hear private conversations from at least fifty metres away. Even farther if I really concentrate. So long as a room or place isn't soundproof, I can hear through it."

"That must be useful."

"Sometimes. Sometimes not. There are things I don't always want to hear."

I imagined there were many things behind closed doors that were better off left secret.

Bronislav ran his finger along the smooth edge of a bar. "So, Miss Zaya Wayward, what is it about you that has the general in a tizzy?"

The fact that he knew my name made my insides shrivel up, and I was too slow to wipe the surprise from my face. "Nothing. It's a mistake. I'm no one."

"No one? You travel with the infamous pirate Annaka Vandergriff, accompanied by the rebellious senator and a disloyal commander. You want to know what I think?"

Not really.

"I think *you* are responsible for what happened north in the sea. I think it had something to do with Morgomoth."

I ignored his dubious tone. "Is that what you think? Or is that what you've heard?"

Bronislav settled back against the wall and closed his eyes. "Better get some sleep, Miss Wayward. The *Vanquisher* is full speed ahead to the Black Palace. We should arrive there a little after morning."

"Morning? How long have I been asleep?"

"About eighteen hours."

"And the Black Palace? I thought we were headed to Muiren."

"Aye, Muiren is the Vukovar capital. It's a Free Zone. That's where the Black Palace is and currently where the general resides."

The saliva in my mouth evaporated.

I'd heard the captain demand his sailors chart a new course to Muiren, but at the time, I'd been too dazed to understand the full repercussions of what that meant.

I was trembling with both worry and fierceness. "That's where the Council of Founding Sovereigns are?"

"Yes." Bronislav sounded sleepy. "General Kravis and his guards will collect you and your friends from the dock and present you to the sovereigns at the Black Palace."

"You heard all of this?"

"I did."

My gut rolled with terror. "What are they going to do to us?"

Bronislav raised a finger to silence me. "Keep quiet, and I may be able to pick it up."

I realised he had no intention of sleeping. He was listening, extending his hearing to lengths that were beyond imaginable for the rest of us.

The Black Palace.

The current residence of the sovereigns and the Council.

The people we'd been doing everything to avoid.

They'll imprison Darius and Macaslan. Annaka too. Maybe even Jad.

What will become of Talina and Marek? What will happen to Macha? Obeahpeople have no place in this world. And Clorenzo and his children?

And me?

Do they know what I am?

I had a very bad feeling the sovereigns did.

CHAPTER 32

Bronislav was right. We arrived at Muiren a little past dawn. At least, that's what I assumed; there were no windows in the prison block, and all I had to go on were the hum and vibrations of the ship slowing down.

Bronislav stretched his arms wide and yawned, as though he'd just woken in a king-size bed in a trendy resort and not in a cell. He wiped sleep from his eyes and offered me a courteous nod. "Good morning."

I glared.

Good morning.

My friends were somewhere on this ship, imprisoned, and I was about to be sentenced to an unknown fate. I had tried to sleep, this time hoping the Dark Divide would pull me into its shadowy depths, showing me more of the memory, but it remained elusive all evening.

"Did you learn anything?" My voice came out with more bite than I intended.

Bronislav strode up and down his cell, reminding me of a caged tiger. "No. I fell asleep."

Again, I questioned whether I could trust him.

The fluorescent lights above flicked on, and I flinched. After so long in the dark, the light was practically interrogation-room-level brightness.

Bronislav laughed. "Don't worry. You get used to it." His smile dropped. "Sorry. That was a stupid thing to say."

Because of course, I wasn't going to get used to it.

I stood from my steel sleeping shelf, trying to get a reading on his mood. "You don't seem worried. Aren't you afraid of what will become of you?"

His expression remained calm. "When you see as much death and horror as I have, you learn to accept whatever fate has in store for you. If I'm to die today, so much the better. At least it will get me out of this misery."

"You're full of positivity, aren't you?"

Bronislav ignored my comment. He stopped pacing and his eyes widened, no doubt his supersensitive hearing catching something my own ears couldn't detect. "They're coming."

My head was already a whirlwind of emotions, but right then, paranoia rose to the forefront. Footsteps thundered toward us. I took a few steps back from the metal bars, wishing I had something to defend myself.

Captain Forsythe appeared in the passage, along with several other Haxsan Guard sailors, all of them equipped with cast-shooters.

I suppose I should see that as a compliment.

The captain's thin mouth curved into a smile. "Come now, Miss Wayward. General Kravis is waiting."

He unlocked the door.

Several soldiers swept inside the cell and fastened my wrists in shackles.

There was little point resisting.

THE FIRST THING that came to my attention as I was escorted down the gangplank was the blazing sunlight. It was still early morning, the sun only newly risen in the sky, yet the air was scorched and dry, the absence of clouds providing no shade or relief. I blinked, trying to adjust my eyes to the incredible brightness. Even the sea, which crashed against the red-gold sand, did nothing to appease the abysmal heat.

I hoped it would be cooler inside the celestial shield. Every so often, I caught a flicker of the barrier in the sky, like a swirling of colour on a soap bubble, alerting me that the shields were active.

My captors marched me down the gangplank onto the dock. I stole a glance over my shoulder, but I didn't see Jad or any of the others behind me.

Where are they?

More importantly, what's become of them?

"This way," one of my captors barked.

My shackles were jerked harshly, and I had to bite my lip to prevent letting a profanity slip. The guards led me through the dock-yard, their grip on my arms tightening until it hurt. The dock was awash with the sounds of province life. Fishermen returning from their early morning catch watched me with narrow-eyed suspicion. Women and young girls, skin as dark as leather from the sun, gutted and salted fish. Some of the women spat at the ground as I was dragged past. My captors never reacted, which meant the women's disgust was aimed solely at me.

There were shouts and clatters from merchants along the docks. Maids and servants bartered and bickered on price for seafood, trying to get the best bargain to appease their lords and ladies. There were sailors and soldiers, on guard and watching for the slightest unrest. The dockyard was home to the lower-class casters, those who lived in the Free Zones only because they served the ruling families.

I was led toward a convoy of sparrowhawks—a sort of four-wheel-drive troop carrier. The one I was pushed into was built like a tank, made of black galvanised steel that drew in the heat like a cloth soaked in water. Two guards sat on either side of me.

As if I can escape, idiots.

If I'd had the energy, I would have rolled my eyes.

The driver sped forward, passing through the city gate and the celestial shield into Muiren. It would have been a beautiful city if it weren't so damn hot. It was built on a mountain, a vertical city of stone plazas, palisades, and towers, all painted in colourful red and gold hues, each building rising as if in prayer to the Black Palace built on top of the mountain. Beyond Muiren was a golden landscape of shifting dunes and burnt-orange rocks. The absence of rain and trees made me feel like I'd stepped into an alien world. Beyond the desert, dramatic cliffs dropped to the ocean. I wondered if the entire Vukovar coastline was like that. If it was, the Haxsan Guard had no fear of refugees or boat people. No one could climb cliffs of that height.

The guard to my right saw me staring at the outside world. "You have no right to gaze upon our city."

"And you have no right to drag me in it as a captive," I fired back, no longer able to hold my tongue. I was growing agitated and fidgety, and when that happened, my sarcasm always won over my common sense. "At least give me a proper sight tour if you insist on driving me around."

A hood was pulled over my head and tightened around my neck, barely allowing me to breathe, let alone see anything.

So much for sightseeing.

THE JOURNEY to the Black Palace was long. Maybe over an hour, but I was judging that on how uncomfortable my backside had become on these less-than-comfortable seats. I swore my cheeks had gone numb.

A guard—I assumed the unpleasant one who had blinded me with a hood—gripped my arm and led me out of the sparrowhawk. Hot, arid air met my skin, my face and hair covered with sweat beneath the hood's thick fabric. I couldn't see where I was going, but I knew the moment I had stepped indoors because the heat was doused by cool air-conditioning. It was a relief, but then my fear spiked all over again. It meant I was that much closer to my unknown fate.

We strode down corridors, up flights of stairs, and through various levels.

Am I really being taken somewhere deep in the Black Palace, or is this just a ploy to disorientate me?

I began to think it was the latter. This time-wasting was just getting ridiculous.

Finally, we came to a stop and the hood was lifted.

I could only gape at what stood around me. I was in a throne room, the walls made of thick onyx. Even the floors were black glass, reflecting the lights like an upside-down night sky. Everything was smooth and solid, which meant nothing could be used as a weapon. The ceiling reached high, culminating in a point. It must have been a spire, probably the largest tower in the entire castle. There were no windows and no other doors save the one I'd entered.

This throne room was not for investitures or ceremonies. It was a place where decisions were made in private, and where they were to remain secret.

Positioned along a dais were seven dark thrones, each made of polished ebony and glass, and on those thrones sat the sovereigns.

My mouth went dry. Up until that moment, I'd hoped Bronislav had been lying, because a private audience with the Seven Sovereigns did not bode well. Even though they were human and physically weaker in strength than casters, they were powerful enough to determine my fate in a heartbeat.

Four men and three women watched me with curious dislike. Their clothes were the finest silks and chintz, and lavishly embroidered. The ladies sat in pastel-coloured gowns, decorated with all manner of lace, ribbon, and flowers. The men wore long narrow coats trimmed with gold braid.

I glanced around the throne room, wishing I could melt into the floor. "Where are my friends?" My voice seemed to echo endlessly across the obsidian walls.

It was a sentry who answered, perhaps the captain of the royal guard. "Chained and in cells. Don't worry." He scoffed at my dismayed look. "They'll see daylight again when they're brought in for questioning."

His yellow teeth grinned at me.

If I weren't shackled, I'd punch all those teeth from his pale gums.

Jad, Talina, and Marek no longer had the Council insignia branded on their palms. Would they be punished? Or questioned and immediately sent to death? I thought about Macha, Macaslan, Darius, and Annaka. They were probably being roasted on a stake right now.

The tightness in my muscles abated when guards entered the room, bringing with them two familiar faces. My relief lasted about half a second. Darius and Macaslan, despite being chained, walked into the throne room with their heads high, as though they belonged on the thrones on the dais. Something dark flittered across Macaslan's face, and I knew she was looking at the sovereigns as impostors.

An usher appeared from behind a black curtain and stood at the edge of the dais to announce the sovereigns. "His Royal Highness Georgen, His Royal Highness Harrior..." He listed their names like a waiter poring over today's specials on a menu.

Georgen was elderly, sallow, and soft-eyed. Harrior was closer to Darius's age, his rust-coloured hair neatly parted at the side. Next to him was announced Her Royal Highness Nehwa, a woman with incredibly long blonde hair, lightly laced with the first strands of silver. The woman next to her, Her Royal Highness Sephia, could have been her daughter. Her curled and pinned hair was elaborately decorated with crystal beads that resembled stars.

None of them could have been described as beautiful. Their perpetual scowls wouldn't allow it. They sat tall in their thrones, intimidating, aloof, and stiff, but it was the three sovereigns in the centre of the dais who truly alarmed me.

"His Royal Highness Rozric, His Royal Highness Alric, Her Royal Highness Toshiko." The usher sounded out of breath.

The last three sovereigns stood from their thrones, the obvious spokespeople of the group. Rozric watched me with a dangerous glint in his eyes. He had long, impeccable copper hair, held back by a gold crown. A cape of white fur hung from his shoulders, which trailed the floor. He looked like a king from the medieval age, and I immediately pegged him as the real decision-maker. The sovereigns were meant to have equal say and voting rights on all matters in government, but somehow, this man looked capable of persuading others to get what he wanted.

The other sovereign, Alric, was red-faced with a bushy moustache. His wizened face appeared bored. He tapped his leather boot, probably longing more for his breakfast than... well, whatever this was.

The woman, though, she watched me with a sharp, contemplative look. Toshiko was different from her fellow sovereigns. She wore a long trailing kimono from a time long ago, her eyes decorated in gold, drawn up from the corners to resemble those of a cat. She had high cheekbones, full lips, and skin so fair it could have been painted white. Her black hair was tied back with a comb. She smiled, but I couldn't tell if it was sympathetic or marked with disdain.

Rozric spoke, his voice jabbing at me like an unprotected eye. "This is the girl?"

From the opposite curtain, General Kravis stepped out and stood beside me, not once making eye contact. He'd aged considerably since I'd last seen him. His dark hair was streaked with grey. He had it brushed back, and the ends touched his shoulders, revealing his rectangular face and pointed jaw. His Vandyke beard, which I remembered as being stylishly maintained, looked like it hadn't been clipped in days. I'd never learnt what accident had caused the deep scar that ran past his nose and through his lips. It could have been a blade. Or an axe.

The general still wouldn't look at me as he spoke. "She is."

"And what is it that you suspect she is?"

"A necromancer, Your Highness." A speck of spittle flew from the general's lips.

I couldn't breathe. Every part of me was braced for an attack. I half expected Haxsan Guard soldiers to storm into the throne room and execute me right there on the spot.

Rozric looked at Darius for confirmation. "Is this true? Is *this*"—he pointed at me—"the reason you betrayed your Council and sovereigns? To join Morgomoth's forces and unite two necromancers?"

Darius chuckled with a shake of his head. It didn't sound amused. "You have no proof that she's a necromancer. And what you suggest is offensive. I would never ally myself with Morgomoth."

"She is a necromancer," General Kravis snapped, venom in his words. "Why else would you protect her the way you do? I've done my research. You and the commander were the girl's legal guardians. You have known all along what she is. *She*"—again a finger was pointed at me—"is responsible for what happened at the Bone Towers. She created that... *thing*."

The senator's smile grew broader "That *thing* is Morgomoth's new kingdom. He's created a dead army. The longer we stand here deciding if a mere girl is a necromancer or not is more time for Morgomoth and his ULD forces to initiate an attack."

There was more arguing, more conspiracies and denials shared.

"Enough." Rozric shouted. His cheeks grew red with indignation. "There is a simple way to know whether the girl is a necromancer or not. Bring in the soothwitcher."

Darius stilled but recovered his composure before anyone else saw. I, on the other hand, felt like I'd stepped in front of a firing squad. Soothwitchers were about as rare as obeahpeople. They could understand a caster's power just by feel. Whatever that meant and entailed, I didn't like the sound of it.

The guards left and returned a moment later with a hooded figure. The newcomer must have been elderly because they were escorted inside by the guards. They walked with a limp. I flinched when the newcomer was positioned in front of me, their breathing heavy and guttural. Underneath the black cowl was a woman whose face was so heavily scarred and thin that it was like staring at a skeleton with empty eyes. I'd always found Macha's appearance distressing, but this soothwitcher looked like she belonged in a grave. Even the wind would be capable of knocking her over.

She stretched a bony hand toward my face, quicker than I would have thought possible for a woman of her age. She touched my cheek, her calloused fingers rubbing across my skin. I think she might have been blind, because her eyes were vacant.

"Necromancer," she droned, causing fear to surge inside me. "This caster is a necromancer."

Five little words had sealed my fate.

The sovereigns stared at me with new-found horror.

Rozric raised a hand to his guards. "Remove the soothwitcher. Put her back in her cage."

"Cage," I repeated before my brain could catch up with me. "You put her in a cage? She's blind and elderly. She needs care."

I was visibly shaking with anger.

Rozric waited until the guards had departed with the soothwitcher. "She's a prisoner. Her magic is banned."

"Meaning she's powerful and you want to use her magic for your own ends?"

Rozric's nostrils flared. "That is an outrageous accusation."

"But it's true," I persevered. "You did the same thing to Morgomoth. You bound him in a sleeping curse and used his magic like a lithium battery to generate power for the entire Athnik region. You want to know why you're losing control of casters? Why so many have fled your rule and joined the United League of Dissent? It's because of the way you treat them. I *am* a necromancer, but I am not on Morgomoth's side. I am not on your side. I think you're all despicable."

Rozric stepped down from the dais and took fast, infuriated strides toward me.

I cringed, thinking he was about to slap me, but he stood very still, breathing hard. "You confess. You are a necromancer?"

I gritted my teeth, wishing I had a cast-shooter in my hand. "I am not ashamed of what I am. I'm the only one who has a remote chance of stopping Morgomoth. Of killing him. That's what we're planning to do. To stop him, not aid him."

I didn't dare look at Darius or Macaslan. I was too afraid of what I'd see on their faces. Shock? Betrayal? After everything they'd done for me, it pained me to even consider how hurt they must be to hear me divulge everything. But the truth always had its day in the end, and today it had arrived.

Toshiko stepped down from the dais. Her golden eyes swept over me. "And how exactly do you intend to defeat Morgomoth? He was asleep for years, and in that time, his followers rallied and grew. Morgomoth's death would not defeat the ULD. It would only strengthen their course. He'd become a martyr in their eyes."

Adrenaline burned through me. "That's why you need to start making the changes first. Amend your laws. Draw up and sign new accords. Grant clemency to those who have fled out of fear, and give casters equal status. Let them choose if they join the Haxsan Guard or not. Revolutionise the Council."

Toshiko regarded me with a small frown. "You say it like it's so easy."

"Speaking is easy. Doing is the hard part."

I snuck a glance at Macaslan and Darius. Macaslan watched the scene play out before her with impassive eyes, her emotions guarded. The senator looked like he was fighting down a smirk. I understood what that look meant. He had come up with a new idea. A new motive.

His gaze settled on Toshiko, who seemed more reasonable than

Rozric. "If you were to change your laws, I would do it quickly. There's already talk in Muiren of the event that occurred at the Bone Towers. Whispers for now, but it won't be long until those whispers are confirmed and everyone learns that Morgomoth has land and a kingdom. You do not want discontented casters flocking to him, seeking a new life where they're promised revenge over the Council and the sovereigns... and, of course, humans."

Toshiko's stance turned stiff. "You hate humans."

"I do not. I merely want humans and casters to live in harmony, and for the former not to enslave the latter."

"And I suppose you have a way to do this, Senator Kerr?"

Darius swept her a gallant bow. "I always have a plan, Your Highness."

Toshiko moved toward Rozric and whispered into his ear. He raised his brows but nodded in agreement.

"Guards," he called ruthlessly. "Take the girl away. We will speak privately with the commander and the senator."

My vision blurred for half a second. "Wait. What?"

Take me where?

The hood was fastened over my head again. Arms forcefully dragged me away.

CHAPTER 33

I expected a dungeon, a prison, gallows. When my hood was removed for the second time, I did not expect to be greeted with a chamber fit for a queen. The walls and décor matched the rest of the palace—dark, obsidian, and smooth, some of the walls painted with gold leaf, the others decorated with giant tapestries. There was a small dining table, a sitting area with deep-cushioned chairs, and an enormous canopy bed.

What the hell?

The guards slipped back into the hallway and shut the door. The jangle of keys told me they'd locked me in, but I checked anyway.

Yep. Locked.

I turned back to my huge bedroom, frazzled.

Why would they put me in here?

Suffering in luxury didn't seem like the sovereigns' style.

I stepped through the room, opening the armoire, the dressers, and the vanity, searching for anything that could be used as a weapon. I only found a letter opener so blunt I didn't think it would even cut paper. Neathror had abandoned me after I used the blade to strike Morgomoth. Regrettably, it had never made an appearance again, even when I'd tried to summon it. The blade only answered when I really needed it. Life or death. Trying to flee a bedchamber didn't qualify.

Sighing heavily, I peeked out at the world beyond the window. All I could see was an impressive view of the ocean. Large lattice doors would have opened to a remarkable balcony, but these were locked too. The sovereigns didn't want me to leave this place.

I had no idea how much time had passed, but judging from the position of the sun in the sky, it was now mid-morning. The heat was still climbing. I needed fresh clothes. I needed a shower. I needed food. Mostly, I needed sleep.

How can I sleep in all this finery when Jad and the others are likely in cells somewhere in the palace?

And what were Darius and Macaslan now discussing with the sovereigns? It infuriated me not knowing.

I felt hopeless and utterly alone.

But I'm not alone.

I kicked my shoes off and sat on the bed, loosely resting my hands on my thighs. I closed my eyes, summoning my magic.

"Lunette? Adaline? Are you there?"

I waited.

No answer.

"Please. I need your help."

Nothing.

Either I was too exhausted and incapable of conjuring their spirits, or they simply didn't want to reply.

Disgruntled, I dropped back onto the bed, giving in to sleep.

WHEN I OPENED MY EYES, I was in the cabin. The Dark Divide had projected my sleepy conscious into Isgrad's—I mean Morgomoth's—memory again. He was sitting at the small dining table. His hair was much longer and unkempt, his face terribly white. I supposed there wasn't a chance to sunbathe in a place like this, or maybe spellrock was taking its toll, altering his physical appearance. I'd heard it could do that.

His mother sat next to him. Opposite, slumped in a chair, was Willieth.

My blood thrummed in my veins. Willieth might have been brought back from the dead, but he still looked... well, dead. His hair, which had been blond and thick, was now white and thin. His eyes were sunken and black, and his lips were still blue. Touching them would have been like touching ice.

He's still dead. Just reanimated.

Willieth stared ahead, unseeing, a spoon resting in his hand. The three of them were eating soup, something that didn't appear remotely appealing. It looked like hot water with a few vegetables in the mix.

Isgrad's mother tapped him on the shoulder. "Will you help me with the dishes, please."

The pair slipped away to the kitchen. I followed, standing next to them at the sink.

"What is wrong with him?" Isgrad's mother stole an anxious glance at her youngest son, who still sat zombielike at the table. "He's been like this for weeks. Is he sick, do you think?"

Isgrad flinched like he'd been struck. "I don't know. Perhaps."

He stared out at the window. Snowflakes swirled at the glass, reminding me of a school of fish swimming through currents. It was terribly cold in the cabin, the fire reduced to burning embers. They had run out of wood. It must have been too wet outside to find anything dry to burn.

"What should we do?" his mother resumed. "We can't take him to a doctor."

Isgrad closed his eyes for a second, guilt weighing heavily in his shoulders. "Let him be. He may just need… time."

Time for what? To recover?

Willieth likely didn't even have a pulse.

I studied Isgrad, wondering if necromancy was working inside him. Could he hear the dead? Were they visiting his dreams? Whispering omens to him? Toying with him as they did me? He kept shooting worried glances at his brother, and I could tell he was genuinely afraid of what his sibling had become.

Morgomoth isn't afraid of the dead or the power he has over them.

What happened in Isgrad's future to make him the twisted lord who presided over the United League of Dissent? I knew Isgrad hated the Haxsan Guard and the Council of Founding Sovereigns, but something much worse than raising his brother from the dead must have occurred for him to become Morgomoth.

Isgrad's mother nodded with a sniffle. "I'll try and get him to eat something. Providence help us."

She departed.

The memory changed. Shadow and dark swirled in like smoke. When it vanished, I was in the woods. Isgrad plodded heavily through the snow, three dead rabbits over his shoulder. He must have caught the family's dinner and was returning to skin and cook them. I shuddered. Rabbits were so cute with their soft velvet ears, round eyes, and little twitching noses that the thought of eating one made me physically ill. But when you were as desperate and starved as Isgrad and his family, cuteness went out the window.

The night was incredibly dark. Nothing was visible in the sky except for thick clouds and heavy snow. The wind was so strong it howled through the trees, making the branches creak with a haunting cry. There was no light except for Isgrad's headlamp, and in the muted radiance, I saw his entire body tremble with exhaustion, his breathing laboured. He shut his eyes, and for a moment, I suspected he was about to fall. Searing brightness washed over his face, bringing him back from the clutches of fatigue.

His eyes widened in dismay. Spotty light bled through the trees ahead, taking on more heat and colour. Isgrad sped forward. I followed, my pathetic ballet flats doing a poor job of helping me keep up. He raced ahead, and all I could do was follow the intermittent light that flashed in and out of the trees from his headlamp.

I reached the tip of the summit, shocked to be greeted with scorching heat. Isgrad was a silhouette framed against the new burning light. He sprinted down the hill, not caring if there were hidden rock fragments beneath the snow. I hurried after him, aghast at the sight ahead of me.

The cabin was on fire. Thick black smoke poured off the roof. Flames surged up the walls. Glass exploded, heavier smoke billowing from the windows.

The worst sight was the Haxsan Guard soldiers who stood around the burning building. After so many weeks, or months, in hiding, Isgrad's family had been discovered. The Haxsan Guard had set the cabin alight to spite them.

Screaming like a madman in a battle, Isgrad charged toward the soldiers. "What have you done? What have you done? You've killed them."

Several soldiers grabbed him, holding him back. He thrashed and swore, trying to break free, but there was no way he could take on the men who surrounded him.

A man, probably the captain of the Haxsan Guard troop, stepped forward. "Is this your home?"

Isgrad spat on the ground the captain stood on. "You bastard. You killed them. You killed my mother and brother."

The captain didn't look fazed. He cast a bored glance over the inferno. "We did not. We were passing through the woods. We saw the fire and came to inspect it. The real perpetrator of this crime is in our custody."

He pointed to a sparrowhawk, which had been parked near the tree line. My mind groped through the chaos, trying to understand what I was seeing. Inside the vehicle was Willieth. He stared back at his brother, eyes glassy, skin watery pale in the flamelight.

"We caught him adding more flames from his hands," the captain continued.

Isgrad dropped to the ground. The soldiers backed away, no longer seeing him as a threat. Isgrad was a distraught wreck, incapable of fighting.

Tears bled from his eyes. "He wouldn't. Not with our mother still inside."

The captain looked down at him without a hint of sympathy. "He did. And now he'll be taken to a Haxsan Guard base to undergo military training. As will you."

Isgrad slammed a fist into the ground. "My mother is dead. My brother needs help, and all you can think about is the reward you'll receive for our capture."

"Be grateful she's dead. Far worse things would have been done to her for hiding Council property."

Isgrad uttered a shaky cry. "We are not property. We are casters."

The captain motioned to his men to pull Isgrad from the ground. They did, holding him tight to keep him upright. Shock must have hindered his ability to stand on his own.

The captain stepped close to Isgrad, a threat in his eyes. "You belong to the Council of Founding Sovereigns. You will always serve. While the Council are in charge, humans will always come first. We are their protectors. It is an honour to be part of the Haxsan Guard. And don't you forget it."

The veins in Isgrad's neck corded. "It's a life sentence. We have no rights. No freedom."

Despair cinched itself into a knot behind my ribcage. Was this the moment Isgrad became Morgomoth? Was this the beginning of his slow descent into madness?

The captain grinned a nasty smile. "Take them away."

The soldiers dragged Isgrad through the snow and steered him inside the sparrowhawk. They chained him to a seat, cuffing his wrists and ankles. He'd gone into a sort of shock, his eyes empty and unfocused.

Next to him, his brother watched the cabin collapse as fire destroyed it from within. For the first time, Willieth's lips moved. They stretched into a thin smile.

I woke, startled out of my sleepy haze. A woman stared down at me.

Correction: an assembly of caster women stared down at me.

"Good gracious," a strict voice announced. "She hasn't even bathed."

I sat up, wiping the sleep and memory away. I wanted to be by myself, to take a moment to think about what I'd witnessed, but the women had other ideas.

Toshiko sat in one of the deep-cushioned chairs. She had a folding fan in her hand, which she used to wave cool air into her face. It was her who'd spoken.

Why is a sovereign in my chamber?

While I'd been contained like a prisoner under house arrest, the balcony doors had been opened for her, allowing me to see the setting sun as it slowly trailed down to the ocean, the night stars already aglow in the sky.

I've slept all day.

The desert temperature had lowered to a heat that was comfortable—for sitting around and doing nothing. As soon as I started moving, I'd be a sweaty mess again.

Toshiko stood and brushed down the long skirt of her kimono. This time her outfit was black silk, embroidered with cherry blossoms, the long patterned sleeves decorated with real peacock feathers. Her hair was tied up, pinned with flowers and gold beads. She turned to the caster women who I assumed were her ladies-in-waiting. "Run a bath and make sure to clean her thoroughly. She will need her hair washed too. You have forty-five minutes to make her look... presentable."

The way she spoke the last word made me want to kick her. "Excuse me?"

I swatted away the various hands that pulled me off the bed as though I were an invalid. "What is this? Where are my friends? Where's Jad? What did you discuss with Macaslan and Darius? What's happening?"

Honestly, I didn't know why I expected any of my questions to be answered.

Toshiko sashayed over to the balcony and looked out at the waves, ignoring me.

The caster women dragged me to the bathroom. Five of them altogether, their combined strength was impossible to outmatch. They ran a bath, undressed me, not caring how my cheeks grew ruddy at my abashed nudity, and forced me into the tub, scrubbing days of filth and muck from my body.

Why are Toshiko's ladies-in-waiting attending to me?

It was useless arguing. These women were so fierce and determined in their actions, I would have liked to see the Haxsan Guard take them on.

I was too tired and still too frazzled by the memory to resist, and honestly, it was kind of nice to have people take care of me for once. When they were finished, they patted me down with towels, covered me in a silk robe, and led me to a dressing room. Then they brushed my hair, clipped my nails, and moisturised my arms and face. It started to get a little invasive.

My senses caught up with me.

"Stop, please." I grabbed the hairbrush from one of the ladies, holding it like a weapon. "What is this? You don't bathe and dress prisoners."

What game is being played now?

Toshiko emerged from the balcony. She crossed the chamber and sat in the chair next to mine, graceful and poised. "Your presence is required at court."

I dropped the brush in surprise. "Court?"

"Yes. Now let my ladies do their work. You look ghastly."

I tried to swallow, but the moisture in my mouth had vanished. "I… I don't understand. Am I going on trial?"

The sovereign's lips tipped into a small smile. "That depends."

"On what?"

She looked like she was biting back a laugh. "On how you behave."

TWENTY MINUTES LATER, I stood in front of the mirror, examining my much-improved appearance and still pondering Toshiko's words. She'd returned to the balcony, leaving me in the hands of her ladies. They had curled and swept my hair into an elaborate updo, powdered my face with make-up, and painted my eyes. I hardly recognised myself in my new dress. It was dark blue and black lace, with swirls of thread on the bodice shaped into roses. Along the wide skirt, silver beads had been woven into the fabric. The dress had a low neckline and was backless, and it came with a matching tiara and earrings made from, of course, obsidian. I would have blended in with the walls perfectly.

Toshiko appeared from around the corner and stood in the doorway of my dressing room. "It's time."

She clapped her hands. Her ladies-in-waiting left my chamber like banished dogs.

"You look beautiful," Toshiko told me.

I glanced back at the mirror.

Beautifully dark is more like it.

My appearance didn't match the princess image girls gushed over. I looked like a dark fairy queen, capable of ruthless and vindictive terror. Again, I questioned Toshiko's motives.

The clock struck six.

Toshiko turned to the door. "It's time to go."

I WAS LED down a grand hallway, Toshiko by my side and an escort of guards behind us.

Surely they wouldn't go to so much trouble to present me like this if they're going to execute me?

But this was the Council of Founding Sovereigns. Maybe even executions were grandiose events.

We approached gold-and-black doors, which had been left ajar a fraction. Beyond them, I glimpsed wreaths, candelabras, and chandeliers that bedecked a majestic ballroom. Someone was speaking on the other side of the doors, addressing a large crowd of wealthy courtiers.

Toshiko's hand was tight on my shoulder like her entire life depended on this going right.

The voice behind the doors was clearer now. I recognised Rozric's hoarse tone. "We will no longer suffer under the hands of Morgomoth and his radical dissidents. Now we have a weapon to match his strength."

Weapon?

The guards threw the doors back, and I was flung forward. Spotlights bore down on me, and it took a moment to blink the stars away. I stood on a mezzanine used to address a crowd and make speeches. Two black marble staircases swept down from either side to the ballroom below. A sea of faces stared up at me. Their gazes were startled, afraid, and curious.

Rozric stepped beside me, his voice raining down over the court. "I present to you our saviour and our weapon against Morgomoth, Zaya Wayward, the sovereigns' necromancer."

Silence filled the ballroom.

The corset I wore suddenly felt tighter.

Sovereigns' necromancer?

For as long as I could remember, I had kept my power a secret. Only my closest friends and those I trusted knew. And now it had been announced to this court, to the most powerful people in the world.

Run. Flee.

But my feet were leaden.

What game were the sovereigns playing?

In the crowd, I caught sight of someone raising their glass in salute. I wanted to race down the stairs and throttle his neck.

What mess have you gotten me into now, Darius?

CHAPTER 34

I grew increasingly uncomfortable the longer people stared.

Rozric's amplified voice filled the ballroom. "Please continue the festivities."

I had the urge to vomit.

Toshiko swept forward and linked her arm with mine. "Come." She gave me a stiff nod and led me down the stairs. The band must have been instructed to play, because music filled the ballroom and the dancing resumed, but there were still more than a few wary eyes on me.

"Go mingle," Toshiko instructed as we stepped into the crowd. "These people are here to meet you."

So many questions burned in my mind, but she sped away, disappearing among the dancers. That was okay. The person I *really* wanted words with was in my line of sight.

I cut through the guests and stalked up to Darius and Macaslan, who were blessedly standing next to each other, champagne flutes in their hands.

That just made me madder.

"Give me one good reason why I shouldn't pull your teeth out, one by one."

Macaslan turned her stony gaze on me.

Darius gave me a glassy stare. "Let's not make a scene. Especially here, of all places."

I drew a rocky breath, my pulse racing. "What the hell did you say to the sovereigns? What did you do?"

"What had to be done," he snapped back, keeping his voice low. "The sovereigns already knew what you were. Our original plan wasn't going to work. We had to make them see you as an ally, not an enemy."

"An ally. They called me the sovereigns' necromancer. A weapon. They made me look like something to be feared."

"Of course they did. The sovereigns are desperate to show they have a strategy to overturn Morgomoth and destroy the ULD for good. You need to play the part. You need to appear as terrifying in these people's minds as Morgomoth is. It'll give them confidence that you can defeat him."

I wanted to fall to my knees and cry. I had no confidence that I could defeat Morgomoth, and now I had the entire expectations and hopes of the Council weighing on my shoulders.

No pressure at all.

My chest was tight. The damn corset made it impossible to breathe. "I suppose you made a deal to save yourselves. That's why you're here, right? Sipping champagne and not hanging at the gallows?"

"Zaya." Macaslan's voice stabbed like ice. "We are still prisoners. We're confined to the palace."

"How awful for you."

"It is. We're here for appearance's sake. The sovereigns have led the Council to believe we protected you on their orders, that we brought you to the Black Palace at their request. We are their pawns now. We must do as they say; otherwise, we *will* be sent to the gallows, along with your friends."

My tongue stumbled. "Where are they?"

Worry lurked on her face. "In the palace prison. If we, or you, divert from the plan, the sovereigns will have them killed. Do you understand?"

"I understand the sovereigns are using my friends as a bargaining chip."

"Not all of them," Darius interrupted.

"Not all of them what?"

He mastered a sly smile. "Not all of the sovereigns are heartless. Toshiko is on our side. She understands that laws must change in order for us to truly defeat Morgomoth. She has Nehwa and Harrior in agreement to write new magic accords. It'll revolutionise the way the Council operates and give casters the chance to choose whether they serve the Haxsan Guard."

I glared stonily. "That's only three votes. You need at least four sovereigns to agree to make new laws and magical binds."

I was not feeling optimistic.

Darius downed the last of his drink. "You do your part and let us worry about the sovereigns."

I crossed my arms. "And what exactly is my part?"

"Tomorrow, Toshiko will take you to the Forbidden Library. It's beneath the palace where all outlawed texts are secured."

"And why would she do that?"

"Because she wants to prepare you for what's about to come. The Forbidden Library contains information about the Isla Necropolis. We need the Bone Grimoire, Zaya. Morgomoth cannot obtain it. If he learns the spell that merges the Larthalgule and the Neathror blades, then he'll create the ultimate weapon. If that happens, there will be no defeating him."

My suspicion flared.

Darius working with the sovereigns made me uneasy.

"Toshiko will tell you everything tomorrow," he resumed. "In three days, you'll be sent to the dead city to retrieve the book... and you will not be going alone."

"Who's coming with me?"

Great. The sovereigns' personal guard, I suppose.

Darius nodded toward someone in the crowd.

I turned, my heart galloping—in a good way.

Jad was talking to a group of courtiers. He wore a dark red coat with black embroidery, looking every part the Gothic prince in a dark fairy tale. His hair was brushed back and shining, his handsome face catching the attention of wandering eyes. He looked like he belonged here, effortlessly captivating his onlookers. Where had he learnt to do that?

The senator's eyes brightened with amusement. He must have

realised my resolve to remain angry had weakened. "I did manage to convince Toshiko that Captain Arden should become your personal protector."

"Protector?" I scoffed. "I'm not some weak little girl who needs saving."

Though it did make me feel a lot safer knowing Jad would be by my side for what came next.

Darius shoved my shoulder lightly. "Go. Mingle. Show these councillors that you're a worthy opponent of Morgomoth. Otherwise, they may turn on you."

So comforting.

Jad spotted me, his eyes betraying his concern. He excused himself and moved in my direction, not noticing—or simply ignoring—the collective sigh of disappointment from the women around him.

"You look... lovely," he decided.

I sucked in a rattling breath. "I look like I'm capable of ordering everyone to slaughter. Did you know about this?"

He took my arm, leading me through the ballroom. "An hour ago, I was in a cell. I've only had minutes to come to terms with the plan myself."

"This is crazy."

"Is it? Before, we were hiding. Now we're hiding in plain sight with the support of the sovereigns."

"Not all the sovereigns," I reminded him. "And our friends? They're in cells?"

"That's why we need to play this game and survive."

He took my hands in his and planted a gentle kiss on my forehead. "I will not let anyone hurt you."

Try as he might, I knew that was one promise he couldn't keep.

FOR THE MOST PART, no one really did talk to me. As the night progressed, I could tell by the way people turned away quickly that they feared me. Even the women, who had stared fondly at Jad, didn't dare send me death stares from beneath their long, glittering eyelashes.

I couldn't blame them. Whenever I happened to catch my reflection in a window, I saw an unknown face staring back. She was the embodiment of darkness. She was a queen who reigned over the dead. A summoner. A conjurer.

This is not me.

The sovereigns had moulded me into something I was not. They had made me into a symbol. One they controlled.

Jad remained by my side for the entire evening. A few brave courtiers attempted small talk. I played the game, acting civilised when really all I wanted to do was stamp my feet and scream.

When the dancing started, I'd never felt such relief. Dancing was not a talent of mine, but at least it meant Jad and I had some privacy, even though we were still watched by a few prying eyes. He led me around the floor in time with the music, his broad hand against the small of my back, guiding me expertly. Neither of us had any inclination to dance with anyone else. I didn't care who that offended.

Balls were meant to be spectacular, and no expense had been spared with this one. Everything had been ornamented in swoonworthy Moroccan style. It was an ancient design that had survived the centuries from our human ancestors and had become the embodiment of Vukovar high fashion. Exquisite, silken tapestries hung from the walls. Many of the dining tables had been ornamented with candle lanterns. The floor, walls, and even the ceiling were crafted with beautiful geometric patterns. This was something only people could dream of seeing, and yet I was about as lively as I would be at funeral.

"Please," I begged Jad. "Can we go outside? I just need some air."

He guided me through the dancers to the terrace, which led down to a roof garden. It was a courtyard with black-and-jade tiles, lush greenery, and impressive water fountains. Music and conversation flowed down from the ballroom, reminding me that there really was no escape. I settled on one of the benches and stared up at the cloudless night. The stars seemed to wink at me, as though they understood my fate and were laughing.

"This is a nightmare," I confessed.

Jad sat beside me. He stared at me for a long time, and I wondered if he could see inside to my troubled soul.

I rubbed my arms, even though I wasn't cold. "Something doesn't feel right about any of this. The sovereigns are far too… calm. Morgomoth has spies everywhere. By now, he would have learnt that I'm here at the Black Palace. He would know you're here with the key."

"What are you saying?"

"Why hasn't he attacked Muiren and the palace? He has the army to do it."

A brief smile played over Jad's lips, but it didn't reach his eyes. "It takes time to organise a raid. Right now, Muiren is the most secure Free Zone in all of Vukovar. He'll strike when we leave for Isla Necropolis. It's what I would do in his place."

I remained silent. A throb of pain started in my lower scalp. A tension headache was the last thing I needed.

Jad frowned. "What's wrong?"

"What's wrong?" Bitter emotion surged inside me. "Everyone is relying on me to destroy Morgomoth, and I don't even have the faintest idea how to do it. Everyone says it has to be me, but when I ask, no one tells me how."

"Only a necromancer can slay another necromancer."

"Great. Very detailed. That explains everything."

"There must be answers in the Forbidden Library."

"Or all the answers are in the Bone Grimoire, and that's another reason why Morgomoth wants it."

A flicker of doubt crossed Jad's face, and I knew that was something he hadn't considered before.

He took my hand. "We'll work it out together."

There was such sincerity in his eyes that I couldn't help it. I leaned forward and brushed my lips against his. The kiss was slow, gentle, then deeper and full of need. I was desperate to feel something other than fear for the future, and with Jad, I felt safe. I felt like I finally belonged. I felt capable of anything.

He kissed me back, the spark between us turning to fire. Jad scooped his arm beneath me and pulled me onto his lap. My hands instinctively gripped his shoulders as I deepened the kiss. His fingers brushed the thin fabric of my sleeve until it slipped right off my shoulder, and in that moment, I wouldn't have minded if the entire dress fell off. Jad trailed gentle kisses down my neck and across my collarbone.

Stop, I warned myself, but my body was filled with too much desire for me to take notice of what my head said.

I pushed his coat down his arms, which he hastily shoved away. The earth seemed to spin around me, making me dizzy in a good way.

Light blazed against my closed eyes. I broke the kiss, gasping for air. "Did you see that?"

Jad's body was rigid beneath me. He was looking out at the sea. I turned, my fear building inside me, feeling tangible enough to be stone. There was a storm on the horizon. Powerful blue-and-purple chain lightning lit the sky in monstrous eruptions. At first, I thought it was a light shower that fell, but it was too warm, and it didn't have the fresh smell of rain.

And it never rains in the desert.

It blew against me, wispy, swirling, and hot.

Ash.

I moved to the parapet, troubled by what I was witnessing. Jad hurried after me. I took his hand, squeezing tight. "It's him. Morgomoth. The Dark Divide is growing out there."

I'd read in the history books how volcanic eruptions devastated civilisations. Mount Bislorn had exploded some centuries ago, and it had plunged the northern hemisphere into a decade of darkness. Crops failed. Starvation followed. Disease ran rife. Millions of casters and humans died in the aftermath.

That was one volcanic eruption. Morgomoth's new kingdom was an island of volcanoes, a ring of deadly, cataclysmic fires. If its effects were already reaching here to Muiren and the coast of Vukovar, what chance did the world have?

And I helped him.

By opening the door, I'd bridged the gap between the world of the living and dead. I had unleashed the Dark Divide.

A crack of thunder tore through the sky, alerting guests in the ballroom that something unnatural was occurring outside. The Council flocked onto the terrace, staring up at the darkening sky. Lightning revealed the horror and surprise on their faces.

If there'd been any sceptics or deniers in the crowd about Morgomoth's return, this display surely made them believers.

The threat was real.

CHAPTER 35

I struggled to sleep, tossing and turning in my silk sheets, but my hurricane of emotions refused to settle down. There were so many expectations on me now, and if I didn't deliver, my friends would pay with their lives. I was fairly certain I would pay with my life, too, either by Morgomoth's hand when I flat-out refused to join him again or by the sovereigns' order when they realised I wasn't up to the task. I could be a thief, a con artist, and a swindler. I could do all that without seriously hurting anyone. But to play assassin? Against the most powerful caster in the world? I really hoped Darius and the sovereigns had a plan B.

The balcony doors had been locked again, all the window shutters firmly closed. Perhaps the sovereigns were worried I'd scale the outside walls of the palace to escape. Ha. I had skills, but I wasn't that good.

The dry heat in my chamber made me parched. I climbed off the bed and ambled to the dining table where someone, probably a servant, had left a pitcher of water and a drinking glass. I greedily guzzled the water down, then poured another.

A shiver of fingers ran up my spine, an instinct that warned me to be aware. My magic was at work. There was someone here.

Someone who was dead.

"Hello."

All the shadows in the chamber seemed to grow darker, bleeding out into every nook and corner. I focused my magic, trying to sense if the newcomer was harmful or simply curious. They could have been a ghost who lived in the palace when they were alive. An icy feeling wrapped around me, and I knew my visitor neither belonged to the palace nor was here simply to be nosy. I sensed purpose at its essence, but for what, I still couldn't determine.

"Hello," I called again. "Make yourself known. Please."

The darkness remained still.

I gingerly returned to my bed to grab my pullover. "Hello—"

Something sprang at me, wrestling me flat onto the bed. A pale hand drowned my scream. Cold, dead fingers curled over my mouth.

The wraith leaned forward. Long brown hair concealed her face, her eyes and nose lost in shadow, but her lips were wide in a fiendish smile. Recognition made fear grip me all the way down to my toes. She was the ghost from the Dark Divide. The one who'd followed me in Isgrad's memories. I thought she'd been a wraith cursed to wander the endless tunnels, but the Dark Divide was a part of the world now, and maybe that meant...

She can cross over.

The wraith bought her face close to my own. I trembled under her weight, my nostrils filling with the stench of her putrefaction. And a trace of something else, so faint I couldn't be certain if I imagined it. Lavender and vanilla. It smelt... familiar.

She lifted a pointed finger to her lips, urging me to be silent. "Dream, little one."

Her voice sounded like the wail of a banshee, causing me to freeze up.

Her hand pressed against my nose and mouth. She was blocking my airway. I convulsed and struggled, kicking with my legs.

She's going to kill me.

She's going to succeed.

A haze filled my eyes, and then the world went black.

I woke gasping, unsure where I was. Certainly not my bed or my chamber. Maybe not even in the Black Palace or Muiren. For one, I was no longer lying down. And two, it was raining. I stood alone in a cobbled laneway slick with puddles and mud. A streetlight behind me cast a dim glow through the miasma that swirled through the lane. Where the light couldn't reach, it was pitch-black. A rat scuttled out from an overloaded dumpster and ran past my feet. I leapt back, holding in a girly squeal, ashamed that something so small could still make me squeamish.

The buildings on either side were brick, covered in crude graffiti about the Council and the sovereigns.

That rules out the Free Zones, then.

This place had to be in a province town, somewhere the Haxsan Guard visited fleetingly; otherwise, who would dare risk writing such obscene language on the buildings? If they were caught, their hands would have been cut off and put on public display as a warning to others.

"You," a voice shouted.

I wheeled around, expecting a confrontation, but the man walked straight past me.

I recognised him.

Isgrad.

He was older now. Maybe in his midtwenties.

I'm in another memory.

I hurried after him, the rain pelting down on me, soaking my nightdress. Isgrad had never been talking to me. There was a homeless man sitting by the dumpsters. I hadn't noticed him at first because he was hidden in the shadows.

Isgrad showed him a slip of paper. "I'm looking for this address. Do you know it?"

The man grinned. There were large gaps between his yellow teeth. "Know it? That's the old mortuary. No one goes in there no more. Too many strange things happened. The building's boarded. Everyone's banned from entering."

"I need to find that building." Isgrad's voice was a scary demand.

"I'm happy to tell ya, but it'll come at a price."

Isgrad dug through his pocket and took out a few silver coins. He dropped them on the ground. "Will that do?"

The man greedily scooped them up. "That should suffice."

"Where is that building?"

"Keep going to the end of this lane. Turn right and then right again. It's the last door on the left."

Isgrad didn't stick around. He walked down the deserted alley, and I hurried after him.

"The door's locked," the homeless man called. "There's no way in. You don't want to go in there. Not if you want to keep all your body parts. Something in the building takes pieces of you."

He continued to shout, but the heavy rain washed the last of his warnings away.

Body parts?

I followed Isgrad between the buildings until we stepped into our destined laneway. Even though this was a memory, I sensed something dead and twisted down the other end. Milky light streamed from a rooftop somewhere, shifting across the shadows like a spotlight, revealing strewn papers and brick walls so thick with black-crust stains that in the rain, it resembled dark, running blood. Even the air down here smelt of decay. I wondered if Isgrad sensed it.

All the windows on the left building were indeed boarded up, but on the outside, as though something inside shouldn't be allowed out. It made me nervous. We reached a black door with gold lettering that had been badly scratched off. I could just make out the word *mortuary*, but the rest of it, a family name perhaps, was gone.

Isgrad tried the handle. The door was locked.

He tapped once.

No answer.

Breathing in deeply, he rapped his knuckles rhythmically in a beat.

A secret code.

The door creaked open, inviting us in. Isgrad took out a small flashlight from his coat and stepped inside. I looked back hesitantly at the lane, questioning whether this was a good idea.

Something wants you to see this.

Squaring my shoulders, I entered with a bravado I didn't feel.

It was a house... of sorts. The wallpaper was thin and peeling, pieces of it shrivelled up like fossilised insects on the floor. From the hallway there was a sitting room, the chairs and settee stained. On the other side was a kitchen. The chequerboard floor and wooden bench top were covered in dust. There were footsteps in the grime. Someone had been here. Recently. A half-eaten sandwich on the table confirmed it.

Isgrad shook his head and continued down the hall. There was a staircase that led to the upper bedrooms and another that descended to....

I shivered, not wanting to think about what might be in the household's basement.

I followed Isgrad down the narrow stairwell. There was a door, which was open a crack. The whirr and buzz of a grind saw greeted my ears. Isgrad pushed the door open.

My legs swayed.

A young man with white-blond hair was at a workbench, cutting into a body with a saw-toothed blade powered by magic. He wore goggles and a white apron, though there wasn't much white left about it.

He looked up from his work. His lips stretched into an unsettling smile. "Brother. So, for once you actually came."

He took off his work gloves, the apron, and his goggles and stepped good-humouredly around his bench, crushing Isgrad in a hug. "It's been... how many years now? Four? Five?"

Willieth was older too. Late teens, possibly. His skin was ashen, his eyes cold and lacking emotion despite his smile.

Isgrad visibly swallowed. "I didn't want to believe what I read in your letter. Please, Willieth. Tell me it isn't true."

"What does this look like? Of course it's true."

Isgrad's gaze lingered on the workbench. "What are you doing?"

"Dissecting, if you must know. I'm interested in seeing how the body works. Apologies for the smell. I ran out of fresh bodies and had to steal one that was buried last week."

"Willieth. You're meant to be at the base."

"I fled."

"And killed six soldiers in the process. You're wanted for murder."

"Oh please." Willieth waved his concern away. "You hate the Haxsan Guard. I'm doing this for you. To strengthen your resistance."

Isgrad made an impatient sound. His high eyebrows arched even farther. "I don't have a resistance. The casters I meet with are intellectuals. We discuss politics. We debate our reflections on society. We converse over solutions to problems we're seeing."

"Which is against the law," Willieth pointed out. "Brother, you have an incredible gift. Why not use it? For instance"—he motioned to the corpse—"you could summon this wretched being's soul back this instant and learn all his secrets. This one was executed, his crimes unknown."

"Your point, exactly?"

Willieth burst out laughing. "The truth, brother. You could ask him what he did, or what he knew, to deserve the death sentence. You could discover information about the Council, the sovereigns, and the Haxsan Guard. How much knowledge the dead must have." His eyes lit up. "And it's all at your command."

"Such things are unnatural. Necromancers protect the dead. They don't manipulate them."

Willieth snorted. "And what do you know of necromancers? You've never used your magic. You prefer to hide it."

"It's dangerous."

A glimmer of rage flashed across Willieth's face. "All magic is dangerous. Why do you think the Council and the sovereigns keep us on such a tight leash? They're happy to use casters for their own ends, but when we try to use magic for ourselves, they turn us against each other. They crush us."

Isgrad's voice was a whip of fury. "What you're saying... it will get you in trouble. More than you're already in."

A knot of anxiety tethered in my lower back. The tension in the mortuary was more charged than an electrical storm. For a moment, I had actually sided with Isgrad, the concept startling. I had to remember who he became. Who he really was. I couldn't feel apathy for him, because soon he would become Morgomoth. The two representations warred in my mind.

A dangerous glint appeared in Isgrad's eyes. "Willieth, if you continue to do this, stealing bodies and cutting them up, it will cost you your life. You need to leave this place. Forget your experiments. Get a ship to Vukovar and start a new life. If the Haxsan Guard find you, you'll die."

He turned to walk away.

"Then perhaps you'll resurrect me." Willieth's smile was smug. "My death might be what you need to finally summon your necromancy."

Isgrad stilled. His face was flushed.

Willieth tilted his head, observing his brother. It was the same way a wolf assessed whether it could take on another animal. "You never asked me why I cut up the bodies."

The older sibling moved to the stairs. "You told me," he said over his shoulder. "You want to learn how the caster body works."

"Oh, it's not just that. I want to understand how necromancy could reanimate the dead. How far decomposed one has to be for necromancy not to work."

Willieth's smile sent goose bumps up my arms.

Maybe Isgrad couldn't bear to look at him, because he quickened his pace up the stairs.

"Goodbye, brother," Willieth called after him. "Next time we meet, I'll have answers for you. I swear on it."

He picked up the saw and continued slicing the corpse with macabre fascination.

The memory changed. The mortuary faded around me like watercolours sinking into a canvas, moulding into new scenery. This time I stood in a cave, one I recognised. Nothing had changed. Herbs, bones, and dried animal parts were arranged on a wooden bench in glass jars. Skulls of strange and misshapen creatures hung from the ceiling. A cauldron bubbled on a hearth, the fire the only source of light. Sitting in a chair beside it was the silver-thorned witch. She stirred the fire and gazed at the wall clock with an impatient huff. I wasn't sure if she was cooking up a potion or making her dinner.

Footsteps thundered from the stairwell. Isgrad appeared, snow covering his cloak. He panted, out of breath. He must have been running through the woods outside all night. When he brought the hood down and his face came into the light, I gasped. He looked older, maybe late twenties. The left side of his face was a mess of purple welts, the skin split across his cheekbone. His nose crooked, and the corner of his mouth had puffed up in a blood blister.

The witch eyed him shrewdly. "Not a second too late."

Isgrad drew in a sharp breath. His eyebrows were white, almost frozen. "You knew I was coming?"

"Of course. I see all things. I assume you're here to be healed."

"No. I want to know what you did to my brother all those years ago."

"Me?" She snorted. "You were the one who resurrected him."

"Under your guidance. Under your trickery." Isgrad's voice was ragged with emotion. "He's a… psycho. He has no conscience. He murders people to experiment on their bodies. He's convinced my circle of intellectuals to side with him, and when I refused to join, he did this to me." He pointed at his battered face. "Their hatred for the Council of the Founding Sovereigns and the Haxsan Guard… it frightens me. They're bloodthirsty. And it's all because of Willieth." He glared at her with raging eyes. "It's your fault. You did this to him."

The witch stood from her chair. "I did not. I gave you a gift. Necromancy was destined for you that evening. You were meant to take responsibility for the dead, to guard and protect souls and ferry them across to the next world, but instead you chose to renounce the magic. It lies dormant in you."

"I didn't want it."

"Stupid child," she spat. "There is a consequence for every action. I am the keeper of the balance. Necromancy was meant to be reborn into the world that night for virtuous purpose. It was meant to go to you, but when you renounced it, the magic refused. It went to the next living source it could find."

"What ramblings are you on about?"

"The magic went to Willieth. He is a necromancer more powerful than any born before him, and if we're not careful, he will destroy the world."

A buzzing formed in my ears as though I'd suddenly been swarmed upon by locusts.

Willieth is… Morgomoth.

I remembered Willieth's sweet, boyish face. The curious eyes. The little boy who idolised his big brother and desperately wanted to impress him. It was extraordinary that someone so innocent could be fashioned into something so dark.

Isgrad stared in blank astonishment. "No."

All the heavy lines in the witch's face hardened in disgust. "You brought him back from the dead, and then, by relinquishing the necromancy, it transferred to him, along with your anger, your hot temper, and your irritability. Didn't you think it was strange that the condition that ailed you as a child suddenly disappeared that night?"

Isgrad sagged to the ground and broke down crying. "Willieth is a fire wielder. He doesn't have necromancy."

Bitterness edged the witch's words. "That's what he wants you to believe. Your brother killed your mother by summoning a dead fire wielder, who he instructed to set the cabin alight. He's obsessed with death. He's fascinated by it. He wants to learn how to manipulate it. And he will succeed."

Isgrad stared at the fire. His eyes seemed to go vacant. "Have you seen my brother's future?"

"Yes. Willieth's still learning his craft. It will take him some years to fully understand his magic, but eventually he'll become the most powerful necromancer the world has known. He'll lead a resistance against the Council, the sovereigns, and the Haxsan Guard. They will call themselves the United League of Dissent, and they'll be responsible for the deaths of millions of casters and humans. At least, that's one future I have seen."

Isgrad looked up. "And the other?"

"The other leads to his death."

His expression tightened with pain. "How?"

"How he dies? It isn't clear."

"No. How do I kill him?" Isgrad was watching the witch now with hardened resolve. "Can it be done with a normal weapon? A cast-shooter? An athame-sabre?"

The witch's face twisted into an ironic smile. "You begged me to do anything to bring your brother back from the dead, and now you want him to die?"

"He's a monster."

"A caster weapon cannot kill your brother. He's already too powerful. Only another necromancer has a chance of defeating Willieth and returning him to the dead."

"I can do that."

"No you can't. The necromancy inside you is dormant."

"Then how do I change that? How do I accept it?"

"You can't. Once renounced, it will always remain dormant. But… perhaps there's a way for you to obtain more necromancy."

A strange chill crept up my spine.

Isgrad nodded. "Anything, please. I'm willing to do it."

I wondered if it was love and guilt that now made Isgrad so determined to see Willieth dead. Or if it was because he was genuinely afraid of what his brother was capable of.

The silver-thorned witch fixed her steel-like gaze on him. "There is a book that contains immense power. It's necromancy magic. The book is called the Bone Grimoire."

I pressed my lips together, trying to repress my mounting hope. Was this the reason I was seeing these memories in the first place? Was the Dark Divide… helping? No, I didn't think so. The Dark Divide was under Morgomoth's command thanks to yours truly, but there had been another strange part about the memories that didn't fit in with the puzzle—the ghost woman with the long brown hair. She'd been present in many of the memories, not part of it, just an onlooker like me. She'd smothered me with her hand in order for me to lose consciousness and wind up here.

Was she, in fact, helping?

There was a long silence in the cave. The only sound was the deep crackling of the fire.

The parts of Isgrad's face not covered in bruises went white with fear. "Tell me."

I drew closer, intent on hearing about the Bone Grimoire.

CHAPTER 36

I sgrad and the silver-thorned witch had settled in chairs around the fire. I sat on the woven rug, both afraid and desperate to hear what the witch had to say. She stoked the fire and added another log. The potion in the cauldron hissed in response to the rising flames.

The witch watched the wispy smoke rise. "Many centuries ago, necromancers were the keepers of the dead. There were huge temples dedicated to worshipping them. Casters would travel far and wide for a necromancer's service."

"And what was that?" Isgrad was staring at the cave floor.

"Necromancers performed burial rites. They conducted the funeral ceremonies and ensured that the soul crossed over to the otherworld. Ten of these necromancers became renowned for their abilities to raise and speak with the dead and were hired as the spiritual advisers to the sovereigns. These necromancers had their own court in the White, Black, and Red Palaces, providing advice and guidance they learnt from the dead. They became known as the Grand Masters. Of course, their success couldn't last. The sovereigns began to fear and grew jealous of how powerful the Grand Masters became. They instructed the Haxsan Guard to arrest all members. The Grand Masters fled, but the sovereigns weren't deterred. A warrant went out to capture all necromancers and seize their assets. Across every continent, necromancers were hunted down and burned at the stake. Loyal necromancers to the Haxsan Guard were turned on, murdered where they stood, or strangled where they slept. These necromancers didn't have the power your brother does. They were helpless to stop it. It was a violent, bloody time in caster history."

Isgrad shifted his feet and leant forward in his chair. "I haven't heard any of this before."

"No, you wouldn't have. It isn't something the Council or the sovereigns wish people to know, so it's been eradicated from the history texts."

"What happened to them then? The Grand Masters?"

The witch shook her head with sad disappointment. "They escaped to the Isla Necropolis. It isn't known how, but, fearing for their lives, they renounced their magic."

"They did what I did?" Isgrad gave an ironic snort.

"Not exactly. The Grand Masters were afraid necromancy would be eradicated entirely. If that happened, it would change the balance, which would have devastating consequences for all magic. The Grand Masters decided that to save necromancy, they would need to transfer their magic and store that power in an object so future generations one day may be able to resurrect it. Each Grand Master cut a bone from their body. They melted the bones down with stagma fire, creating a book."

Isgrad gripped the armrest on his chair. "The Bone Grimoire."

"Yes. They wrote their spells in the book and hid the grimoire in the dead city. They left clues so that, in time, someone might find the book and learn the magic again, but it proved fruitless."

"Why?"

The witch scrunched her face, as though there was a bad smell beneath her nose. "When the Grand Masters surrendered, or were captured—it isn't clear what happened—they were powerless. The sovereigns did not grant them clemency, and the Grand Masters were burned at the stake. Necromancers continued to be hunted for centuries. If you were born a necromancer, you did not reveal it. Eventually, the magic died out."

"So, the book was lost?"

"The Bone Grimoire is somewhere in the Isla Necropolis. It takes a key to open the doors to that city—which, incidentally, is lost too. Another preventive measure set by the Grand Masters."

Isgrad's brown eyebrows shone against the fire's ray. "How do you know this isn't just some sort of fable?"

"I don't."

"Then how does it help us?" He ground his teeth together, his agitation making him shake. "We can't rely on a story."

The witch surveyed Isgrad with a stare that could shatter glass. "The Grand Masters were real. Therefore, it's likely the Bone Grimoire is real. The book contains their combined necromancy. It can be transferred. To you," she added with hard resolve.

"That's impossible. My powers are dormant."

"But it is still inside you. The grimoire would recognise that. All you would have to do is enact the spell, and you would receive the Grand Masters' magic. You would be powerful enough to destroy your brother."

Isgrad stared at the witch for an absurdly long time. Then he laughed. It was the dry, humourless kind. "He'd kill me before I could find any clues. I defied Willieth tonight. I refused to join his United League of Dissent. I barely escaped with my life."

The witch stood, the veins in her neck strained. "Then join his forces. Pretend you're on his side. Keep him close. Learn his plans. Be a spy and, in the process, learn everything you can about the Bone Grimoire. Find the book. Take its power. Return your brother to the grave."

"I don't think it's that simple."

"And that's your reason not to do it? Necromancers are important for restoring the magic balance. Many of them died because the Council and the sovereigns spun a story to make people afraid of what they were. Your brother is about to prove that necromancers are something to be feared. Casters will unite with him. They will fight against the Council of Founding Sovereigns and the Haxsan Guard. It will be innocents who lose." She eyed him sternly. "Are you willing to let that happen?"

Isgrad held his head in his hands. "No, I'm not." He made a deflated sound. "How do I find the book?"

"Good boy." The witch drew her chair closer and sat down. "We start by—"

"Miss, wake up."

Someone was shaking me.

No.

The memory was fading. Isgrad and the silver-thorned witch were slipping into darkness. I reached out for them, trying to hold on to the memory, but I was being ripped away.

"Miss, please. Someone, please help. I think she's having a seizure."

I woke up gasping.

One of Toshiko's ladies-in-waiting was staring at me with large eyes. "Oh, thank providence. Miss, you were having a fit or something. I could hear you from the hall thrashing about and crying."

You fool, I wanted to shout, but my voice felt like it had been blocked by something solid.

I'd been so close to hearing an answer. I was certain the witch would have told Isgrad where to start searching for clues, how to find the door to the Isla Necropolis, and maybe even how to absorb the magic from the book. Devastation settled deep in my stomach.

A man I assumed was a healer entered the chamber. Behind him was Toshiko. She stood in the doorway, watching me with hooded eyes.

Did she know what her sovereign ancestors had done? Did she understand what the Bone Grimoire really was?

I wasn't sure if I wanted to find out.

I'D BARELY CLOSED my eyes when I heard the click of a lock. A pair of maids entered my chamber. One ripped the lightweight blanket from my bed, exposing me to the morning heat, while the other tossed the drapes back, welcoming the desert sun. I winced. After the dream last night, I'd been assessed by the healer. Once I'd been given the all clear, he'd instructed me to rest. I'd only been too happy to oblige, keen to see the rest of the memory, but no dreams had visited my sleep.

I groaned, burying my head in my pillow. "Can you please close the curtains?"

"Leave us," a voice demanded.

The maids scampered out into the hallway.

Toshiko glided into the chamber. She sat at my small dining table, her spine and shoulders straight, as though she were sitting on her throne. She was wearing a dark-purple-and-green kimono, tied with a gold obi belt, the loose flowing sleeves decorated with embroidered roses.

Three young servant girls slipped into the chamber with trays. They set several dishes on the table, bowed politely to the sovereign, and left.

Toshiko watched me with a simpering smile. "Come. Have breakfast."

Breakfast? With her? In my chamber?

Invite yourself, why don't you?

I slid to the edge of the bed and made my way to the small dining table. There was grilled fish wrapped in a large leaf I didn't know the name of, a bowl of rice, something that appeared to be scrambled egg rolls, and a heavy-looking teapot with matching cups.

I sat down, suspicious of her motives. Sovereigns did not breakfast with commoners. "That's an interesting tea set."

It was black with peonies painted in a floral design.

She bowed her head. "It has belonged in my family for decades, perhaps centuries, and has been used to honour esteemed guests."

"Well, I'm not an *esteemed guest*. I'm a prisoner. All of this"—I waved to the aesthetically organised breakfast—"is over the top."

Especially considering I was used to skipping meals, eating on the run, hunting for food, or outright starving.

The kindness in Toshiko's eyes dimmed. "This is a traditional breakfast. I follow tradition. This is the food of my ancestors."

I could almost feel her irritation crawling toward me from across the table.

"I'm sorry. I didn't mean to cause offence. Thank you for sharing it with me." I took up one of the egg rolls, not entirely sure how I was meant to eat it. It came with a dipping sauce and something that resembled mashed-up horseradish. It was spicy and too tangy for my tastes. "Speaking of ancestors, how long has your family been part of the sovereigns?"

Becoming a sovereign was a hereditary role, but on occasion, the heir could abdicate. If that happened, the Council voted a new member into the position of sovereign, often by backstabbing, betraying, or destroying others' reputations in an endeavour to promote themselves for the role. An election had never happened in my lifetime. I didn't think one had occurred in Macaslan's or Macha's lifetime either.

Toshiko toyed with the gold bangle around her wrist. "My father was a sovereign. And my grandmother before him. And her mother before that. House of Okano have been rulers for five centuries."

"You must have quite the family tree."

The history was probably tapestried somewhere in the palace.

Toshiko nodded, the only answer she offered.

"Where are you from?" I persevered. "I've never met anyone with your traditions before."

Her gold eyes flicked up. Her painted face made her appear as cold and hard as a statue. "After the change, the history of my ancestors' homeland was lost. All I know is it was an island, but its name has been forgotten. It is probably now at the bottom of the sea, like so many other lands before the change. House of Okano was one of the few to survive, or so the legend says."

She changed the subject by pouring the tea. "Did you sleep well?"

I took a sip. It was bitter. "I did manage to fall asleep again, thank you."

I wasn't sure what game we were playing, or why we were being so polite.

Her dainty fingers picked up one of the egg rolls. She took a small bite and nibbled, her eyes never leaving mine. "That was a strange attack you suffered last night. Has that happened before?"

I'd had many unusual and warped experiences in my sleep, but I wasn't going to share that with her. "First time."

"Curious." She stirred her tea with a silver spoon. "The healer said it was not a seizure but something else. Astral projection of some kind."

I swallowed more tea, giving myself a moment to collect a response. "It's all a blur. I can't remember. Sorry."

Her smile was fake. "Well, at least you are okay. After all, that is all that matters." Her eyebrows narrowed ever so slightly, hinting that my answer was not the one she sought.

Darius and Macaslan might have become chummy with Toshiko and the sovereigns, but I didn't trust any of them. Two days ago, we were traitors and the most wanted casters in the world. Did they really think I was stupid enough to believe we had all become best friends overnight?

Toshiko raised her head regally. "I have been meaning to ask you about your childhood. Darius has informed me that you have no recollection of it."

So she is snooping.

I wiped my mouth on a napkin. "I remember as far back as Brendlash Orphanage. I was ten when I arrived there."

"You do not remember your parents?"

I crossed my arms, not caring how unseemly it appeared. "Amnesia means no memory."

Why is she so interested in my past?

Her expression held a tight smile. "Darius warned me about your sharp tongue."

Pity Darius didn't warn you about my hatred for small talk.

She sipped her tea. "Rena will be here shortly to take you to the Forbidden Library."

"Who's Rena?"

My suspicion was flaring.

"She is the palace librarian. She is keen to meet you. The Forbidden Library is off-limits to everyone in the palace. This is an excellent opportunity for her to quench her curiosity."

"Are you joining us?"

"No. I am required at court."

Well, at least that's one good thing.

I ran my fingers along the smooth curve of the table. "I would like to see my friends before my visit to the library, please."

She looked up with a cheerfulness that didn't fit the situation. "That will not be possible."

"Why not? They're in the palace's prison. It wouldn't take me long to see them."

"The other sovereigns will not permit it. You are to focus on your study in the Forbidden Library."

"Will Captain Arden be joining Rena and me?"

"No."

"No," I repeated. "Why not? You let him join the festivity last evening."

Disdain flashed across her gold eyes for a second. "Captain Arden joined the celebration last night to assure the court that you and he are united in our efforts to destroy Morgomoth. He will remain in his chamber until your journey to the Isla Necropolis."

"I need his help."

Actually, what I needed was a chance to tell Jad about the memory. I knew with certainty now that Morgomoth wanted to absorb the Grand Masters' powers. Only then would he be able to merge the Larthalgule and Neathror blades into the ultimate weapon.

What troubled me was how Morgomoth had come about this knowledge.

What happened to Isgrad?

A young woman with bushy brown hair and large spectacles appeared at the door. An assembly of guards waited behind her. I counted six, but judging by the long shadows in the hallway, there were more.

"Ah, Rena. Please do come in." Toshiko waved the librarian forward. "This is Zaya Wayward, the sovereigns' necromancer."

I flinched, still not used to the term *necromancer* being spoken so liberally. I recalled Darius's words of caution from last evening. *"The sovereigns are desperate to show they have a strategy to overturn Morgomoth and destroy the ULD for good. You need to play the part. You need to appear as terrifying in these people's minds as Morgomoth is. It'll give them confidence that you can defeat him."*

Darius never did tell me if I or my friends would be granted clemency after Morgomoth's defeat. *If* I defeated him.

I started to think all of this was one big witch hunt.

CHAPTER 37

The Forbidden Library had been built into the palace's catacombs. Rena led me through the rows of books, two guards behind me at all times, holding torches to light our way. It was evident no one had been down here for a long time. Dead rats littered the floor. Spiderwebs lined the shelves, and dust mites danced in the muted torchlight wherever we turned.

I was amazed the library had a card catalogue.

"It should be just down here." Rena's bushy hair bounced behind her as she sped ahead.

We need a map.

The Forbidden Library was a city of papyrus scrolls, clay tablets, and leather-bound books. Some volumes were permanently shut with locks made of iron. There was no sign of a key to open them. Some books were so old that the gold script on their spines was unreadable. It was incredible how many confiscated texts there were in the catacomb. Many books had been burned throughout history. I was looking at the only surviving copies. This was caster history, chained away. Forgotten. Never to be seen unless it was to service the sovereigns.

"Here." Rena ran a hand across a set of dusty volumes. "This is everything on necromancy."

I gawped at her. There had to be over a hundred books in this section. "Can't you search specifically for the Bone Grimoire?"

"Oh no. The card catalogue is organised by banned magic types, not by subject. Unfortunately, this collection hasn't been digitised, which means searching the traditional way. Nose in book." She let out a squeal of delight.

"You have got to be kidding."

It was a good thing I already knew a great deal about the Bone Grimoire from Isgrad's memory. What I really needed to learn was how to find the entry into the Isla Necropolis. It was no good having a key if you couldn't find the front door.

Rena frowned. "Don't you like books?"

"I like books when they're not held prisoners."

"Oh, yes, I understand. In any other circumstance, I'd be outraged, but these books are too dangerous for the public."

"Says who?"

"The sovereigns."

"And you believe everything the sovereigns tell you."

"Of course." Rena didn't look like she understood why I was being testy. "The sovereigns are wise and must be respected. Books are precious, but the information in these volumes instructs the most abominable of magic practises."

She retreated a step, as though just realising I was part of that detestable magic.

I took up a book. "Fine. Let's start."

Rena would be lucky if I didn't hit her over the head with one of the hefty tomes.

So much for going to the Isla Necropolis in three days' time. Three days turned into a week. A week turned into two. The sovereigns said learning everything there was to know about the Bone Grimoire was of the greatest urgency, yet no one would explain to me why things had taken such a slow turn.

They were stalling. But why?

My days consisted of studying in the library, most of the books so badly damaged they couldn't be read, or they were written in such an ancient language that there was no hope of interpreting the words. In the evenings, I was locked away in my private chamber. The only people I saw were Rena, the guards, and the occasional maid who brought my meals. They never answered me when I inquired about Jad or the others. Toshiko never visited. Darius and Macaslan never visited. Even the dreams had abandoned me.

On the evening that marked my two-week anniversary at the palace, I stared at the ceiling in my chamber, sleep elusive.

Aren't they worried Morgomoth will attack?

Jad had said it took time to organise a strategic ambush, but Morgomoth was clever. His forces had destroyed the White Palace. He could do it again. I was fast beginning to understand that he was capable of conquering every province and Free Zone. He was just biding his time, waiting for the opportune moment to strike. The sovereigns surely knew that.

There's a game being played here.

At a little past dawn, my door was unlocked, and two maids entered. One lady carried a tray of food, which she neatly set on the table. The other dropped a set of folded clothes on my bed.

"It's a little early, isn't it?" I was annoyed at being disturbed, even though I was itching to get out of the chamber.

"I am to help you dress, Miss Wayward. You are to eat your breakfast, all of it, and then the captain of the guard will arrive to escort you to the palace's landing pad."

"Landing pad?"

Normally I spent my days in the Forbidden Library, reading and breathing in dust.

The maid kept her face carefully expressionless. "Please, miss. I need to dress you. The captain will not be pleased if he has to wait. We are on a tight schedule."

The clothes turned out to be a pair of black trousers, a grey undershirt, and an insulated jacket. There was also a pair of lightweight boots.

"Am I going hiking?"

The maid didn't answer my sly attempt at humour.

I refused her help dressing—who needed someone to dress them? —and disappeared behind the screen to change. Looking at my appearance in the mirror, I felt more myself in these clothes. They weren't to the Haxsan Guard military standard, but they were comfortable compared to the dressy garments I'd been forced to wear, which had been ridiculous because I saw no one but Rena and the guards.

A pinch of anxiety squeezed me.

It's today.

They had kept me in the dark for so long, but I knew instinctively that they were sending me to the Isla Necropolis. I had discovered no new information from the Forbidden Library. The sovereigns had to know that. Rena would have reported it. So why was this happening now? What had been the real motivation behind the two-week delay?

"Miss, please." The maid's head popped around the screen. "You need to eat breakfast."

Breakfast turned out to be scrambled eggs with bacon and porridge with blueberry compote, accompanied by juice and tea. All foods high in protein to give me energy. I'd been eating like a queen since I'd been in the palace and had enjoyed all my meals, but today everything tasted bland. I didn't feel ready for this. Instead of reading books and collecting dust on my fingers for the last two weeks, I should have been training.

After breakfast, the captain of the guard appeared. He was a caster with a square jaw and a no-nonsense façade. I was swept out of the chamber and down various hallways. No one had given me a proper tour of the Black Palace. It was an enormous building and made Tarahik look like a kid's park in comparison.

I probed the captain, trying to get answers, but he was regrettably silent. We came to a solid obsidian door, which was drawn open by magic, and stepped out to the landing pad. Hot wind whipped at my face, fine grains of sand scraping my cheeks. The pad jutted out precariously from the tower, providing stunning views of Muiren and the coastline.

The landing pad was an incredible architectural feat, but it paled in my eyes when I saw the carrier-hornet that waited. The planes in the Haxsan Guard forces had been built like airborne tanks. They were scratched, dented, and spoiled by battles, but this one was sleek and impermeable, which just made me more panicky about the task at hand.

Darius and Macaslan stood in front of a platoon of soldiers.

If the Haxsan Guard are coming with me, then that means we must be facing hostile forces.

Has Morgomoth made his move?

Several seconds passed before I realised I'd stopped breathing. My hands turned clammy.

It'll be okay. Jad is coming with you.

But out of all the faces I saw, his was painfully absent.

I headed toward Darius and Macaslan. I wasn't afraid, but I tasted my breakfast coming back up. "A little bit more warning would have been nice."

The senator took my arm, steering me closer to him and the commander. His voice was deliberately low. "Zaya, find the Bone Grimoire. Bring it back to the palace. Don't do anything else. If General Kravis orders you to give him the book, don't."

I drew in a frazzled breath. "General Kravis. He's not coming with me, is he?"

Something in Macaslan's expression changed. I was used to her scathing looks and her scorn, but never had I seen her watch me with such... pity.

I stared at the pair of them. "What aren't you telling me? Where's Jad?"

Neither answered.

The captain of the guard appeared. This time he led me away with more force than was necessary.

"Where are my friends?" I shouted over my shoulder, demanding Darius and Macaslan answer. "I want to see Jad and the others first. Where are they?"

"Do not worry," a dispassionate voice answered.

Toshiko stood by the carrier-hornet's boarding ramp, looking every bit the queen from an ancient time. "Your friends are going with you."

I had no time to respond. That, or I'd simply lost my voice.

Going with me?

While I was numb from shock, the captain of the guard led me inside the hornet.

Sucking in a deep pull of air, I stared at the soldiers seated in the cabin, unnerved by how many of them there were. Streaks of hair were plastered to my face. I was sweating.

"My friends?" I asked.

The captain of the guard swept me down the aisle and pointed to a line of seats where Talina, Marek, and Annaka were settled uncomfortably, shoulders jammed against each other, their wrists and ankles chained. I was relieved to see they looked healthy. No bruises or weight loss, but the magic binds over their mouths were... concerning. Their eyes communicated a hint of panic as I was shoved past. I knew why the sovereigns had ordered them on board—to make sure I behaved. If I didn't, it would be Talina, Marek, and Annaka who suffered the consequences.

"Sit here."

I was shoved into a chair at the back of the cabin, right next to... Jad. A bittersweet ache flared in my chest.

He turned to me, exasperation clear in the lines of his shoulders. His dark eyes assessed me for injuries.

"I'm fine," I lied.

"You don't look fine."

Before I could reply, the guard strapped a pair of heavy-duty manacles around my wrists. He grunted and left.

Jad had a similar pair secured around his own wrists. I was taken back to the time when we first met. Jad had been the one to retrieve me from the Gosheniene internment camp and deliver me to Tarahik. I had been uncouth the entire journey and probably deserved to be chained up. It felt like an age had passed since then, yet here we both were, only now Jad wasn't in the pilot seat.

I dabbed my tongue against my lip. Soldiers stole quick glances at us over their seats. Some outright glared at me. It seemed not everyone believed in the sovereigns' necromancer.

I tilted my head closer to Jad. "Do you understand anything that's happening?"

There was a hard edge to his voice. "I've been confined to a chamber for the past two weeks, only allowed out to exercise in the early morning and at noon, and surrounded by no less than ten guards. Something's happened. You can sense the fear in the soldiers."

He was right. I felt it the moment I'd stepped into the carrier-hornet. The energy in the cabin was restless. I recognised it as war anxiety: the pent-up energy, the adrenaline, the fear that your life might be over in an hour, a minute, the next second. Tension coursed through the entire cabin like electricity.

Yes, we're definitely expecting to encounter hostile forces.

I flexed my hands, trying to calm the anxious tingling in my fingers. "I'm surprised they allowed you to join."

The corner of Jad's lips lifted. "I have the key, remember? The key chooses who can have it."

No wonder we're sitting together. We're the sovereigns' most important assets.

My jaw quivered a fraction. "You'll have to tell me how you found the key."

"Another time." Jad's focus was directed to the front. General Kravis had risen to address his soldiers.

I swallowed, tasting only sticky froth in my mouth.

We were updated on the mission and task at hand. The soldiers were to remain outside the dead city, guarding the gates, while Kravis, Jad, and I, plus a small team, went inside. The general never explained what would happen once we entered the dead city. I guessed that would remain a mystery until we arrived, which would take a little over two hours. Kravis assured the platoon that there would be no real danger of attack.

Jad kept his voice low so only I could hear. "A lie. Everyone is heavily armed."

Despite my handcuffs, I grabbed Jad's hand, cradling it in my own. His fingers were warm and calloused from years of training and battle. He was my only comfort at that moment. "Do you trust Darius and Macaslan?"

Because I'm not sure if I do anymore.

His dark eyes were unreadable, and I wondered what thoughts

were transpiring in his mind. "I believe they're making the best out of a situation beyond their control."

"You would tell me if you knew what they were up to, right?"

Because I was certain Darius was hatching a new plan.

"Of course."

I settled back in my chair. At least I still had Jad on my side.

His voice was soft at my ear. "Darius did manage to get a message through to me. You're not going to like this. Macha will be sentenced for obeahcraft. Her punishment is yet to be decided. Clorenzo has been arrested and detained. His children are now in an orphanage just outside Muiren."

Rage made my blood fizz "But that's…."

I didn't have words for how unreasonably cruel that was.

"Get the book," Jad advised me before I could open my big mouth and shout something obscene. "If you have the Bone Grimoire, you can use it as a bargaining chip. You can request Macha's and Clorenzo's freedom, as well as everyone else's."

"That's what I plan to do, but there's something I need to do with the grimoire first." I hesitated, not sure how to start the rest of what needed to be said.

Jad's dark hair fell across his forehead. "What aren't you telling me?"

I bit my lip. I both loved and hated that he could read my inner thoughts so clearly. "I know what the Bone Grimoire is."

I explained Isgrad's memory, and how I was witnessing fragments through dreams.

"I just need to know how to absorb the Grand Masters' magic," I confessed, "and then I might be strong enough to actually defeat Morgomoth, because that's what's coming next."

Jad's eyes were shining. "No one else knows?"

I shook my head.

"Then you need to absorb the book's magic in the Isla Necropolis. If you're more powerful than the sovereigns, more powerful than Morgomoth, they'll have no choice but to answer your demands." He was silent for a moment. I wondered if he was considering a plan. "Once we're in the dead city, we need to find a way to ditch Kravis and his team."

"How?"

"I don't know yet. No one knows what the Isla Necropolis looks like or what's inside. We'll have to devise a strategy on the spot."

I closed my eyes, wanting to slap myself. "I have been so stupid. All that time in the library, I should have been trying to find information about the Isla Necropolis."

"It's too late now. The best thing you can do is go to sleep and try to see the next part of that memory."

"It doesn't work that way." I glared up at the ceiling, hating all my troubles. "The memories come to me when they please."

"Is Isgrad dead?"

The question startled me.

Jad's eyes pinned me in place. "If you're seeing his memories, do you think it's because he's dead? Are you summoning these recollections somehow?"

"Unconsciously?"

He nodded.

"I suppose it's possible."

It was something I'd never considered. I didn't know what the limits of my necromancy were. I had thought it was the Dark Divide. But what if it was me? Or the ghost woman with the long brown hair?

"Why don't you try it?" Jad advised. "Go to sleep, because in two hours, we'll arrive at the Isla Necropolis."

I squeezed his hand, lacing my fingers with his. "We're in this together, right?"

"Always." He pressed his lips against mine, the gentlest of touches.

The cabin shook as the carrier-hornet lifted off the landing pad. Every bump and jolt juddered through me acutely, sending uneasy waves through my gut. I could just make out the Black Palace and Muiren through the window, fast becoming a distant dot as the hornet ascended. We shot across the sky, winds tearing and rocking the vessel, enough to leave me nauseated. Silence stretched through the cabin.

I shut my eyes, ready to dream.

CHAPTER 38

I tried following Jad's advice, but my mind wouldn't drift off. I was too wired up. Too nervous. Too afraid. Time itself seemed to slow down, the two hours becoming the longest in my life. I fidgeted, shifted in my seat, stretched my legs more times than I could count. The captain of the guard shot me a nasty look when I accidentally— all right, purposely—lodged my knee into the back of his seat. I was surprised Jad was able to tolerate all my wriggling.

He'd been deep in thought, probably imagining various scenarios that could occur and thinking up strategic ways to work them in our favour. He looked out the window at the blue sky beyond. "We're coming in to land."

"How do you know?"

At this height, we were above the clouds. I couldn't see anything but sky.

"I can feel it in the hornet."

A moment later, the gentle purr of the engines grew into a myriad of whirs and screeches as the landing gear was deployed. We dipped lower into the clouds, then hurtled over specks of what appeared to be volcanic rock. The hornet landed with a tremble, as though it, too, were afraid of this new land.

The soldiers disembarked. Jad and I remained in our seats. I arched my neck to see if Talina, Marek, and Annaka were still on board. Their seats were regrettably empty. I would much have preferred they remained safe on the plane.

Twenty minutes must have passed before Jad and I were finally led out of the carrier-hornet by two soldiers. We'd landed on a mesa, the flat rock stretching far and bordered by steep escarpments. I gaped at the alien landscape. It was a world of soaring pinnacles, rugged canyons, and massive rock fins. To my amazement, the sand dunes moved like waves in the ocean, cresting against rocks in a powerful swell.

I sputtered a disbelieving laugh. "What is this?"

Jad squinted against the hot sunshine. "Aureus Oceanus. Otherwise known as the Golden Ocean."

"*This* is the Golden Ocean? The place you and Marek were going to try and trek on your own?"

That fast started to look like a joke.

"It's sand," I announced dumbly.

Before Jad could answer, General Kravis appeared. His hooded eyebrows alerted me that something was amiss before he grabbed Jad by the shoulder in a rage. "Your senator gave us the wrong directions. There's nothing here. This is just one huge barren rock. Where is the city?"

Jad's eyes coloured with red fire. "Darius gave you the correct coordinates. It's not my problem if you and your soldiers can't read them."

His hands bound, Jad couldn't strike the general, but that didn't stop him from shoving Kravis with his elbow. He let out a whimper, horrified by Jad's lycanthor strength. General Kravis toppled to the ground, biting his lip and howling. His arm didn't look right in his sleeve, and when he started screaming, I realised why. His shoulder was dislocated.

He shouted an order at his platoon, and in less than five seconds, we were surrounded by soldiers, their cast-shooters aimed at our chests. In the hot sun, the weapons shone with well-oiled care.

Jad was trembling beside me, and I sensed he wanted to take on every soldier and rip them apart. I didn't doubt that he could.

"Stop," I demanded. "The city is here."

Somewhere.

"Where?" General Kravis rose to his feet, his face scrunched in ugly pain. He brushed sand off his dark uniform, cringing whenever he moved his shoulder.

"Remove the handcuffs and maybe I can find out. Captain Arden's too."

"The handcuffs remain."

I rolled my eyes to the sky. "And what exactly do you think we'll do without them? We can't run away."

Not unless I wanted to take a sand bath. Somehow, I suspected falling into the Golden Ocean would be like slipping into quicksand.

Kravis's face was lined with tiredness, but his eyes were bright and mean. He jerked his chin at Jad. "That boy's got unnatural strength. The handcuffs stay. So do yours." He levelled his heated gaze on the soldiers. "Everyone on the hornet. This is a failed mission."

"Wait," I cried. "The Bone Grimoire was hidden for a reason. It makes sense that the dead city would be concealed too. It's here. I just need to...."

"Need to what?" Kravis mocked in his deep, irritating voice.

Maybe I should let Jad dislocate the other shoulder.

I swept the satisfying thought aside. "I can find the city. I know I can. I need to tune in to my necromancy."

"Tune in?" The general looked at me like I was speaking a foreign language.

I sighed heavily. "I need to open my mind to the dead."

There was a collective inhale of horror from the soldiers.

The general gave a short, grisly laugh. "Melshor. Gamar." Two soldiers swept forward to his side. Kravis's eyes never left mine. "The moment she does or says something dangerous, you have permission to shoot her in the foot."

My jaw dropped, but the only thing I could achieve was an offended scowl.

"You have an hour to find the city," Kravis told me. "You do anything to try and escape, anything to hurt my soldiers, and Captain Arden and your friends pay the price. Understand?"

I knew "pay the price" meant a cast-shooter bullet in the head. "Understood."

About a dozen soldiers had settled beneath a large outcrop of rock next to the mesa's edge, savouring the shade from the sun. Among them were Talina, Marek, and Annaka. They were on their knees, hoods over their heads. A trio of soldiers forced Jad to sit among them. The guards kept their weapons levelled on him. Jad was capable of tearing them all apart with his bare hands, but against heavy-duty restraints and three cast-shooters, even he probably knew it was better not to test those odds.

"What are you staring at?" Kravis spat at me. "Find the city."

Filled with terror at what the consequences might be if I didn't succeed, I turned and faced the desert.

Melshor and Gamar never let me out of their sight as I wandered around the large, flat mesa rock, which was practically an island surrounded by the Golden Ocean. The one I thought was called Gamar had gone so red in the face, I would be surprised if he could shoot anything. Melshor hid behind his heavy hood.

The pair split apart, walking in a broad circle around me as I closed my eyes, opening my mind to the dead. I called out to any spirits who might be bound here, but there was never an answer. I tried various locations around the mesa, but there wasn't a cold spot present to indicate a wraith was here.

Darius wouldn't lie about the location, would he?

This isn't some sort of ploy?

The sun was a white-hot orb that rose too fast in the sky. The odds of finding a city that had been lost for centuries in one hour were stacked against me. Lifeless, dry earth stretched as far as I could see. There was no life out here. There was nothing dead out here either.

I sat down in defeat. I'd been concentrating so hard that a dull throb had started at the back of my skull.

"Zaya."

Melshor crouched beside me. He raised his head slightly, his face apparent beneath the hood.

My chest hitched. "Bronislav?"

He lifted a finger to his lips, urging me to be quiet, and waited until Gamar was a safe distance away before he continued. He cracked a smile. "You didn't think Darius would leave you in the lurch, did you?"

"I did, actually." After everything that had happened in the past two weeks, I hadn't spared a thought for my poor cellmate from the *Vanquisher*—who, it turned out, wasn't poorly in the slightest. "How are you here?"

"I got the real Melshor drunk last night. He's now sleeping off a hangover in the palace's cellars. They won't find him for a long time." Bronislav beamed, proud of himself.

I glanced over my shoulder, hoping Kravis or the other soldiers weren't suspicious of our conversation, because the real Melshor would probably never talk to someone like me, but they weren't looking. Still, I felt safer whispering. "I thought you were headed for a detention camp."

Bronislav shrugged. "I was, but I was kept in the palace prison before my transfer. Darius found me there. He made me an offer to help."

"What kind of offer?"

Now I was really curious. And hopeful.

Bronislav squeezed his eyes shut against the desert's white brilliance. "He told me to request a word with the general and swear my allegiance to him. It worked. As far as Kravis is aware, I'm a dutiful Haxsan Guard soldier." He lifted his hand, which was heavily bandaged. The dirt and dust made the dressing look like ancient mummy wrappings. "I had to cut my mark of oath from my palm afterward. It hurt like... well, you know what I mean. But it was worth it."

I cringed. The mental image made me squeamish.

His chuckle was dry. "I serve Darius and Macaslan now. I'm helping you. I'm here to make sure you remain safe. Darius's orders."

He dug into his pocket and handed me a note.

I unfolded it and recognised the senator's neat handwriting.

"The sun works with the moon. Don't you hate it when what you're looking for is in the most obvious place? Oh, how the sun shines, hiding what is in plain sight."

I scrunched the paper, not in the mood for poetry.

Thank you, Darius. Your words of wisdom are useless.

But were they?

I unfolded the note, reading it again.

Moon. Obvious place. Sun shines. Plain sight.

I stood, my gaze arcing wide around the mesa.

It had been so bright that I'd kept my eyes screwed shut most of the time, trying to block the discomfort. My skin felt like it was melting in the hot sun, but I searched the sky, hoping it might have an answer. A sphere of white caught my attention. It was the moon, dull compared to the wonderful luminance she cast at night.

The moon.

A memory stirred. I recalled what Darius had said on the *Velorosa*. *"Legend says that the Isla Necropolis only appears during the course of a full moon. If that's true, then that means it's only accessible for three days."*

That's why the mission had been delayed.

I forced my lids not to squint, my eyes watering in complaint. The mirage ahead, which had appeared deceptively like reflections of water, became clearer. Hot air shimmered in front of it, moving across the mesa as though it were steam, blurring everything close to the ground.

No. Not steam.

The more I stared, the more I realised what it was. A glamour. Old and ancient, hidden from caster eyes, but incapable of hiding against the sun's strong glare. Beyond the glamour was a jagged outline, which I had no doubt was a cluster of buildings.

I broke my gaze and turned to the others. "It's there."

I pointed ahead, unable to contain my excitement.

General Kravis and his platoon trudged across the flat, rock-strewn ground, dust rising from their boots. They brought Jad with them, the barrel of a cast-shooter pinned to his back. I wasn't sure if it was regrettable or a mercy that they left Talina, Marek, and Annaka behind with a team of soldiers.

Kravis glared at the distance ahead. Someone had pushed his shoulder back into place. I hoped it was painful. "I don't see anything," he growled.

"Don't squint," I instructed. "Just look. It'll hurt at first, but if you persist, you'll see it."

Gasps of wonderment filtered through the platoon.

The general raised his eyebrows, not impressed. "How far do you think that is?"

One of his men lifted a mapographic and scanned the distance. "Just over two kilometres, sir."

Kravis's gaze travelled back to the carrier-hornet. He pressed his lips together, indecision apparent across his sweaty face.

I guessed what he was thinking. Carrier-hornets were designed for long-haul flights. A two-kilometre journey would eat up more fuel and magic than was necessary. It would hardly be worth starting up the engine.

"We walk," he announced.

We marched forward with heavy steps, dust and sand sticking to my clammy skin. It was hard work trying to keep the Isla Necropolis in sight while also fending off wind and sand from my eyes. I silently cursed that the dead city was here, of all places.

We must have walked for ten minutes when shadow settled across the mesa. I tilted my head to the sky, panicked that we'd lose sight of the city if a cloud coasted over the sun.

I shivered, something I didn't think was possible in the sweltering heat.

It wasn't clouds that settled across the sun like a black fog.

A galactic storm was on the horizon.

CHAPTER 39

At least, the storm had been on the horizon a moment ago. It was closer now, charging forward in a wall of thunder, lightning, and fire, hellbent on destroying everything in its path. It reminded me of a volcanic ash cloud. Arrows of hot fire scorched the mesa, leaving terrible fissures through the flat rock.

This was no normal galactic storm. This was…

Morgomoth.

He's here.

Kravis's face was a mask of horrified surprise, the gleaming sweat on his cheeks reflecting the fierce explosions in the storm. His shout was barely audible over the thunder and lightning. "Everyone to the hornet."

We ran back in the direction we came, pelted with sand, grit, and rock. There was no way we could reach the hornet in time. No way we could ever fly. The storm expanded out in all directions, forming around the mesa and casting us in a secure dome. The sun was entirely eclipsed now. There was no light except for the fire and jagged streaks of lightning.

The ground bucked and lurched. I toppled onto the hard earth, grazing my palms. The entire mesa was rumbling like a hornet about to take flight. It rattled my skull and shook all my bones until even my joints felt like they'd come loose.

Someone yanked me onto my feet.

Jad.

The beautiful dark of his eyes had been replaced by a bloodthirsty red, his hands no longer chained. He must have summoned enough lycanthor strength to break the manacles apart, but there wasn't time to ponder it, because at the moment, chak-lorks emerged from the storm. Their horrible screeches amplified across every stone, sending shivers of terror over my skin. They appeared from the left and then the right, bodies burnt and crisp, animated by necromancy. Fire danced through their exposed veins.

Forming into a second line behind the creatures were dissent rebels. I would have loved to know how they travelled through the galactic storm, but all I could focus on were their ruthless battle cries. They charged forward with their weapons. Hex-grenades erupted, throwing up massive amounts of charred earth. The mesa had become a battlefield, the desert smelling of ash, blood, and fire in a matter of seconds.

Jad clasped my arm, his fingers digging through my jacket from tension and strain. "We need to get to the city. We need the book."

I had no argument there.

We ran through the battle, scuffling our way past skirmishes. I recognised some of the soldiers from the platoon. Worse were the faces I saw staring lifelessly up from the ground, eyes glassy, already succumbed to death.

I have to reach the Isla Necropolis.

I have to absorb the magic from the Bone Grimoire.

It's the only way to make me strong enough to stop all this.

I still had no idea how to do that, but that was a future-Zaya problem. For now, Jad and I needed a fighting chance to reach the city. And there was only one way I knew how to give us that opportunity.

I crouched down to the ground, pressing my hand onto the cracked earth. There had been no spirits on the mesa before, but now that so much death had occurred, I sensed the dead acutely. Dead Haxsan Guard soldiers and dissent rebels, their ghosts now lost and unsure on the battlefield. I felt their fear and shock, so many confused emotions running through them as they hovered over their bodies, lips parted without words. It was unfair to treat them this way. They should have been ferried to the world beyond, their souls laid to rest, not resurrected into weapons, but I was running out of time and options.

"What are you doing?" Jad sounded frantic.

I curled my fingers into the hard soil, amazed it broke at my touch. "We need our own army."

I focused on my necromancy, sending a wave of energy into the ground. My magic hissed and fizzed like electricity, lines arcing out, tethering the souls to me. I clenched my teeth, sweat inching down my spine. There was so much dark energy inside me that even my skin felt like it was about to peel off. My vision clouded.

No. I can't let go.

I had the souls. I just needed to control them.

I sent more power through the earth. My nerve endings were on fire, but I broke through the veil that shrouded the dead, now hearing their wailing screams.

"Return to your bodies. Fight."

Their souls were sucked into their corpses like a vacuum. One after another, the dead soldiers picked themselves off the ground, legs and arms more mechanical than natural, their movements disjointed as they returned to the battle.

This time, the shouts across the mesa were from the living.

"Come on." I clutched Jad's hand, forcing him to run with me and not looking at the startled shock on his face. I wasn't a monster, but at that moment, seeing his alarmed expression made me feel like I was one.

Sand beat my skin. The dust seemed to want to choke me. My eyes were riveted to my destination, which was now a short distance away. Whenever the lightning struck the ground or a series of chain flashes swept through the churning clouds, the light reflected off the glamour and I caught a glimpse of the city beyond, becoming more apparent with each step closer. There were columns and stairs, decorated with murals that looked incredible even from this distance.

We're nearly there.

We're going to make it.

Something heavy collided with my head. Pain erupted down my neck, paralysing all my limbs below. All I could think about was that terrible, raw, aching pain. The ringing in my ears grew louder. I realised with belated horror that I'd lost contact with my resurrected souls and no longer had control. But none of that mattered, because gracious darkness closed in, washing away all my troubles.

I WASN'T ENTIRELY sure where I was when I woke.

If I even have woken.

I was staring at a cave ceiling riddled with tree roots and dripping water. That was, in fact, what had forced my eyes open. Cold water had dripped onto my forehead, running down in an icy trickle past my nose and over my lips.

I sat up, my head still spinning. At least the awful pain was gone. A fire licked and spat somewhere, wonderfully warm, not scorching like the flames from the mesa.

Wait. Where am I?

I blinked the sleepy haze from my eyes. I recognised the wooden bench, covered in glass jars containing herbs, bones, and dried animal parts. All the skulls hanging from the ceiling still made me squeamish, and I avoided looking at them for long.

I'm back.

Sitting in a chair beside the hearth was the silver-thorned witch. Isgrad sat opposite her, his head in his hands. He raked his fingers through his blond hair. "Where do I go to find clues about the Bone Grimoire?"

The memory. It was playing right where it had left off.

"Good boy." The witch drew her chair closer and sat down. "We start by understanding what it is you're willing to lose."

Isgrad blinked. "I've lost my brother… and my mother. What more could possibly be taken?"

The witch sat back in her chair, assessing him quietly. "There is no point in going on a search for this book if you're not willing to pay the price. Absorbing the Grand Masters' necromancy is simple. All you need to do is offer the Bone Grimoire what you value the most. It will take it, and in exchange, it will give you the magic."

"But that's... crazy."

"Is it? The Grand Masters wanted to ensure that their necromancy would be passed down to someone who was worthy. Someone willing to make sacrifices. Giving up what you value the most is a fair exchange."

Isgrad stared at her blankly. "But I don't know what that is. Everything... everyone I care about is gone."

Sad amusement shone in the witch's eyes. "It could take years to find the Bone Grimoire. Time makes changes in one's life."

Isgrad's heavy eyebrows rose. He didn't look like he fully understood what she was alluding to, but I did. In time, Isgrad would come to value something precious to him, and that would be what the Bone Grimoire would demand in payment.

It was so easy. And so ironic.

If I wanted to absorb the Grand Masters' necromancy, then I had to give the book what I valued the most.

MY EYES PEELED OPEN, everything a stunned blur as my senses woke. Searing heat beat down from the sun above. The wind drove dust up my nose and into my eyes, which then watered and formed a messy gloop.

The sun.

I forced myself to stand, wincing with every painful move. The galactic storm was gone, the sun now a gold disc in the sky. I couldn't see much of anything beyond the sand-riddled landscape.

How long have I been out?

Jad?

Where is he?

There was no sign of the chak-lorks. To my left, I could just make out what appeared to be the aftermath of the battle. Bodies were strewn through the sand, crows and other birdlife already in an assembled pecking order. The wind picked up again, and everything was shrouded in a brown haze.

"All dead," a voice announced.

The bitterness in the tone couldn't have been stronger.

I flinched. That proverbial voice made my blood pound in my ears like drumbeats.

Vulcan and a team of dissent rebels stood blocking my way to the necropolis. I counted seven. Among them was Lainie. She had her head down, refusing to look at me. She reminded me of a little girl who'd been severely reprimanded and was now too afraid to do anything but stare at the ground. Sadness seeped through me. She'd made one terrible decision, and it had reduced her into a shell of her former self.

"Beautiful, isn't it?" Vulcan continued. He raised his hand to the necropolis.

It was a massive rock-cut temple. Colossal-sized statues of ancient kings and queens stood at the façade. They were excavated from the stone and at least twenty metres in height. Their hands were raised in warning, cautioning onlookers to stay away.

Not a great sign.

A single entrance stood in the centre, flanked by the statues. It was made of solid gold and carved with reliefs of the dead, their hands raised in worship at the rising sun and the moon.

Vulcan was right. From the outside, the necropolis was beautiful. And intimidating. I wondered what dangers lurked inside.

My eyes travelled across the rest of the dissent rebels. Apart from Lainie, I didn't recognise any of them, not until I saw the last one.

Misery gutted me. Jad. His hands had been bound with silver chains, the metal burning into his wrists to leave horrible red scorches in his skin. His pupils and irises were a deep, dark red, like demon eyes in a twisted nightmare. He'd succumbed to the lycanthor power inside him.

A weird mix of emotions settled inside me. Memories of fear and despair, and horror at witnessing the atrocities he'd committed as Trajan Stormouth.

No.

Please, no.

But there were no gods in this lifetime to pray to.

I took it as a good sign that he was chained. It meant he hadn't turned into Trajan Stormouth fully. Jad was still inside somewhere;

otherwise, he'd be standing beside his father, a perfectly conditioned zealot.

The small composure I'd managed to hold snapped. "What did you do to him?"

A slow grin spread across Vulcan's face. It looked wolfish and cruel. "Nothing. This is who he really is."

I knew, to a certain point, that it was true. It was anger that triggered the lycanthor power inside Jad. I only hoped that he could contain the fury, because if he didn't, then he would turn fully, and I'd be facing another adversary.

A nasty pain at the side of my head made my vision teeter. My guess was that one of Vulcan's minions had snuck up and knocked me out cold with the barrel of a cast-shooter. I'd suffered worse injuries, but yellow dots still danced across my sight, my body heavy with weakness. Damned if I was going to let it show, though.

I summoned all the defiance I had left. "Morgomoth sent you here to do his dirty work, did he?"

The sun bathed Vulcan's angular face in pale luminance. His skin appeared almost translucent, bones and veins apparent under the milky colour. He would have looked perfectly at home in a coffin. "We're going to enter the necropolis, Zaya. We're going to find the Bone Grimoire, and we're going to take the book to Morgomoth. You can either join us as an ally or a prisoner. The choice is yours." He turned to Jad and unfastened the silver chains. "Open the door."

Indecision flashed across Jad's expression, but in the end, Trajan won. His wrists now free, he took the key out from his shirt and walked to the entrance. A moment later, there was the tense sound of pulleys and chains rattling after centuries of long disuse. The door groaned open, welcoming us to the dead city.

CHAPTER 40

The necropolis turned out to be a series of long, stretching tunnels. It was an extensive funerary complex where the dead had been laid to rest in the walls on stone slabs. The slabs ascended in levels like bunk beds, possibly to the ceiling, but I couldn't be certain. It was completely dark up there.

A few of the rebels brought flashlights, casting elongated shadows along the walls, the flickering shades causing me to jump. Some of the dead had been embalmed and preserved in wrappings; others had been left exposed to the air, reduced to skeletons now blanketed in cobwebs. Rats scurried in and out between the bones.

Vulcan's face scrunched into one of pure disgust. "What is this?"

"Seriously," I deadpanned. "It's the city of the dead. What did you expect?"

"Yes, but who are they?" He held his nose to rid himself of the stuffy, fetid stench.

My guess was that these people were the protectors of the necropolis and possibly some of the first Haxsan Guard soldiers, but I didn't tell Vulcan any of that. I shrugged, pretending I didn't know.

Jad was watching me, or maybe it was Trajan. His eyes were red, but they held no expression. There was nothing inside. He was a zombie, going through the motions. Emotion hit me hard, and I had to look away.

We continued our journey through the city. Sometimes we

stepped through ascending passageways, and other times the channels dipped so low, we were forced to turn back. It was claustrophobic and maddening, especially because we had no idea what we were actually looking for. The Bone Grimoire was an important artefact, so it would likely be contained in a chamber. But never once did we find a door. Only rows upon rows of the dead.

"This is ridiculous," Vulcan snapped. "We need a mapographic."

One of his rebels took a small device out from their cloak and let the gadget scan our surroundings. "It's coming back empty, sir."

Of course it is, idiots.

I highly doubted modern magic would work at a site so ancient.

Vulcan stormed toward me. "Summon the dead now and find out where that book is."

My mouth twitched into a smile. "It doesn't work like that."

Actually, it did.

Sometimes.

"Keep moving," he barked at everyone. "We'll find that book in this maze."

He sounded confident, but his eyes shone with hesitance.

We kept going, tunnel after tunnel, turn after turn. Jad led, keeping his distance. Lainie walked beside me, always leaving space between us. She never lifted her head once. It was as though she were incapable of it.

I moved closer, speaking quietly. "You're a harmonist. You can soothe Jad's emotions. Calm his anger." I had never pleaded for anything more in my life. "Please. Help him."

There was an edge to her eyes when she gazed at me. Then she shook her head and sped away, leaving me in a moment of silent astonishment. The Lainie I knew would never walk away from a situation where she could help. She really had changed.

She really is on Morgomoth's side.

One of the rebels hit my shoulder, shouting at me to stop dawdling.

After the heat of the desert, the farther we trekked through the passages, the surprisingly cooler they became. Even the air I breathed seemed to burn my lungs with icy cold. I shivered, a chill running over my scalp. I stole a glance at my companions. None of them seemed to be affected.

If I'm the only one feeling the cold, then that means….

The first contact came as a whisper, long and drawn out.

"You should not be here."

"Go back," another hissed.

"Leave this place," a third warned.

"I can't," I communicated back.

"We know why you are here," the voices stated, all of them rolling into one thunderous cry. *"We cannot let them find the Bone Grimoire. He is not worthy of its magic."*

The hair on the back of my neck stood up. *"I have no intention of letting them steal the book. I want to absorb its magic. I need it to defeat Morgomoth."*

Silence.

"Please," I begged. *"Show me the way. Unless you think I'm unworthy, what reason do you have to hide the grimoire?"*

Their voices, powerful and deep, circled around me. *"Absorbing that magic will come at a price."*

"I know. I'm willing to pay it."

"Then follow the path at your own cost."

Blue radiance lit the passage ahead. Runes appeared along the walls in swirling patterns, lines, and whorls. I had seen this once before in the Otturin Cave. It was the language of the dead, long forgotten and capable of only being seen by necromancers.

"Thank you," I said, having to wipe away a grateful tear.

"We are helping you, but we cannot let the others pass."

I froze, taking a moment to comprehend their meaning, because I was certain there was something hidden behind those words.

That's when the passage shook. Dust, grit, and rock pelted us from above. Lainie screamed and dodged the path of a large boulder. Jad flattened himself against one of the walls. Vulcan and his rebels shone their flashlights to the ceiling, as though it would reveal what was happening above. The walls shuddered. The ground lurched. It was like we were in the epicentre of an earthquake. I imagined the ceiling about to cave in, the walls closing, flattening us into pancakes.

A loud boom exploded from the end of the passage. Sand, tonnes of it, appeared at the end of the tunnel, shooting toward us in a massive wave.

"Run!" I shouted.

Forcing aside my swelling panic, I followed the runes, skirting down the passages, turning past sharp corners, glancing over my shoulder whenever I could manage it. Jad and Lainie were behind me, feet pounding hard on the trembling ground. Beyond them, I could just make out Vulcan and his rebels, their flashlights sputtering on and off. The sand was a monster of a wall, its speed incredible.

I focused back on the runes, concentrating on where they led while swatting away the fine grains of sand that blew in my hair and face. Several screams ran out behind me and were quickly silenced. I didn't dare look back. Judging by the sudden lack of light, the rebels had met a sandy end.

The runes ahead shone brightly, a beacon lighting our way. I slipped through a doorway, waving frantically for Jad and Lainie to get inside. At the last possible second, Vulcan crossed the threshold. I cursed my ill luck. The four of us pushed the door back, which had to weigh a tonne, and shoved it into place with a resounding bang that seemed final.

I panted, trying to get air back into my lungs, my skin coated in sweat.

"Sweet providence," Vulcan muttered.

He was looking behind me, his eyes alight with wonder. He wasn't the least bit fazed that he'd lost several loyal rebels.

I turned. We stood in a decorative chamber, every wall adorned with frescoes, the columns inlaid with carved marble. Runes glowed on the ceiling. In the centre of the chamber was the most bizarre and spine-chilling plinth I'd ever seen. A series of humerus, radius, and ulna bones had been assembled into two giant hands, the phalanges bones shaped as the fingers, which held the Bone Grimoire. The silver-thorned witch had told Isgrad that each Grand Master had sacrificed a bone to transfer their magic to the grimoire. Even from this distance, I could see how ornately crafted the book was. It was smooth, clean ivory. Two skeleton hands rested on top. Where the backs of the hands should have been, exquisite sculptings of the sun and moon had been etched.

I stepped forward, intending to finish this right now. Hands seized me, nails biting impossibly through the fabric of my jacket. I struggled and kicked and almost fell when I realised who had taken me captive. Jad.

No.

Trajan.

He held me with a grip like iron. His lips were thin lines, his expression impassive, but in his eyes, I detected ruthless enjoyment. Trajan relished pain. It sickened me to see him reduced to this blood-hungry monster.

I cast a beseeching glance at Lainie, desperate for her to use her magic and calm him, but she looked away.

I twisted and writhed in Trajan's grip. Then Vulcan stepped forward and slapped me hard across the face. Pain radiated all the way down my cheek to my neck. For a split second, I questioned if my jaw had been fragmented from my skull.

He grabbed my chin, forcing me to look at him. "You knew where this chamber was all that time, didn't you?"

I cursed fate at that moment, wondering why it had let such a madman live.

"We've wasted enough time," Vulcan snapped. "Only a necromancer can claim the book."

A small shiver of uncertainty passed over me. "Then let me go so I can do it."

He smiled, cunning all over him. "Not you."

Vulcan set a small metallic device, about the size of an acorn, on the ground. There was a soft click, and the device opened like a locket. A dark, flowing substance rose. It grew larger, expanding through the chamber and thickening into clouds.

Fear made my insides turn liquid and soft. This wasn't some sort of hysterical hallucination cooked up by panic. What I witnessed was impossibly real. A galactic storm.

How?

The amorphous darkness transformed, taking on a shape. It appeared to be a mirror, shiny and reflective, but I couldn't be certain. The silver glass rippled, and the image inside it changed. I held my breath, not believing what I was seeing.

In the mirror was a dead land. A wasteland of fire. A surreal world of black rock and steaming craters, of rivers of lava and vats of boiling lakes. A ring of volcanic cones dominated the landscape, and in their centre, the smoky outline of a castle, its windows gleaming red. Towers and spires pierced the sky, disappearing in the black clouds. An indescribable wailing resounded across the land—the screams of a thousand souls tortured into submission or death.

The longer the image remained, the more the chamber became pungent with the smell of fire and volcanic gas.

It's a portal.

Somehow Morgomoth, probably through his sinister accomplice Hadar, had managed to create a gateway through a galactic storm. They had trapped that storm in a portable device. What I was looking at was his land. His kingdom.

This was the Dark Divide.

And I helped him make it happen.

Before I could dwell on the guilt, a figure emerged from the portal. He'd rejuvenated since I'd last seen him. There was now some flesh on his bones, but the shapeless darkness was still part of him. Morgomoth looked like something that had climbed out of a grave. Knowing who he was now, I recognised the bright glint of savagery I had witnessed on Willieth's young face.

Vulcan dropped to his knees, as though he were in the midst of royalty. "Your Grace."

Your Grace?

I'd have laughed if I weren't so afraid.

Vulcan's expression revealed how proud he was of his accomplishment. "The book is waiting—"

Morgomoth held up a ringed finger, silencing him, then made his way across the chamber.

I struggled again, but Jad's muscled arms draped around me, holding me tight enough to leave bruises.

I couldn't let Morgomoth claim the book. I'd come this far. I wasn't ready to fail.

I shut my eyes, doing the only thing I knew might help, even though it would cause me pain.

"Neathror."

I called out to the athame-sabre, urging the weapon to assist me. I still had no idea where the dagger disappeared to most of the time, so I pictured its pristine black hilt and its smooth dark blade, imagining how it would feel in my hand.

"Please. I need your help."

The blade had no reason to answer me; it was loyal to both Morgomoth and me. I forced more energy into my request. No. Into my demand.

"Save him. Now," I cried, fuelling all my power into the command.

Neathror materialised in my hand.

I was trembling all over, convincing myself this was the right thing to do. Jad was still inside there somewhere, but Trajan Stormouth had taken over.

Trajan Stormouth had to die.

This is a merciful act.

This is what Jad would have told me to do.

I plunged the athame-sabre into Trajan's shoulder with a speed he wasn't ready for. I might as well have used the dagger to pierce my heart for the pain it caused me. His eyes widened in shock, lips parting with surprise. Hatred settled on his face, and I knew that look would forever haunt me.

I twisted away from his falling body, not giving myself a chance to look back because if I did, I would surely drop to the floor beside him, begging forgiveness. No one survived a wound from Neathror, no matter where they were struck on their body. She was the blade of death, and she guaranteed it. I only hoped that she killed Trajan, not Jad.

I ducked Vulcan's reaching hands, kicking him hard in the shin to knock him over, and raced across the chamber floor to the grimoire. Morgomoth was so close. His hand was nearly on the book.

His sharp eyes fell on me, a spasm of rage burning inside them. He let out a roar of savagery as we both touched the grimoire at the same time.

An explosion of white light erupted from the book, the energy knocking us both backward. I hit the floor hard, but the pain was minimal compared to the scalding heat that ran through my body. It was agony. Pristine light was all around me, tethering me to the grimoire like jagged lightning. It filled all my veins with fire and rattled my ears until they were numb. It felt like my bones were melting inside me.

Morgomoth was engulfed in the same searing light, his eyes open in astonishment. Deafening thunder filled the chamber, resonating across the walls. In it... was a voice. Deep. Powerful. Persuasive. It sounded like the haunted echo from the bottom of a well. It came from the grimoire.

"Two necromancers claim the Grand Masters' magic. In exchange, you must sacrifice what you value most. Are you willing to do this?"

It took a second for my brain to compute what was happening. Despair spread through me, thick and fast. The grimoire was going to divide the power between us. If I didn't accept it, Morgomoth would be granted all the Grand Masters' necromancy.

"Yes," I answered, not allowing myself to think about what it was I next most valued, because the person I truly treasured might have been lying dead on the chamber floor.

Lightning continued to spill like arrows of fire from the book. It was coursing through me, filling every fibre of my body with renewed magic, more powerful than any force I'd encountered before. I felt like I was being pulled apart and stitched back together with fire. This transfer of necromancy would surely kill me.

I was on the verge of passing out when the grimoire closed with a resounding snap. I realised I'd blacked out for a few moments, because when I found the courage to open my eyes, I had to twist out of the path of tumbling rocks. The chamber's ceiling was collapsing. Large chunks of stone plummeted like rain. Several columns toppled, sending a shower of dust over me. The floor, too, had terrible fissures cracking through the marble.

I climbed onto my feet, fighting vertigo.

Why do they never build these temples strong enough?

I blinked, struggling to make out what I saw at first. Fury ripped through me. Vulcan had a supportive arm wrapped around Morgomoth. The pair moved as fast as they could to the portal, Vulcan doing most of the work. They slipped through the rippling light, disappearing into the shadowed land beyond.

They'd left me behind. That figured. I'd made it abundantly clear through both words and actions that I would not join the United League of Dissent. Better off leaving me here to die.

What seriously hurt, though, was Lainie's torn expression. Hesitation was written across her face. When she spoke, her voice was full of regret. "I'm sorry, but he's my master. If you won't join us, then you have to die." She grabbed the disc and took a swift step back through the portal.

"No, you coward." I stumbled forward, but it was a joke to think I could reach Lainie in time.

She shut the device. The portal imploded in on itself with a resounding crack, then disappeared into a thin stream of smoke. My only way out of this crumbling chamber had evaporated into nothing.

Spiderwebbing cracks fissured in the floor around my feet. The door was sealed by sand.

A seizure of panic twisted inside me.

I was trapped.

CHAPTER 41

Shattering marble cracked around me. I reached my arms out, trying to steady myself on the pitching floor. It felt like I was standing on a seesaw. Thoughts of a long, plunging fall to my death made me break out into a cold sweat.

A shout drew my attention, startling me that I wasn't alone.

Through the dust, I could just make out the silhouette of a figure gingerly lifting themselves from the chamber floor.

Jad.

I sidestepped the splintering cracks in the floor, jumping over fissures to reach him. A part of me warned caution. I had no idea if this was Jad or Trajan. I could have been running to salvation. I could have been running to death.

He caught me as I flew forward, wrapping his arms tightly around my waist, securing me in comforting warmth. I knew in that single moment that Trajan was gone. There was no red in his eyes, no savageness in his expression. This was Jad.

Had Neathror killed Trajan like I'd hoped?

I felt an ache in my chest as emotion momentarily overcame me. "I'm sorry I stabbed you. I'm glad you're not dead."

Jad's gaze swept over my face. "I'm grateful I'm not either."

He clutched his shoulder. A steady flow of blood spilled out from the stab wound, growing like an oversized poppy on his coat. He lost his balance, and I had to hold him tight to keep him upright. His strength was fading fast.

A woozy dizziness spun over me. "What a mess we both are."

His eyes travelled to the plinth. "Where's the grimoire?"

I hesitated to look over my shoulder. The grimoire was gone. In its place was ash. "I think it must have burned itself after it transferred its magic."

At least, that's what I hoped had happened. I didn't even want to comprehend what the repercussions would be if Morgomoth had somehow gotten his hands on the grimoire and taken it to his kingdom.

Jad didn't respond. He was looking at the door, blocked by sand on the other side.

My voice was shaky. "We're trapped."

"There'll be another way out." Jad observed the walls, or what was left of them. "There always is. All temples are designed with escape routes for this very reason."

I opened my mouth to say something, but the floor caved in beneath us.

I screamed, my chest fluttering like there was a bird inside it trying to break free, my insides reduced to water, sloshing around in sickening circles.

My hip and shoulder struck packed earth. Rocks and stones pelted me. I groaned, wriggling my way out of the debris. I must have bitten my lower lip, or something sharp had cut it, because I tasted blood.

I coughed, wheezing against the dust that filled my throat. "Jad?"

"Over here."

He'd fared much better than me. That, or he was faster and stronger at getting himself out of the rubble. Even with a stab wound, his strength was double that of the average caster man.

He still has lycanthor abilities.

I was ashamed of how much that disappointed me.

"Come on." He tucked his hand in mine, doing a quick assessment to make sure I was all right.

"I'm fine," I lied, struggling to keep my feet steady beneath me.

We'd fallen into a lower passage. The walls were filled with the dead, these bodies in worse condition than those in the upper tunnels, the bones blackened and crisped. Hopefully, they'd been burned after death.

How many levels down does the city go?

There was no time to find out the answer. A familiar tremor hit the passage, nearly toppling me into the wall.

"Zaya." Jad squeezed my hand so tight, I thought he would break it.

Sand was coming down the passage. It moved like a raging river, drowning everything in grit and gravel and riddling the air with dust. Signs of fatigue were all over Jad, but he pulled me forcefully into a run. My feet complained, but I kept pace with him, gasping for air the entire time.

How are we in this situation again?

We were underground. Was there even a door out of these lower passages? Or were we merely wasting our time running from the inevitable?

We sprinted down a slew of right and left turns, no doors or palls of sunlight in sight in the passages. My legs were weakening every second, but I fought to stay on my feet.

As we rounded another corner, I caught sight of light ahead between two connecting passageways. It was blue, beaming brightly.

"This way," I cried, hightailing toward it.

Jad couldn't see the runes, and it meant something that he trusted me enough to follow. I took a moment to appreciate the fact that I hadn't called on the dead for guidance. The runes grew alight for me, flaring brighter, guiding my way.

Is this because I'm stronger?

Can I see the magic without the help of the dead now?

Is this because I possess the Grand Masters' necromancy?

Half of it, I reminded myself.

The thought sobered me.

Jad's elated voice caught up to me. "Up ahead. Daylight."

He was right. There was a staircase, split halfway down the middle by a crack, probably from all the seismic activity that had shaken the temple. The closer we neared it, the more the acrid smell of desert air filled my nose, driving me with hope.

I clambered up the stairs, Jad right behind me. The steps shuddered and bucked, nearly tossing me to my knees. I shifted my weight, straightening my balance.

A monotonous creak groaned above. I looked up to see the ceiling crashing down. We moved, unsteady yet swift, up the last of the ancient steps worn flat by centuries and burst into the desert's searing heat.

When I looked over my shoulder, I saw what was left of the necropolis collapsing in a giant dust cloud.

IT TURNED out we had exited the necropolis from a side door. Jad was right. There was always a way out, just not in the way we'd expected.

Based on the sun, we were able to navigate our way across the mesa. The flat expanse of barren land was harsh and uninviting. Light bounced off every rock, amplifying the heat a hundred times over. My nose felt like it was clogged with sand. Grime and dirt stung the cuts on my hand. I really hoped the hornet hadn't been compromised. I double-hoped my friends weren't part of the bodies strewn about on the battlefield, being pecked at by birds and other desert life.

Now that Jad and I were out of immediate danger, exhaustion caught up with us. We plodded heavily, concentrating on putting one foot in front of the other. What really made me afraid was Jad's stab wound. His left shoulder was saturated in blood. It was trickling down his fingers and dripping onto the lifeless dry earth, making a terrible red paste in the sand.

Did Neathror really answer me and kill Trajan?

It was another curiosity that I had to add to my list of mysteries about the athame-sabre.

Our progress was slow. A few times, I shook myself awake; otherwise, I would drop into the sand and never get up again. I recalled Kravis saying that the necropolis had been just over two kilometres away. That was a walk easily achievable in twenty minutes. I estimated we'd been staggering across the mesa for the last forty-five. It didn't lift my spirits.

Just when I thought the sun couldn't possibly reach any higher in the sky, I heard the drone of a distant motor.

Jad stood still. "Do you hear that?"

I strained to see through the bright sunlight. Something dark hovered in the sky. Joy filtered through me. It was the carrier-hornet. It dipped awkwardly, the whirling blades gusting sand over us as it approached. The boarding ramp lowered from the hovering ship. Jad and I clambered up together, holding each other for support.

Annaka beamed at us from the cabin. "Please present your boarding pass."

I wrapped my arms around her, crushing her in a fierce hug.

"Okaaaay," she drawled, a little mystified but clearly pleased. "I didn't think we were that good of friends."

Talina was buckled in a seat but undid the belt the moment she saw me. She squeezed me tightly, perhaps in a desperate need to be close to a friend.

There was a world of questions in her eyes, but I spoke before she could.

"Are you okay? How are you here? What happened?" I turned, looking at both girls for answers.

Annaka laughed. "Calm down. One question at a time, please. We have been hostages, you know." She settled in a seat. "To answer your first question, yes, we're okay. Second, some soldier called Bronislav found us. He led us away from the fight into the hornet. We waited here until it was safe, and then Marek started the engines and did a few flyovers in search of you." Her eyes settled on Jad, her good humour vanishing. "Is he all right? Wait. Is that blood?"

Jad sucked in a sharp breath. Then his eyes shut and he fell. Both Annaka and I stumbled to catch him, but he was too heavy, and all three of us ended up on the cabin floor. Blood pooled onto the carpet.

"Out of the way," Talina ordered. "Someone find me a first-aid kit and some wrappings. I need to heal him."

She set to work, pulling Jad's thick coat off. I threw a hand over my mouth, desperately fighting the sick back. Swollen skin puffed up around the wound, bruised in shades of black, purple, and brown. The blood that ran out now was so thick it was almost black.

I ran to find a first-aid kit, my panic suffocating.

TALINA MANAGED to stop the bleeding but warned that Jad still needed proper medical attention. She couldn't guarantee that there wasn't an infection, and if there was, it would likely be poisoning all of his insides.

"We need to get him to a hospital," she instructed.

We were sitting in the hornet's cabin. Jad was asleep, sprawled across the chairs. I sat next to him, stroking his dark hair away from his face. Annaka watched on from the aisle, her arms crossed.

Talina's emerald gaze locked onto her. "You know Vukovar better than any of us. Are there any hospitals nearby?"

"Out here in the Golden Ocean?" Annaka narrowed her eyebrows as though she'd been asked a stupid question. "It's a Free Zone he needs. Or a military base. There's nothing out here." She exhaled a resigned breath. "After everything that's happened, we would be crazy to return to the Black Palace. We have this ship. We have freedom. We can go anywhere now."

"He needs a hospital," Talina cried with surprising hostility. "Are you suggesting we just let him die?"

"No, of course not. But there is no way in hell that I'm going back to the Black Palace."

I dropped my head into my hands, indecision grating at me. Annaka was right. This was a chance for my friends to flee, but in doing so, Jad's life was on the line. I shut my eyes, wishing there were alternatives. "Drop Jad and me off at the nearest base. The rest of you leave. Get as far away as you can. Dump the hornet, find another. Make new lives for yourselves."

"No way," Talina cried. "Not without you."

"I'm not leaving Jad." I spoke with resolve. "And my task in all of this isn't finished."

I thought about the Dark Divide in the portal. Morgomoth's new kingdom. His new seat of power. We had both absorbed the Grand Masters' magic. We were equal now. I had to finish what I started. I had to defeat Morgomoth. I owed it to Jad. I owed it to everyone.

"Well," Annaka said cheerfully, "your sacrifice is greatly appreciated. Imprisonment doesn't agree with me."

"I'm afraid that is exactly what's going to happen," a new voice confirmed.

Marek appeared from the cockpit. Bronislav stood behind him, leaning against the door.

"Shouldn't you be flying the plane?" Annaka asked with a hint of sarcasm.

Marek's face looked grey in the fading light, his scar taking on a silvery sheen. "The Haxsan Guard have taken over the hornet. They're in control. Some kind of signal to steer us back to the Black Palace. All the controls are locked."

Silence settled in the cabin, the air thick with dashed hope.

Annaka slapped her hands on her thighs. "Well, there goes freedom."

CHAPTER 42

I was confined to the same bedchamber in the Black Palace. Days passed without hearing a word from anyone. The only people I saw were the maids when they brought in food and fresh clothing. They never answered my questions.

When the carrier-hornet had landed, soldiers had stormed into the cabin. Talina, Annaka, Marek, and Bronislav were seized and taken away. Jad was put onto a stretcher, and a crowd of healers had rushed him into the palace. I still didn't know if he was okay.

Me? I'd undergone hours of questioning. The sovereigns wanted to know every detail of the events that had occurred at the Isla Necropolis. I explained as much as I was willing to tell, keeping some things in the dark, but they had a truth seeker, a caster who could detect if you were lying by merely touching your skin. Truth seekers were about as rare as the obeahpeople or soothwitchers. I wondered if she also lived in the palace's prison, only allowed out when it benefited the sovereigns. Prisoner or not, she wasn't on my side. She'd forced me to reveal the truth. The sovereigns weren't impressed that the Grand Masters' magic had been divided between Morgomoth and me. After questioning, they had ordered me returned to my chamber.

To prevent my mounting anxiety, and to stop myself from going crazy out of boredom, I concentrated my efforts on summing the Neathror blade. Perhaps I could have used it to escape this place and find some answers, but every time I tried, my magic came up empty.

It seemed the athame-sabre only appeared when I needed it the most —when I was in danger.

When summoning the blade failed, I tried sleeping, hoping my mind would drift back to Isgrad's memories. He'd never found the Bone Grimoire, but he must have learnt weaknesses about his brother. I needed to understand those vulnerabilities, but just like the athame-sabre, even dreams were elusive.

On the fifth morning of imprisonment, I woke to two maids—I still didn't know their names—scrambling to get me out of the bed and fitted into a black gown that fell to the floor. The dress was uncomfortably tight. It was laced at the back, the gown's satin itchy over my skin. The bodice made me appear too thin on top, and the pleated skirt was too wide.

I frowned, hating my reflection in the mirror. "Off to another party, I suppose."

Which courtiers do the sovereigns want to fool this time?

One of the maids dropped her jaw in surprise. "Oh no, miss. A funeral."

Several guards appeared—more than last time—and whisked me out of the chamber. They rushed me through the palace corridors, ignoring me when I asked questions like "Whose funeral am I attending?" and "Is it someone I know?"

Someone I know?

No. Please, no.

I couldn't breathe. It felt like I'd just been pushed off a precipice.

Not Jad.

Cold despair spread through my veins. I asked again whose funeral I was attending, but the guards remained stone-faced and silent the entire time, which only served to infuriate me.

My pulse was screaming in my ears when we arrived at an enormous hall the size of a ballroom. It had a vaulted ceiling that appeared to have been painted in gold, glossy obsidian floors, and colourful stained-glass windows. It could have been a church from ancient times. Maybe parts of it had come from the ruins of cathedrals and basilicas. The walls were painted with frescoes of old saints and gods who were no longer worshipped, and the friezes had sadly never been touched up and were fading from sunlight.

Crowds had gathered at the sides of the hall. I scanned people's faces, hoping I might see Jad's among them.

I would know if he was dead. I'd know it.

My guards led me through the crowd to the front. There must have been over thirty coffins, all works of art. All of them open. The caskets were strung with black banners and wreaths of white flowers.

Relief flooded me. Jad wasn't one of the fallen.

In the centre on a raised bier, General Kravis was lying on a shroud with the Haxsan Guard insignia embroidered in gold. He was ornamentally placed with his arms across his chest, his athame-sabre fixed in his hand. It was creepy to see him that way, preserved to appear as though he were sleeping.

Guilt grappled inside me. I hadn't liked the general, but I hadn't wanted him to die either. I hadn't wanted any of his platoon to die.

My guards steered me into a seat at the front where the sovereigns and the Council members sat. The men wore traditional black dress shirts and ties that were ceremonial for mourning. The women were adorned in black gowns similar to my own. Toshiko's outfit was the only novelty in the room. It was a simple dark kimono with a grey belt. There were others in the room too: uniformed Haxsan Guard soldiers carrying banners, and people I assumed were family members of the deceased. They were the only ones who cried.

People whispered and pointed at me. I imagined word of what happened at the Isla Necropolis had gotten around. I wondered if anything they'd been told was true.

When the funeral started and talk about General Kravis and his platoon's great sacrifice to defend the sovereigns' necromancer was spoken with respectful formality, I knew I was here for appearance's sake. What they were saying was an outright lie.

My protectors?

I was their prisoner.

I saw Darius in the corner, looking solemnly down at his feet. He appeared calm, and I had to remind myself that this was all part of the game. He was on my side. I wished I could find a chance to talk to him.

After the funeral, which turned out to be a sordid two-hour affair of falsehood and major dishonour to the dead, my guards returned to chaperone me back to my chamber. I spotted Macaslan through the parting crowd. She kneeled at a small altar, which struck me as odd. One, because she was far too shrewd and strict in her ways to believe in a higher power. And two, because there were no gods.

I turned to my guards. "A moment, please."

I was surprised when they nodded in acquiescence, but really, I shouldn't have been. The sovereigns didn't want me to be seen as a prisoner but as a valued guest in need of twenty-four-hour protection.

Two-faced slimes.

Macaslan didn't say anything when I kneeled on a harrow beside her. "Who are we praying to?"

She rewarded me with one of her no-nonsense frowns. Her dark eyebrows rose, accentuating her storm-grey eyes. "Did you know this was Saint Leandra?"

She gestured in the direction of a fresco above the altar. The painting had faded, parts of the gold leaf peeling. From what I could make out, Saint Leandra had been a slim-faired caster girl with radiant blonde hair. There was a hint of informality in her dark eyes. She'd been depicted balancing a globe of water above her hand. She was a water wielder.

I conceded a smile. "There isn't much of her left to look at."

Macaslan arched her neck to examine the fresco, as though she were trying to understand the artist's motivation. "She was one of the first sovereigns."

My tongue locked up. "But that's… impossible. The sovereigns have all been human."

"That's what the Council want you to believe, but the first sovereigns were casters. They've been forgotten from history—deliberately, of course. No one in this palace, except for Darius, would know who Saint Leandra was. Look at what she's been reduced to. Saint Leandra's murder marks the beginning of all caster suppression."

"Careful," I cautioned. "Those words will get you into trouble."

Her voice was grim. "I heard about the events at the Isla Necropolis. The *real events*. You did well."

"Did well? The book was destroyed."

"But you did acquire its power."

"Half its power," I corrected. "The other share of the magic went to Morgomoth. The mission was a massive failure."

"We're working on a plan." She focused on the fresco, her gaze never leaving it once.

"And?"

She didn't answer.

"So, your plan is to keep me in the dark? That worked out really well last time, didn't it."

"Our plan is to keep you safe," she confessed in a quiet voice.

"How? By keeping me locked away in a chamber?"

She grabbed my arm, her swift movement surprising me. She snuck a glance over her shoulder, making sure no stragglers remained in the hall. "There has been work going on behind the scenes. Tonight, a private conclave will take place in the sovereigns' hall. A new accord has been drawn up, one that will replace the Conscription Act. It means military training and service will no longer be a mandatory requirement. Casters can choose whether they want to join. It's the first step of many to ensuring unity among casters."

A small surge of elation filled me. It was the first good news I'd heard in a long time.

"You should know," Macaslan continued, her voice low and full of secrets, "that there are people in this palace who will not be pleased. The sovereigns will sign the accord tonight, along with the support of a majority of councillors."

"I want to be there."

I'd already guessed what the answer would be and braced myself for a fight.

"Yes."

I blinked, the argument sinking inside me. "What?"

"Toshiko has granted you permission to attend."

"I bet she came up with this entire plan."

The heavy lines on Macaslan's face deepened. "I believe it was Rozric who settled all of this."

Rozric?

The last time I'd seen him, he'd seemed in favour of keeping conscription. Maybe he'd had a change of heart. Maybe I'd judged him too quickly. Or maybe he simply understood that this move was the only way to ensure unity and peace among the casters.

Someone had opened a window to relieve the rising heat in the room. A warm breeze blew across my skin and doused the three candles that had been lit at the altar. Macaslan leaned forward, quickly lighting them again with a taper.

I studied her closely, trying to discern her quiet attitude. "Who are the candles for?"

The flames reflected in her eyes, small dots that reminded me of fireflies buzzing in the night. "One is for General Kravis. The other is for Colonel Harper."

A wave of remorse settled through me. So much had happened since the *Velorosa* was set alight and sunk that I'd never really had the time to mourn Colonel Harper properly, or to even understand how his death might be affecting the commander. They had been friends. Comrades. Allies. She'd lost someone she'd trusted wholeheartedly. That had to be difficult.

I swallowed. "Will there be a funeral for him?"

Macaslan's jaw was tense. "No. Darius and I might be pardoned in the future if we continue to work alongside the sovereigns, but in their eyes, Colonel Harper was a traitor. They have refused him the proper memorial rites."

I placed a consolingly hand on her arm. "There's been something I've been meaning to ask you. Was the colonel sick?"

She looked at me, her stern gaze fumbling for a moment. "Why would you think that?"

"When I was an essence, I saw him drinking a potion on the *Velorosa*. I was the one who called for help that night. He wasn't well. The potion was a hex."

I had actually wondered if the colonel had drunk the poison to deliberately harm himself.

Macaslan focused back on the fresco. The slightest shade of pink lit her cheeks. "Colonel Harper had his difficulties. He faced them alone... in the end."

I didn't understand what that meant, but I could tell it was a subject the commander didn't want to dwell on.

"When all this is over," I started, "we'll have a memorial for him.

Not here, but out in a garden. He was an earth wielder. He'd have appreciated that."

When all this is over?

What would that even look like? When would that even be?

Macaslan only nodded.

My eyes travelled to the third candle. "And who is that one for?"

"My daughter."

Surprise rippled through me. I didn't know Macaslan had a daughter, let alone that she was dead.

The commander rose to her feet. "She died a long time ago fighting the ULD. Now, if you'll excuse me, I have a conclave to prepare for. And you have some impatient guards wishing for you to leave."

She was right. My guards had crept forward, uncomfortable the longer I was out in public. One of them raised his eyebrows at me, giving me the "hurry along" look.

"I'll see you tonight," I told Macaslan.

"Yes." The tightness in her lips increased. "It will be an evening to remember."

My GUARDS FLANKED me out of the memorial room. We entered a long hallway, the heat climbing now that it was the middle of the morning. I could already feel my skin starting to itch under my make-up, my pores clogging with sweat.

Walking around a corner, we came into contact with a friendly surprise. Jad. He was accompanied by his own set of guards, who monitored him with a keen eye.

Seeing Jad made my chest tighten. I was relieved to see he'd recovered from his wound. My lips lifted into a smile, and I ran to him.

His expression had been calm, but once he saw me...

He averted his eyes and walked the other way.

What the hell?

He said something to his guards, and they immediately followed.

"Hey, wait." I caught up to him, astounded that he hadn't recognised me.

Because that's what it had to be, right?

My eagerness froze the moment he turned. The dejected look in his eyes was a stab straight to my chest.

I stepped closer. "What's happened? Is something wrong?"

He took a step back, raising his hands in a placating gesture. "Please, could you keep your distance from me?"

Distance?

I didn't. "Jad, what's wrong? Tell me."

Why is he acting so strangely?

He slowly shook his head. He was looking at the floor, at the wall, at the ceiling—basically anywhere but at me. I'd never seen him appear so... distressed.

"What's wrong?"

He closed his eyes for a second and expelled a breath. "I need you to stay away from me."

I stared, dumbstruck. This had to be a joke.

"Is this about what happened at the Isla Necropolis?" I persevered. "I'm sorry I stabbed you, but you were Trajan Stormouth. I asked the blade to kill him, not you."

"It's not that."

"Then what?"

I stared at him pleadingly, desperate to understand what was happening.

There was a catch in his voice. "It's been coming on gradually, but now... I just can't be near you. It makes me physically ill."

His tanned face was turning greener by the second. He wasn't meaning it figuratively. Being near me was literally making him sick.

My breathing grew rapid. "Do you mean as in a hex?"

Had someone cursed him? Against me?

He took another step away. "I don't know, but even being this close to you is giving me the worst headache. Zaya, please. Just let my guards lead me back to my chamber."

"No, we have to talk about this."

He turned away with a dismissive gesture.

I grabbed his arm before he could leave. I was tongue-tied and embarrassed, but mostly confused.

He flinched. My hand had burned a hole right through his sleeve. The material was smoking. His skin was blistered, as though someone had doused boiling water over it, only it was in the shape of my hand.

My blood thinned, making me dizzy.

How could I have caused that?

Anger burned in Jad's eyes. In that very moment, he reminded me of Trajan Stormouth.

"Get this in your head," he said in a voice levelled with menace. "Stay away from me."

The statement was loud and clear for everyone to hear. It amplified down the hallway. It was a wonder the walls didn't shake.

This time when he walked away, I let him.

Emotions I didn't know how to contend with tore my brave façade down, and I burst out crying. Ugly, sorrowful tears that I was not proud of. Someone might as well have sliced my abdomen for the pain Jad's very public confession had caused.

Who would hex us like this? Who would have the audacity to make Jad's feelings turn against me?

He said it had been coming on gradually, but for me, it had been a fast slap in the face.

And then it hit me.

The Bone Grimoire took what I valued most.

Jad's love.

I watched his retreating figure disappear, his guards stepping up behind him to barricade my view.

Seeing him fade away, recalling those blunt words, made me want to tear every furniture piece apart in the Black Palace.

This was the price of the Bone Grimoire.

CHAPTER 43

It was a good thing there was no alcohol in my chamber, because I probably would have drunk myself stupid. Jad's harsh words spiralled in my mind, the sorrow of losing him plaguing my every waking minute. I let myself fall into a heavy sleep, refusing to get up whenever I woke, preferring to just slip back into the dull blackness where I was safe from the brutal reality. I told myself that after everything I'd been through, I had a right to be pathetic and upset for a day. After the initial shock was over, I'd become myself again. I'd find an answer to solve this hex. There had to be a way.

When the sun started to settle and night drew in, I grudgingly got out of bed.

Darius and Macaslan will know what to do. I'll be seeing them soon. It'll be okay.

My maids entered not long after with a meagre dinner—which I didn't eat, much to their annoyance—then took me to the dressing room to clean me up and prepare me for the conclave. Once again, I was dressed in a stunning gown of black satin and silk, my eyes bold and smoky, hiding the fact that I had been crying all afternoon. When I looked in the mirror, I appeared the very image of a dark, avenging queen. The sovereigns' necromancer was a doll playing a part. Act out of character, and it would be my friends who paid the consequences. Marek, Talina, Annaka, and Bronislav had regretfully been returned to their cells. If I did anything wrong, the sovereigns would make them pay.

The accord is the important thing here.

Act brave tonight.

Work out a plan tomorrow.

The knock at the door informed me that my guards were waiting. They were different tonight. Perhaps my usual escort was having the night off. Maybe they only did the day shift.

"This way, miss," one of the men said.

They led me down the hallway, the opposite way from the usual route.

I frowned. "Isn't the sovereigns' hall in the east wing?"

"It is, miss, but security has been increased, and we have been ordered to use a more discreet path. You can never be too careful."

They took me past several passages, down a staircase, and into a room that appeared to be a servants' hall.

I gave the guard beside me a sharp look. "I think you might be lost, because this is definitely not—"

A hand closed around my mouth.

A hand with a cloth.

I struggled, barely having time to understand what was happening before sleepiness dragged me under.

I WOKE with a hell of a headache. For a few muddled seconds, I struggled to understand where I was. The night stars were bright in the sky, the air warm but no longer imbued by the earthy aroma of sand. No, it smelt briny. Even my ears were assaulted with the heavy susurration of waves. I recognised that sound.

No. Not possible.

I clambered onto my feet. I was on the deck of a ship, drifting farther away from the coast. Plumes of smoke permeated the sky above Muiren. The entire city was cast in red light.

Fire.

Everything inside me seized up. The Black Palace was burning.

Flames shot up into the sky. Towers collapsed. A wall of flame moved steadily from the ruins into the city like an unrolling carpet. Even from here, screams carried on the wind.

Jad.

Darius and Macaslan.

My friends.

Everyone I loved and cared about was in that palace.

I ran with swift steps in the direction of the stern.

There has to be a lifeboat somewhere. There has to be a way off this damn ship.

A hand latched onto my arm. Rock-hard fingers bit into my skin.

I spun around, so frazzled that it took me a moment to recognise my captor. "Toshiko."

She watched the city burn, her eyes reflecting the flames. Her painted face, which had always reminded me of a statue, shone with pride and satisfaction.

A river of despair washed through me. "You did this?"

Her eyes snapped to mine. "That accord could not be signed. It was a threat to the true sovereign's plan. The Council of Founding Sovereigns are dead. Anyone who knew about that accord is dead. There is only one ruling power now."

The true sovereign's plan?

I stared at her for a long time, my horror climbing. "You work for Morgomoth."

My brain was hit with a sudden surge of evidence. The sovereigns had fled the White Palace because Toshiko had inner knowledge of the attack. It had all been part of the plan to get the Council to Vukovar and to the Black Palace.

And the Black Palace? That's why the ULD forces had never attacked, because Morgomoth already had a mole in place, right in the middle of the Council. It was no wonder that Vulcan and the dissent rebels ambushed us at the Isla Necropolis when they had. They knew exactly when we'd be there. Their aim had been to either turn me or kill me.

It all made horrible, undeniable sense.

I stared at the burning palace, tasting ash on my lips. I imagined the councillors banging their fists on the doors, trying to flee the fires.

I imagined Rozric and the other sovereigns sitting on their thrones in confounded silence as the flames soared around them. I couldn't bring myself to think about Jad and the others. I would surely crumble and die of grief if I did.

"Why?" I cried, still in too much shock to formulate any other response.

Toshiko didn't have to answer because I suddenly understood. She wasn't wearing a radiation-resistant suit or gas mask, something humans couldn't survive without outside the Free Zones.

"You're a caster."

Her smile was toxic. "House of Okana were human once. The change started with my grandmother. Even though she was a sovereign, the others ordered her execution because she was mixed. They feared caster magic in a human. When my father took her place on the throne, he was subjected to torturous tests to prove he was human. The other sovereigns were satisfied that the disease in our family had been eradicated. But he never forgot, and when I was born a caster, he vowed that I would have a safe future. He understood the age of humans was over. He understood Morgomoth's cause."

She grabbed my shoulders and spun me around, walking me toward the bow. "And now we are headed for Orthrask, the new world capital. Morgomoth's kingdom. You will renounce all your magic and gift it to him. If you are lucky, he might even let you live in a prison cell for the rest of your miserable existence. Actually, now that I think about that, dying might be luckier."

Black storm clouds rolled on the horizon out at sea. Searing white-and-purple flashes detonated the sky, the world erupting in jagged streaks and thunder.

Toshiko whispered into my ear. "Welcome to the new world, Miss Wayward."

THE STORY CONTINUES

THE
BONE
GRIMOIRE

THE WAYWARD HAUNT SERIES

THE BONE GRIMOIRE

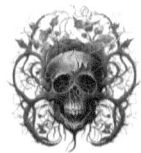

Zaya Wayward has survived battles, dark magic, and bloodthirsty rituals. But she's still not safe. In the escalating war against Morgomoth, now she must play the most vital part in the final battle. Zaya must use The Bone Grimoire to unite the Larthalgule and Neathror blades and defeat the ruthless leader of the United League of Dissent.

Fighting against old enemies and new, Zaya and friends will have to gather their strength and survive the gruelling and maliciously brutal world of Orthrask as they navigate their way to Morgomoth's Kingdom, but determination might not be enough. As armies collide and secrets, lies, and betrayals are exposed, fighting for freedom will cost Zaya and her friends the ultimate price.

ACKNOWLEDGMENTS

Indie publishing isn't a solo task. It has taken a team of people to help me get this book into the world. A big thank you to Gillian, Stuart, Tom, Stacey, and the Brisbane Nightwriters for taking the time to read and critique samples from the book. I always appreciate your feedback and the improvements that you make.

Thanks must go to my two wonderful critique partners, authors Shan L. Scott and Lisa McNeil. You ladies have been a big part of my author journey. Thank you so much for all your help, advice, feedback, and suggestions. I appreciate all of it and will always cherish our friendship.

What would I do without my wonderful Beta Reader team? Thank you for taking the time to read the book and offer your valuable feedback. I loved some of the ideas that you came up with.

I thank my editor, Kristen Scearce, and final eyes reader, Kim Deister. These ladies' time and patience made the story stronger and better than the previous four drafts. I have learnt so much about editing just from these two ladies alone.

Thank you to the Brisbane Young Adult Writers Group. I always love attending our sessions, discussing marketing and social media ideas, and just chatting in general about writing and publishing.

Thank you to everyone who has read and provided a review for this book and the previous two novels in the series. I always value the thoughtful reviews and the time taken to write them.

And finally, thank you, reader, for taking a chance on this indie author. I appreciate your wonderful support and look forward to writing more fantasy stories for you.

ABOUT THE AUTHOR

Cas E. Crowe is an admirer of all things spooky, quirky, and witchy. She enjoys writing YA and NA dark fantasy, horror, and romantasy stories filled with magic and adventure. Cas lives in Brisbane, Australia and, when she is not reading or writing, is often daydreaming about her next story or creating art with Photoshop.

www.casecrowe.com

BB bookbub.com/authors/cas-e-crowe?

a amazon.com/author/cascrowe

g goodreads.com/casecrowe

instagram.com/casecroweauthor

X x.com/CroweCas

f facebook.com/casecroweauthor

tiktok.com/@casecroweauthor

pinterest.com/casecroweauthor

LEAVE A REVIEW

If you enjoyed The Dark Divide, please consider leaving a review on Amazon and Goodreads through the links below. Authors depend on reviews to get the word out about their books.

Amazon
https://books2read.com/u/4A2Yqk

Goodreads
https://www.goodreads.com/book/show/195523476-the-dark-divide

NEWSLETTER

Sign up for Cas E. Crowe's Author Newsletter

Get access to
Author Interviews
Sample Chapters
Bonus Book Material
Book Recommendations
WIP (Writing in Progress)
Book Reviews
News and Social Events
Reading Lists
Exclusive Reveals
Upcoming Events
https://casecrowe.com/contact/

BOOKBUB

Follow Cas on BookBub to get notifications about upcoming releases, preorder availability, new book launches, and limited-time discounts.

bookbub.com/authors/cas-e-crowe?